Bar T. Rancher

A novel

by

Matthew W. Adam

I would like to thank My Lord and Saviour, Jesus Christ.
I also want to thank my wife, Eileen, and the rest of my family for tolerating me,
pushing me, and most of all
believing in me. Thank you.

A Papa's Press release

ISBN Number: 978-0-615-24883-7

Cover Photo: By Eileen Adam, all rights reserved.

Published by Papa's Press
Contact Information for Papa's Press and this work:

Matthew Adam
2062 West Center Street
Cave City, AR 72521
870-834-9350
email: paparoniadam@hotmail.com
www.lulu.com/paparoniadam

Publisher's Note: This novel is a work of fiction. Names, characters, places, and incidents are either products of the author's imagination or used fictitiously. All characters are fictional, and any similarity to people living or dead is purely coincidental.

Printed in the United States of America

Bar T. Rancher

By

Matthew W. Adam

CHAPTER ONE

Brother Bart Rancher, pastor of the First United Christian Church, leaned heavily over his pulpit and scanned the solemn sea of faces that stretched out before him. As he gazed out at those in attendance, looking, no searching, for those two people who were always present, he allowed his mind to wander momentarily down the side path through the forest of names. He thought first of the church name and how odd it must sound to someone who didn't share their beliefs. As a fairly new pastor, there were a limited number of things, theologically speaking, that he could claim to be certain of. One of them was the fact that they were not the "first" Christian church. Since Christianity had begun with Jesus over two-thousand years ago, he could be doubly sure that they were indeed not the first. He began to wonder how many first churches there were, but decided that would only provide him with a headache, something he had far too many of as it was. He was almost as certain that they were not united. Oh, they came together, for the most part, in a clinch, but that was far from being united. He had only been a pastor for just over a year, and a Christian for just four years before that, but he knew that every church was made up of squabbling, imperfect, self-centered, people. That fact alone precluded any chance of the church being truly united. His own congregation was currently separated, like the literal sheep and goats, by the left and the right. The current division concerned the shade of the new carpet to be purchased. On the right side, the goats, who wanted the carpet a deep, dark shade of brown. On the left, the sheep, who wanted a creamy, mellow shade of brown. Until that decision was made, everyone endured the putrid green carpeting that looked like it had been ripped from a mobile home just this side of the inferno. Brother Bart couldn't care less, so as far as he was concerned it served them right to have to face a floor of pond scum green. As

2

for being Christian, well, he didn't think Jesus would squabble with his disciples about the color of carpeting.

Then there was his own name to ponder on, which presented it's own unique set of problems. Each time he spoke, even briefly, about the sin of lying and deception, he felt like the world's biggest hypocrite. His very name was a lie. Well, not exactly, as he once again tried to justify his actions. All of the letters for his birth name were included in his chosen moniker. They were even in the right order. But his name as it appeared on his birth certificate was Bar T. Rancher, the T. stood alone. He was not the Bart Rancher he had introduced himself as to his congregation. The woman who birthed him (he could not bring himself to call her mother, mama, or any other nomenclature closely associated with parenting) wanted to name him after the man who had donated the other half of the DNA necessary for his conception. Unfortunately, she had been overly friendly with most of the staff of the ranch where she worked as the maid, so she couldn't recall which saddle tramp had ridden her during the donation time. But she figured Bar T. Rancher was a great improvement over Bar T. Cook, or Bar T. Owner, or Bar T. Visitor, each of which were likely donors. So, with the downsizing of one letter and the omission of a period, Bart Rancher was born.

Finally, he spotted them. Darryl was on the left side, with the sheep, while Leonard found his place among the goats. Obviously they had chosen

3

sides in what would be called throughout the annals of history as the great

carpet shade revival. Bart was pretty sure that the sheep of his congregation

could handle the shock of his name and background. They were the more

forgiving and understanding of the two groups. He didn't think, however, that

either group, no matter how forgiving and understanding they might claim to

be, could condone the fact that he saw two men in the congregation who

didn't exist outside of his own somewhat twisted view of reality. Darryl was

the leaner of the two, and the better dressed. He wore dark slacks, a blazingly

white pinpoint oxford shirt and a tie that spoke to you without shouting. At the

moment he was scrunching in close to Sister Margaret because Sister Louise

had come to claim her usual Sunday morning spot. Darryl had complained

time and again to her that she ought to try harder to make it to the services on

time, but since she couldn't see or hear him, she ignored his advice entirely

and showed up her usual five minutes late.

Leonard, on the other hand, believed that God was casual. He wasn't

dirty or unkempt, just casual. This morning he sported a pair of jeans that had

only been moderately faded by washing and wearing, along with a T-shirt that

displayed a rather flattering view of Mr. Potato Head. He had the pew to

himself, except for Brother Ben, who lived by himself for the better part of his

seventy years and never had the benefit of a wife to teach him about proper

hygiene and regular bathing. Since Leonard was a figment of the pastor's too

4

fertile imagination, he didn't seem to mind the odor as much as those whose

nostrils were actual flesh and cartilage.

Just ahead of them sat Bro. James Holden, the local banker and the

church song leader. His wife of ten years, Mrs. Bonnie Holden, along with

their children, Lucy and Ann, sat quietly next to him. They stood when others

stood, sang when it was time to sing, and even actually bowed their heads and

closed their eyes, without peeking, at the end of the service. All of the Holden

women were gifted with voices like angels, and were willing to share their

talents when called upon to do so. To all outward appearances they were the

perfect church family, with an existence to be envied. But Bart knew that

appearances could be deceiving. They were the epitome of a loving family; a

successful businessman, a doting wife, and two adorable children, but Bart

sensed tension underneath the otherwise calm waters. He knew all too well

that the old saying about a book and its cover was all too true. His own story

could hardly have been guessed by the slip jacket of his life.

He was single, and happily so. He wasn't homosexual or against

women in general, he just hadn't met the one that lit up his darkened life. A

dark cloud passed over his thoughts. There had been one woman who made

him want to give up being a bachelor, but that was in a land far away and in a

time he desperately wanted to forget. Weighing in at just under two hundred

pounds on a six-foot frame, he wasn't at an ideal weight, but broad shoulders and the fact that even at age forty-two middle age spread was well in check,

he was pretty content to still be able to eat what he wanted most of the time. If

asked he wouldn't have admitted to being handsome, although several of the

single girls around town would have argued the point. Of course, to some of

them all a man had to do to be considered handsome was have a pulse.

According to his own perception, he was fairly sure that he wouldn't stop any

clocks with his rugged good looks, but he wouldn't bust any either.

His gaze fell upon the Holden family again, as if they held him under

some kind of spell or hypnotic trance. The harder he tried to pull away from

them, the more he found himself looking that direction and wondering what

storms brewed below the calm seas they displayed. And again he found

himself thinking of his own rather placid exterior with the storms of life that

he had endured. Being born to a sociopathic liar with a tendency to believe

that any man who wanted to bed her also wanted to marry her hardly gives a

young man a leg up on life. Couple that pleasant thought with that same

woman blaming you for the men who ran out of her life like a cat with

kerosene on it's tail and you begin to have a recipe for total disaster. Blend in

foster homes, uncaring relatives, grandparents who had a whole lot to do with

their daughter confusing sex for love, and a mixed bag of deviant men, bake

for ten to fifteen years and you have the perfect recipe for raising a juvenile

delinquent and future career criminal. He should have been the poster child for becoming a burden on society. He probably would have, too, if it hadn't been for the Printer's, his last foster family. He remembered going to their home thinking that they were like the rest of the world, wanting him because with him came a monthly check for his care and well being. Instead he found a couple who gave him everything a young boy needed. Love. Acceptance. A sense of pride. A deeper sense of responsibility for his own wrong choices. An introduction to the God of the Bible. He had vomited on them all of his years of hatred and self-loathing and they wiped it clean with showers of love and forgiveness.

A cough from the congregation awoke him from his self induced trance. He glanced at the clock in the back of the sanctuary and was relieved to see that only five minutes had passed. He decided to use the pause as an object lesson for his sermon for that day.

"Silence," he began, "we don't hear enough of it these days." He paused to see if anyone picked up on his humor. A few smiled. That was about as good as he could expect. He spoke about Elijah's experience in the cave, Samuel hearing the voice of God as he prepared for bed, David's time tending sheep, and mostly about the times Jesus withdrew from the crowds to spend time alone with his Father. Finally, he drew it to a close by asking everyone to bow their heads and close their eyes. He was always amazed at how many people peeked around to see if anyone else raised their hands for prayer or other spiritual needs. When the invitation was over, he asked Bro. Thomas Bell to close out the service with a word of prayer while he walked toward the back to shake hands with the congregation as they left. He chose Brother Thomas because he was rather long winded with his prayers, calling upon God with several names before he even began his prayer and always somehow managing to extend God from a one syllable word to at least five syllables, sometimes as high as seven. Bart needed time to think and gather his thoughts before hearing the usual, "Good sermon" or "I really enjoyed that one." He had a deep impression that something was amiss with the Holden family but he didn't know what or how to approach them. They were usually one of the last families to leave since James always paused to pick up candy wrappers left behind or straighten up song books left askew. He was a neat and orderly man and expected others to be as meticulous about the church as he was. Unfortunately, he was disappointed Sunday after Sunday. He rarely complained, though. He just went about putting right what he saw wrong. By the time they arrived at the back, Bart had formulated something of a plan.

"Good sermon as usual, Pastor," James commented, grabbing Bart's hand in a vise like grip. Bonnie nodded and agreed, adding her own comments about the service. The girls just took his hand lightly for a moment before rushing outside to join their friends.

"Thank you," Bart said, then added, "I was thinking of Christmas. I

8

know it's still months down the road, but if we're going to do anything special, we need to get started on it right away."

"That's true," Bonnie agreed.

"I thought I might stop by this afternoon and discuss some ideas I have. If it's alright with you, of course." Bart didn't actually have any ideas about Christmas or anything else, but hopefully he would by the time he got to the Holden's house that afternoon for coffee, cookies, and Christmas.

"Sure," James said, "Why don't you come around three or so? To be honest, I was thinking of a few ideas of my own, but I'd love to hear yours."

"Then three it is," Bart said and stepped back to let the Holden's past. He shook a few more hands, went through the routine of turning out lights, turning down thermostats, and locking doors before heading out to the car. As he was heading to the back, Darryl caught his attention. He was pointing excitedly to something on the pew where the Holden's had been sitting.

"What is it, Darryl?" Bart asked.

"A clue," Darryl responded.

"Jinkies," Leonard chimed in, although he really had no idea why. Bart walked over and found a slip of paper lying on the pew. On it was written several scripture references, all of them from the Pentateuch, or the first five books of the Bible. The verses were Genesis 49:19, Exodus 31:18, Leviticus 24:12, Genesis 47:27, Numbers 33:22, and Deuteronomy 9:15.

"So one of them wrote down some scripture references," Bart said. "What's the big deal about finding those in church. At least someone was awake enough to write them down."

"But that's just it," Darryl countered. "You don't find them anywhere else because Mr. Holden picks them all up, along with the candy wrappers, and anything else that seems out of place."

"That's true," Leonard added, his curiosity now a little piqued. "I wonder if there's a reason he only wrote references from the first five books. There could be a pattern there." He knew that in speaking about a pattern, Bart would have to look. One of the gifts that came in the bundle of his neuroses and psychosis was the ability to distinguish patterns in an otherwise chaotic world. It was also one of the gifts the Printer's had passed on to him. When he first began seeing patterns in the world around him, he had almost gone mad. It was as if the entire world was speaking to him, and it began to drive him towards paranoia. He would see his name written over and over again in Alpha Bits or in alphabet soup. Number patterns appeared in his mathematics textbooks, causing him to nearly fail the class. One of the few times that his talent aided him was on his final exam in History. Mr. Hardin gave multiple choice tests throughout the year, and Bart was able to spot a pattern of answers. On his final, just as a lark, he filled out the test based on the pattern he had seen. It wasn't foolproof, but he scored a ninety-five.

It was with the Printers help and by the grace of God that Bart was able to distinguish between true patterns, such as those found in nature or on history exams, and false patterns. With prayer, along with the Printer's and a few confidantes, Bart was also able to distinguish between real and imaginary people. Darryl and Leonard had joined him when he was about ten and the three of them grew up together, so even though he knew they weren't real, he kept them around anyway. He managed to make it through high school and into college, where his talent for pattern discernment got him noticed by recruiters from the CIA. With their help he graduated early and began work with them on code breaking. Once in a great while, he would have the opportunity to spend some time in the field. It was there that he met Maria Ramirez.

She had hair the color of a full moon night sky, and the jewels she almost constantly wore for decoration completed the feeling that as you looked at her you were looking into the midst of the Milky Way. Her eyes did nothing but add to that illusion. They were dark as well, but sparkled in any light like prisms from a chandelier, especially when she laughed, which it seemed like she was always doing. The only thing she loved more than laughter was people and the only thing she loved more than people was her faith in God. It wasn't right to say that served God, because work done with such joy could hardly be called service. She was constantly giving of herself.

In his line of work, she was called an incidental. She worked as a maid for the people that the agency was after. It was thought that she might provide information that would help Bart crack a particularly difficult code by providing sensitive personal information about her employers. It was a long shot at best. Bart bumped into her at church, introduced himself as a visitor to the country and let the nature of Maria Ramirez take it from there. From the moment the assignment began he hated it. He already hated the nature of the work he was in. He was able to justify it by telling himself that he only worked on the codes and that good people needed to stand up against those who would harm the innocents. But he had a horrible time trying to justify lying to an innocent woman whose only crimes were working for someone who may or may not be spying on the U.S. and being naïve enough to believe that a visiting American wanted only a little company and information about his new surroundings.

She caused him to rethink his entire life. He had always considered himself to be a Christian. Well, at least since his time with the Printer's. But she was a horse of an entirely different color. She lived it every moment of every day without even trying. It was as if she were tapped into an unlimited power source that fed her constantly. Bart had always struggled with his faith, forcing it as much as living it. He blamed it on his upbringing, on his afflictions, on his precarious mental state, but, watching Maria, he knew he could have more if he only had what she had. They spent hours together, sometimes talking into the late hours of the morning at a coffee shop, about God and other philosophical subjects, but mostly about God. It was during one of those late-night sessions over what seemed like the thirteenth cup of cappuccino that she laid a true revelation on Bart.

"You try too hard," she said with a compelling smile. "Why do you work so hard on something that God made so easy?"

"I don't see anything easy about trying to please the God who created everything. It's like trying to buy a gift for a multibillionaire when you only have a few pennies to your name."

"Si," she answered, "but if you are the child of that multibillionaire, would he not be as pleased with a card decorated with crayon drawings? You are the child of that God. He loves you no matter what. It is His very nature to love you. He cannot do anything else."

"But some of the things I've done," he said sadly, thinking of the very thing he was doing now by lying to someone who he found himself caring deeply for.

"He knows all that you have done and all that you will do," she replied. "He still loves you. His love is not based on who you are, but on who He has always been. I tell you, it is His nature to love you." They spoke for hours. Bart confessing things he had done or seen, her countering with the same emphatic theme; God loves you. They sang together, laughed together, cried together. By sunrise, Bart knew this would be his last assignment. He didn't know that by sunset Maria would be standing with the God she loved so desperately.

"Do you see a pattern or not?" Leonard asked, awaking Bart from his painful stroll down memory lane.

"I think so. I need a songbook." Darryl handed him one. Bart knew in the recesses of his mind that it was his own hand that had grabbed the songbook from its perch on the back of the pew, but his mind's eye saw Darryl hand it to him.

The preacher began flipping through the songbook, sometimes humming a quick tune as he passed by a familiar melody or a favorite tune. His companions, who knew his singing had been compared to pig's screaming, chided him for causing noise pollution that might bring the head of the EPA to their little town. After about fifteen minutes he sat looking at the paper he had been scribbling words on, scratching his head and wondering if maybe this time his intuition was off. When he was finished, he had the six words him, eternal, living, praise, unto, and shall.

"It's just a list of random words," he told his imaginary compatriots.

"That's because you're stringing when you should be stacking," Leonard insisted. Bart appreciated the invaluable insights that both Leonard

14

and Darryl had given him over the years. Darryl was a wealth of knowledge, most of it trivial, like who were the guest stars on sitcoms or the words to the theme songs, but there was also a vast wealth of useful knowledge deposited there. Even the trivial knowledge proved to be useful at times since he also had an uncanny ability to piece together seemingly unrelated events into a logical and plausible theory. Leonard, on the other hand, looked at the world just a smidge off of kilter. It allowed him to see people, concepts, and theories outside the box of normalcy. The three of them often collaborated together to solve puzzles and riddles, each contributing their own particular talent to the effort.

Bart took the paper and rewrote the words, making a column instead of a row. Giving a list that now looked like:

him
eternal
living
praise
unto
shall.

"Capitalize them," Leonard suggested. Bart went back through and capitalized each of the words he had taken from the songbook. As he did, the message became crystal clear, and frightening. It spelled, "HELP US."

"Who do you think left it here?" Darryl asked.

"And who is 'us'?" Leonard wanted to know. The three sat in stony silence for a moment, each of them pondering the possibilities.

"It could be the girls," Leonard offered. "The note came off a computer printer, and teenagers are more proficient with computers than adults."

"How do you figure that?" Darryl wanted to know. "Besides, Bro. James is a banker, and has access to computers and printers. He's also the song leader, so he's the obvious choice. Someone is probably threatening his family. Maybe he's being blackmailed to rob the bank or release vital information about banking codes. I think we should call the FBI."

"Not until we know more," Bart replied. "He could have written the note, the girls could have, or Sis. Bonnie might have written it. We don't know if it's the entire family being threatened by someone on the outside, or if it's a portion of the family being abused by those who are supposed to protect them. Until we have more than a piece of paper with what might be a sick joke, we can't go anywhere."

"Except to the Holden's. We have an appointment there this afternoon, remember?" Leonard reminded him. "I think if anyone is abusing anyone, it's him. Think about it, what kind of creep wears long sleeves all the time, even on church picnics and stuff. And what's with those turtle necks he wears sometimes. Does he think we're still in the seventies? Next thing you know he'll want to install a disco ball in the fellowship hall."

"Just because a guy wears long sleeves doesn't mean he's abuses his family," Darryl chided. "Maybe he's got a skin condition or something."

"Yeah," Leonard muttered, "like leprosy."

"Okay, that's enough," Bart stated flatly. "I need time to think. I've got to sort this whole thing through. If you guys don't mind, I'm going to take a drive."

"Shotgun!" Leonard shouted.

"I think he means without us," Darryl said sadly. Bart assured them that he was right. It was time for him to gather everything together in a single congealed mass, and he wouldn't be able to do it while they argued about turtlenecks and leprosy.

Bart walked outside and slipped behind the wheel of his sixty-one Rambler. In the rearview he could see Leonard and Darryl standing on the steps of the church, each with puppy dog eyes and lips that stuck out like they'd been stung by a bee. He hated to leave them, but he really needed time to clear his head and a drive in his baby blue would help him do exactly that.

She was a beauty, at least in Bart's eyes. Most people saw her as a dinosaur, a throwback to another era that should have stayed in the tar pits. But to Bart, she was a reminder of a time when things maybe weren't right in the world, but they were certainly closer than they are now. He had restored her to her showroom glory, complete with a powder blue paint job and clear plastic seat covers. The plastic was hot and sticky in the summer, and cold and brittle in the winter, but it kept the seats in pristine condition. Even when he carried kids, with all of their junk food all he had to do when he was finished was wipe the seat, vacuum the carpets, and spray a little air freshener.

He wondered sometimes why he liked the old tank, but then it occurred to him. It was because it was an old tank. This thing could hit a deer at sixty and it wouldn't even scratch the paint. Besides, even though it was built in a time when gas didn't cost much more than air, it still got a respectable twenty-six miles per gallon, if it wasn't hot-rodded.

"Ola, Senor Rancher," a voice called to him gently from the passenger seat. He should have been startled, but strangely he wasn't. In fact, he had been expecting his charming guest.

"Ola, Maria," Bart returned the greeting. "I've been expecting you. But call me Bart, por favor." She was just as beautiful in death as she had been in life, but then why shouldn't she be? This wasn't a spectral reminder of sins far past. She wasn't a menacing spirit come to haunt the man who had brought her to her untimely death. She was another figment of his more than lucid imagination, a haunting of his own design, so to speak.

"You know that you are forgiven for all of your sins," she reminded him, as if she were reading his mind, which was natural since she flowed from the same thoughts.

18

"I know that God has forgiven me, and I know that you have as well. It's forgiving myself that I'm having a hard time coming to grips with."

"When you do, perhaps you will be able to let me go," she offered.

"Perhaps," he agreed. He looked again at her. She was grace and beauty incarnate. Her raven hair with its iridescent shine still sparkled like a glorious moonlight night, all of the stars decorating the flowing locks. The olive complexion glided as smoothly over her face as the wind flew over the wheat of Kansas, without a blemish or wrinkle in sight. She still wore the same maid uniform he had last seen her in. It wasn't one of those cheap French maid jobs that are sometimes seen in low budget comedies where the top comes too low and the hem is way too high. It was a simple, even drab, gray uniform with a high collar and a hem line that came at least close to the knees, utilitarian in design. But on Maria, it was transformed into Cinderella's evening gown on the night of the ball. Bart was almost sure that if he looked at the passenger floorboard, he would see glass slippers.

Her uniform, her lack of any adornments that spoke of outward comeliness, gave Bart pause to think about the source of her beauty. No, source wasn't the right word. It would come to him. Just think. Focus. Focal point. Yes, that was it. Where was the focal point of her beauty?

Most women have a feature that draws a certain amount of attention to them. For some it's a fetching smile that welcomes a man into her presence

19

like a candle glowing in the window, for others its eyes that captivate a man's attention until he's totally lost in them and can't think of anything else, for still others there are more prominent physical features that grab a man's eyes. None of those things, however, fit Maria. It was true that she had a smile that said, "Hello, I'm a person you would like to know." And she had eyes that sparkled a thousand different colors all at once. She also had her share of other prominent physical features that would not disappoint most men. But none of those things touched on her real beauty. It wasn't any outward appearance that would bring a man toward her, but something inside. A spark. A glow. A luminescent shine that poured out of her from her smile, her eyes, from every pore of her olive skin. Her outward appearance might make some men turn for a second glance, but her inward grace and style came through to make you a second glance, and a third, and finally a lifetime with her. Bart decided that there were far too few women who possessed that kind of beauty, and far too many who had all the outward attributes, but lacked the inner qualities to be called a true lady. There was a vast difference between being a woman and being a lady.

"Tell me, Bart," she said, bringing him back to the present, "have you thought much lately about John?"

"You mean Big John?"

"Si, Senor Grande John." He wasn't sure that her use of Spanish was entirely proper, but since it came out of his head and he had only barely

squeaked by with a 'B' in high school, he thought it little wonder that her

Spanish was this good.

He hadn't thought of Big John McNamara in years. He was the closest

thing to a father he had known in his short time with the woman who had

given him birth. He lived up to his name in every way. Bart was sure that his

size was not as enormous as the imaginational memory of a five year old

insisted that it was, but he was a big, big man. He would lumber in from his

workday at the sawmill, rattling the porch as he approached the front door,

swing open the door and fill the doorway with his body. Bart remembered that

almost everyday bits of sawdust and woodchips clung not only to his flannel

shirt, but to his beard and hair, bits of white and light brown flecked among

the blackness of night. Big John reminded Bart of a bear, mostly because of

his size, but also because his hair seemed to cover every bit of his face, with

only enough space left for his twinkling eyes, a ruddy nose that had seen it's

share of barroom brawls, and a mouth that was only visible when the big man

was laughing, which, fortunately, was often.

When Big John came home, the games began. While everyone was

gone, Bart was expected to sit still and behave, and he didn't dare do

otherwise. Seeing John come up the driveway, Bart flew off the couch and

began running for his life. Big John would give chase, bounding through the

21

house like a wild animal after its supper. He could have caught the little boy in mere seconds with a mighty swipe of his hand, which also had enough hair on it to resemble a huge bear paw. But that would have ended the game way too soon. Instead he let the boy run into the kitchen, past the dining room, down the hall, and up the stairs to his bedroom. It was always there that the big man caught up to the little boy.

"Fee fie, foe fum," he bellowed from just inside the doorway. Having already spotted the lad under the bed, he made a long pretentious search throughout the room, checking drawers, closets, and behind doors before finally coming to the bed. Once there he lifted the bed from the floor and cried out with a tremendous roar that shook the windows. Bart screamed and ran again, but this time was caught swiftly, deposited on the bed that was back on the floor where it should be, and tickled without mercy. This went on until they heard the downstairs door open, at which point Big John transformed into a little boy.

"I'm coming," he called plaintively, as if he were a twelve year old being called in from a game of sandlot baseball for supper. "I'm coming." Bart heard him hit the stairs two or three at a time, tripping over himself to get to the door. Then it started. She yelled at him for the sawdust on the floor. She berated him for acting like a child again. She screamed at him for not having dinner ready for her after she had put in a hard day of filing and typing. If the truth were told, her work day ended at noon when her and her boss found themselves having a 'business' lunch in close proximity to a discreet hotel. Big John could not apologize enough. He assured her that dinner would be ready shortly and that he would have the carpets vacuumed and the kitchen cleaned before going to bed that night. Bart wanted to scream, but he dared not. The less she thought about the child she had given birth to, the better it was for him. He crept quietly into his bedroom, closed the door behind him, and played there quietly until Big John called him down for dinner. After dinner and helping Big John gather the dishes, he did what he could to straighten up the living room and make things as easy as he could for the big man. Even at the tender age of five he didn't think he would lift a finger for the woman who gave him birth unless it was life or death, and there were times like tonight when he wasn't sure that he would even then. After doing what he could to help, he climbed the stairs stealthily and read comic books until his eyes refused to stay open any longer.

It was sometime in the early morning darkness when he awoke. The night was so dark that he felt like the darkness wasn't just around him, but permeated him, like he had become as dark as the sky itself. He stretched his hand before him and it was swallowed up in the penetrating darkness. There were other times when he had been awakened in the middle of the night for various reasons. Sometimes his bladder called to him, usually just before it was too late. Other times he needed a drink of water or an evening that had started warm became suddenly chilly and he needed another blanket. Tonight, however, was different. It wasn't his own needs that had opened his eyes, but the needs of another. He lay there still, hoping he would hear it again, just so he would know it wasn't a part of a lost dream or a figment of his over active imagination. There it was!

It was a cry. A sad, mournful cry, one that digs deep into the fabric of your compassion and claws its way inside. The cries were so mournful and pitiful that Bart felt his own eyes begin to well up with tears. He couldn't tell where the cries were coming from. The big house echoed every creak of every board and every squeak of every door until you were sure that a houseful of ghosts and goblins had taken up residence and were throwing themselves a housewarming party. He might not be sure of its source, but he knew who could make it stop. Big John wouldn't tolerate someone harming a child. The big man believed in spanking, and he had proved it a time or two with Bart, but he wouldn't allow anyone to inflict the kind of pain that Bart knew this little boy was in. From the sound of his screams, he would have to be in total agony. Big John would put an end to that.

Bart tossed aside the covers, swung around, and let his feet drop down onto the cold hardwood floors. Instantly a shiver went up his spine, but not from the chill of the floor. It was the last wail he heard. It sounded like it had come from just this side of the grave. He had to hurry. Whoever that little boy

was, he was in big trouble. He ran to the door, nearly knocking his head into it

before finding the knob and turning it. Down the stairs he sped. Down the hall

he ran. And sprang into the bedroom Big John shared with the woman who

gave him birth. Almost instantly, he wished he hadn't.

A bedside lamp cast an eerie glow through the room, and even though

the light was dim, to a boy coming out of almost total darkness it was like

staring into the headlights of an oncoming car. After his eyes adjusted, he

rubbed them to try to readjust them to what they were seeing. Big John was

huddled in a corner, his bareback riddled with slash marks and blood that

slowly crawled down, cascading in small streams before dripping to the floor,

forming little diadems as they splashed onto the hard surface below. His eyes

were wide with fear. They were, at least, until they caught sight of the little

boy he loved standing in the open doorway. Then they shut for an instant, then

lowered into glistening pools of shame and remorse. The woman who had

given him birth stood behind Big John, the instrument of his torture clutched

in her right hand. Bart didn't know exactly what it was, but he knew it wasn't

meant to be used by one human being on another. Big John towered over her

normally, but here, in the macabre glow of the bedside lamp, she appeared

larger than him, larger than the room she was standing in, larger than anyone

Bart had ever seen. Larger, and evil. Not the evil of the coyote trying to catch the road runner. That evil, though bad, was understandable. The coyote was

hungry. The bird was food. That was simple. This, however, could not be

explained nor rationalized by an adult, much less by a five year old boy who

was witnessing the cruel torture of the only person he had ever loved. It was

more than he could take. Five years of frustration, hate, bitterness, and

confusion tore through him like steel knives ripping through paper. His fury

was unleashed in a flurry of flying fists, kicking feet, and a slew of screams.

He tore at the woman who had given him birth with every bit of anger he

could muster, scratching at her skin, bruising her shins, and damaging her

eardrums. In shock, she stood and took it for a moment. But only for a

moment. Without warning, she backhanded him and sent him sailing across

the room like a discarded piece of paper. Then she turned that instrument of

torture on him. Instantly, Big John was transformed again into a man with the

heart of a lion and the strength of a bear. He stood between the evil queen and

her unwanted prince.

"Enough!" he cried with sufficient force to make everyone know that

it was indeed enough. Before she could respond, he flung a shirt over his

bloody back, scooped up the boy and headed out the door and into the night.

Without looking back the big man strode to his sixty-five Mustang and began

buckling Bart into the passenger seat. Almost as if by instinct he took the boy

from the car and gently deposited him into the cab of the pick up he used for work. It smelled of pine chips, cedar shavings, and a mixture of gasoline and oil. To Bart it was the sweetest scent this side of heaven.

Bart sobbed himself to sleep with his head resting on Big John's powerful legs, the exhaustion of emotion draining him like the plug being pulled from the bathtub. He awoke sometime the next day, so he wasn't sure how far they had driven. He noticed that Big John's eyes were red and swollen, but he didn't know if it was from being awake all night or from tears. It was probably a combination of both.

They stopped at a roadside diner and enjoyed a lunch of cheeseburgers, fries, and the thickest shake Bart had ever known. If it hadn't been for the specters of the previous nights memories haunting the back lot of their brains, they could almost believe that they were on a grand adventure or at least a small holiday. When they were through eating, he and Big John went to a park and played until almost sundown. It was after an afternoon of fun and excitement that Big John took little Bar T. Rancher to a nearby orphanage run by a group of loving nuns. Bar T. hated them, hated the world, hated Big John for leaving him, and most of all hated the woman who gave him birth, both for giving him birth and then for not caring for him. It wasn't until his time with the Printer's that he stopped hating and started forgiving. By the time he surrendered to preach he had forgiven everyone, even the woman who had given him birth. But just because he had forgiven her didn't mean he had to like her, or did it? Maybe one day he would have the answer to that and a thousand other questions.

"So you're saying…?" he asked Maria, the tears welling up in his eyes cutting the question short.

"I am only asking if you have thought of Big John," she replied sweetly. "And now that you have, I must be going. Adios, mi amor." And with a kiss blown to him, she was gone.

Bart pulled the car over to the side of the road, where he wept for Big John. He pulled himself together, started down the road, pulled off again and wept for Maria. When he finally pulled himself together, he knew where he had to go. To the home of Sheriff Jake Plunkett.

Sheriff Jake Plunkett, at ten years junior to Bart's forty three, was one of the youngest sheriffs in the state, but he was also one of the most capable, wisest, and most caring in the country. People often saw his youth as a weakness, and Sheriff Jake was glad to let them do so. He was glad when people underestimated his abilities. There were several people in the state penitentiary and several more in local jails that wouldn't make that mistake again, but it only took one time for them to end up behind bars.

Bart knocked on the door and was greeted by Sheriff Jake's lovely wife, Melissa. She was blonde and petite, with lovely green eyes that reminded Bart of a day on the ocean. Melissa taught English at the Junior

High School, and Bart was glad that his teacher didn't look anything like her since he had a hard enough time concentrating on his studies. She smiled warmly and invited Bart in, telling him that Jake was in the living room watching the races.

"He'll be glad to see you," she assured him.

"I don't think he will be this time," Bart replied. She understood that this was business, not pleasure and took their toddler boy, Jake Jr., out to play in the backyard before telling him to go on in to the living room.

Jake was sprawled across the couch, remote in hand. His lanky frame took up most of the couch. Even in this reclining position, it was obvious even to the most casual of observers that Jake Plunkett did not fit the description of the stereotypical southern sheriff. He was lean and athletic, his body tanned and hardened by years of working on his families dairy farm. The years of hauling hay, running the deer woods, and working the garden had already given his body an athletic head start in life. Later, his work on the farm coupled with his natural abilities of being able to run and play football, adding grace and agility to an already athletic body. That body, mixed with his thick, sandy blonde hair and smooth tanned skin made him look more like a lifeguard on Malibu Beach than a sheriff from the rolling green hills of Arkansas. Upon Bart's arrival, he sprang to his feet, dropped the remote and extended his hand in one smooth motion.

"How's my favorite preacher?" he asked, and even though the question was asked in an easy going, how do you do manner, Bart knew he actually wanted to know the answer. Sheriff Jake was the first person he met on the way into town. Unfortunately, it was when the good sheriff stopped him for a burnt out tail light, but since that time they had become the best of friends. Bart even shared the story of his life with the easy going sheriff, telling him everything; including his time with the CIA and his two other best friends, Darryl and Leonard. After Jake had assured himself that the new preacher wasn't a threat to himself or anyone else in town, he dropped the issue of imaginary people and concentrated most of their early talks on Bart's time as a spook. Bart tried to dissuade him from the idea that he had done much more than break codes, but Jake remained firm in his use of the word spook. As to his other friends, he merely said, "Whatever it takes for you to keep both oars in the water."

"I've had better days, Jake." He told him of the paper he found, what he thought it meant, and his final suspicions.

"Whew, talk about ruining a man's Sunday afternoon," he said with a sly grin. "What do you think we should do from here?" Jake was the sheriff, but he also trusted the older man, both because of his time with the intelligence community, and even more so because of the wisdom that God bestowed upon him naturally. Then again, most of that wisdom was earned through the school of very hard and often bruising knocks.

"I have an appointment with them at three," Bart said. "I was hoping you and I could go together. Maybe let you hang back a piece until I go inside and see how it plays out."

"Sounds like a plan to me," Jake answered. "So, it'll just be the two of us?" Although Jake never had a problem with Bart's idiosyncrasies, he didn't much care for sharing a room with two people he couldn't see or hear. He knew in his head that they weren't real, only figments of his friends somewhat tortured imagination, but they still gave him a case of the creeps. He looked around Bart, peering first over the left shoulder, then the right, squinting as he looked, as if by sheer force of his own will power he could see what only existed in someone else's head.

"I left them at the church," Bart assured his friend.

"Good. I'll call for Johnson to sit on the corner of Vine and Elm, just down the street from the Holden's. That way I'll have someone close if we need any assistance."

"I hope there's no problem, but I'm glad we'll have someone close by in case."

Jake kissed Melissa goodbye, telling her that he'd only be gone a couple of hours at the most.

"Where have I heard that before? Oh yeah, a month ago when the two of you left for a couple of hours and came back two weeks later," she scolded.

Unfortunately, she was right. The two of them had gained quite a reputation in

their short time together as a couple of people who seemed to find trouble in

the least likely of places.

"Well, that maybe true," Jake backpedaled. "But didn't I bring you

those lovely flowers when I came back?"

"Yes, from Ecuador as I recall."

"It's the thought that counts," he said, as if that made his unexcused

disappearance acceptable. He patted JJ, as he called Jake Jr. on the head and

went out to the car before she could retaliate. He climbed into the backseat of

the blue monster and told Bart to hit the gas before Melissa could hit them.

After seeing her dander raised after their last escapade, Bart didn't need to be

told twice.

The Holden home was far from a mansion, but in a small town in north

central Arkansas, it sure could come close to passing for one. The drive pulled

in through a gated entrance that was timed to close at dusk and open at dawn

unless overridden by someone in the house. The lawn was neatly manicured,

with huge shade trees of various oaks and elms lining the drive as well as

placed strategically in the five acre front lawn so as to both provide shade to

picnic areas that had been set up and block the view from the street. It may not

have been a mansion, but it did everything to give a good impression of one.

As they pulled up the drive, Jake slid down in the back seat in case anyone was looking out through the windows. They hoped that if there were a problem, Bart could defuse it before it got out of hand. If not, well then Sheriff Jake was there and Deputy Johnson was just up the street.

Bonnie opened the door almost the instant Bart rang the bell. Her sudden appearance startled him, causing him to flinch back.

"I hope all men don't jump when they see me. I did put on make-up this morning, you know."

"I'm sorry," he muttered. "I just didn't expect you to answer so fast."

"Oh, I was watching you pull up the drive," she responded, which made Bart doubly glad Jake had slid down in the seat before they had made their turn. She welcomed him into the den, where she had finger sandwiches, small cakes, and coffee already prepared on the exquisite coffee table, which no doubt cost more than his weekly salary. He started to make a mental note about preaching more on tithing and giving, then chided himself after remembering his reason for his visit. It was hard to remember that something was amiss in the Holden household because there didn't seem to be anything, absolutely nothing, out of order in their orderly world. Although he couldn't prove it, he was sure that a quick peek in areas like under the couch or behind the refrigerator would show that they were just as spotless as the rest of the house. Maybe there was something amiss after all. Maybe the total absolute absence of chaos was in a sense a form of chaos.

"Sorry, Reverend," James said as he entered the room, "I didn't hear you come in."

"It's alright," Bart replied. "But please don't call me reverend. It sounds so pretentious for a simple man like myself."

"Sorry, but I kind of have a hard time saying Brother Bart. Somehow it sounds like a character on an educational program, or one of those puppets on religious kid's shows. You know, watch out everyone, it's Brother Bart and his gang of nasty outlaws."

"Oh, James," Bonnie clucked. "Sometimes you're absolutely horrible." Bart just chuckled.

"I can see your point. How about you just call me Bart. Most everyone else does. Maybe now I know why." The three of them talked in easy going fashion about the weather, current events, and church, finally bringing it around to the Christmas program Bart was considering.

"I've got a rough sketch of what I was thinking about in my bag here," Bart said, fumbling about in the black satchel he carried every Sunday. He continued fumbling, muttering under his breath about not being given the gift of administration as little beads of sweat popped up on his forehead. More fumbling, more muttering about it should be there somewhere, where else could it be.

"Something wrong, Pastor?" Bonnie asked politely.

"I guess I've misplaced the program outline I was working on," he answered, and it was the truth, since he had actually been working on a Christmas program and had misplaced earlier in the week. The timing was a little off, but the truth was there. He hoped God would be gracious about his lack of forthcoming on the time of his error in handling.

"You really need a good woman to take care of you," Bonnie said sweetly.

"Now, Bonnie, don't you start matchmaking."

"I'm not. I'm just saying that the right woman would do wonders for our pastor. Don't you agree?"

"That is a loaded question if I've ever heard one," Bart interrupted.

"But I'll gladly answer," James said. "A good woman can do wonders for a man. And I know God has the right woman already prepared for you. But until she comes, is there anything we can do for you?"

"I hate to be a bother, but I might have left it on the front seat of the car. Would you mind going to take a look while I dig in the bottomless pit of this bag?"

"Not at all. I'll be back in a jiffy." As he went out the door, Bart started replacing the contents of the bag and began preparing himself for the next few minutes. He had begun earlier fortifying himself in prayer, calling to mind scriptures that would come in handy and calling upon his Heavenly Father to help him in this time of crisis. Like Nehemiah, who had also prepared with prayer in advance of his audience with the king, Bart gave a final short prayer that consisted of only three words, "Help me, Father."

He stood, helped himself to another sandwich, which would probably be the last one he was served in this household, walked quietly over to the window, and peeked through the blinds. What he saw almost caused him to choke on his tuna salad. James had removed his shirt in order for Jake to examine his back. It was a mass of bruises, scars, and almost fresh cuts. They were almost certainly put on today, probably within the last hour. It was like some macabre scene of connect the dots, only Bart found that he couldn't connect the dots between a highly respected banker and pillar of the community, his lovely and supposedly devoted wife, who served on numerous charitable committees, baked cookies for school and church bake sales, and the wounds on the back and arms he was now seeing. He supposed, and rightfully so, that there were more wounds that couldn't be seen, not to mention the wounds that would only be seen by the counselor that James would need to be able to put this behind him and go on with his life.

"Is something wrong?" his hostess asked, probably supposing that she had prepared the sandwiches a bit too early, allowing the tuna to spoil.

"I don't know," Bart asked, memories of Big John washing over him like a monsoon rain. He felt a deep compulsion to scratch at her and kick her shins the same way he had done the woman who had given him birth. He was a man now, though, not a frustrated little boy. As a child, he did childish things.

"What is it?" she asked insistently. "Is something wrong with James?" How was he supposed to answer that one?

"When did it start, Bonnie?"

"When did what start?"

"The beatings."

"James has never laid a hand on me. He's too good of man. Better than I deserve."

"No doubt about that," he replied before his brain could stop his tongue. That one came out of an angry bitter heart. But it seemed to have rattled her. With trembling fingers she set down her coffee before she managed to stain the rug a deep brown.

"I'm not sure what you mean by that, Pastor Bart. And I don't think I like what you are implying." The time for subtleties was over. Either he was right, in which case James was out there getting ready to file formal charges with Jake, or he was totally bonkers and he would be sued, run out of town on a rail, and end up in an institution someplace having tea with Napoleon while discussing what went wrong at each of their respective Waterloos.

"Bonnie, you are abusing your husband. From what I can see, it's been happening for quite awhile, probably the whole time of your marriage, if not longer. It may have started as something that only happened in the bedroom between the two of you, but sometime or another you stepped over the line and began to abuse him." He watched with almost morbid fascination as the façade of gentility and grace slipped off of her like skin off of a molting snake. Beneath the cheer and charm of a southern belle there lay a strange combination of fire and ice. Her eyes virtually shot fire at him, while her words came straight from the Arctic trade winds.

"So what," she spat. "So I beat that poor, sick, pathetic fool. He likes it. He always has. His momma beat him, too. He doesn't know anything else. And what's more, he never will. He may have told you, but he won't tell anyone else."

"He's telling Sheriff Jake right now," Bart replied quietly. Sometimes the force of a whisper can penetrate where a scream won't dare to go. It had the desired impact. Her back stiffened, momentarily subduing the raging inferno in her eyes.

"He won't press charges," she declared defiantly. "He'll come crawling back to me like the worm he is and after a month or two with me, we'll be able to put this ugly child back to bed and together we will run you out of town." Bart knew she might be right. He thought of Big John the night

38

he was dropped off in the orphanage. Somewhere underneath the glistening tears of a man who had rescued a child was another child who would go back to the only love he ever knew, even if it were a sick, sadistic love. He never heard from Big John after that night. He had always hoped beyond hope that the big bear had found some woods to hibernate in until a new spring could have a chance to thaw the icy love he felt. But somewhere deep inside he knew the bear went back to that lonely and dark cave.

"You might be right," Bart agreed. "But," he began to say

"But it won't matter because we will press charges," he was interrupted by one of the girls. She stood in the doorway, defiant. Bart had hoped that he didn't see or hear from the girls that they were at a friend's house. He should have known better. To someone like Bonnie, children are meant neither to be seen, nor heard.

"You get back to your rooms this instant!" Bonnie screamed. Sometimes a scream never truly leaves the lips of the screamer. The girls went around the room to where Bart was standing, positioning themselves behind him.

"You'll protect us, won't you?" the other girl asked. They were both scared, with good reason, but the younger of the two didn't have the steel in her backbone the older one possessed. Still, she was here and that said a lot about how much metal went through her spine.

39

"He will," Lucy assured her. "Long enough for the police to come and take Mommy far enough away so that she can never hurt us or Daddy again."

"I don't want Mommy to go away," Ann pleaded, causing a smile to play across Bonnie's lips. It only played for a moment.

"I know, but we talked about this, remember? Mommy will only get help if we make her. You don't want to hear Daddy cry anymore, do you?" Lucy had experienced more beatings than Ann, and it had stiffened her resolve about what needed to be done. It had also given her a wisdom beyond her twelve years. She knew just what to say to strengthen Ann's resolve.

"No!" she cried. "I hate hearing Daddy scream like he does. I don't want him hurt anymore. You're a sick, sick woman, Mommy. And you need help." Coming from the lips of the little eight year old, the words almost sounded comical. Almost.

"You're right," Bonnie said with just a hint of a tear in her eyes. "And I will get help. Here, with you two and Daddy. We'll work this whole thing out together as a family, without outside intrusion." The snake had put her skin back on, and the cobra's charm was working on at least one of the two little mice hiding behind Bart.

"What do you say, girls? Do you really want Mommy to go to a nasty old jail? Wouldn't it be better if Mommy and Daddy stayed here together and Mommy got help here?" Their resolve was starting to melt under the warm words hissing forth from the snake's tongue.

"I don't think so," Sheriff Jake answered from the doorway. "In fact, I think it would be better if you'd just come with me right now." He walked over to Bonnie and extended a hand to help her out of the chair. Always the sheriff, but he never stopped being the gentleman. Bart heard him whisper to her, "I'll be glad to wait until we're out of sight to put the cuffs on, if you'll promise to come quietly without trouble." Bonnie must have promised, because they walked out together, without cuffs. She only stopped briefly at the doorway.

"The girls, who will watch my girls?"

"Bart will stay until Miss Lillian from social services comes. She's already been called and should be here momentarily." That last part was for Bart's benefit, since Jake knew he didn't feel comfortable being left alone with two little girls. True to Jake's promise, Miss Lillian arrived on the heels of Jake's departure.

Bart Rancher went to his waiting sixty one Rambler, with it's powder blue finish and clear vinyl seat covers, satisfied that he had done what he could to put a family back together. Despite the personal animosity he held against Bonnie, one that stemmed back to his own childhood, he truly did hope and pray that she would get the help she needed. He also hoped that with that help, and despite the odds, that her, James, and the kids could reunite as a family someday. Until then, James, Lucy, and Ann would need some extra attention. He made a mental note to make some phone calls that evening after services. The service that evening, he decided, would consist of prayers for the Holden's and a planning strategy to meet some of their immediate needs, like making sure a hot meal was on the table each evening and that the girls got off to school each morning. Some of the men would gather around James. They would fish, work on cars, do whatever it would take to help him through. They might divide over the shade of carpets or drapes, but they would unite on this front. His work wasn't quite done, but he was still satisfied that it would be. With that satisfaction in hand, he opened the door so he could make the drive to church.

"I'll drive," Leonard offered, having positioned himself behind the wheel.

"How many times do we have to go over this?" Bart asked. "Real cars and imaginary people don't mix. Never have, never will."

"Fine," Leonard said sullenly, scooting over to the passenger side, squishing Darryl against the door as he did so. "But I've got shotgun."

"I called shotgun," Darryl protested.

"Boys, let's not argue. There's room for all of us up here."

"Okay," Leonard agreed, his pouting almost over. "I just wish you would imagine a car for me. A Porsche, or maybe a Corvette."

"On my salary, I can't even afford those kinds of cars in my dreams."

"Well," Darryl stated, "if he gets a new car, I want a place of my own. I'm tired of sharing my room with Leonard. He's such a slob. I can never find my things. He's always borrowing them without asking, and he never returns them."

"Do too."

"Not."

Bart drove slowly to church, enjoying the imaginary argument he was hearing as evidence that for now, at least, his life was back to what passed as normal for him.

CHAPTER TWO

Unfortunately, Bart Rancher had been unable to make rest a companion. They were less like good friends and more like passing acquaintances who happened to pass each other on the street and nod to one another. That Sunday evening the nod came during the services, which contained about a third of the number of people as the morning worship service, which was typical for most churches. The fewer number of people, and the fact that those who came for the later services were more dedicated and interested more in learning Biblical doctrine than they were in rules and decorum gave Bart the chance to relax and do what he loved to do, teach the Bible. They read scripture, discussed it with Bart telling what he had learned from his own experiences along with the knowledge of various commentators on the scriptures, and then members of the congregation spoke as they were moved. Doctor Emmett Smythe, recently retired from a practice he had begun shortly after graduation from Harvard, gave a short lecture on interpreting the scriptures from the cultural context of the time in which they were written. Bart was allowed for a moment to simply step back and allow another to pour out his knowledge while those faithful sponges in attendance soaked it up. Bart was feeling a little spongy himself. Dr. Smythe had studied extensively on his own, having never attended seminary, but probably capable of teaching at several if he had chosen to. He read and spoke Hebrew, and read Greek.

Sometimes Bart wondered why they hadn't chosen the good doctor as pastor.

But then, as he listened to Emmett slip into a monotone lecture style, he

realized that some people might be gifted with knowledge, but be lacking in

other areas.

The clock was rapidly working its way to eight o'clock and Bart took

the chance to wrap things up with prayer requests when Dr. Smythe paused to

catch his breath. It was a little rude, and normally he wouldn't have done it,

but tonight he wanted to check on the girls before heading home to a hot

shower and a soft bed. During prayer requests, he mentioned only that the

Holden family was in need of a touch from God's grace. He could have said

much more without gossiping since he had been there during most of the

afternoon's ordeal, but he chose to remain discreet and allow Jake to

disseminate the information as he saw fit officially. Of course he knew that by

the time he lathered up, most of the town would think they knew what had

occurred in their sleepy little community. Backyard fences and party line

phones had been replaced by police scanners and instant messages on home

computers. Either way, whether it was person to person, or pc to pc, the word

got out. At least they wouldn't hear it from him, which would give them the

confidence in his discretion to be able to come to him if they had their own

problems.

They bowed; Bart leading them in a prayer that he knew reached the ears of the Creator of the universe. It always amazed him, no matter how many times he did it, to know that when he spoke, God listened. It wasn't confidence in himself or the loftiness of his words that allowed him that assurance, but confidence in God and his written word. He prayed fervently for the Holden family, with a special emphasis on Bonnie, who needed the embrace of a loving Father the most, but probably wanted it the least. With amen being said, he dismissed the congregation, shook hands as always at the back door, and went about the business of shutting up the building until the Wednesday evening service, Darryl and Leonard walking along with him as he went. Afterwards, he went to his office to call Jake, who told him the girls were already bedded down for the night with friends of the Holden's. Mr. Holden was with them, which relieved Bart. He was worried that James would either spend the night at the county jail, defending his wife's actions and trying to get her released, or do something utterly stupid and leave his two little girls with no parents at all. It seemed that for right now, at least, he could indeed rest easy.

Part of taking it easy for Bart was a long walk through town. He preferred a long walk in the country, with the sun at his back and the wind in his face, but opportunities like that were rare for him, since he and rest were not the best of friends. So he took opportunities as they came. Tonight was such a chance. He left his Rambler parked beneath the sign that read,

"THOU SHALT NOT COVET THY PASTORS PARKING SPOT"

The sign was corny and mostly unnecessary since no one parked there, but it was kind of cute, not to mention a gift given for his first anniversary at the church. He dared not to use it. He assured himself that the car was locked, not that anyone would steal such a car, but it did have a decent stereo system which might tempt someone looking for a quick ten bucks. Having double checked, he left the parking lot and wandered into the arteries of his small adopted town. He had grown to love it here. The people, the town and it's buildings, the old fashioned manners and mannerisms all added up at times to make him feel like he had wandered into a Rockwell painting. If this was an episode of some old television show, he wasn't looking forward to a commercial break.

There were times, like this morning, when a bout of cynicism took hold of him like a dog grabbing hold of an old shoe, thrashing him about and slobbering all over him. The events of that afternoon, and how they scraped away years of scabbing meant to keep his emotions buried safe and deep under layers of self made bandages, could have driven him further into the depths of despair and misery. Instead, they served as a catharsis for his own pain, making him realize that each event in his life, no matter how painful they were in the moment, could be used by a loving God to help someone else along the path. He had heard that before, even preached it himself, but it took going through it to make it as real as it was now. No doubt in the coming years he would shelve the memories and the lessons learned with them, forcing God to teach him again and again until it stuck, if it ever did. He was a slow learner at times. Still, for now anyway, he not only had the knowledge that he had helped divert a man from a lifetime of suffering, detoured two little girls from learning lessons that would have harmed them and their future mates, and brought a woman to justice and hopefully rehabilitated, but he had seen his church come together to help a fellow brother. Things worked as they should.

"Penny for your thoughts," Darryl said, interrupting Bart's basking in the glow of his warm feelings.

"Wait a minute," Leonard protested. "Since we're a part of his thoughts, ain't that kind of selling yourself into slavery?"

"A philosopher," Bart commented. "Now there's a discussion we could all sink our teeth into. Of course, others might say that perhaps I'm the imagined one and that the two of you are real."

"Hmm," Darryl said thoughtfully, stroking his chin as he always did when they began their journeys into altered states of thought. It was part of Bart's process of unwinding. Others might enjoy a movie or good book. He enjoyed spending time with his childhood pals, those men who had grown up with him and had rescued him from times of sheer madness, even if others might think that they were in themselves indicators of madness. Bart thought

of that possibility, but he also thought of the years he had spent in almost total

isolation with the right Reverend Billy Sunday Thompson, pastor of The

Independent Pentecostal Church of Talowah, Mississippi, just below

Hattiesburg. Reverend Thompson and his church weren't affiliated with any

organized denomination. The good Reverend believed that all major

denominations had been corrupted by the harlot found in the book of

Revelation, and that he alone was able to carry on the truth through the visions

given to him by the angel, Ariel. It was more likely the visions given him by

the spirits he brewed himself from corn, sugar, and yeast, but those in his

small but fervent congregation didn't care. When the Reverend spoke, it was

as if God himself breathed through his lungs, moved his tongue and parted his

lips as He had done with the Red Sea in the Exodus.

Bart became associated with him when he stopped at the orphanage a

week or so after he had been dropped off by Big John. The Reverend came to

minister to the needs of the boys and girls there, bringing gifts for birthdays

and Christmas, as well as food, clothing, and other necessities throughout the

year. It was a good ways from his church, but Billy Thompson the preacher

had to make a living as Billy Thompson the over the road truck driver. His

congregation was zealous in their beliefs, but poor in their giving. Actually, to

be fair, they were just poor and so had little to give. Brother Billy, as the kids at the orphanage called him, kept the church alive through his earnings as a

trucker and a sideline of smuggling booze, drugs, or other contraband as he

was able. To him the ends of keeping the church alive and spreading the only

true gospel with a tape ministry was worth the means of having to deal with

the low life people who peddled such products and the fools that bought them.

If they were bound and determined to destroy their lives anyway, why

shouldn't the Good Lord and he prosper from their idiocy?

Bart liked the man at first. He was always bringing things to the

orphanage, including games and laughter, something the sisters who ran the

orphanage had little for themselves, and surely none to spare for little urchins

like him and the other kids. It wasn't very long until Bart found himself in the

passenger seat of the big eighteen wheeler, heading south for Talowah.

Shortly after his initial run, he was adopted out and became Bartimus Isaac

Thompson.

It was a good life at first, but Bart learned quickly that the nicest

people in the world can become the meanest drunks in just one swallow. He

didn't know why, but he knew soon that Billy Thompson was not a man able

to hold his liquor. With only one shot, he was transformed from the saintly Dr.

Jekyll into a hideous Hyde, who found no greater pleasure than inflicting pain

on Bart. He would open a hatch in his floor, tossing Bart into a crawlspace

filled with cobwebs, bugs, and other creatures who inhabit such places. The things that were missing included light, food, and human companionship.

After coming to his senses, which sometimes took days, the good Reverend

would remember what he had done and where Bart was. He would release the

boy; apologizing over and over and swearing in the same way that he would

stay away from that devil's brew and treat Bart as a king. Bart usually ruled

his kingdom for two or three days before being tossed off of his throne and

back into the dungeon. It was during one of those exiles that he met Darryl

and Leonard. They came to him as little boys, just as he was, and played with

him down there. They would make up games, solve puzzles and riddle, and

laugh at the stupidest jokes. They were so much fun to be with that Bart often

was able to forget about the torture of bug bites and the heartache of an empty

stomach.

One Sunday night after services, Bart watched his adopted Daddy go

out to the shed where he kept the bug juice, as Bart had started calling it. He

knew that within an hour he would be back under the house if he didn't do

something fast. The thing he did was run, and kept on running. He ran until

his legs couldn't carry him anymore, rested only for a moment or two before

getting up to run some more. He didn't know exactly where he was running

to, but he knew where he was running from, so his only thought was to put as

much space between him and his adopted home as he could. He also knew, or

at least thought he knew, that the sisters would return him right back to

Reverend Thompson, so he made sure that he didn't run in that direction.

"I know why we're imagined and you're real," Leonard stated. "Because I have a better imagination than you do, and if I were going to invent a friend to talk with, he would be taller, better looking, and smarter than you."

"Leonard," Darryl chided. "That's an awful thing to say to Bart. I thought you were supposed to be his friend."

"I wasn't talking to him," Leonard corrected. "I was talking about you." Darryl punched his counterpart in the arm, who returned the punch with greater force. Soon the two of them were wrestling on the ground, with Bart refereeing them.

"Break it up you two," he whispered. "Someone's liable to get hurt."

"That is a possibility," a voice said out of the darkness. The voice stepped from behind a tall wooden fence and Bart realized that it belonged to a young black man torn blue jeans, a t-shirt printed with the emblem of some music group he had never heard of, a denim vest, and a red bandana pulled to one side and tied pirate style. He also realized that the voice came with companions, most of them bigger than the body the voice inhabited, which wasn't very small. Bart estimated that he stood at least as tall as his own six foot frame. And he was solid from top to bottom. If he had any fat at all, it was well hid under several layers of hard earned muscle.

"I wasn't looking for any trouble, guys."

"Well, you found it any way. Ain't this your lucky day." He stepped forward menacingly, forcing Bart to back up into another body that didn't seem to have a voice, and didn't seem to need one. The sneering smile and eyes that seemed to come alive with the anticipation of causing pain and/or grievous bodily harm said all that needed to be said.

"I didn't realize where I had wandered to," Bart said, hoping he could talk his way out of at least what looked like a night in the emergency room, if he was lucky. "But since I trespassed on your turf, the least I can do is offer what I have to pay for any inconvenience I've caused you." He carefully reached for his wallet in the back left pocket where he always carried it and pulled out a twenty dollar bill, wishing he had more in the way of a peace offering.

"It's not much," he acknowledged. "But it's really all I've got, so if you'd be willing to take it, I'll just be on my way."

"Check it out, fellas. Whitey here is trying to pay some toll. Well, let me tell you something, whitey, your daddy owned my daddy. And the way I figure it, you owe us a lot more than any twenty dollars."

"And the way I figure it is that you just need to get over it. Your daddy graduated from college, has a good job and makes good money. His daddy worked hard as a farmer to make sure that could happen. The only slave I see around here is you, and you're just a slave to your own selfishness." This was

a new voice, one that seemed to boom from the sky like thunder. It didn't yell,

but carried through the air with a force that rocked the ground underneath

their feet. The body carrying the voice stepped from behind the fence and Bart

understood why the voice was so huge. It had to be to fill the body it came

from. He was darker than any of the youths harassing Bart. In fact, he was

darker than anyone he had seen before in his life. It was as if light bounced

away from him. He stood at least six foot four or maybe six by Bart's

estimation and probably weighed close to three hundred pounds, with just

enough fat to round out the hardened muscles rippling beneath his t-shirt and

cut off denim shorts.

"Aw, come on, Marc. We didn't mean no harm. We was just scaring

the brother." He talked like a scolded school boy, who had just got caught

smoking in the bathroom.

"Maybe you didn't mean no harm, but you caused some anyway. Now

you go and tell this brother about the love of Jesus after you done played

yourself stupid in front of him. How's that going to play out?"

"Guess I didn't think about that," he conceded.

"No, you never do. Now you boys apologize and head on home. I'll see

you Wednesday night." They dropped their heads and shuffled their feet back

and forth before finally mumbling an apology. The wall who had appeared from behind the fence made them say it over and over until it sounded good and proper to him. Then he dismissed them and they ran off in different directions.

"Yo, Mikey," he called. "You gonna bring game Wednesday, or am I gonna have to school you again?"

"Yo, old man. I got your game," Mikey called back before turning the corner. Bart realized that the two of them had a deep respect for one another, something that went beyond the normal bonding of different generations.

"He don't have a father," Marc said, answering Bart's unspoken question. "Most of these boys don't. I end up being a surrogate for half the community down here. And speaking of down here, what's a white boy like you doing here? My boys were just spooking you, but there's a lot of boys who would kill you for insulting them by not bringing them enough money to steal."

"Sorry, I just found myself wandering around, enjoying the cool breezes, when we found ourselves down here."

"We?"

"Oh, long story," Bart excused himself, not wanting to explain to a total stranger that he had imaginary childhood friends who still stayed with him, even though Darryl and Leonard were standing by to be introduced and were thoroughly disappointed when they weren't.

"Well, I'm Marcellus Johnson, most folks call me Marc." The big man put out a hand that looked large enough to swallow Bart's head and squeeze it like a lemon. Bart returned the gesture and found his hand in a firm, but not crushing, vigorous handshake.

"I'm Bart Rancher. I pastor the First Christian Church. I guess you're a youth leader at a nearby church." Marc laughed with a roar that seemed to shake the clouds from the sky.

"No, sir, not youth leader. I pastor the Holiness congregation down the road. Me and the missus have been serving there about fifteen years now."

"Fifteen years? How come we've never met before? Aren't you in the local ministerial alliance?" Again the roaring laughter.

"With the right reverend Angus McFarland as head of the alliance? I don't think I'd be welcomed there. Or maybe they just lost my invite in the mail." It was obvious from his words, body language, and facial gestures that Marc was disgusted by his fellow preacher. Bart was a part of the alliance, attended the monthly meetings and even preached at their annual community revival held in the city park, but as he thought about Reverend McFarland, he realized he hardly knew the man. He was distant and aloof, as if he were somehow better than his so called peers. Bart had never thought of him as prejudiced. He thought of him more as seemingly superior to everyone.

"I've got an idea, if you're up to it," Bart said.

"I'm up to most of anything," Marc replied. "What'cha got in mind?"

"I'm scheduled to speak at the back to school revival coming up in about a two weeks. The thing about it is that I can either preach it myself or bring in someone if I choose."

"And you want me to preach in your stead?" Marc finished.

"Like I said, if you feel up to it." Bart answered.

"Brother, if I have the chance to preach Jesus, I'd do it from the Dome of Rock with a thousand of them Moslems throwing rocks at me. You've just earned yourself a piece of Georgia Johnson's pecan pie. That is, if you're up to it." Darryl urged Bart to accept the invitation. Leonard could care less. He liked Marc and all, but he was allergic to nuts. Darryl wasn't though, and he loved everything about a good pecan pie, from the crunchy nuts to the melt in your mouth corn syrup based filling. Bart couldn't disappoint him. Besides, he had no other plans and he enjoyed Marc's company.

"I'd eat pecan pie at the Dome of the Rock cafe, if they served it," he replied. Marc pointed the way and they headed off, discussing preaching, prejudice, and the problem of over cooked pecan pie as they went along. But Bart had a pressing question he had to ask.

"Marcellus isn't the kind of name most folks would call their child. How'd your parents come up with it?"

"Parent, not parents," Marc corrected. "My Momma named me. The

57

full name is Marcellus Cass Johnson. Daddy was there, but not most of the time, if you get what I mean."

"Not really," Bart answered.

"He was hiding his self inside of a bottle, only coming out to beat one of us kids or Momma from time to time."

"I'm sorry," Bart said, knowing what it was like to have a parent so trapped within themselves that they couldn't see the hurt they were causing others.

"Don't be," Marc answered. "He's the one that led me to the LORD."

"How's that?" Bart wondered. "Did he get saved?"

"Yeah," Marc answered with a chuckle. "But not until after I did. You see, cause I didn't have a father, so to speak, I went looking for one. The only one I could find was God. I got saved at the age of six, and by the time I was nine, I had led all my family to Jesus, including my Daddy. I led him out of the bottle and into the light."

"Wow," was all Bart could say, while tears streamed down his cheeks. Leonard and Darryl both cried as well, holding onto each other for support as they turned the corner to Marc's house.

"Here we are," Marc said as he swung open a small wooden gate, part of a white picket fence, of course.

Georgia Johnson was probably one of the most beautiful women Bart had ever seen. Like Maria, she possessed both an outward and inward beauty, both of which were apparent at first glance. She was tall, almost statuesque, not nearly as tall as Marc, of course, but taller than Bart with her heels still on.

"I thought you'd still be at choir practice," Marc said, bending over to give his lovely wife a kiss on the cheek, as well as a sly pat on another cheek that Bart was embarrassed to have seen.

"Not in front of company," she scolded; although it was obvious she had enjoyed the attention and didn't really mean the scolding.

"This ain't company. He's just another reprobate preacher like me," Marc answered.

"Ain't nobody like you, Marcellus Cass Johnson," she replied, enjoying each syllable of his name as it rolled off her tongue. "You is one of a kind, break the mold, we don't want no more of his kind different." Bart thought that if she knew him very well, she would have the same opinion of him. The men went into the living room while Georgia went to the kitchen to serve the pie. Bart watched her as she made each move a symbol of grace. He thought how much she looked like a dancer, making even mundane moves like getting a plate from the cupboard look like it belonged on stage with a band playing and other dancers adding background support. She was not as dark as Marc, but more of a chocolate brown, with absolutely no flaws or imperfections in her skin. Bart estimated that she might have weighed maybe twenty or thirty pounds over the century mark and that just because of her height.

"Ain't she something?" Marc asked, interrupting Bart's thoughts. He was slightly embarrassed at having been caught staring at another man's wife, but he wasn't lusting in the slightest. He studied people in the same way others studied butterflies. He found their movements and idiosyncrasies captivating in a way, realizing that God made everything just a little bit different, although deep down they were all the same. It amazed him how people could be so alike and yet so different.

"She sure is," Bart replied. "How'd you guys get together?" Marc laughed again, as he was prone to do. He seemed to find humor in almost everything and genuinely enjoyed life in general.

"We met while I was playing football for Georgia Tech. I got sidelined with an injury during my senior year, dashing any dreams I had of playing pro ball. Georgia was a volunteer at the hospital. It's funny, but she was a senior at Tech as well, but we had never met until then. I didn't know she existed until she came to my hospital room with some newspapers and magazines."

"What he ain't' telling you," Georgia said as she glided into the room carrying their pie and coffee, "is that I didn't start volunteering at the hospital until after he got hurt. See, I knew he existed even if he didn't know I did. The big, dumb ox would have never given me a second look if he hadn't gotten injured."

"Looks like the hand of the LORD brought you together," Bart commented.

"The hand of the LORD and a big linebacker from Arkansas," Marc corrected. The three of them talked for nearly two hours, sipping coffee that Georgia managed to keep filled to the rim as quickly as they brought it down and savoring both the sweetness of the pie and the sweetness of the fellowship. Sometime during the course of conversation, Bart had gotten up and helped himself to a second piece of pie. Darryl and Leonard hung around the kitchen, engaged in their own discussion of current events and eating their own imaginary pie, cooked just the way they liked it.

"Actually," Darryl commented to Bart as he walked into the room, "I wish the filling wasn't quite this chewy. I like it when it just sort of melts in your mouth before finding its way to your throat and down into your belly." Even though

"Well, its fine with me," Leonard stated flatly.

"Of course it is," Darryl said. "You're not eating any."

"Can I help it if I'm allergic to nuts?" Leonard asked.

"Then why are you hanging around him?" Darryl replied, pointing to Bart and shoving another helping of pie into his mouth. "Besides, since we're eating imaginary pies, why don't you just imaging yours is a coconut or chocolate cream pie?"

"Hmm," Leonard said thoughtfully. "Maybe that's not such a bad idea." He furrowed his brow and within seconds a huge piece of chocolate pie was on a plate in front of him.

"Don't eat too much," Bart warned, "I don't want to have to clean up after you later."

"Did you say something?" Marc called from the living room.

"Just commenting on the cabinets," Bart replied, hating the lie, but not yet willing to risk telling a new friend about his affliction.

"Marc built them," Georgia said, with just a hint of boasting in her voice.

Bart almost ran into Marc as the two met in the doorway, Bart exiting while Marc was entering.

"Thought I'd have me another piece of pie," he told Bart.

"I wouldn't do that, Marshmallow," Georgia warned playfully. Despite his best efforts, Bart found himself snickering. He stopped when he felt Marc's eyes boring into the back of his head. He sat down quietly and began devouring his pie, no longer savoring the sweetness, but rather devouring it to keep himself occupied while the tension in the room built.

"You know I don't like that name, woman," Marc said, returning from the kitchen with an empty plate.

"Then you best leave that pie alone," she replied. Bart ate the last bite of his, the taste suddenly turning sour. It resisted his efforts to swallow and he had to get a drink of coffee to force it down.

"Don't you tell me what to do," Marc answered, his hands on his hips in defiance.

"I ain't," she said sweetly. "You just go ahead and eat that pie, gain twenty pounds, let your blood sugar go sky high and die on me. It's alright. I got some good insurance on you." He moved towards her menacingly, and Bart found himself wondering how he was going to stop a freight train from moving. Before he could react at all, however, Marc dove in for Georgia and began tickling her mercilessly.

"Stop, stop!" she cried, unable to catch her breath as the big hands moved up and down her ribs, grabbing her legs just above the knees, and then going back to the ribs for a second helping.

"Can insurance money do this?" he asked. "Huh? Come on, girl. Tell me something I want to hear."

"I love you, baby," she finally managed between peals of laughter. He stopped. Then, after she caught her breath, she said, "But you still better leave that pie alone or I'll stand and testify in the midst of the congregation that my husband used to be called Marshmallow."

"You wouldn't."

"You just grab that pie and see if I wouldn't," she said, cocking her head back and forth in a manner of defiance that said you know I will. Bart tried, but again he found he couldn't resist. His mouth opened long before his brain could stop it.

"I know I'm risking a new and wonderful friendship," he said, wiping away the last bit of pie crust crumbs from the corners of his mouth, "but I gotta know where Marshmallow comes from. Let's face it, that's the last thing I'd think of calling you." Marc and Georgia both broke out in spontaneous laughter.

"Toasted marshmallow, maybe," Georgia was finally able to say. Bart tried to explain that he didn't mean it that way. He wasn't talking about the color of Marc's skin, but his tremendous size and hardened physique. He tried, but his own laughter impeded him.

"I wasn't always this big," Marc answered after a time.

"Oh yes you were," Georgia interrupted. "I seen the school pictures. Believe me, baby, the size was the same, but where it all hung out was different."

"She's right. Up until I was twelve or so, I was still hungry for something."

"Anything," Georgia interrupted again. She hushed when Marc shot her a glaring look.

"As I was saying, I was hungry for something. I had God in my life, but it still felt like something was missing. So I ate my way through life, trying to find something to fill the emptiness. It was about that time that I saw a movie, the one about all them bodybuilders."

"'Pumping Iron'?" Bart asked, having seen it himself.

"Yeah, that's the one. Well, I had the size, like Georgia said, but it was soft and in all the wrong places. That's why kids called me Marshmallow."

"That ain't the only reason," Georgia added. "He wasn't just soft on the outside, but on the inside, too. Kids sensed that and some kids can just be cruel when they find someone easy to pick on. The other kids did like most folks, just playing along to get along. Besides, for most kids growing up, you're either a predator or prey."

"Sad, but true," Bart commented.

"That's why I decided to spend one summer becoming the predator. I saved my birthday and Christmas money to buy me a weight set. Daddy found a bench press at a yard sale, and Momma picked up some hand grips and a jump rope at the local five and dime. The whole family got healthy that year. But I got more than healthy. I dropped about thirty pounds of fat, picked up about the same in muscle and went back to school ready to join the football team. And I figured out that if you're big enough and play your stuff right, you don't have to be predator or prey. You just swim through the waters going your own way."

"But did you ever figure it out?" Bart asked.

"What's that?" Marc asked back.

"What you were hungry for all that time. Did you figure out what made you eat to begin with?" Marc and Georgia both laughed, Marc with his trademark shake the rafters roar, while Georgia giggled quietly like a shy little schoolgirl.

"It's funny, but the one thing I wanted was the one thing I was keeping myself from getting." Marc answered between spells of laughter.

"Huh?"

"He was looking for friends. People he could be with, hang out with," Georgia explained. "But his food addiction kept him from the one thing he was hungering for."

"I think we all do that in one way or another," Marc said, bringing his laughter under control and gaining a more serious attitude. "Them boys tonight wanted your respect. They got fear." Bart agreed with that. "But they didn't have your respect. And they won't get it acting like hoodlums. They're keeping themselves from the one thing they want the most."

"God sure is funny," Bart commented. "He creates within us wants and desires, but then somehow they get all warped up inside."

"You can't blame that on God," Georgia disagreed. "We been like that since the beginning."

"How's that?" Marc asked.

"Adam wanted to be a little god, didn't he?" The men both agreed. "But he was in a sense, already a little god. He had control over all the world. God gave it to him. But he goes and eats the one thing that takes away the thing he says he wants. Don't make no sense, but folks have been acting like that ever since."

"And as for Angus," Bart began, "what is it he wants and what is he doing that stops him from getting it?"

"Don't know for sure," Marc answered. "I do know he don't want me or my kind around."

"He's allergic to marshmallows?" Bart asked innocently. Georgia giggled.

"Alright now," Marc responded. "I'd hate to have to kill you on the night we met, but if you keep that up, I'll find a way to get over it. And I can get over you, too, woman."

"Don't you threaten me, big man. I'd hate to have to shame you in front of our guest and all, but I'll put a bad hurting on you if you ain't careful."

"Seriously," Bart said. "Is Angus prejudiced. I can't believe a man who preaches God's word could entertain any notion of prejudice. At least in this day and age."

"The day and age may have changed, but men's hearts are still the same," Marc answered. "I wish I hadn't brought it up cause I don't want to talk evil about a fellow brother. So if you want to know any more about Angus, you'll have to learn it from someone else, alright?"

"Good enough. But I do have one more question. The fall community revival is in less than a month. Can you have a sermon ready by then?"

"I don't think I'm on the speaking list," Marc responded.

"You are now," Bart replied. "Our church is responsible for providing the Friday night speaker. I was going to do it, but we have the option of bringing in someone."

"A white church voting on a black man to preach at a revival. That ought to be interesting."

"Now who's prejudiced?" Georgia chided. "Do you thing your church will really vote for Marc to preach?"

"Don't know why not. They've always trusted my judgment. Besides, about a third of the congregation is black, so we're not a white church."

"Oops," Marc said shamefaced. "Guess I just assumed."

"We all make mistakes. Don't sweat it." They talked for a couple more hours before being interrupted by an invasion of loud yawns and long stretches.

"Guess I'll head back to my car," Bart said, heading for the door.

"I don't think so," Georgia stated flatly. "We've got a guest bedroom you can sleep in. Then Marc will drive you to the church in the morning." By her tone of voice, both men knew the verdict was rendered and that there would be no chance for appeal. Marc showed Bart the rest of the house, including the rest room, which he took time to inspect more carefully while Marc waited outside. Meanwhile, Georgia put fresh sheets on the bed and found one of Marc's old t-shirts for Bart to sleep in. It swallowed him whole, but it was better than sleeping in his old clothes and he wasn't that comfortable with the idea of not having some sort of shelter between him and the rest of the world.

He slipped between the sheets, basking in the scent of fresh linens. He should have drifted into dreamland immediately, but his thoughts were impeding his journey. He wondered about the right Reverend Angus McFarland, and what he was keeping himself from that he truly craved. Then he listened to the quiet snores of Darryl and the loud rumbling of Leonard as his two constant companions slept at the end of the bed and wondered if they were keeping him from the one thing that he truly craved. Then he wondered what that might be. Would he even know it if he saw it? Had he found it in Maria, only to lose it again because of some twist of fate? But he didn't believe in fate. He believed in the sovereign hand of God. Would God show him the one thing he longed for, only to take it away again? He thought about

Moses and how God showed him the Promised Land, only to tell him he couldn't go in. The situation was different, though. Moses had sinned. But he was a sinner, too, wasn't he? By now the thoughts were too deep and he began drowning in a sea of philosophy that was better left to better swimmers than he was. Instead of continuing to fight it anymore, he let the waves pull him under. He slept restfully, not one more thought entering his head until late the next morning when he thought he smelled bacon, eggs, and that nectar of the ages, coffee.

CHAPTER THREE

It was almost noon when Marc dropped off his new friend and fellow brother-in-arms. Bart thanked him for his hospitality and Marc thanked him for the opportunity to preach at the community revival, which was something he had longed for since coming to town almost fifteen years ago.

"You let your members do what they want, you hear?" he ordered Bart.

"They are my members, but I'm their spiritual leader, and you better know which direction I'm going to lead them."

"Fair enough," came the response. "But don't you go preaching to them if they don't see it your way."

"I'll preach to them if they don't see it God's way," Bart replied.

"Again, fair enough." The two men embraced, unashamed of the fountain of love that had sprung up within each of them for the other. This was what Jesus had intended for them. Bart almost felt like Jonathan to Marc's David. It was as if in one chance meeting their souls had been knit together. But then both men knew that with God there was no such thing as a chance meeting or coincidence. The chaos theory that said the flutter of the wings of a butterfly in Africa could affect events across the globe was true in a sense, but it had nothing to do with chaos and everything to do with the God of order and creation. He knew the falling of a sparrow and the hairs on the head of each

71

man, so why would it seem a big thing for him to orchestrate events to His

chosen desire?

After they departed, Bart got in his car and headed for Dixie's Diner,

even though he was still stuffed from the breakfast he had eaten less than three

hours previous. The second helping of biscuits and gravy was probably a bit

much, but the cooking was so good that he couldn't resist. He decided that his

church and Marc's needed to have a day of fellowship to introduce the

congregations to one another, capped off of course with a pot luck dinner.

Every service should be capped off with a pot luck dinner on the grounds if

the cooking was that delicious. He wondered how Marc maintained any self

control.

He didn't need any lunch, but he had made Dixie's a regular stop on his

daily routine. He liked to get there earlier, while some of the chicken house

hands were coming in during their break, but he had missed that chance. Still,

he would be able to catch up on some of the local news and find out how the

town had reacted to the arrest of Bonnie Holden. After he left there, he

planned to go see the family.

He made it almost eight blocks before steam came pouring out from

underneath his hood and the needle was moving toward the red danger zone

on his thermostat. He pulled the car over to the curb and popped the hood,

despite the fact that he had little to no mechanical skill. He probably couldn't tell the radiator from the carburetor, but the manly thing to do when your car broke down was pop the hood, look at the engine, jiggle some wires or hoses, and then get back behind the wheel and hope you fixed it. If you had a wife or other capable female assistant, you told her to try it again at various times after you had jiggled the wire or hoses, then told her what you thought the problem was even if you didn't have a clue.

After the steam cleared, Bart peered down into the engine compartment hoping there would be an arrow like the one on the map at the mall that pointed out exactly what was wrong and then give detailed, even an idiot who doesn't know a open end wrench from a socket set of instructions to follow on how to fix the problem. He was hunched over the area where the steam had been thickest when he jumped at the sound of a voice calling behind him. He nearly crashed into the open hood before regaining his senses.

"What'cha doin' there, preacher?"

"Praying for a mechanic to pass by."

"Then you're in luck. Guess the big guy was feeling generous today, cause you happened to break down just a few feet from my driveway, and I'm a mechanic. Strictly shade tree, but I'm good and reasonably priced."

"Great!" Bart proclaimed. "I'm Bart Rancher, by the way," he said offering his hand to the stranger.

"I know," the other man replied. "Guess you don't remember me. I'm

Clyde Fowler. We met at my niece's wedding last year. She's Tamara Rivers

now, was Tamara Peterson."

"Yeah, I remember the wedding. I was wondering how they're doing. I

usually do a follow up visit with those I marry, but they moved away shortly

after that. Have you heard from them recently?"

"Just the other day. She's dropping a bundle sometime around the first

of the year. He's working steady and they got a roof over their heads, so I

guess all in all they're doing pretty good."

"Glad to hear it. Hey, I was heading to Dixie's for a little lunch. Care

to join me? I'm buying."

"I guess. I gotta let this thing cool down before I can get into the shop

anyway. I'll go get my car and we'll be on our way."

"Don't bother," Bart said. "The cafe is just a few blocks away. It'll give

us a chance to talk." Clyde agreed against his better judgment, not being

someone given to regular exercise. Besides, he didn't like the thought of being

seen with a preacher in public. It might hurt his image and give people the

wrong kind of idea. Soon though, he lost all thought of Bart being a preacher

and just started thinking of him as a regular kind of guy who happened to

preach. It was funny, because Clyde had been raised in church and had met

every kind of preacher under the sun. There were those who preached hell fire

and damnation at every drop of a hat, while others spoke in lofty platitudes no matter what situation arose. If your mother died, as his had, then God had called her home with a purpose. What purpose could God possibly have for taking the only decent person a nine year old boy knew home? Still others spoke of doing one thing, while they practiced another. Like the youth pastor that had gotten his cousin pregnant and then suddenly felt God call him to another ministry somewhere else, and no doubt another young, vulnerable girl.

Bart, however, didn't speak in trite quotes about the goodness of God or talk about everyone going to hell in a hand basket. Instead, he talked about the weather, sports, how long Clyde had been a mechanic, who was who in their little town. Clyde was working on a second piece of pecan pie when the conversation took on a more serious tone.

"What do you know about Angus McFarland?" Bart asked, lifting his coffee to his lips for another drink. He had only eaten a light salad, a few bites of pie, and probably close to a pot of coffee.

"The pastor at Riverview? What about him?"

"Nothing really. It's just that you were born and raised here and Angus has been here as long as anyone can remember. So I thought you might know a little something about him."

"I know he's the reason I quit going to church," Clyde answered.

"That's a lot of responsibility for one man," Bart replied. "What could he have done that was that bad?"

"Alright, he ain't the only reason I quit. I reckon he's more the straw that broke this camel's back. You sure you got time to hear the story?"

"Where am I gonna go? You got my car so I guess I'll walk back to the church and see if I can rent a car or something. But, yeah, I got time and I'm interested."

"Don't sweat the car. I got one or two I can loan you until I get yours finished. As for Angus, I guess it's not that long of story. I was really into church when I was a kid, even though most of the preachers I knew were hypocrites or boring as paint drying."

"Which category do I fall in to?" Bart asked.

"Well, you ain't boring. We'll have to see about the hypocrite part. Anyways, me and some buddies went visiting. You know, handing out tracts, going door to door."

"Wish I could get some young people interested in that today."

"Well, we weren't interested long. We went to the black community and invited some of them folks to join us the next Sunday."

"Black community?" Bart wondered.

"Yeah, this is the south and that was a few years before segregation. There's still a kind of black community across town. There's folks of all colors around town, but in that area, it's mostly blacks."

"So what happened?"

"Huh?"

"When you invited them to church. What happened?" Bart wondered.

"Brother Angus, who was my pastor at the time and a few deacons met them at the door, but not to welcome them into the congregation. They told them folks that they were at a white church and pointed them to another church down the road that was more to their particular persuasion."

"They turned them away because they were black?" Bart asked incredulously.

"Like I said, this is the south, and that was a long time ago. Thanks for lunch. If you'll drop by later, I've got a sixty-nine VW bus in the yard you can drive while I fix yours. The keys are in it."

"Thanks, I'll take you up on that. Hey, you said that was a long time ago, right?"

"Yeah," Clyde answered.

"So people change, right? Maybe Angus has changed."

"I wouldn't count on it," Clyde disagreed. "I didn't tell you, but after that incident, I found out he was into more stuff. The Klan, the Aryans, that kind of stuff. I wouldn't be surprised if he wore a swastika and a cross. With the swastika coming in first."

"She's been watching you," Darryl told Bart.

77

"Who?" Bart wondered.

"Angus, of course," Clyde replied.

"The waitress. She's been watching you the whole time you've been here."

"Jenny?" Bart asked.

"Yes," replied a sweet young girl with bright blue eyes and an even brighter smile. She came with a carafe of coffee and filled both of their cups. Bart thanked her and she left. This was getting out of hand.

"No," replied Darryl. "Not Jenny, the other one. The one with the set of luggage under her eyes and more wrinkles than your old basset hound."

"I've never had an old basset hound," Bart corrected him.

"Nice to know, preacher, but I don't see what it has to do with Angus or his brother Shane."

"Sorry," Bart said lamely. "I was just thinking out loud."

"He's right," Leonard added. "She's been watching you and now she's on the phone, probably calling in to her report on you."

"You're just being paranoid," Bart stated.

"Well, maybe, but I always say that even paranoid people have some real enemies," Clyde answered, totally unaware of the conversation that was going on around him. Darryl was at his left, peering over the back of the booth at Linda Falstaff, the older waitress that was now on the phone and occasionally peering back in their direction. Bart thought that his two friends might actually be on to something, but then dismissed the thought as delusional. Leonard was pacing around the table like a caged lion and Bart thought it best to get him out of there as soon as he could so he motioned for the bright eyes to come his way.

The waitress came back by to bring their check. Bart had known her since she joined the church shortly after his arrival. She was a cute blonde or redhead, depending on her mood and the latest bottle bought from the department store, with a dazzling smile and the kind of bubbly personality that made people warm up to her immediately. With her currently blonde hair up in little pigtails, she looked like she should be home having a tea party instead of serving up coffee and pie.

"No classes today?" Bart asked as he picked up the check and handed it back to Jenny along with his credit card.

"I've got English this afternoon," she replied. "But tomorrow's my big day. Three classes, including Algebra. Yuck."

"Don't overload yourself," Bart advised.

"Yeah," Clyde added, "or you might end up a grease monkey like me." Jenny smiled without comment, and then turned to run the card through the machine for payment. Bart told her to add a generous tip to the bill. He knew her well enough to know she wouldn't cheat him. After her return, Bart and

79

Clyde went outside and parted ways, with Bart promising to be by that afternoon for the VW bus. He walked down the street, heading first for the library to study up on Riverview Church and it's one and only pastor, Angus McFarland. Sometime in the course of their conversation, Bart had learned that Angus had started Riverview right after his seminary graduation. The congregation of ten to fifteen people exploded within a year to nearly a hundred. Now they were a mega church, complete with a day care, school, and a fleet of buses running every Sunday that would rival the local schools fleet. There was even talk of Angus and his brother Shane starting a community college that would be run in conjunction with Shane's ministry, a drug rehabilitation ministry that was run on a six hundred acre camp west of town. The image of Shane McFarland made Bart shudder involuntarily. Bart always tried to see the best in people, and he admired the work Shane was doing, to a point, but when he saw Shane the first time, there was an aura of pure evil around him. Normally Bart could differentiate between things he saw only in his mind and things that were real. But when he saw Shane, there was an unearthly glow that emanated evil, one he was sure that no one else could see. He asked Jake about it later.

"He gives me the creeps. That's for sure," Jake replied. "But I gotta admit he keeps getting results. They've graduated a lot of people through that camp. People that are now clean and sober."

"Where are those people now?" Bart asked.

"I don't know," Jake replied. "I think some work at the camp; others have made their way into town. Some went back home, wherever that is. Why do you ask?"

"I was just wondering," Bart replied, letting the conversation turn to sports or weather. That was back in spring, shortly after graduation. Since then, Bart had avoided the subject, and avoided Shane. It wasn't that he didn't like the guy. There really weren't any feelings one way or another. They didn't know each other well enough to develop a friendship or enmity with one another. But Bart still saw that evil emanation come from him and couldn't stand the thought of it. Even now, while he walked down the road on a bright fall day, full of fresh air and sunshine, a cloud hung over his head at the image of Shane McFarland. He decided to purposefully think of something else, another image to superimpose on his current thoughts. His mind ran to the sixty-nine VW bus that Clyde was going to loan him, and another one he had known during his days in college.

It was summer break of nineteen eighty-three. He had made a couple of friends during his Philosophy class that year that were almost as strange as he was. In some ways they were even stranger. For one thing, they thought it was totally cool that he saw people no one else saw, something he admitted to while they were up until four a.m. playing Risk. They wanted to know how he

81

did it, like it was a trick he could turn on and off at a whim, a game he played that he could quit if he wanted to. Their names were Elmo Jessup and Elvis Cornelius. Bart called them the Blues Brothers. Elmo was tall, lanky, and a bit clumsy. He walked like his body hadn't yet realized that his legs were as long as they were. He was constantly seen with a Detroit Tigers baseball cap and dark sunglasses, even at night. Someone asked him once about the baseball cap, since he was born and raised in Arkansas, and he replied that he preferred tigers over pigs and that it was as simple as that. Elvis, on the other hand, was round and jovial, like a young Santa Claus. To offset his appearance of jolliness, or at least that was what everyone supposed, he wore dark navy suits, complete with a white shirt and solid colored tie, usually a matching navy or black. He looked like a door to door Bible salesman, which he tried one summer with nothing to show for his efforts but sore feet and phone numbers of several bored housewives. He never called them as far as Bart knew.

They had a VW bus they drove around campus and were planning on taking it to California that summer for a music festival around the San Francisco area. They wanted him to go along so he could take a turn driving and they could make better time. He figured out shortly that they really wanted him to go so he could do most of the driving while they sat in the back passing a joint back and forth to each other. Bart had to keep his window open to avoid a contact buzz.

One memory played upon another, like a cassette tape rewinding itself in his mind. He thought of the concert, head banging music so loud it felt like his insides were turning to Jell-O. He thought of Elmo and Elvis being arrested along with about a dozen others on drunk and disorderly charges after they were spotted in one of the nicer neighborhoods urinating on people's flowers.

"They needed watering," Elvis claimed. The police would have preferred they used a different sprinkler system. It took all that he had, money that was supposed to be used for the return trip, to bail them out. It was the thought of them locked up in a crowded cell with their fellow watering partners that made Bart shudder involuntarily with fear. He remembered another inmate, one that was quiet and sat by himself in a corner. When Bart came in, he raised his head to look directly into Bart's eyes. He had the same emanation of evil surrounding him that Shane did. Later, after they were safe back home, Bart called back to San Diego to make some inquiries. With a little luck and a lot of lying, which he later regretted, he found that the man with the haunting stare and aura of evil was a serial pedophile who had killed at least three children and probably many more. Bart didn't think Shane was a pedophile, but there definitely was something about that commonality of an evil presence that made Bart think the guru of drug rehab was capable of unspeakable acts. He decided at that point that he and Jake needed to visit the facilities in the woods, just to see what they were really up to. Jake, of course, couldn't go in any official capacity, but he could accompany a pastor who was considering asking his church to support their efforts financially.

Bart was so lost in his train of thought that he nearly knocked over Joe Thompson, the mail carrier on his appointed rounds.

"Go...," Joe began to say angrily, then realized who he had bumped into and changed directions, "...sh darn it. Sorry, preacher, I didn't realize it was you."

"Don't apologize to me," Bart responded. "It wasn't my name you were about to use in vain. Besides, it's my fault. I was pretty deep in thought."

"No harm done," Joe replied lazily. "We all step in it from time to time." Joe was a cowboy who had been born about a hundred and fifty years out of his time. He should have been riding for the Pony Express instead of driving a jeep around town and walking up and down the streets delivering mail door to door. He was born to avoid wild Indians, not stray dogs. He stood about five foot eight, with big burly arms, an expansive chest full of coarse red hair, with a bushy mustache and eyebrows to match. Bart thought how much he would look like a sheep dog when those red hairs turned gray and almost giggled. His expression of stepping in it came from the small cattle ranch him and his wife ran.

"Like I said, I was deep in thought," Bart apologized. "I should have been watching where I was going."

"Like I said, preacher, no harm no foul," Joe replied and walked on down the street. Bart watched him walk away and something caught his eye. Despite the objection of the calendar and common sense, Joe was still wearing his short sleeve shirt and baggy shorts. It was the shorts that clicked with Bart. He had promised Clyde that if he ever showed up at church, which he was likely to do just to check, that he would find the preacher wearing Bermuda shorts and a flowery shirt. The only problem was that Bart had neither.

"You can borrow some of mine," Leonard offered.

"Thanks," Bart responded. "But somehow I don't think the congregation would think kindly of me if I went to the pulpit wearing imaginary clothes that only I could see."

"Why not?" Leonard wondered.

"Because he would be naked, dummy," Darryl answered. "Haven't you ever heard of 'The Emperor's New Clothes'?"

"No, but since he's got new clothes, maybe he's got some shorts and a flowery shirt that we could borrow."

"Sometimes you're impossible," Darryl replied wearily.

"That would make a good sermon," Bart said to no one in particular.

"What's that?" Leonard wondered.

"The thing about the new clothes. A lot of time people will look ridiculous for one reason or another, but because of peer pressure or because everyone else is afraid that they also look ridiculous, no one says anything. I might work that up for this Sunday." Darryl gave Leonard a disdainful look, which prompted a tongue from Leonard. That brought a big raspberry from his partner, who in turn responded with a gesture of his own. And so it went down the street as the two imaginary friends tried to outdo the other while the one real person began preaching out loud as he walked down the street. This was one idiosyncrasy the townspeople had gotten used to. Bart often practiced his sermons while on long walks or driving down the street. It was strange to people at first, who thought that he was waving when in reality he was beating the dash of his car just as he would beat the pulpit that following Sunday.

Coming to a corner, Bart stopped to gather his bearings. He remembered the night before and even though it was only about two in the afternoon, he didn't want to end up back in a bad part of town. Besides, without transportation, wherever he walked to, he would also have to walk back from. He was on Main Street, in the old part of town. Well, the old, statelier part of town. The oldest part of town consisted of shotgun housing and run down shacks. Some of the descendants of the original settlers still lived there, having lost the drive for exploration and the search for a better horizon that had brought their great grandparents there a hundred years or so before.

The housing Bart was surrounded by was built by the merchants and

bankers who came after the explorers had cleared the way. They came with

their wealth and wares when the manganese mines opened and rail and river

traffic began flowing through town. They prospered off the hard work of

others and their homes reflected it well. They were stately, elegant and

refined, with a sense of history and culture seen in things like marbled

columns, ornamental wrought iron gates, and sculptured carvings over the

doors and windows. This was opulence at its small town best, and it was

almost lost forever when subdivisions began popping up along the edge of

town. Some developer would build a small lake, usually not much bigger than

a farm pond, sell one plot to a relative for a cheap price, and then rake in the

dough as pride forced the wealthy of town to try to outdo each other. Main

Street became passé. It was where the old money, and, consequentially, where

the old people lived. As they died off, those with less money could come in

and buy up the property in estate sales. The houses went relatively cheap since

there was little interest from the real money of town. The only problem was

that those who bought the homes couldn't afford the upkeep and property

taxes. One or the other suffered, usually the maintenance. Houses were falling

into disrepair and ruin, giving the whole town an image of being run down. It

wasn't until some bright politician came up with the idea of having it all declared a historical district that things started turning around. Those who truly wanted to stay in their new homes could now get grants for repairs. Others opted to sell for a handsome profit to those of the upper class who found it more appealing to own a piece of history than a piece of so called lake front property. Angus McFarland owned one of the larger of the homes Bart was now passing. He wished he knew for sure which one, since the good Reverend might just be paid a visit by a fellow pastor and two of his friends. But, since he couldn't very well knock door to door to find Angus, he just kept walking down Main Street, heading for the library and a second hand store where he hoped to find his new wardrobe.

The transition from historic housing to historic shopping came suddenly, buffered in between by two of the oldest churches in town. One was a large Methodist church, complete with sanctuary, family recreation center, and small school for children in first through fifth grade. Facing it, on the other side of the street, was a matching Baptist church. Its sanctuary was just as large, perhaps a bit larger, but it lacked the area necessary for school and recreation center. Instead, it opted to buy a few of the smaller shops next to it and convert them to counseling offices for women in need and those who were drug addicted. It lacked the funding and public eye of the McFarland's venture, but it still managed to help a great deal of people break the savage cycle of dependency.

The second hand clothing store was set in niche between a hardware store and a beauty school. The entrance was unassuming, just a single glass door with a handwritten sign telling the name of the store and it's hours. Bart knew the profits, which were few and far between, helped the local battered women's shelter and tried to shop there as often as he could. Besides, he wasn't too proud to buy decent clothes at a bargain price even if someone else had worn them first. He had found some items that still had the original store tags on them, usually right after Christmas. They probably came from people who didn't like what Aunt Martha gave them, and were afraid of hurting her feelings if they re-gifted within the family. Better to give clothes away than to offend Aunt Martha.

The ding of the bell on the door was the cue for the store manager, Miss Marsha Mae, to come out swinging. She dropped whatever she was doing to come and greet her new customer. Bart was used to her hovering about while he shopped, telling him about the latest bargains they had just gotten in and about the latest gossip she had heard, which she reported as prayer requests, of course. Miss Marsha Mae was in her sixties, but still had the energy of a twenty year old. She began the store as a hobby to fill her time after the passing of her dear Edmund just over a decade prior. And even though her work was solely on a volunteer basis, she worked as hard as Donald Trump or Bill Gates. The shop was kept clean and orderly, with "a place for everything and everything in its place," according to Miss Marsha's strict standards. With her round figure, pleasant smile, and blue gray hair tied neatly in a tight bun, she could have passed for Mrs. Santa Claus. Her plump figure spoke about her love for food, especially fried chicken and sweet treats, but her sparkling eyes and rosy cheeks told about her love for people. That was another reason Bart loved to come and shop there. He had sometimes bought things he had no need for just to visit with Miss Marsha. Later, on a Friday when he knew she visited Edmund's grave and wouldn't be working, he would come and return anything he had bought, but never asked for his money back. To him, it was well spent.

"Brother Bart," she cried out, dropping her duster on the counter, "what a pleasant surprise! What can I help you find today? We just got in an almost brand new electric skillet. It would be the perfect thing for a bachelor like you. Easy clean up, enough room for you to cook your bacon and eggs at the same time. And with its non-stick surface, clean up will be a snap. At five dollars, this bargain won't last." Bart thought about how much she sounded like a late night infomercial host. Just three easy payments of ten dollars and this fifty dollar value will be yours for a lifetime. Hurry, quantities are limited. The next ten callers will receive a free supply of baby shampoo.

"No, thank you," he replied. "I'm looking for a pair of Bermuda shorts and a flowery shirt to match."

"Whatever for?" she wondered. "Bart, dear, if you haven't noticed, fall is coming. I know summer is trying to hang on, but it's going to let go soon, and it's not exactly going to be weather for shorts. Besides, I've seen your legs, it's best to keep them covered." Miss Marsha Mae was not one to mince words, even if it cost her a sale. Bart smiled, unsure of whether to thank her for her advice, which was sound, or to be offended by the implication that his legs were ugly. He knew they were, but it wasn't right to go around telling people they had ugly body parts, even if it were true.

"I realize that, Miss Marsha, but I made a promise to a man and I intend to keep it. If you'll just point me in the right direction, I'll let you get back to your dusting. Thank you." Bart went back to the bargain rack, since Miss Marsha was sure that Fall would attack with blustery winds and colder temperatures any day now, and had put the seasonal items such as shorts on a half price sale. That suited Bart, since he intended to wear his hideous outfit once and only once. With his new clothes properly bought and bagged, Bart headed across the street to the county library.

The library was housed on the first floor of an imposing brick edifice. The basement held various county offices and served at times as a shelter in case of emergency. The building was built in the fifties, during the time of the Cold War, and was built with the thought of a nuclear holocaust in mind. Accordingly, there were accommodations in the basement for housing and feeding fifty people. It was built with the thought of saving the local leaders, who would be needed to bring order back to the mutated mob after the holocaust occurred. Common sense reigned during the seventies, and the area was converted to offices and a recreational center for clubs and civic groups to use for their meetings.

The second floor housed the county court house and associated offices such as the prosecuting attorney and legal aid. Bart had visited there only once, when called upon for jury duty. He found the surroundings overwhelming. The courthouse itself was built with high cathedral type ceilings, complete with mahogany carvings attached to the beams supporting the ceiling. The judge sat high on the bench, looking down upon the offending criminal, and everyone else for that matter, like they were mere ants he could squash with a smack of his gavel. Since this was the second Monday of the month, he was fairly sure Jake would be up there, either giving testimony or guarding prisoners. He didn't like the idea of going back up there, but he needed to talk to Jake about his plans for visiting Shane's place.

He looked up, shielding his eyes from the afternoon sun, to see if he could spot the sheriff in one of the windows. He thought he saw him, but with the glare coming off the windows, it was hard to tell. He was still looking up when he stepped off the curb and onto the street. He didn't look down again until he heard the squealing of tires and the screams of Miss Marsha Mae, who had chased after him because he had forgotten his change.

The car screaming toward him was a dark sedan. Bart stared at it, thinking to himself that he probably felt the same way a deer did when it faced the possibility of a vehicle onslaught. He told his legs to move, to jump, bolt, run. He told them to do anything except just stand there waiting to be hit. His body begged them to move, knowing it would face the greater portion of the impact, but the legs refused to budge. For some reason that defied logic of any sort, he decided to close his eyes, maybe with the possible thought that if he didn't see the car as it crashed into his body and rolled over his lifeless and mangled form, it wouldn't hurt, or at least not as much.

Then he felt it. The impact knocked him down and crashed him into the sidewalk, barely glancing his shoulder on a parking meter as he went down. It was funny, but the closing of the eyes must have worked. The car was much softer than he imagined it would be. It was also warmer than he thought it should be, and smelled of jasmine and wildflowers instead of gasoline and burning oil. Instinctively, he wrapped his arms around the car and found that it was curved and felt nice underneath his fingers.

"Hey," the car called out in a husky, yet definitely feminine voice, "watch where you put your hands. Just because I saved your life doesn't mean you can do what you want with me."

Bart finally gathered the nerve he needed to open his eyes. As he did, he found that staring back at him were the darkest, deepest, most beautiful green eyes he had ever seen. They seemed to swallow any light that came near them and then glow back with an eerie incandescence. They were set in a field of lovely, light olive skin, flawless and glowing. Despite everything that he was, despite the character he had carefully carved over the years from the stone of his soul, Bart found himself craning his neck towards her for a kiss. He kissed long, deep, and passionately, and was pleasantly surprised to find his kiss returned by one of her own.

Her kiss spoke to him of everything that she was. She was wild, reckless, untamed by any man. But, at the same time, she was drawn in by her own restraints. It was power in check. She kissed him intuitively, matching her moves to his, countering his parries with her own dodges or thrusts. It was as if a connection had been made between the two that defied the physical plane, yet had not reached to a higher spiritual one. No, this was transcendent of mere physical desire, beyond the mortal realm of understanding, but not reaching upwards to higher planes. This reached back, deep into the recesses of who man was, of who Bart Rancher was. It was emotional, raw and unbridled. It was deeply primitive, forcing him to move with the stealth of a hunter on the trail of prey for the family dinner, and then reacting savagely once that prey is found.

Her lips were soft and sensuous, inviting a man to probe deeper and deeper into the cavernous reaches; not knowing that lying within was the means for his own demise. Her hair poured down over him like a soft summer rain, caressing his cheek, snaking its way down his neck and tickling the backs of his ears. Her aroma enthralled him. It was part flowers and lace, all pretty and girly, and part the sweet sweat of savage desire. The more that deep inside he tried to run, the more on the outside that he dove in deeper and deeper, oblivious to all that was around him. He was oblivious to the car that had just tried to run him over. He was oblivious to the crowd that gathered around them. Oblivious to the fact that he was the pastor of a church and should be setting a proper example of behavior to his congregation. He was totally oblivious to even Leonard and Darryl, who stood over the pair practically squealing with childish delight. He was oblivious to everything until he heard the sound of his friend's voice, Sheriff Jake.

"Am I interrupting something?" he asked bemusedly. Bart practically tossed off his savior, then realized what he was doing and began helping her up before getting up himself, standing in front of the sheriff like a schoolboy standing in front of the principal after getting caught putting a frog down a girl's back. Only it wasn't a frog and it wasn't down her back.

"This isn't what it looks like," he lied.

"It looks like the two of you were lying on the sidewalk making out," Jake commented.

"We were talking about the car," Bart continued to lie, wondering why he was even as the words came out of his mouth. He felt like a dummy, with ventriloquist's hands up his back, moving his mouth and speaking for him. What did he hope to gain by lying to his best friend? He was caught with his hand in the cookie jar and crumbs spilling down his cheek and onto his shirt.

"Well," Jake smirked, "if you were talking, I'd guess you swapped from Baptist to Pentecostal."

"What's that supposed to mean?" Bart asked, sounding irritated despite himself.

"It means that from what I seen, the two of you were speaking in tongues," he answered. Bart's partner in the great cookie caper laughed quietly. It was just the kind of laugh Bart would expect from her, and he loved it. In fact, he loved everything about her, or maybe he just lusted everything about her. At the moment, his mind and heart were reeling and racing together and he couldn't tell who was in the lead. To make matters worse, he didn't care. It was horrible. He had gained mastery over his heart years ago as a matter of practicality. Too many people getting in and carving their initials on his heart like lovesick vandals had left him at times hollowed, at other times simply scarred and hardened. He had allowed a few in to the waters of his soul, but only deep enough to get their ankles wet and test the waters. Most left, either unimpressed by the temperature of the water or impatient to go deeper. Jake was one of the few who kept trying to get in deeper.

"Are you going to introduce me to your girlfriend, or do I have to arrest the two of you for public indecency and take you downtown for interrogation?" Jake asked.

"Sorry, this is...." Bart trailed off, embarrassed by the knowledge that the woman who had just saved his life and captured his heart, all in one swift move, was a total stranger to him.

"The name is Cassandra Green," she replied, holding out her hand. Jake took it, bowed gracefully, and kissed the top of it.

"My gratitude for your kindness," he stated. Bart felt like he was going to be sick. Jake was being a gentleman, thanking her for her heroics, and all he had done was practically rape her for the public's amusement and pleasure. Of course, she had responded, which meant it wasn't sexual assault. It didn't make it right, either. He was totally confused and wanted nothing more than to crawl into a deep hole until things could be made right again, like possibly after the next ice age. Where was a crashing meteor when a person needed one?

"I just did what anyone would do," she responded. Jake looked at the crowd of gawking onlookers, glaring at them for both their incessant curiosity and their lack of moral fortitude in doing what was right. Most of the people he saw had been helped by Bart at one time or another, either directly or

97

indirectly. And some of them were close enough to have acted on his behalf, but none gave so much as a shout of warning. He knew that most people were incapacitated by fear. Even Bart, who stood in the path of vicious onslaught, had been unable to move. But to gather around afterwards like vultures looking for a tasty morsel to share at the corner grocery or beauty shop was more than he could fathom. They dispersed with a wave of his hand.

"Not anyone would risk their lives for another," Jake commented. "So please accept my deepest gratitude. Believe me; friends like Bart don't come along every day."

"So that's your name," she said coyly. "I was wondering if we were ever going to be properly introduced."

"Shoot me and label me as a clod for my lack of manners," Jake stated. "Bart Rancher meet Miss....?" he trailed off, hoping his guess was right.

"Yes," she said. "It's Miss."

"Miss Cassandra Green," Jake continued. "Miss Cassandra Green, may I present Mr. Bart Rancher, of the jolly ranchers." She laughed again, and Bart found himself getting jealous over a girl he barely knew, and yet one he knew all too well. He knew the graceful curves of her hips that his hands had found, in spite of being told to leave them alone. He knew the feel and touch of her lips, finding them warm and totally inviting. He knew the aroma that surrounded her and captivated him. He knew so much about her physically, all gained in just a fraction of time, a wrinkle in the fabric of eternity, and yet

knew so little about Cassandra Green the person. He wouldn't let that stay.

"Pleased to meet you, Bart Rancher, of the jolly ranchers." It was

funny when she said it, irritating when coming from Jake.

"And I'm most pleased to meet you," he responded, "especially since

if I hadn't met you, I would have become very familiar with that passing

automobile. Speaking of which, did anyone see what kind of car it was."

"I figured you'd know, with your gift and all," Jake answered.

"What do you mean, gift?" Cassandra asked.

"Nothing," Bart responded, giving his friend a look that told him to

shut up about gifts and such. "I just have a knack for cars, that's all. But it

happened so fast and my mind was a thousand miles away."

"It was a late model sedan, either navy or black," Cassandra said. "I

didn't get a license number because it didn't have plates." Jake wrote down

the information and called to one of his deputies on his shoulder radio.

"It's probably stolen," he informed them. "Which means it'll end up at

the edge of Finley Woods when they're through with it. I've got Rogers

headed that way now, but he's across the county from there. They'll have it

dumped and gone before he gets there."

"So you think that's what it was, a careless joy rider?" Bart asked.

"Maybe, but even if it's not, they'll want it to look like it was. And anyone familiar with this area knows Finley Woods is the place to dump a car

and have it found. When we pick it up, I'll have it towed in so our forensics

team can go over it, but I doubt we find anything."

"You have a forensics team?" Cassandra asked, impressed by the

facilities of a small town.

"Well, actually it's just Deputy Rogers, me and a kit we ordered from

Acme products, but we usually get the job done."

"Maybe you should have been a comedian," Cassandra said, locking

her green eyes on Jake's.

"How's your wife, Melissa?" Bart asked.

"Huh?" Jake replied. "I guess she's ok. Unless something happened

since I left her after lunch. We had lunch together in the school cafeteria. Why

are you asking?"

"No reason," Bart answered. "Just haven't seen her for awhile and I

was wondering."

"You were at our house yesterday, chum. Did you hit your head back

there?" Bart felt his head, but it wasn't that end that took the brunt of the fall.

He dearly wanted to rub the other end, where the true soreness was, but

couldn't bring himself to do it in front of Cassandra. Funny, he made out with

her in front of everyone, but he wouldn't rub his own rear end in front of her.

Suddenly, the thought of what he had done hit him like lightning from heaven.

He had kissed a woman. No, he had publicly and flagrantly made out with a total stranger in public view. What was he going to tell his congregation? What answers could he provide for his deacons? And even worse, what would he tell his youth? Those people that he exhorted daily to remain chaste and pure. How could he explain to them what had happened? He felt like crawling into a deep, dark, damp hole and staying there until all memory of this incident could be erased from existence. He should only have to stay until the next ice age. Where was a marauding meteor when it was needed? Objects hurtling through space and policemen were just alike, neither one showing up when they were needed. That wasn't true. Jake could have been a little quicker, but he did rescue Bart just before he had thrown off all restraint and drowned in a sea of passion.

"Maybe you should get checked out," Cassandra commented. "You did break my fall on that concrete."

"Listen to you," Bart said. "You save my life and make it sound like I did you a favor."

"I wish you two would stop saying that. I'm not a hero, just a girl who happened to be jogging by when I saw someone in trouble. That's all." Until now, Bart hadn't noticed that she was wearing a jogging suit, and then he wondered how he could have missed it. It was bright yellow, with a hood hanging down it's back. Bart recognized it at once. It was the same kind of sweat outfit he had worn when he was in physical training with the agency. They claimed that the suits were that bright because of the dangers of passing motorists as the cadets ran down the sides of roads and highways. Others thought it was so escaping cadets could be spotted and caught easily. Other rumors included that they were that color because the directors uncle or cousin had produced an abundance of ugly outfits and needed someone to unload them on. Bart's favorite theory was that they were designed purposefully repugnant so no one would steal them. That backfired, however, when some of the kids from a nearby school borrowed them from their parents. A fashion trend was started and pretty soon banana suits were spotted all over the state of Virginia. The director's uncle, cousin, or other relative must have made a fortune.

The outfit didn't look the same on her though. Bart tried to figure out what had changed in the design and finally came to the conclusion that the man, or woman in this case, did make the clothes. Most women have a body that is slowly molded over the course of their lifetimes. Age, genetics, diet, exercise, or the lack of the latter, all have a hand in molding and shaping the body. Cassandra, however, Bart decided, had not been cast from a generic mold. Her body was sculptured by a master craftsman. Each line, every curve, was placed in perfect symmetry and proportion. The clothing, that usually hung on a body like a set of cheap drapes, caressed over her curves like a rippling waterfall, lengthening each line, accenting every asset.

"Hero or not, thanks for saving my life," Bart said. He looked uncomfortable, not knowing what to say or do next. Jake realized what was going on and decided it was time for him to be the hero and step in to save his friend's life. It wasn't like they hadn't done the same for each other before. Bart had saved Jake's skin in more ways than one. He had saved it literally during a gun battle shortly after his arrival. And, more recently, he had saved it emotionally when he brought Jake and Melissa in for counseling, something neither thought they needed, despite the cold shoulders and hot arguments they had.

"Are you new in town?" he asked.

"Not really in town," she replied. "I'm just kind of passing through, taking care of matters along the way."

"Personal or business?" Jake asked, truly intrigued at how little information she was providing. He was about to set his best friend up on a date and he knew so little about the woman he was getting his friend involved with, other than the fact that she saved total strangers from car accidents and then made out with them. This might be some kind of elaborate scam.

"Yes," she replied, being decisively secretive.

"Right," Jake answered, then turned his attention back to Bart. "I don't suppose you'd know anyone that would like to make you a permanent addition to Main Street?" Bart thought about it. He had made enemies during his short life time, more than most, not as many as others. Still, most of his enemies were shadows of another day's sun. They were past and gone. He had made a few during his time with the agency, but he had left them with his gun, badge, and assorted knick-knacks that decorated his desk. Surely none of them would take the time or effort to track him down to a small town in northern Arkansas. And they would have used a speeding bullet with a silencer, not a speeding car with a loud muffler. There was something. That car had a definite misfire, or backfire, one of the two. It also had a hole in it's exhaust. There was something else, something just outside his mind's field of vision.

"He threw some trash out the window," Darryl came to his aid.

"Jake," Bart said. "Look over here, in front of the jewelry store."

"What are we looking for?" Jake asked. Cassandra walked along behind, stopping traffic with a hand and glare.

"Not sure, but I think our driver is a smoker. Here it is!" he exclaimed.

"It's still smoking," Cassandra commented.

"We'll get this to the state crime lab," Jake said, picking up the burning butt with a pair of tweezers he kept in his front shirt pocket. He used the tweezers to snuff out the remaining fire, then dropped it into a plastic evidence bag.

"You always carry that stuff with you?" Cassandra asked.

"Just being a good boy scout," he replied. He was also thinking of how to be a good boy scout and earn a merit badge in matchmaking. His friend was a good man, but shy and backwards when it came to people. Jake knew that without intervention, either divine or through his own efforts, this fish would jump off of the line before Bart had a chance to set the hook. He wondered at one point how a good guy like Bart could get through life without being snared by the trap of some woman. He knew Bart had problems, but so did everyone else. He knew Bart probably better than anyone, and yet he didn't really know him at all. Every time he tried to get Bart to open up about his past, he found himself getting shut further and further out. He finally decided, mostly by way of Melissa's advice, to drop the interrogation techniques and just be there when Bart needed a friend. That worked. Right now, though, it was time for interrogation techniques so Bart could find out where Cassandra was staying.

"I'm at the Scenic," she said, as if reading his mind. Jake didn't know if she said it for his behalf or Bart's. And he really didn't care.

"They have a terrific restaurant there," Jake stated. "But I bet you wouldn't mind some good home cooking."

"Anytime," she agreed.

"Good, then Bart will pick you up around six." Bart wasn't sure about any of this. He was already contemplating his tactics on dealing with an upset congregation, and having dinner with the woman he had made out with wasn't part of his strategy. Forgetting he had ever met her had come to mind, but that was easily dismissed by the fact that she had been indelibly etched into every recess of his damaged psyche. Besides, he didn't have a vehicle. That was it. That was his way out.

"I don't have a car. Mine's at Clyde's. It went down in front of his shop. Water pump, I think he said." He was rambling, but unable to stop. "He said I could borrow a rig, but it's a sixty nine VW bus, not much to look at. And you know Clyde. I'm liable to get arrested for no tags, no insurance. Who knows what he has stored in there? It might be full of oily parts, greasy rags, and who knows what else?"

"I'll be waiting in the lobby," Cassandra interrupted him. "Now if you two will excuse me, I have a date for dinner and I have to finish my workout and get cleaned up so I can be presentable." With that she trotted off, leaving Bart with his mouth hanging open and his heart hanging out. Presentable? She would be presentable wearing nothing but filthy rags. In her ugly, bright yellow sweat suit she looked better than the Queen of Sheba on her best day and with her finest garments of robes and jewelry.

"I better get back to the courtroom," Jake said. "See you at six. Don't be late or you'll hear it from Melissa." And with that comment, Jake was gone, heading up the courthouse steps, leaving Bart alone with his thoughts and two imaginary friends.

"Bart's got a date," Darryl teased.

"Bart and Cassandra, sitting in a tree," Leonard added. "K I S S I N G." The two of them continued on for a few minutes before Bart shut them up. He was trying to think of ways out of dinner, out of her life before he ever got in, and a way out of town. Not being able to come up with any plausible solutions, he decided that it would be best to just make his date, let her see what a loser he was, then go merrily on her way out of town. Besides, she said she was only passing through. What harm could come from a couple of nights of fun and relaxation.

"She might be a killer," Leonard said. "Maybe she set the whole thing up just to get close to you."

"And what point would that serve?" Darryl demanded.

"Maybe she's using Bart to get to someone else."

"Who else? He's not with the Secret Service. He's not even with the agency anymore. He's just a small town pastor. You're just being paranoid."

"Even paranoid people have some real enemies," Leonard countered.

"Come on, you two. We've got some research to do and then I have a date to get ready for." He put a special emphasis on "I."

"Does that mean we're not invited?" Leonard wondered.

"Duh," Darryl said. "It's at Jake's house, and we don't get to go there anytime, especially when it's a date."

Bart was trying hard to forget about Cassandra for the time. He would deal with that problem later. Right now, he was focused on Angus McFarland and his plans for the town. He forced the passion he was feeling aside, quieting his mind and heart so he could focus on the problem at hand. Angus may not be evil, but something was wrong, and Bart was going to figure out what.

CHAPTER FOUR

Bart was just beginning to dive into the murky depths of the history of Liberty County, well on his way to finding the treasure of knowledge he hoped to find beneath the waters of time, when a tap on his shoulder brought him back to the surface of the here and now. It was Oliver Cratch, a young teenager from his youth group. This was the moment Bart had been dreading since kissing Cassandra on the sidewalk almost half an hour ago. He rechecked the clock on the wall. It had been nearly an hour and a half. He was going to have to keep a check on the time. He was supposed to pick up Cassandra at the Scenic in less than two hours, and he still needed to go to Clyde's and pick up his loaner vehicle, go home to clean up, and then make it out to the hotel. He was glad for the interruption, since he probably would have stayed back in this corner until the lights went out at six.

"What is it, Oliver?" Bart asked the young man.

"Nothing, pastor, I can see your busy," Oliver responded and turned to leave.

"Whoa," Bart called after him. "I'm never too busy for a member of my congregation. Pull up a chair." Bart looked over at his young guest and thought about how much alike the two of them were. Oliver was a straight out of the box, everyday, run of the mill, nerd. Bart tried and tried to think of another word to describe him, but that one kept coming back time after time.

109

He had all the hallmarks of living in Nerdville, including bad clothes that were obviously hand me downs that were not well taken care of by their original owners, glasses that were desperately in need of repair and held together by superglue and tape, and a bad hair cut ala a bowl and clippers. Along with that, he had a horrible home life. The home life being bad wasn't a prerequisite for hitting bottom on the social caste system of high school society, but it didn't do anything to alleviate the problem either. If a man's home is his castle, then a boy's home should be as well. The man should be the king of the castle and the boy it's prince, an heir apparent to the throne. At the very least, the home should serve as a refuge, a fort, a harbor to seek shelter from the stormy seas of the world. In Oliver's case, it was the center of the storm.

Oliver's mom was a tyrant in a dress. At just under six foot, and weighing in at just over two hundred pounds, she could out work, out drink, and just plain out any man at the warehouse where she loaded and unloaded trucks. Oliver's dad, on the other hand, was a mousy little man who worked as a bank teller, a position he had held since high school graduation. He should have been promoted several times, but he was simply a body filling a space and thereby went unnoticed by upper management. In fact, there were people who had worked at the bank for several years that didn't even know Oliver Sr. worked there.

"Are you sure it's okay?" Oliver asked timidly.

"Yeah," Bart answered. "In fact, you just saved me from being late for a date. If it hadn't been for you, I probably would have sat here until closing. So, how can I help you?" Oliver sat down, looked down, and shuffled his feet nervously. Whatever the problem was, it was obvious that it was weighing heavily on his scrawny shoulders. He took out an inhaler and took a few puffs. Bart shifted positions, matching Oliver's position and posture as closely as he could. It was an interrogation technique he had learned during his time with the agency. It was also widely used by counselors around the world. When Oliver finally looked up again, he saw what his mind perceived as a reflection of himself. It made speaking his mind more comfortable.

"I think I'm gay," he blurted out.

"Really," Bart said amusedly. "I am too." Oliver looked puzzled.

"But, that can't be. I mean, I kind of wondered, since you're not married and all."

"What's that got to do with being gay?" Bart asked. "I know lots of married people who are gay. Well, some of them aren't as gay as when they were single, but they are gay." Oliver was truly perplexed. He didn't know how his pastor would respond, but he really didn't expect him to admit his own preferences and talk about other people and their preferences as well.

"Are we talking about the same thing?" Oliver wondered.

111

"I guess," Bart replied. "I know a lot of happy people and you happen to be one of them."

"That's not what I'm talking about," Oliver fumed, obviously upset that his pastor would make light of such a serious subject. "I like guys."

"Me too," Bart replied enthusiastically. "I really like guys."

"You're not just yanking my chain again, are you? I mean, you really like guys?"

"Sure I do," Bart answered. "I like you."

"Eww," Oliver said in disgust. "You don't want to kiss me or anything gross like that, do you?"

"Gross," Bart responded. "No, but I like hanging out with you. You're a neat guy to be with. You're smart and funny. You don't talk bad about other people, even when they've hurt you. I've seen you help girls at your high school with their homework, even though they won't give you the time of day during class time. And I don't know anyone who knows more sci-fi trivia than you. That's why I like you."

"But you don't want to have sex with me?"

"Like I said, gross. I like other guys, too. I like Jake. He's got a weird sense of humor. He can hunt and fish and knows all the best fishing holes in the county. He plays a mean game of one on one. Besides, I can tell him things I wouldn't tell anyone else. And no, I don't want to have sex with him."

"I don't understand," Oliver groaned.

"Have a look here," Bart urged, pulling out the Gideon's New Testament he carried, complete with Psalms and Proverbs. Bart read him a verse from the Proverbs.

"What's that mean, iron sharpens iron?" Oliver asked.

"It means that men become men by hanging out with men. No offense, Oliver, but your dad hasn't been much of an example of manhood."

"He's done the best he could!" Oliver proclaimed defensively.

"I know, and I understand," Bart said sympathetically. "But somewhere down the line, he and your mom trained each other to act the way they do. Your mom yelled at him, and he let her get away with it, probably just to keep the peace. She pushed back even harder, trying to get him to put her back where she belonged, but he just kept taking and never giving back. Now they're stuck in a rut they either can't get out of or don't want to."

"What's that got to do with me being gay?" Oliver asked with tears in his eyes. He knew his home life was a wreck, but it hurt to see the truth through another man's eyes.

"You're not gay, Oliver. You're just confused. And you're taking feelings that are perfectly normal and sexualizing them. You see women like your mom, Attila the Hun on roller skates, and think all women are like that, or they will be after you marry them."

"So all gay men have bad moms and weak dads?" Oliver wondered.

"I don't know about that," Bart confessed. "But I do know what I see in your life, and I've seen you and how you look at girls. You are definitely not gay. By the way, what brings this up anyway?" Oliver wiped the tears away and tried to filter through the information he was just given and sift it along with what he was told earlier that day at school.

"We had a rally today at school," Oliver began. "Shane McFarland came to speak, along with some of his graduates. Afterwards, they asked if anyone had questions or problems they wanted to talk about. I'm sorry, Pastor, but I was feeling down and needed someone to talk to."

"Don't sweat it. We all need people in our lives, and I can't be there all the time for everyone." He meant what he said, but he wished the boy had found someone other than Shane or one of his cronies to talk to. But even though he didn't like them, he wouldn't talk bad about a fellow servant without having more than a gut feeling to go on. After all, there were people out there who thought he was a bit odd and maybe even strange, and he wouldn't want them talking about him, even though they probably did.

"Thanks. Anyway, I was telling them about Mom and Dad, and how I felt about girls, and that's when they told me what was really happening. It never occurred to me, but they felt so sure about it."

"What did they say?" Bart asked

"He said I had the spirit of homosexuality, and that I should come to their camp so they could cast it out."

"He said what?" Bart asked, standing to his feet, knocking his chair over as he did. The chair fell across the hard wood floor with a resounding thud that reverberated through the small library and echoed down the halls and up the stairwells leading to the courthouse. Bart regained his chair and his composure just as the librarian came around one of the bookshelves to see what had caused such a calamitous uproar. Bart apologized profusely, and she went about her duties, clucking like a hen about impertinent people who had no regard for rules of decorum.

"But now I don't want to go," Oliver stated. "I don't think I have that spirit at all. Not after talking to you."

"Did you make an appointment?" Bart wondered.

"Yeah, for Wednesday night," Oliver answered.

"Then I think you should keep it."

"But...."

"Don't worry, I'll be with you. I'll get Harry to cover for me during Bible study. What are you doing now?"

"I was about to head home, but I'd rather not."

"Then how about joining me at Jake's place? I'm supposed to go over there for dinner."

"Are you sure it will be alright with Jake?"

"Sure it will," Bart answered truthfully, but he wasn't at all sure that it would be alright with Melissa, and even less sure that it would be alright with Cassandra. He desperately wanted to make a good impression on her, but he had a young man who was even more desperately in need of help and in need of good male companionship. He knew that Jake and Oliver shared a passion for video games, and thought he could put the two of them together after dinner. Again, he was sure that Melissa would disapprove, at least until she understood the situation. Once she understood that, she'd probably ask Oliver to spend the night and eventually move in. Once she was on someone's side, she was there all the way. As for Cassandra, Bart could only hope she was as understanding.

"I'll have to ask Mom?" Oliver said woefully. "And you know what she'll probably say."

"Tell her I need you for some church business," Bart informed him.

"But we're going to dinner at Jake's. Isn't that lying?"

"No," Bart replied. "I want you to tell Jake about the rally. He and I are kind of interested in what goes on at that camp, and you are going to be our ticket in. So I do need you for church business." Bart had often used Oliver for church business, having him run errands, visit people, and do light handiwork around the church grounds. Most of it was things that he could have done

116

himself, but it offered Oliver the chance to get out of his home life for a little while, and it put a little money in his pocket. Bart paid him from his own pocket, so he didn't feel guilty about hiring him without consulting the deacons or the church body. It freed him to do other things and gave Oliver a sense of purpose.

Bart walked Oliver home, continuing their conversation from inside the library. Now that Bart had assured him of his status of manhood, the young man was much more at ease, as if the doctor had called and told him there had been a mix-up in the x-rays and he didn't have cancer after all. Bart understood. He knew the pressures of keeping up appearances while living in a small town. They parted ways and Bart kept walking towards Clyde's, where he found the old VW just where Clyde said it would be, with the keys in the ignition. Small town life was pressure filled, to be sure, but it was also trusting.

He looked over the vehicle. It was clear that Clyde had done a cursory cleaning of the interior. Bart had been right to assume that parts were stored in the back, as evidenced from the grease marks on the shag carpeting that covered the floorboard. The carpet had been installed with the idea of matching the broad horizontal orange stripe that had been a part of the original paint job. Whoever installed it had a good idea for color, since the carpet still matched in places where the grease hadn't spotted it and the sun hadn't come in to fade it. The rest of the exterior was a bright white stripe. Bart thought

that whoever the original owner was had cared for the van greatly. He

examined the engine and even found it to be fairly clean. An idea began

forming in his head.

"You're not getting rid of old blue, are you?" Darryl pleaded.

"He can't," Leonard assured him. "That car is a part of who we are."

"No," Bart said, still looking over, under and around the little van. "I

won't get rid of old blue. I was just thinking about adding a car to our

collection, that's all."

"Can we afford it?" Darryl wondered, always the practical one.

"Not much of a chick magnet," Leonard said with disgust.

"We don't need a chick magnet," Bart scolded. "We do need a way to

transport some of the kids to camp and activities. We also need a vehicle that

can haul equipment and one I can sleep in if we ever get a chance to hit the

road again. Wouldn't it be nice to take a vacation and just sleep under the

stars?"

"I'd rather sleep in a hotel room with cable TV and room service,"

Darryl moaned.

"Me too," Leonard agreed. "I'm too old to play hippie."

"You guys are just spoiled sports. Clyde said he took this as trade for

work, so maybe he won't be asking too much for it. Besides, I've got some money saved up that should cover this and the cost of repairs to old blue. And I was thinking about one more thing."

"What's that?" Darryl asked.

"I was thinking that Oliver is getting close to driving age and won't have anyone to teach him to drive. This thing is a stick shift, and old enough that I won't worry about him wrecking it."

"You're always thinking ahead, boss," Leonard complimented. "I'm with you on this one." Darryl agreed as well. Moments later they were headed down the road for home. After a very quick shower and shave, Bart was on his way to pick up Cassandra, calling Jake on his cell as he headed out the door to give him a head's up on the night's plans. He transferred the information to Melissa, who, after hearing the story, was more than happy to set an extra plate for their young guest.

"What about Cassandra?" Jake asked. Bart could hear Melissa's answer in the background.

"If she's worth keeping, she'll understand. If not, then Bart's only lost one evening with a beautiful woman. It's worth the risk." That was good enough for Bart.

Bart picked up Oliver before making the run over to the hotel to get Cassandra. Mrs. Cratch stood on the front porch, arms crossed and eyes glaring, but she said nothing when Oliver entered the van with a handful of hand picked flowers.

"I thought you might need a peace offering," he told Bart as he laid the flowers between the two front bucket seats. "And I didn't think you would have time to make the florist shop before you picked up your date."

"Thanks, Oliver. They're beautiful, but won't your Mom be mad about you picking her best flowers?"

"They're not hers," Oliver explained. "I grow them alongside our vegetables in the backyard. They help keep some of the vegetables shaded and they provide the critters something else to munch on besides the good stuff. You're lucky, though, because most of the good ones were gone. I really had to look hard to get a decent bouquet for your date."

"And I'll let her know who her knight in shining armor truly is," Bart assured him. "She should be waiting for us outside."

Cassandra was waiting at the entrance of the Scenic Inn. She was dressed stunningly, making Bart feel like a pauper in his faded jeans and pull over shirt. He was dressed for a quiet casual dinner at an old friend's house. She was dressed for a night on the town with all the bells and whistles that accompanied such an occasion. She had on a black, strapless evening gown that came down low enough to make a man expect to see more, but high enough to disappoint him if he actually looked. The gown was slit slightly up one side, teasingly revealing the most gorgeous legs Bart had ever seen. Her hair, which was tightly wrapped at the top of her head earlier that day, now

cascaded down in a softly flowing, dark brown waterfall, gracefully pouring

itself out down between her shoulder blades.

Bart parked the van, hurried to get out, fighting a stubborn door handle

while continuing to stare at the goddess who had deigned to dine with mere

mortals for the evening. She smiled coyly at him, causing even further delay

as he fumbled with the handle. Finally, after agonizing minutes which seemed

more like hours, he thrust open the door and burst out of the van like it had

caught fire. He practically ran over to Cassandra, almost knocking down a

businessman, who was already getting knocked down by his date, who didn't

care for where his eyes were traveling. Bart noticed that several men had eyes

that were driving down the same road as his and the businessman's. He also

noticed, with some appreciation that Oliver's eyes were revving their way

down that highway. He opened the door for her, and if she was surprised by

the intrusion of a third party into their date, her demeanor failed to reflect it.

"Hello," she said casually. "Who might you be?"

"I'm..I'm...I'm...," was all that Oliver could manage to say. Bart had

regained his composure and was easing his way under the steering wheel.

"My semi-mute friend back there is Oliver," he informed her.

"Hello, Oliver. My name is Cassandra." She turned and extended her

hand. At first he limply took her hand in his, but then grabbed on like a

121

drowning man who's been thrown a life preserver. For better than a minute, he still refused to speak, his brain forgetting in the presence of such beauty how to properly activate his tongue.

"Your gorgeous," he was finally able to mutter, but he still refused to let go of her hand.

"Thank you, Oliver," she said shyly. "It's too bad others in the car have forgotten how to pay a compliment." Bart turned several shades of red. Like Oliver, his brain and tongue refused to cooperate with one another. He was searching for the right words to tell her how beautiful she was, but was unable to locate the exact phrase he was searching for. In his simplicity, Oliver was able to find what he had lost. Now he was afraid anything he said wouldn't be taken seriously.

"I'm sorry," he said lamely. "I was hoping to find a poetic phrase or something to tell you just how wonderful you look. Instead, I went blank and let a boy speak for me."

"Don't be so hard on yourself," she said. "I was just teasing."

"I know," Bart stated. "It's just that it's been so long since I've dated. I'm not sure if I know how to act. By the way, do you need your hand back?"

"My arm is starting to go numb in this position," she admitted. Bart told Oliver to let go, and he complied, letting her hand go and his hand drop limply onto his lap. He was like a zombie in a voodoo trance.

"Oliver," Bart called. "Snap out of it."

"Sorry," Oliver said. "It's just that I don't think I've seen anyone so beautiful before, except on TV, movies or something. You look like something out of a magazine," he told Cassandra, and again Bart scolded himself for not saying something similar. He was being outshined by a pining schoolboy.

"How sweet," Cassandra said shyly. "Bart, I don't know where you found him, but he's a keeper." The rest of the trip to Jake's was a history lesson of their small town. Oliver would point to a landmark of local interest and talk about the legend of one of their local heroes and fill in the gaps with the true story of events as they actually occurred. Even Bart was amazed to find out how little he knew about the town he lived in. Oliver continued as their tour guide until they pulled into Jake's driveway. Smoke was rising up from beyond the cedar fence.

"Is he barbecuing," Oliver asked.

"Either that, or his backyard is on fire," Bart answered. He hopped out, heading for Cassandra's door. He might not have been Don Juan in the complimentary department, but at least he knew how to be a gentleman.

"I'm afraid I'm not dressed for the occasion," she confessed.

"You are dressed for any occasion," Bart assured her, satisfied that he had finally hit the mark on compliments. Oliver had clambered out of the back

123

seat and was headed to the door, drawn by the enticing aroma of grilled steaks and vegetables coming from the backyard. He waited impatiently at the door for Bart and Cassandra to catch up.

"What's your hurry?" Bart asked.

"I'm afraid he'll overcook my steak," Oliver explained. "I like mine a little bloody in the middle."

"Ugh," Cassandra moaned. "I think I could have done without that information."

"Sorry," he said just as Melissa opened the door.

"I saw you pull in," she explained. "Come on in and make yourself comfortable. You must be Cassandra. Wow, are you a knockout or what? Can I get anyone something to drink? We have soda, lemonade, and water of course."

Just as Melissa was finding places for everyone to sit, Jake jumped through the open doorway from the kitchen, wearing nothing but a camouflage apron, with the words, "Grill Sergeant" printed in bold, capital letters across his chest.

"Hey pretty lady," he called, oblivious to his guests, who sat in stunned silence as the drama played out before them. "How about we do a little cooking of our own before the guests arrive?"

"Hmm," she purred. "That sounds good tiger, except for one thing."

"What's that, pussycat?" he whispered in her ear, still ignoring the people filling his couch and chair.

"They're already here," she whispered back as she drew away from him to see the response play across his face. It was one of those moments when you wished for a video camera. She was sure the redness of his face, together with his dropped jaw and bulging eyes would have been worth a ten thousand dollar prize easily.

"Why didn't you tell me?" he wondered, doing his best to back out of the room without anyone seeing something they shouldn't.

"And miss this moment?" she responded.

"I almost forgot!" Cassandra exclaimed. "My cell phone has a camera."

"No," Jake cried. "You wouldn't."

"Sure I would," Cassandra countered. "Who's going to stop me?"

"I'm the sheriff," Jake pleaded, slowly backing his way through the open doorway and to the sanctuary of the kitchen beyond.

"I don't see a badge," Cassandra argued, as she dug through her purse for her cell phone. "Why can't I ever find that thing?" The slamming of the kitchen door let her know it was too late. "Oh yeah," she recalled. "I left it at the hotel." She heard Jake holler something about that not being the only thing that should have been left at the hotel, but she wasn't at all sure what he could be talking about.

After the false start, things proceeded fairly well. Everyone made an extra effort to make Oliver feel at home. Bart was happy to see that Cassandra was making it the point of her evening to spend time with him. He wasn't sure if it was just lust or real love that he was feeling, and he wasn't sure that he even cared at the moment. That last thought scared him. He wasn't a man of the cloth. He was real flesh and blood, and as such, had needs that had been denied most of his life for one reason or another. On the other hand, no one had promised him or anyone else that life would be a bed of roses, although most of the time he would just settle for getting out of the briars. He noticed that the women and men had paired off for the evening. He had expected as much. Oliver and Jake had retired to the living room to play the latest shoot the bad guy game, while the women gathered the dishes and were in the kitchen rinsing them off and, no doubt, talking about the men in their lives, including him. He was, as usual, left to his own devices to entertain himself. He thought about joining the guys for a round of shoot, maim, and destroy, but he found that playing games that blurred the line between fantasy and reality had the effect of moving his own frail boundaries. The giggling pouring between the whispers and running water told him he dare not venture into the realm of womanhood. Only the bravest, or most foolish, of knights dared such an audacious venture, and he counted himself to be both wise and cowardly. So he sat at the bar, making the most of his after dinner coffee, and enjoying the atmosphere of normalcy that surrounded him. This is what he wanted his home to be like someday. Perhaps, with a woman like Cassandra, it could be.

"Penny for your thoughts, handsome," Cassandra offered. Bart nearly jumped off his barstool.

"My thoughts, madam, are worth much more than that. You'll do well to keep that in mind when you make such offers in the future."

"Pardon me, sir. I didn't realize I was in the presence of such genius," she said, stooping in a mock curtsy.

"Arise, peasant. To be sure, genius is not what you are in the presence of."

"I didn't think so. But I didn't know what I might have stepped in."

"How is it you came in to my life?" Bart asked. He knew down deep that she wasn't much more than a stranger who had managed to put herself at the right place at the right time, and that this dinner could be considered as nothing more than a show of gratitude for that salvation, but he wanted it to be much more. He wanted a chance to have happiness again with a woman, the kind he had once had with Maria. Perhaps, if God was good, which he was, and if love was truly blind, he might have that chance with Cassandra.

"Who says I came in to your life?" she asked. "Maybe the fates

127

orchestrated things so that you came into my life. Maybe you're just what they've ordered for my momentary happiness."

"Who says it has to be momentary?" Bart wondered. "Why don't you marry me so we can spend the rest of our silly lives together?"

"Whoa, you don't believe in wasting time, do you?" she asked, amazed at his audacity. She was only partially sure that the offer was made teasingly. Even with that in mind, she entertained the thought, if for no other reason than idle curiosity. Could there be such a thing as love at first tackle? There was an extra beat in her heart that she hadn't felt for a long time, not this decade that much was sure. She didn't have a problem attracting dates, no more than a flame has a problem attracting moths. But like the flame, all she seemed to attract lately was fluttering bits of fluff that dissolved when they got too close. Even so, she wasn't ready to marry a guy she had only met that afternoon, despite the fact that her heart was screaming at her to grab him, throw him in the car and take him to Vegas before he changed his mind.

"I was kidding," Bart replied. "I like you and all, and you are a great kisser, but I don't think we can build a relationship on that alone."

"I don't know," she teased. "We could go back to my place and at least build a night on it."

"Look, there's something I should tell you," he started.

"I'm sure there are a whole lot of things we need to tell each other," she replied. "But right now, I'm just interested in you telling me that you'll still respect me in the morning."

"I plan to, but…," came Bart's response, which was cut off by Melissa calling out from the kitchen that dessert was ready. "Let's just take things a little slower. We need to know each other a little more before we know each other, if you know what I mean."

"Whatever you want, cowboy. I'll be ready when you are. That is unless I've already ridden out of town. I am here on a limited engagement, you know." Bart assured her that he understood that her offer came with an expiration date. He didn't, however, tell her the reason he couldn't accept her offer. He wanted to, but after his flagrant disregard for morality and decency that afternoon, he found it hard to tell her that he was a preacher, a moral pillar of the community who couldn't offer his body on the altar of pleasure, no matter how much he might really want to. He would tell her, he told himself. He would tell her before the night was over. But he wouldn't do it now. The time would have to be right. People don't just blurt out over hot fudge brownies that they are preachers. Why not? What was the difference between telling someone that you're a construction worker, or a doctor, or any other profession for that matter? Why did it have to be difficult to tell a girl you liked that you spend Sunday mornings preaching to others to not do what he did that afternoon? That was the crux of the problem. He had already

129

stepped over the line with her, giving her a wrong impression of who he was and what he stood for. Now he had to backtrack, reverse course and set a new direction for their relationship, if they were going to have one.

"What time is your appointment with the counselor tomorrow?" he asked Oliver, who was busy slurping down his second helping of ice cream.

"He just said to drop by sometime around six," Oliver answered, wiping the melting ice cream from his chin. "Are you thinking about coming out with me?"

"Well," Bart answered, "you do need someone to drive you out there. Besides, I was hoping Jake would join us. What do you think, Jake?"

"I have been curious about that place for sometime now. You know they have security measures out there that would put Fort Knox to shame. An eight foot fence, complete with razor wire at the top and cameras mounted in strategic locales. They chose a spot with excellent natural cover and where it lacked, they planted trees and shrubs to offer better concealment. They also have dogs and run patrol guards all through the night."

"I thought this was supposed to be a rehabilitation center, not a prison or gulag?" Cassandra offered. "What kind of place are they running, and why hasn't anyone asked questions before now?"

"The usual reasons, I suppose," Jake answered. "They've gotten a lot of good publicity. That, coupled with Angus' political connections, has kept most people from making any real inquiries. Why the interest?"

"Remember I told you I was here on business and pleasure? The business part has to do with the camp. I'm a freelance reporter doing a piece on the camp. I wanted something beyond the sugar coated fluff you normally see about places like this. I was going to visit the camp on my own, but I wouldn't mind having a police escort when I go."

It was decided that they would meet Oliver after school and drive to the camp. Oliver told them that he didn't have any classes after noon, just study halls that weren't mandatory. The only reason he went was because he didn't have a job and would rather stay there than go home. They all agreed that the earlier they got there, the better chance they had to catch them doing something other than what was shown on their sales brochures.

"Meanwhile," Cassandra said, "I'll spend tomorrow on the phone with contacts and doing research at the library."

"I have some things on my schedule that can't be rearranged," Bart said. "But I'd like to meet you for lunch. We can go over anything you find and I might be able to fill in some blanks for you."

Everyone said goodnight, with action plans in mind for the next couple of days. Bart drove Oliver home first, but he was nearly asleep when they pulled into his driveway. Then he took Cassandra back to her hotel.

"The offer still stands," she told him through the window.

"And it's tempting," Bart conceded, "but I still have to say no. I guess I'm just old-fashioned. I think we should date, get to know one another, fight and argue a little, and then get married before we go to bed."

"Ouch! You are right out of the fifties, aren't you? If you change your mind, you know where to find me."

Bart drove slowly away, watching her walk to her room in his rearview mirror. Once again, he chastised himself for simply not telling her that he pastored a church and couldn't give in to the moral temptations she offered. He also chastised himself for having feelings for a woman whose sense of morality didn't come close to matching his own. He had often preached to his flock about being unequally yoked with an unbeliever. Relationships and marriage were hard enough to maintain without sabotaging them before they even began. His and Cassandra's relationship, if there was going to be one, had already been damaged by his kissing her and then further damaged by his lying by omission. Before he realized what he was doing, he pulled over at a gas station and asked to use their phone.

"Is it an emergency?" the clerk asked.

"Sort of," Bart replied. "I need to call a girl and I left my cell phone at home."

"Dude," he answered. "Why didn't you say so? Use the one in the office." The clerk lifted up the hinged portion of the counter that separated the workers from the customers and allowed Bart to duck underneath. He looked

up the number in a tattered phone book lying on the desk and called before he

lost his nerve.

"Scenic Inn, how may I direct your call?" Bart hesitated, still unsure of

what he was going to say, then asked for Cassandra's room.

"Hello," she replied.

"Hi, Cassandra, it's me, Bart."

"Are you calling to tell me you're coming back?" she teased.

"No, I'm calling to tell you why I can't accept your offer. Cassandra

I'm a preacher. I pastor a church in town and I shouldn't have kissed you the

way I did. I know I should have told you sooner. It should have been one of

the first things out of my mouth and I'm sorry that it wasn't." Silence. There

was nothing on the phone but silence. For what seemed to be an eternity, Bart

heard only thundering silence. Then he thought he heard something else. He

wasn't sure, but he thought it was her giggling. And what he thought was

giggling turned into riotous laughter. She laughed herself silly for over two

minutes before regaining enough composure to speak again.

"I'm sorry," she managed to say before breaking out into more

spontaneous laughter. Bart wasn't amused at all. He had called to apologize

and have a serious conversation with a woman that he hoped to have a deep

and meaningful relationship with one day, and she couldn't do anything but snort, giggle, and guffaw. Before long, he found himself doing the same thing. Her laughter, however annoying it might be, was also highly contagious. The station attendant must have thought that he had lost his ever loving mind.

"Want to let me in on the joke," he managed between spells of giggling.

"I knew all along," she answered, having regained her composure to the point that she could again carry on a conversation. "Jake told me you were a preacher. I was stringing you along to see how long it would be before you told me yourself. I gotta say, it took you longer than I expected. I'm a bit disappointed."

"You and me both," Jake agreed. "I shouldn't have waited so long before saying something. Forgive me?"

"This time, preacher man," she answered. ""for that matter, you're going to have to be completely honest with me. Got it?"

"Got it," he affirmed. "I guess you'll want to know that I see things most people don't see and that I live with two imaginary friends named Darryl and Leonard." There was an eerie silence on the other end of the line. A long pause made Bart think that she might have hung up.

"Right," she at last responded. "And I think I'm Josephine Bonaparte. We all got our problems."

"But I really," Bart started to say, but then let it trail off. "Good night,

Josephine. I'll see you at Waterloo."

"Good night, my little general. Say good night to Leonard and Derek."

"That's Leonard and Darryl," he corrected.

"Whatever, just blow me a kiss and hang up the phone." Bart did as he was told, painfully aware that the clerk had reentered the room and was watching everything he did. He felt like a five year old dealing with his first crush. He hung up the phone, bought a large soda from the fountain and a candy bar before heading home for what he hoped was a good night's rest.

CHAPTER FIVE

Bart awoke after a fitful night's sleep, full of images of Cassandra and himself in provocative scenes, each of them interrupted by Mrs. Miller, the town gossip, with a camera crew and microphone that she shoved in his face, demanding an explanation for his congregation and her viewers. Even after his eyes were opened and he was well beyond the realm of REM, his thoughts involuntarily turned back to the images that seemed to be burned onto the backs of his eyelids. The harder he concentrated to erase them, the more they insisted on staying, like holiday guests that stuck around longer than the leftover turkey. He decided that in order to dispel what his mind saw, he had to turn it to other things, so he swung his feet over the bed and assumed the position for his morning prayers. He found that it was hard for his heart and mind to reach out to God when his mind was still reaching out for Cassandra, but by concentrating on others he knew needed prayer, he was able to slowly erode the stony edifice that had erected itself on the plateau of his thoughts. He began praying for the Holden's, naming each of them in turn, starting with Bonnie, next Oliver and his family. Then he continued with those in the church he knew were sick, either physically or emotionally. Finally, just before the final amen, he prayed for Cassandra. By the time he was finished, his dreams were burned away with the rising of the morning sun. He arose feeling whole, clean, and refreshed. Well, spiritually speaking, anyway. A quick sniff reminded him that the best of prayers may remove the stain of sin from your life, but they won't do much about the scent of sweat.

The tub was an old claw footed metal monster that looked like it belonged on one of those home fix up shows that seemed to permeate the cable channels. It reminded him of how old the house itself was. Someone had once commented that Billy Sunday or Dwight Moody had probably stayed there during their years of ministry. Looking around at the cracked ceilings and rolling hardwood floors, Bart gave credence to the theory that the house had been built with lumber salvaged from the ark. He usually didn't mind the dilapidated condition of the old structure. It had a sense of style that was all its own, much like him. But today he was considering the possibility that he might actually meet a certain someone that he could share the rest of his life with, and since he also planned to pastor that same church until the day he died, she would have to share the parsonage as well. He did what he could to fix up the old place, but he was no Bob Vila. He was closer to Pancho Villa when it came to home repair because what usually happened was criminal. The old adage about measuring twice and cutting once didn't apply to him. He could measure the same distance with the same tape measure a dozen times and come up with thirteen different measurements, one of them thrown in extra just to confuse him.

He stepped into the tub and pulled the clear plastic curtain around. He made sure to point the flexible shower head away from his body since he knew the first thirty seconds of the spray would run the gamut from scalding hot to frigid cold before settling in to a comfortable temperature range. He had just worked the shampoo into a frothy lather when he heard her voice. He thought at first that it was Cassandra, but he realized that he had locked both doors before settling down the night before. Besides, what would she be doing in his house this early in the morning? Or any time of the morning, for that matter. Wiping the soap from his eyes, he dared to sneak a look through the bubbles to the world around him. He wasn't ready for what he saw. She stood about five foot eight, with a slender, but not skinny body, and long blonde hair that draped over her shoulders and down to nearly her bare bottom, which was hid only by the clear shower curtain that she had pulled around herself. She turned to look at him with eyes that were piercing blue, like the sky on a perfect summer day. She smiled and he smiled back, not knowing what else to do. He had no idea who this woman was or how she managed to come into his home, much less his shower, totally unexpected and totally uninvited. He consoled himself only in the fact that her modesty, for what it was, had caused her to turn herself away from him, keeping most of her bare skin beyond the reach of his probing eyes. She reached up with her free hand, keeping a tight grip on the shower curtain with her other hand, and grabbed her hair from her back and pulled it forward.

"There," she declared, "I'm ready for you to scrub my back. Be a good boy and make sure you get that spot in the middle that always drives me crazy when it itches. Ooh, I can almost feel it starting to itch right now. Do hurry, love." Bart didn't know what else to do. Almost as if running on instinct, his hand began reaching for the washcloth and liquid soap, totally ignoring the stinging suds that were creeping into his eyes. He applied the soap to the washcloth, worked up a good lather, and reached out for her back, which promptly disappeared, along with the rest of her into rising steam. He finished showering and wrapped a towel around himself before calling out to his two roommates.

"Darryl. Leonard," he called out. "Get in here, now." They walked in from their bedroom, each of them wiping the previous night's sleep from his eyes. Darryl was wearing his usual Scooby Doo pajamas, while Leonard dragged in behind wearing a Superman costume, complete with cape and red boots. Bart was used to them and didn't comment at all on their choice of sleeping attire. There were times when he wished that Darryl would show a little creativity since he was tired of looking at the same old pajamas. The least he could do would be to find another set of Scooby pj's.

"What is it?" Darryl demanded. "I was planning on sleeping in today."

"Yeah," Leonard agreed. "We had a late night last night. Darryl and I had some guests over for poker night. I took them all."

139

"In your dreams, mister," Darryl corrected. "As I recall, Diane walked away the big winner."

"Only because she bluffed me on that last pot. I can't believe I folded against a pair of twos."

"She conned you, man, that's all there is to it."

"What does Diane look like?" Bart wondered.

"You remember her, don't you?" Leonard asked. "She's that raven haired beauty we met in Vegas. She was just passing through last night on her way to Atlantic City." Bart knew in his heart that all of what he was currently hearing was just a part of his mixed up imagination. There was no raven haired beauty named Diane whom they met in Vegas and she wasn't on her way to Atlantic City. That was in his heart. Right now, his head wasn't so sure. He had seen someone in the shower with him. And then she vanished like a puff of smoke.

"Who else was here?" he asked. "Were there any blonde's here? Someone with long hair maybe? It was a kind of ashy blonde, not totally blonde. It had hints of a light brown to it, like soft corn silk. Long, straight. She was tall, and from what little I could see she was curvy, with soft, rounded curves that sort of flowed easy down her body."

"Oh, from what you could see?" Darryl asked. "Did you happen to notice what color her eyes were?"

"Yeah," Bart answered. "They were the most magnificent blue. Piercing, searching. An innocent blue that carried you back to good childhood memories if you have any."

"I wish you had gotten a better look at her," Leonard commented. "We'll never find her with that description."

"Very funny," Bart commented. "Was she here last night?" Both of them said no. They had never seen a woman even coming close to that description, but Leonard said he wanted to and he would definitely keep an eye out for her. Darryl agreed and was asking about the possibility of her having a sister when he noticed how shaken Bart appeared. There was a wild, almost incoherent look in his eyes that Darryl hadn't seen since the death of Maria. It scared him.

"You okay?" he asked.

"I'm not sure. I'm thinking about going back on my medicine." That thought did shake the duo. Bart wasn't even close to being himself when he was on his meds. For one thing, they disappeared into a formless, dark and foreboding void when he was taking his medication. It put his mind into an impenetrable fog that dulled his senses and kept them from communication of any sort with him. It wasn't a place they wanted to be.

"Hold on," Leonard said. "One episode doesn't mean it's time to grab the nets and put on the funny jacket with the long sleeves. You had quite an ordeal yesterday, what with almost getting run over and then kissing that girl in public. Besides that, you're starting to check out that camp and you know any time you start investigating it opens portals in that ship you call your brain that aren't usually open. Maybe she was just a stowaway from last night's dreams. Is that a possibility?" Bart wasn't even sure what he was asking, much less what the answer would be. But the more he thought about it, the more he was convinced that he had overreacted. It was just a one time hallucination brought on by the stress of the day before, along with the stress of things to come, or at least that's all he hoped it was. He wasn't ready to resign his church and check into a halfway house. That was the worst case scenario. The best he could hope for while taking the medication would be a sort of dulled perception of events around him. He wouldn't be able to counsel anyone, that much was for sure. And his preaching would be about as exciting as watching clouds floating by on a lazy Sunday afternoon.

"We'll just take a wait and see approach to this," Bart told his two compatriots, who were deeply relieved to hear the news. They didn't have much of an existence. After all, their only link to the real world was a somewhat touched pastor who managed to keep the imaginary friends from his childhood. It wasn't much of a life compared to others, but it was the only life they knew and they wanted to keep a hold on it for as long as they could. Besides, in their own way, they cared deeply for Bart and wanted what was best for him. If that meant taking medications and losing their touch with him, then that's the road they'd travel.

With that decision made, Bart went about the business of preparing for the day's activities, which included his weekly visit with Sister Agnes, one of the original matriarchs of the church. She was in a nursing home, since she had fallen last year and was no longer able to take care of herself, but at one time she had been the mainstay of the church, managing to keep the doors open even when the membership consisted of her and two other blue haired ladies. That was shortly before Bart arrived. The pastor who had served before him had brought attendance back up to around fifty, which wasn't bad in comparison, but wasn't near what they were capable of. Under Bart's leadership, the church had grown to around a hundred and fifty members, give or take a dozen on any given Sunday, and more visitors were coming each week. Bart had a unique style of preaching that utilized his mental liability, turning it into an asset for God's work. Bart thought of it as God making good from bad, as he had done for Joseph when his brothers had tossed him into a pit and sold him as a slave. His childhood wasn't one he would choose to relive, so he didn't. Other people with bad memories chose to relive them every day, rehashing bits and pieces of their lives in a stew of bitterness. Bart chose instead to take what he had been given and make something better out of it. Sister Agnes had helped him to do that. She knew about his malady, and had convinced him to make it a part of his ministry, which he managed to do

through the skits he performed while preaching. He played off of Darryl and

Leonard, sometimes with material he prepared the week before, other times

they would do improv. Either way, they managed to make the congregation

either laugh or cry, depending on what they performed, and always managed

to make them think. He would always be thankful to her for that gift and

wanted to show it by making the time to visit her at least once a week. They

called it their Tuesday date.

The one thing he didn't like about the visit was the location. He didn't

mind the elderly people. In fact, he liked being around them for the most part.

But the home itself was something else altogether. It reminded him of

something that might be seen in an old movie about an asylum where the

patients ran the facilities. He didn't like the idea of nursing homes in general.

The ideal situation would be for the children to take care of their parents in the

home when they couldn't stay by themselves any longer. But economic forces

often drove both husband and wife out of the home and into the workforce,

not leaving them any time to take care of their children, much less their

parents. But when the ideal couldn't be met, there should be a better

alternative than Ivan the Terrible and Attila the Hun running up and down the

halls like they were running across the fields of Europe raping and pillaging.

Most of the nurses and staff at the home weren't like that. For the most part it was a pleasant place to stay, and a decent alternative for those who really

didn't have any other place to go. But the few bad apples had a tendency to

spoil the whole barrel. It was one reason Darryl and Leonard never came with

him. It was too bad, because Agnes really missed them. Bart wasn't sure why

it was, or how to explain it, but she formed a bond with the two of them. She

could only communicate through Bart, but even with that limitation she

formed a deep attachment to them. She claimed that she had even included

them in her will, which was bound to cause her lawyers a great deal of

consternation after her passing.

He pulled into the parking lot, and parked the bus into one of the two

spots reserved for clergy. He noticed that Brother Guy Marvell had filled the

other spot. He liked Brother Marvell. He was a cowboy in preacher's clothing.

Actually, on second thought, he kept the cowboy clothing and just preached

anyway. He had hair nearly long enough to braid, but he never wore one, at

least to Bart's knowledge. It was always pulled back and laid down in crested

black and gray waves over the collar of his black duster, which he wore

through most of the year. It was only during the hottest days of summer that

the coat was hanging on a nail. The duster, with jeans, a western shirt, and a

pair of cowboy boots was his usual costume. During funerals or other special

occasions he would add a bolo tie to complete the ensemble. Bart liked him

because his attitude came from the same period as his dress. Everything was just kind of laid back. There was no need to rush because there was always tomorrow to take care of what you let go today. His philosophy on life was basically that you shouldn't sweat the small stuff, and most everything in life fit into the category of small stuff.

As soon as Bart opened the double glass doors leading into the Sunnyland Nursing Home, he could hear that Guy was coming towards him. The clippety clop of cowboy boots on hard linoleum was unmistakable. Bart went in and saddled on up to the nurses station to wait for his saddle partner to mosey up the hallway. Guy Marvell wasn't big by any man's measure, but there was a certain swagger in his stride that made him appear taller than his five foot ten and look larger than the one hundred eighty pounds he weighed. Bart had watched him cower much larger men with nothing more than a stare from beneath the brim of his hat. He had what they referred to in western lore as 'dead eyes', a look that made others feel like he was a man who had not only met death face to face, but had invited him in for dinner and a movie. On the other hand, Bart had seen the same man running around the playground with such fervor and zeal that it was hard to tell him apart from the children.

"Well, bless my soul," the old cowhand said with a grin bigger than the Texas panhandle, "if it ain't my old friend, Bart Rancher. I think I'd die for a name like that. Instead, I get stuck with a name that sounds like a number cruncher at the bank. How'd you come up with that name, anyhows?"

"Long story," Bart told him for the hundredth time. "Let's just say that the woman who gave me birth was a bit more creative with names than most folks. What have you been up to lately?" Bart asked, hoping to change the subject. He liked Guy, but he wasn't ready to share his life story with him just yet.

"I was trying to arrange a little outing for some of the folks here," Guy answered. "I got me about a dozen buggies and teams all lined up for some Saturday afternoon. I figured we'd take as many as we could hold out for a look see at the trees changing colors. This warmer weather we've been having has slowed 'em down a bit, but it won't be too long afore they shed their leaves. Reckon a city feller like yourself could drive a team?" Bart hadn't really thought of himself as a city feller, but then compared to someone like Guy, he guessed that's exactly what he'd be. Guy was all outdoors all of the time. He would have been happier than a tick on a dog to have been born a hundred years or so earlier, but Bart was content with the modern days, and the conveniences they provided. He probably wouldn't have lasted a week in the old west.

"I don't know," Bart answered hesitantly. "That's a big responsibility."

"Ain't nothing to it," Guy reassured him. "Them horses have been doing this kind of thing for so long, we're just there as window dressing to please the folks. Them horses are used to walking one behind another. As long

as you ain't the lead wagon, you got nothing to worry about." Bart still wasn't

too sure, but Guy was a hard man to say no to. He would have made an

excellent side show carnival barker, or a salesman of any trade. Bart finally

relented, mostly because he didn't want to disappoint any of the older folks

who might not get another fall to see the leaves. He knew everyone had the

possibility of dying before the next season, but some people had increased

their odds by living so long.

"I'll see you around noon, then," Bart called as Guy was heading out

of the door. He headed for Sister Agnes' room, which was down the hall and

to the left. He passed by the nurses station, nodding to the nurses on duty as he

went by, who didn't even notice him because they were so enthralled with the

imaginary characters of the soap they were watching to notice the real

characters around them. Bart couldn't understand how people could be so

caught up in the lives of contrived crisis that they missed out on the lives of

real people around them. Then again, maybe he could understand. Maybe he

wasn't that different from anyone else who walked on the planet. His only

malady was that his television only got a limited number of channels and he

was the only one who could see it. It was his personal version of digital

quality cable television. He consoled himself in the fact that there were also

dedicated nurses and other staff going about taking care of patients and tending to needs as they arose. He thought about church, where around ninety percent of the work got done by about ten percent of the people and realized that they were just a reflection of the larger reality around them. The problem was that they weren't supposed to be a reflection of the darkness, but a prism for the light to pass through.

Sister Agnes' door was closed, as usual. And, as usual, Bart waltzed right in, only to be shooed out again by a much younger woman than Agnes. Bart thought she looked familiar, but he was out of the room and into the hall before he could get a clear look at his bouncer.

"Can't you see I'm trying to give Aunt Agnes a bath?" she called after him. But Bart couldn't see anything except the badly painted landscape portrait that ended up being about three inches from his nose by the time he came to a stop. He wondered if perhaps whoever painted the donated picture also donated a large sum of money to the home. He couldn't see any other reason for hanging something so hideous on the wall for public viewing. In his opinion, it was the artist who should have been hung instead of the picture.

"How do you like it?" The woman who shooed him out of the room asked. He had stood, transfixed at that spot until he heard her voice. Again, it sounded vaguely familiar to him. It wasn't the voice of an old friend, but belonged to someone he had just recently gotten acquainted with. He started to tell her exactly what he thought of the picture when he saw the tiny plaque at the bottom that gave credit to the artist as being Miss Agnes.

"It's a beautiful picture," he lied. Actually, it wasn't technically a lie. Now that he had a chance to get a second look at it, there were qualities in the painting that drew him in. He saw things in it that didn't strike him as lovely at first, but with a closer examination he was able to judge brush stroke qualities and color choices that really made the painting come alive.

"It's as ugly as homemade sin," the girl said. She was right. "But since Aunt Agnes is staying here and endowing the home with a portion of her estate, they wanted to give it a place of prominence. I feel sorry for the person who occupies this room next. Hopefully, though, it won't be for a long time. The old gal seems to still have plenty of time left." Bart was staring stupidly, which he wasn't normally prone to do, but there was something about this girl that poked and prodded at his mind. He knew that he knew her from somewhere, but he couldn't for the life of him remember where. He started reviewing places he'd been recently to determine if the two of them had crossed paths within the past six months or so. He concentrated mostly on church activities and other social functions where two people might bump into each other without truly meeting. He thought that since she was Agnes' niece, it was a good possibility they had met at one of the church socials that Agnes had been able to attend. Her health was failing and she wasn't able to go to all of them, so that eliminated a number of possibilities.

"There," she stated, "I'm ready for you to come in now." That was it.

He examined her again, just to be sure, but he knew where he had seen her before. She was the girl from the shower; there was no doubt about it. She had the same soft, warm, hair with a color that was not quite blonde, but not yet brown either. Although the clothes masked a lot of the shape of her body, he was still able to see that it was curvy, not fat nor plump, but definitely not skinny either. And most telling of all were those piercing blue eyes that probed straight to a man's heart and sunk hooks deep into it.

As she turned her back, Bart reached out and poked her in the back, unintentionally making her stumble to the point that he was forced to catch her in his arms. He was hoping to prove to himself that she wasn't real. He had hoped that she would simply disappear the way she had done in the shower. Unfortunately, the fact that she didn't vanish away proved absolutely nothing. Bart was able to shake hands with Darryl and wrestle with Leonard. They felt as real as they looked.

"What's that all about?" she demanded, looking up at him with those lovely blue eyes.

"Sorry," he stammered. "I thought there was a bug on your back."

"Well, the way you were poking me, it could have been on my chest and you'd have still got it." Bart felt like such a fool. He should have just gone along with the fantasy, knowing that sooner or later it would play itself out.

Now he was stuck somewhere in the middle between reality and make believe. The best he could do now was just hope for the best.

"I am sorry," he repeated. "Let's go in and see Aunt Agnes." That was it! He truly felt like a fool now. If Aunt Agnes didn't see her, then she wasn't real. All he had to do was wait a few minutes and get her reaction.

"We have a visitor," she called to the woman lying in the bed. Sister Agnes didn't respond. She was fast asleep. "Poor dear. I must have worn her plumb out with that sponge bath. I hope you didn't travel far to see her."

"No," Bart assured her. "I live in town. I'm her pastor. Oh, by the way, my name is Bart Rancher. Sorry I didn't introduce myself before poking you in the back."

"So if I had known your name, poking me in the back would have been perfectly fine to do? Is that a game you play with all your friends?"

"No. I just meant that I should have introduced myself when we first met." He held out his hand for her to shake.

"And my name is Shalina Marie Baxter, lately of Memphis, Tennessee. But most of my friends just call me Shelly. I'm just in town for a few days to visit my Aunt and take care of a little business. It's a pleasure meeting you, sir." They found a couple of chairs and chatted while Aunt Agnes slept. Bart was sorry she was sleeping for a couple of reasons. First, he missed their weekly date. She had insight on church goings on and on people in general that most people only dreamt of. He loved to probe her mind and glean her wisdom when things happened at the church that shouldn't be happening. Normally her calm demeanor and quick thinking combined to bring about the perfect solution to any crisis. Besides that, he wanted to know for sure if Shalina, which he preferred to call her over Shelly, was real or not. He was just beginning to think about Cassandra as a possible candidate for dating, and now he was thinking that the girl in the room with him could be another possibility. Maybe it was the fact that neither girl was going to be in town for long that drew him to the attraction. Or it could be that both girls were extremely attractive in their own ways. Cassandra was a roaring fire, full of life and shooting off sparks in every direction, attracting the attention of every man within a five mile radius by her fiery beauty. Shalina, on the other hand, was like the warm glow of a candle in the window, attracting weary travelers to come in and lodge for the evening so they could rest from their journeys. Cassandra was a shout that grabbed the attention of everyone, while Shalina was a whisper that called out only to those who were willing to hear. He found within both women a strength all her own.

"Do you intend to stay in town long?" Bart asked her. "Because I thought if you were, that we might run into each other again, like at the dinner or lunch or some other meal where two people ate together."

"Uh-huh," Shalina said nodding. "I guess we might bump into each other that way, just a sort of happy coincidence."

"I'm a preacher," he told her. "I don't believe in coincidences, just divine appointments." Unlike his time with Cassandra, he told her he was a preacher without any hesitation whatsoever. It came completely natural to him to let her know almost everything up front. Almost everything, anyway; obviously he didn't tell her about the two friends he had waiting for him back at his house, although instinctively he thought maybe he could tell her and that she would understand.

"Tell me where you preach," she said. "I still should be in town Wednesday night, so I'll come by and hear you preach then."

"Sorry," Bart told her. "I have business with a young man that night, so I won't be there. It's an unavoidable appointment. Maybe you'll still be here Sunday?"

"Sorry," she apologized. "I plan to be gone by then. I was planning on being back in Memphis by Friday night so I can rest up over the weekend before going back to work."

"Then I guess we'll have to have dinner Thursday night. That is if your husband doesn't mind you having dinner with a new friend."

"Is that what you are, a new friend?" she asked coyly.

"I could be," he answered. "But I noticed you bypassed the question about your husband."

"Hmm," she began. "I don't remember you asking if I had a husband. But if you did, I'd have to tell you I've never been married. A few boyfriends, some closer than others, and one fiancé, but he's out of the picture and has been for awhile. Any other personal questions?" She peered at him over her glasses.

"Yes," he answered. "You never told me where to pick you up for dinner Thursday, or what time."

"I also never told you I'd have dinner with you."

"True," he admitted.

"At the Scenic, room nineteen. I'll be ready at six." That worried him somewhat, even though it shouldn't have. He and Cassandra had kissed, but only in a moment of emotional release; a time when neither of them were thinking straight. They weren't dating, per se. Sure they had the one date at Jake's place, but that was just supper with friends. It couldn't be said that they were an item or even seriously dating. Still, it might be awkward if he was picking up Shalina and ran into Cassandra at the same time. He thought about suggesting a different meeting spot, but that would cause her to ask why, and he didn't know if he was ready to explain to a possible date that he might run into another woman he might also be dating. He remembered now why he didn't like relationships and dating. He was much more comfortable with people that came out of his imagination.

"I'll see you Thursday then," Bart told her. They talked awhile longer before deciding that they were wasting one of the last warm days of fall sitting inside a room with only a small curtained window. The filtered sunshine beckoned to for them to join him outside for a bit of warmth. Its clear invitation wasn't to be ignored. They were on their way to the patio when Shalina remembered her purse was still in her aunt's room.

"What do you need it for?" Bart wondered.

"I might want a soda or something," she responded.

"I'll buy you anything you need."

"Men!" she exclaimed. "Sometimes you just don't understand anything. A woman just isn't dressed without her purse. It's not just an accessory. It's an extension of who she is. Why can't men understand simple things like that?"

"Probably," Bart responded, "because we just think our wallets as a place to carry our money and credit cards. A purse is nothing but a big wallet in our minds."

"Well," she countered, "it's much more than that to us womenfolk, so I'll be on my way back to Aunt Agnes' room to retrieve my third hand. You go on ahead to the patio. I'll join you there in five minutes."

"I'll go back with you," Bart offered.

"I'll be fine on my own, thank you. I've been a big girl for quite some time now." She turned and went back to the room, leaving Bart standing alone in the hallway. But he wasn't alone for very long.

"Hey," Jake called. "I've been looking all over town for you. I should have known if it was Tuesday, you'd be here."

"Hey," Bart said, "I'm glad you're here. There's someone I'd like for you to meet. She's Agnes' niece, in from Memphis for a visit."

"Not sure we have time," Jake answered. "I need you over in the ruins." The 'ruins' was a nickname for a part of town that most people wanted to forget about. It wasn't just on the other side of the tracks; it was on the other side of the bayou, a leftover remnant of the days of the plantation owners and the sharecroppers that followed. people who lived there lived in a world all their own.

"Come on," Bart urged. "It won't take a minute. She's right over here in Sister Agnes' room. We're supposed to go out to dinner this Thursday."

"What about Cassandra?" Jake asked, causing Bart to drop his head down.

"We're just having dinner," he defended himself. "It's not like I'm going to marry her or anything. Besides, me and Cassandra have just had one date. It's not like we're engaged or something." The prospect of his friend, Bart, dating at all made Jake happy. There were plenty of women in Stony Ridge that wanted to date the eligible preacher, but for some reason or another, none of them appealed to him. Melissa had played matchmaker on

several occasions, only to have her efforts shut down tight after only one date.

So the fact that Bart had actually found not one, but two women, to date

intrigued him. There was a murder investigation going on, but meeting the

woman who had captured his friend's heart that quickly was worth a couple of

extra minutes.

"Lead on," he told Bart. They went to Sister Agnes' room and knocked

lightly on the door.

"We have to be quiet," Bart advised. "Sister Agnes was sleeping when

we left."

"Come in," Agnes called.

"Looks like she's awake now," Jake commented. They could hear the

television playing as they entered the room. Sister Agnes was sitting in her

rocking chair, watching an old black and white movie.

"Do come in," she said sweetly. "I'm just watching an old favorite of

mine. It's 'The Ghost and Mrs. Muir'. It's about a woman who falls in love

for a dead sea captain. Have either of you seen it?" They told her they had.

"I guess you started watching it after your nap," Bart asked.

"Nap," she said quizzingly, "I haven't been asleep all day."

"But when I was here earlier, with your niece, you were asleep."

"Bonnie was here? I haven't seen her for years. Sweet girl. The two of

158

you would have lots to talk about. She'd be much too old for you of course,

being in her sixties and all."

"No," Bart said as calmly as he could. He felt like there was something

horribly amiss. "I was talking about your other niece, Shalina."

"Shalina? My, what a pretty name. But Bonnie is my only niece. Well,

wait, there is one other niece."

"Shelly?" Bart asked, using the nickname Shalina had told him of. It

was a long shot, but he was desperate at this point. It appeared to him, as it

must to Jake, that he had just made a date with an imaginary woman. He

didn't want to believe it, refused to believe it, but the facts were staring both

of them in the face.

"No, not Shelly," she stated. "Her name is Lucy. Actually, it's Lucille,

but she's always hated that name. I don't blame her, do you?"

"No, Agnes, I don't blame her a bit," he told her. "We better go now

and let you get some rest."

"I think that would be a good idea," she agreed. "I'm unusually tired

today for some reason. You boys run along now, but come back soon and

we'll have some cake and a good cup of coffee."

"Sounds good, Miss Agnes," Jake said. "Maybe we could have some

hot cocoa instead of coffee, though." Jake and Bart went outside, leaving a

yawning Agnes in her bed, snuggled in for a late morning nap. Bart knew she would barely have her eyes closed before one of the aides would come by to wake her for lunch. It was another one of the things he disliked about nursing homes in general, even the nicer ones, and that was the fact that you were told when to eat, what to eat, who to eat with. Your freedom, for the most part, was waiting for you in the parking lot when and if you were able to leave. He was sure that if he ended up in this kind of facility, or even a more restrictive one, that he would not only be given directions about his dining, but about his medicines. He couldn't handle the thought of not being able to choose between the captive state the drugs kept him in and the freedom of living in his own little world, but if Shalina was indeed a product of his imagination, he might not have much of a choice. There were worse things to contemplate, of that he was certain, but he couldn't think of any at the moment.

"We need to get go," Jake urged him. "I hope you feel up to helping."

"Yeah," Bart stated with little certainty. "I'm fine." He wasn't anything of the sort, but he couldn't let Jake know that, not yet.

"You know," Jake began, "Miss Agnes is getting up in years. I hate to say it, but her mind isn't everything it used to be. She might not remember us visiting her either." He was trying to reassure his friend that everything was alright with the world, but he wasn't too sure himself that it really was. Bart was acting out of character, if that was possible for someone who kept the imaginary friends he had from childhood. But since that attempt on his life, he had been acting strange, including kissing a woman passionately in public,

and now setting up a date with another woman, who may or may not really

exist, while trying to develop a relationship with another woman. Bart

Rancher was many things, but a player wasn't one of them. At least he hadn't

been up until now. Jake hoped he was doing the right thing by having him

come to the crime scene. It was a gruesome sight, not something most people

could handle. He hoped he wasn't about to drive his friend the short distance

from reality to fantasy.

Bar T. Rancher

CHAPTER SIX

The drive from the nursing facility to the crime scene at the ruins was silent, punctuated only by the stop signs and small amount of traffic that interfered with their journey along the way. Bart's silence came with his contemplation of his recent past actions and their meaning to his future. If Shalina were real, then why didn't she stick around long enough to meet Jake, and why didn't Sister Agnes remember her. On the one hand, Jake was right; she didn't always remember their visits together. Sometimes she would scold him for missing one of their dates when he had been there. Still, he couldn't help but think that a normal visit from your pastor couldn't compare with seeing a niece you only see once in a great while. But he didn't want to believe she was only a product of his mind. He truly liked her and wanted the opportunity to know her better. Besides, he was already having a tenuous grasp on reality without it being further eroded by a make believe girl friend. Life was complicated enough with real people.

Jake's thoughts were along the same line as Bart's, but not nearly as pleasant. He was truly concerned about his old friend and his seeming inability to discern between real and imaginary. He understood about Darryl and Leonard and accepted them as part of Bart's life. But even Bart knew they weren't real. He understood that they were a part of who he was, an extension of his mind that manifested itself from time to time, but was for the most part

163

controllable. The girl, however, was a different matter altogether. Shalina, or whatever her name was, didn't exist as far as he was concerned. And that meant Bart was starting to show signs of mental deterioration. He was beginning to lose control over his ability to live in the shadows between the light and substance of reality and the darkness of imagination. Jake didn't think that Bart was capable of hurting anyone, at least not yet. But what if the day came that he saw something unreal and acted upon it as if it were real, possibly injuring someone in the process? And now he was taking his friend to a crime scene, asking him to do something that could push him further over the edge. How could he justify that to himself?

He never had the chance to answer that question since he was pulling into the driveway of Holly Swenson, the current and yet former resident of 119 Maple Drive in the suburb of Stony Ridge known as the ruins. He pulled in the Crown Victoria as if it were running on auto pilot, his mind too engaged in concentrating about the well being of his best friend to be bothered with such frivolities as driving defensively. He nearly knocked over a small jockey decorating the front lawn, a bygone relic of the days prior to political correctness that was still overlooked in the south by most people. It was probably a leftover of the prior tenant, as was the hubcap collection that covered three quarters of the outside walls of the shed behind the house. The rest of the yard was clean and well trimmed, making it stand out from her neighbors, whose idea of a well manicured look was to burn the lawn off in the spring and do it again with the leaves in the fall. Their idea of lawn decorations included tires, transmissions, and various lawn mower and bicycle parts. Unlike other neighborhoods in town that had garnered a less than savory reputation, the ruins was an equal opportunity employer of the cast offs from the rest of society. Here whites intermingled with blacks who in turn intermingled with the legal and illegal immigrants from the south of the border. No one saw color in the ruins. In fact, no one saw anything here, which is why a crime as horrendous as the murder of Holly Swenson could take place without a single witness. She was killed in the privacy of her own home, but she could have been killed in the middle of the street during high noon and there still wouldn't have been any witnesses.

They were met at the door by Deputy Clarence Allen, who had taken an instant dislike to Bart upon meeting him. Bart usually was able to get along with almost anyone, but Deputy Clarence fell into the beyond almost category of people. He was mean spirited and head strong, which Bart could overlook in most people, especially those in law enforcement, since the job had a tendency of either attracting that kind of people or shaping those who were malleable into that kind of person. Clarence, however, was not just a deputy. He was also a Baptist minister at one of the smaller congregations outside of town, with a congregation of around twenty, most of them related to Clarence, and most of them just as mean and ornery as he was.

"What's he doing here?" Clarence demanded, his mouth stained with tobacco laden saliva. He wiped the spittle away with the back of his hand and flung it to the ground near Bart's feet.

"I've asked him to come," Jake answered, standing toe to toe with his deputy. "You got a problem with that? Cause if you do, you got a problem with how I do my job, which means you got a problem with me." Jake was easy going, almost to a fault, and he tolerated too much horse play on the job to suit most people, especially those on the county quorum court and the county judge, but he knew his men and how much leash to let them have before yanking them back in. They were a crack team of professionals, even if they didn't always act like it. Clarence was no exception. He was a top law enforcement official, with a lot of commendations and experience to his credit. But one thing Jake would not tolerate under any circumstance was one of his deputies undermining his authority in any way. Bart remembered one such poor fellow who threatened to kick Jake's behind halfway across the state if he ever caught him without his badge and gun. Jake gladly obliged the young man by taking off his badge, gun, and uniform shirt before heading out the door. The younger officer gained a greater appreciation of his boss' abilities, along with several contusions and even more stitches. He left the force later to take a job with a larger city force, but the memories and scars stayed with him.

"I got no problem with you," Clarence finally muttered, leaving the door open for doubt as to whether or not he had a problem with Bart. Even if he did, he wouldn't say so in front of Jake anymore.

"Yeah, well I got a problem with you contaminating a crime scene with your DNA," Jake retorted. "I train professionals to act professionally. If you can't do that, maybe you need to take a job with one of the local factories working night shift security."

"Sorry, Sheriff. I guess I wasn't thinking."

"No, because you were too busy minding my business to mind your own. Now you better hope you haven't done anything to harm our investigation any further." Jake shoved him aside and stepped toward the house, leading Bart along the way.

"I doubt there's any DNA evidence out here," Bart said.

"Me either, but that's just plumb stupid," Jake answered. He wrote a mental note to himself to go over the rules of crime scene protocol once again. They were a small town force, used to handling department store thefts and busting meth labs, but that was no excuse for being sloppy with evidence, especially when the crime was murder. And even though all murders were gruesome to some extent, Jake found this murder was particularly heinous. Within seconds of entering the front door, Bart knew why.

There was blood all over the room. It was as if someone filled several water balloons with red dye and unleashed them with the fury of hell in a torrent on the walls, the hardwood floors, the curtains, and the furniture. But that wasn't the first thing Bart noticed. He saw the quality of the furniture, the newly painted walls, and the unmarred finish on the floors. He asked Jake about the condition of the interior, which was well disguised by the appearance of the yard and surrounding homes.

"It was part of a renovation project done by the camp," Jake answered. "They chose several of the homes in the area and had some of the graduates and several of the recovering addicts come to do the work. They talked local businesses into donating most of the material, others donated monetarily to fill in the gaps."

"Seems like they've almost got the golden touch over there," Bart commented. "I've seen other churches try to do the same thing, only to get the sliding glass doors shut in their faces. Why does he rate such treatment?" It wasn't just a rhetorical question. The answer truly puzzled him. He had seen others start projects only to stop them because of a lack of funding or community involvement, and yet every project began by Shane and the members of his camp came to complete fruition without a hitch. Bankers loaned them money without collateral, sometimes without even charging interest. Stores opened their doors for them. Other businesses and prominent individuals opened their hearts as well as their wallets to Shane without blinking an eye. It had been a splinter in his heel for some time, but now it was a thorn in his side. There was something amiss about a man who could do so much with other people's money and not be held accountable for how the money was spent or where. As far as Bart knew the camp didn't have a board of directors or others to answer to. The only ones who really knew where the bones were buried were Shane and his brother, Angus.

Bart forced himself to set that puzzle aside so he could focus on the one before his eyes. It was hard to set a focus on any one part of the scene, since blood was the focal point and it was everywhere the eye went.

"Something's not right here," he told Jake.

"Congratulations, Sherlock," Jake answered sarcastically. "What was your first clue, the blood or the dismembered corpse lying in the middle of the living room floor?"

"There's more," Bart answered. "I'm not sure what it is yet, but I'll let you know in about ten minutes. Can I have some time?" Jake knew he meant time alone, and he wasn't sure he wanted to grant it, not given the fragile state of mind that he seemed to be in at the moment, but he also knew that if Bart were going to be any help, he would need to work his magic alone.

"Ten minutes, no more," Jake replied. "And if I hear anything weird, I'm coming in, you understand?"

169

"Jake, I talk to imaginary friends and now I'm going to talk to a dead woman. What could possibly be weird about that?" Bart smiled, but it was the smile of a clown who hates the circus he's performing in. Jake left the room, taking the rest of the entourage with him, despite their protests. It left Bart alone in the room with the remains of what used to be a lovely young woman. She was someone's daughter, quite possibly a sister or maybe even an aunt. Someone somewhere knew this woman and would want answers about the monster that killed her and mutilated her body so horrendously. Bart took the time to process the photo in his mind before he went to work. The girl was on her back, blindfolded and gagged. She was cut multiple times, with cuts on her arms, legs, body and face. The two most notable cuts, though, were the ones the slit her throat, allowing her to bleed to death, and the one that disemboweled her, exposing her entrails for public viewing. Bart had been privy to more crime scenes, including murders, than he cared to remember, but he couldn't remember any that were as horrific as the one before him. He would be surprised if Deputy Clarence was the only one to contaminate the crime area. He figured there were probably several others who had heaved ho as soon as they seen the victim. If they didn't when they looked, he was sure most of them with noses did as soon as the scent reached their tender nostril hairs. It was all he could do to keep breakfast down once the door was closed and the air turned upon itself. Focusing on the task at hand, he walked over to the corpse that had once been Holly Swenson and reached out his hand to her.

She reached up and took it readily, happy to be out of the body that had held

her captive.

"Yeah," she said happily, "I am so glad to be coming out of there. That

much if for sure."

"Happy to oblige," Bart responded. "I don't suppose you could tell me

what happened?"

"Vell," she replied, "it looks to me like I vas killed." Bart decided

against answering her sarcastically. She was dead and he had learned a long

time ago that sarcasm was lost on children and the deceased.

"Yeah," he answered, "I had figured that much out for myself. I was

really looking into who might have a motive for killing a beautiful young

woman such as yourself."

"You think I'm beautiful?" she asked shyly.

"Well, I can see where you were before." He let the rest of the

sentence trail off. She tried to straighten out her blouse and comb back her

blood matted hair with her fingers, but there's only so much a corpse can do to

look presentable when part of her that should be inside is hanging on the

outside.

"I really am a mess, aren't I?" she asked. Bart had to be honest and tell

her that she was indeed a mess, but that he needed her help to find who had done this to her. She was trying to help, but she kept getting sidetracked by something that was bothering her. She looked under the couch, then under the chair, and then began walking around the room, peeking here and there for something that Bart could only guess what was.

"Can I help you find something? One of the officers might have taken it if it was evidence of some kind."

"I'm looking for my baby doll," she replied, still looking around. "I need to find my baby doll. I vas carrying it ven this happened to me. I hope someone didn't take my baby doll." Bart couldn't imagine a girl as old as this being attached to a baby doll, but there were stranger things happening in the world. People bought sweaters for their Chihuahuas and called them their children. It was a good thing he didn't believe in reincarnation because if he did he would want to come back as someone's pet dog, complete with a sweater and little chocolate treats.

"What kind of baby doll was it?" he asked, hoping it would be a clue.

"You know, just a normal baby doll. I am not so sure even if it vere a boy or a girl, but it vas my little baby doll. I vas carrying it for about three months or more." Suddenly it occurred to Bart what it was she was talking about. It also explained, at least in part why she had been cut open like a strung up deer. Someone didn't want there to be any evidence of her pregnancy. That didn't make sense unless whoever the father was didn't want

172

to be a father, or couldn't afford to be compromised by the demands of a young girl who refused to have an abortion. The crosses and other religious symbols made Bart think that she wasn't the kind of girl who solved her problems by having them removed surgically. Judging by her name, he assumed she was more than likely Lutheran, although that was just a guess on his part.

"What else can you tell me?" he asked.

"This floor," she clucked. "They verk and verk on the floor, but still it is not even. It has dips here and there." Bart looked down at the floor. It wasn't evident at first, but when he turned his head and looked sideways he noticed what she was talking about. He pulled a coin from his pocket and carefully rolled it across a section of the floor that didn't have any blood stains, which was not easy to find. He watched it as it gradually dipped and rose several times. This was a clue as well, but he had no idea what it meant. Then he noticed the blood pool near the body. There was an outline of dried blood that was flowing back toward the body. That wasn't possible. The blood should have flowed away from the body, not towards it. It looked to him like someone had poured the blood on the floor after the body was there. That didn't make sense unless this wasn't the place of the murder.

"Thank you, Holly."

"Vat? I am only complaining about the floor and you say thank you. I am not understanding you men sometimes."

"That's ok, Holly. Sometimes we don't understand ourselves. Would you mind coming a little closer?"

"Yeah, sure, if it vill help you. I am glad to be helping."

She came and stood close to Bart, allowing him to explore the wounds on her body. It wasn't a pleasant experience for either of them, but it confirmed his theory about the location of the murder.

"I should really have these walls painted again," she commented. "They are all wrong."

"I couldn't agree more," Bart stated. He compared what he knew about blood splatter with the wounds on her body. Most of the wounds were superficial, and he suspected that the coroner would find that a number of them were put there post mortem to make it look like she had struggled with her attacker more than she actually had. Either way, there was no way that those wounds would have caused the blood splatter he was seeing on the walls. He was convinced that someone had taken a bucket, or some other container of blood, dipped a knife in it, and then cast off the blood to make the patterns they were seeing on the walls. Whoever did this wanted them to think the murder took place here. That left the question of the day to be, "Why?" He couldn't think of a good answer except that wherever the murder did take place would implicate the killer, and possibly the father of her unborn baby, a baby that was now in Heaven with its mother.

Holly was leaving the room, still seeming to be looking for something. Bart hoped that she understood the baby doll she was searching for wouldn't be found here. But she wasn't looking for the doll anymore. Her searching seemed to be more purposeful, as if she knew exactly where the object she was looking for was, but it wasn't where it should be.

"Dat's funny," she said.

"What's that?" Bart asked.

"Vell, this here panel on the door," she said, pointing to one of the wooden grain quarter panels on the heavy oak entrance door, "the grain on it doesn't run the way the other panels do. Do you vonder vhy that is?" Bart did wonder why that was. He walked over to the door and reached out to inspect the misplaced panel. By prying on it slightly, he was able to remove it, revealing a stash of letters hidden in the hollow space carved behind it. Bart carefully looked over the letters, but didn't find a signature on any of them other than the pet name cookie. He wasn't sure who cookie was, but he was probably her lover and the father of her baby.

"I'm glad you pointed that out to me," he told her.

"I'm just doing vat I can," she replied.

"Just the same, thank you. But I think it's time for you to go now."

"Yeah, I agree. I am so tired." Being dead can make a person tired.

"One more question. If you don't mind, that is."

"If I can help," she offered.

"This is kind of hard to explain, but it's for my own peace of mind."

"Yeah, sure, peace of mind," she agreed.

"I've been talking to you for about fifteen minutes, but the fact is you're dead. I'm not really supposed to be talking to dead people. You could say it's against my religion."

"Mine too," she replied.

"I guess my question would be about you being dead and me talking to you. I'm not talking to a ghost, am I?" He knew the answer even before he asked the question, but he needed some reassurance from someone other than himself. Although, in truth, if the answer came from her, it was coming from himself. It was a complicated system, and at times it hurt his head to try to wrap his brain around it. Normally, he didn't even consider the issue to be relevant, but with the problem of Shalina appearing and disappearing, he wanted to be sure he was still on stable footing when it came to the possibility he was delving into necromancy. He knew he wasn't, but he wanted to be double sure. He couldn't afford to have God mad at him. The rest of the world might be crazy. He might be crazy, but if he could count on his relationship with God, everything was still right in the world.

"You are so silly," she answered. "Do you really think because my name is Swenson that I talk vith such a silly accent?"

"Is it that bad?"

"I sound like a bimbo from a 'B' movie," she answered.

"Thanks, I needed to hear that."

"Ei se mitaan," she replied.

"What's that?" Bart wondered.

"I just say, that's ok in Finnish."

"But I don't speak Finnish," Bart protested.

"Vell, isn't that odd," she answered and laid back down in her body where she belonged. Bart left the house quickly, both to report his findings to Jake and to get out of the house as quickly as possible. He told Jake everything, including his lapse of judgment in perusing through the letters before letting forensics get their hands on them, but he also assured the sheriff that he was wearing gloves so no evidence should have been damaged. He also told him about his suspicion that the girl had been pregnant. Jake told him that the coroner should be able to confirm that with blood tests.

"I know that wasn't easy for you, buddy," Jake said.

"You don't know the half of it," Bart replied. He hadn't told Jake about the Finnish phrase that had left the lips of the girl and frozen in his mind like a tongue on a flagpole. He was pretty sure that trying to pry it from his mind would be almost as painful.

"Are you telling me everything?" Jake probed.

"Everything that relates to the case," Bart answered. "I need to go home now, Jake. It's been a long day."

"I understand. I think we can take it from here. But will you be around if we need you?"

"You know I will."

"I shouldn't have asked. I'll have a deputy drive you back to your place."

"Better make it the nursing home," Bart stated. "That's where I left the van, remember?"

"Along with Shalina, if she's still there."

"Or if she exists. Isn't that what you really mean?" Bart was really beginning to wonder if somewhere along the way he had crossed the center line on the highway of sanity and was now driving on the wrong side of the road. Of course, he reasoned, if he were in England, he would now be on the right side of the road. But, he supposed, if you crossed the center line, no matter which country you were in, you would be on the wrong side of sanity.

"Just because I didn't see her doesn't mean she doesn't exist," Jake tried to reassure him. He was trying to reassure himself as well. He had several people that he counted as friends, but only one or two people he cared to confide in. Bart was half of that team, and he couldn't afford to lose him.

178

"Sister Agnes didn't remember her," Bart countered.

"Whose side are you on?" Jake demanded. "Besides, it's like you said, she doesn't remember half the people who visit her."

"A long lost niece?" Bart wondered.

"Look, I don't have all the answers, but there's one thing I'm sure of, and that's that in this crazy, mixed up, upside down world, you are one of the few people with their head on straight, even if it does come with a few optional accessories."

"That's just it," Bart said, turning aside to go to the waiting police car, "I'm not sure that the accessories are optional anymore. When they were optional, I could handle them. Now, who knows?"

"I know," Jake stated. "You get some rest, because tomorrow we need to go out to that camp. By the way, do you think they had anything to do with this?"

"It would explain how they could bring in a dead body without anyone noticing," Bart answered. "Of course, in this neighborhood, they could bring in a dozen bodies without anyone noticing."

"Shoot, they could rise up from the cemetery and no one in this place would see a thing. You go home, and thanks again for your help."

"Ei se mitaan," Bart replied.

Bar T. Rancher

CHAPTER SEVEN

Bart, Cassandra, and Jake met at the hotel the following day around noon. While they ate Jake updated Bart on the investigation, which was basically in a stall pattern over the runway while they waited for test results to come back from the lab. The letters Bart found didn't have any fingerprints on them other than Holly's, which made all of them wonder what kind of man sends love letters to a woman while wearing rubber gloves. They were just wrapping up the discussion when Oliver joined them.

"I thought we were picking you up at school," Bart said.

"I thought about that," Oliver explained, "and I came to the conclusion that I have enough of a geeky reputation at school without being picked up by a preacher and a cop. Know what I mean?"

"I could have roughed you up a little and thrown you in the back of the squad car," Jake offered. "It might have helped some."

"Hmm, I hadn't thought about that."

"I could have picked you up," Cassandra said. "I think a woman picking you up and not roughing you up would help your reputation more."

"Maybe," Oliver concluded, "but I think most of the guys would know a babe like you wouldn't be messing with a geek like me."

"Don't be so hard on yourself," Cassandra countered. "You're too young for me, but other than that, I think you've got a lot more going for you

181

than most of the guys at your school. Ten years from now, most of them will be working minimum wage jobs flipping burgers or turning screws at some local factory. You, on the other hand, will have a degree and be their supervisor." Bart was thankful for Cassandra's intervention. She was boosting Oliver's ego, which he needed, but she wasn't filling his head with empty flatteries that would have created a false self image for him. She played upon his strengths without either downplaying or falsely uplifting his weaknesses. He found his feelings towards her growing stronger, building upon more than just the obvious physical attraction he had towards her. He knew that with time he could cultivate a relationship with her, but he wasn't sure that he wanted to until recently. And even then he wasn't sure which direction he wanted that relationship to grow towards. He knew that at the very least he wanted her as a friend, but there was a portion of his heart, or some other part of his anatomy, that wanted so much more. That part, for now anyway, had to be held in check.

"Are you going to eat those fries?" Oliver asked Bart. They hadn't considered that their young friend might have come straight from school without eating. Bart called the waiter over so he could order some lunch. It only took a few seconds of arm twisting to convince him that they had time to wait for him and that they could afford to pay for it. It was only after Jake promised to take it out of his official budget that he conceded. He ordered two double cheeseburgers, a large order of fries, a milkshake, and an extra large drink.

"I'm glad you weren't hungry," Jake commented. "We'd have to ask the quorum court to put a tax increase on the November ballot."

"Sorry," Oliver managed to force through between shoving in fries a fist full at a time and huge bites of burger. "I guess I was hungrier than I realized. Is it ok?"

"Sure kid, I was just messing with you. I'm just glad to see a skinny kid like you has an appetite."

"Yeah, but you better watch it," Bart warned. "One of these days, your body will mutiny on you behind your very back and begin hoarding calories like Pharaoh saving up for the seven lean years. Next thing you know, that size 28 waist has happily blossomed into a size thirty four."

"Don't you mean thirty six?" Jake teased.

"Not yet, but it's on its way," Bart conceded.

"Well, I like that little bit of meat you have there," Cassandra said, reaching over to pat his sides. "When I marry someone, I want it to be a real man, not some boy or a poster child for a romance novel." Bart wondered if she was dropping hints already or if he was just being too eager. He hoped it was the former, at least then he wouldn't feel so foolish for the feelings that were involuntarily developing inside of him. Of course, she might just be making casual conversation, which was probably the true case.

"That might be more than just a little bit of meat," Jake said. "It looks to me more like a side of beef. You might want to think about converting to one of them religions that don't have potlucks every Sunday."

"No way," Bart countered. "Love feasts are in the Bible."

"Love feasts?" Cassandra asked. "It sounds more like something from the sixties." After a good laugh and after Oliver finished his second milkshake, they began the trip to the camp.

"What's the name of the place anyways?" Jake asked as they drove out of town. "It's gotta have a name, but I've just always heard it referred to as the camp."

"It's called Megiddo," Bart stated.

"Like the valley of Armageddon?" Cassandra wondered. Bart was impressed that she was that familiar with the Bible. Of course, after the proliferation of material on the end times that had flooded the market in recent years, it wasn't surprising that she should have at least a basic understanding of so called apocalyptic scriptures. Most people in the world seemed to have a better grasp on prophecy than people that had been filling the pews of churches for years.

"It's called the valley of decision," Oliver chimed in. "A fitting name for a camp where people go to face their addictions. You have to come to

184

some kind of decision about which way you want the direction of your life to go if you're going to try to kick some bad habits." Bart was again surprised. Oliver had a better grasp on life issues than he had realized. Maybe the adversity of living in a war torn household wasn't fair, but it did a lot to shape the character of the children who grew up there. Or maybe it just revealed the character that God had placed within their hearts already. He wasn't sure and even more importantly, he wasn't sure he cared. People were who they were, whether they were born with inbred characteristics or whether those characteristics were molded into them by time and circumstances. It was probably a combination of the two. Either way, Bart was determined to enjoy the people around them as well as the scenery around them.

"The trees are beautiful this time of year," Cassandra commented.

"I don't know," Jake countered. "It seems like finding beauty in the leaves is kind of like finding beauty in death. That's what it is, you know; the death of another year, meaning we're all a year older and a year closer to dying ourselves."

"Whoa," Bart said, "when did you become such a philosopher?" Jake smiled. He liked the idea of being thought of as a philosopher. Most people looked at cops, no matter their status on the force or other accomplishments, as something just above Neanderthals. Even if it was just for a moment, he was going to revel in it. Besides, having said one thing intelligent doesn't always lead to another intelligent statement. It was better to let them chew on

that thought for a bit before giving them something they might choke and gag

on.

"But it's not about death," Cassandra said. "Or not strictly about death.

It's about death and the promise of new life to come. You know, everything

comes in its season." Bart hadn't yet talked to her about her feelings and

thoughts on death and the afterlife, whether or not she believed in Heaven and

God, so this seemed like a perfect opportunity. He quietly thanked God for

giving him the opening he needed, along with a captive audience.

"The symbolism only works, though," he started, "if you have the

promise of life to come. Most people think they have the promise with nothing

to back it up with except things they've done for themselves, like good works

or joining a church. Do you have anything to back up your promise?" He was

in the backseat with her, giving him the ability to look her directly in the eyes

as she answered. He had learned a long time ago that when people answered

such a question it was important to see their eyes, otherwise it was too easy

for them to just say what they thought you wanted to hear.

"I've got my faith in Jesus Christ," she answered firmly. "Is that

enough? I mean, don't get me wrong, I've done my share of things wrong,

before and after meeting Jesus. It's possible that I've even done more wrong

after than I've done before, if that makes sense to anyone." Everyone agreed that it made perfect sense, if for no other reason than the fact that you're more aware of the wrong you do after than you are before. For awhile, everyone fell silent, somehow feeling awkward about talking about anything else, as if that moment were somehow sacred and needed to be held in awe. It was only after Oliver passed gas that the magic, or whatever it was, of the time was gone.

"Oliver!" Jake yelled. "For pity's sake, roll down the window or something."

"Open the door and jump," Bart called from the back seat, holding his nose against the stench. Cassandra was laughing uncontrollably, even as she held her nose. Despite his own embarrassment, when Oliver saw her laughing, he began laughing as well. That made Jake laugh, which caused his own fury of flatulence, causing even more laughter, along with more windows being opened, by everyone in the car. The rest ten miles along winding country roads consisted of rude noises, raucous laughter, and the free wind of the open road breezing through the open windows of the sedan.

"I guess maybe the onions weren't such a good idea," Oliver said.

"Now Einstein thinks of it," Jake said.

"It seems to me you had some grilled onions on your steak," Cassandra reminded him. "It looks to me like Oliver isn't the only genius in the car."

"Hold it, princess," Jake countered. "Unless Bart is a fantastic ventriloquist, you're not as innocent as you'd like for us to believe." She

blushed, but didn't argue the point.

They made the final turn off of the main highway onto a dirt road that

led to Camp Megiddo, the home of Shane McFarland and his famous band of

recovering addicts and former addicts. As far as anyone in the car was

concerned, Shane ran a wonderful ministry that enjoyed the kind of success

that brings public accolades and the perks that go with those accolades. But

each of them had confessed a deep gut feeling that said there was more to the

camp than what was visible on the brochure and the web site. Some things

didn't add up. For one thing, no one, not even Jake, knew where the graduates

of the camp went after the successful completion of their rehabilitation. Some

hung around town, working at jobs that Angus had arranged for them. Bart

wondered about the wisdom of putting addicts, even former addicts, in some

of the positions of trust that they now held. Jake agreed. He thought every

man should have the chance to prove themselves, but not at the risk of the

safety and welfare of his people.

Another sticking point was the cost of the camp. It seemed to take in a

lot more money than was necessary for the daily operation of feeding and

housing a small cadre of men and women. Bart felt sure that such an operation

could be run, even lavishly so, on much less money than was being

contributed to the camp on a weekly basis. Most of the churches in the area gave money to the camp. Some of them, many of them in fact, had made the camp a designated mission project, meaning that a large portion of their mission's budget went there. And they knew of several businesses in town that tithed regularly to the functioning of the camp. That, along with a substantial amount of private contributions and grants, as well as public grants, should have kept the operation in the black for decades to come, and yet they always seemed to have more and more needs. Bart, much to the dismay of his own congregation, refused to allow a representative from the camp to speak from his pulpit to ask for them to consider funding the camp. He couldn't stop them from sending money, if they chose to, but he could do everything in his power to dissuade them from doing so.

"Just over this hill and we'll be there," Jake informed them. Bart was surprised by the enormity of it when it came into view. As they were coming over the hill, Bart saw that the entire valley that lay before them was filled from one end to the other with dorms, storage buildings, and other facilities that he could only guess the use of. He also noticed that there were several areas of seclusion that were hidden from view by strategically placed pines and fencing. He wondered what a camp that was supposed to be dedicated to the rehabilitation of drug addicts needed to hide from prying eyes. The cameras dotting the top of the fence and the constatina wire running over it were not beyond his range of vision either. The place had more the feel of a military training camp than a spiritual boot camp.

"Are you on the list?" the guard at the gate asked as they pulled up.

"I'm Cassandra Green," Cassandra called from the back seat. "Mr. McFarland is expecting me."

"And I'm Oliver Cratch. I'm supposed to come for counseling." The guard looked over his list, looked at the passengers of the car, then looked at his list once again before ushering them through the gate with a wave.

"Friendly sort," Jake said. They drove down the road, flanked on either side by tall pines that seemed to wave to them as they drove by. Every once in a while they would see one of the residents doing menial labor. One was mowing a field that already looked better than most golf courses; another one was trimming branches while his partner gathered the fallen branches and fed them through a chipper. A third man raked and bagged the chips of wood, supposedly to use as mulch around the trees or some other garden project. On the outside, everything appeared to be absolutely normal, a vision of a utopian society safely at work. But each of them, especially Bart, knew that outward appearances went about as deep as the skin of an apple. It gave the fruit a bright shiny look, but it did little to tell about the sweetness or tartness hiding inside.

"That's him," Oliver said as they pulled the sedan into a parking space designated for visitors.

"Who?" Cassandra asked.

"The guy who told me I had the spirit of homosexuality," he replied. Bart was out of the door and around the car before Jake could shift it into drive. He could only recall seeing Bart truly angry once before this. He was ticked at times, annoyed at others, but there was only one time that he could remember seeing him truly angry, and that time Jake had to pull him off of another man before he was killed or seriously injured. It was funny though, because the man was a bouncer and outweighed Bart by at least thirty pounds. If this guy wasn't a black belt in several forms of martial arts, he was in serious trouble. It might not hurt if he was carrying a weapon as well. There was one thing Jake had learned about his friend over the years of their friendship, you could hurt him and he wouldn't bat an eye. In fact, he might try to counsel you to find out where your anger was coming from and eventually make you a deacon in his church. If, however, you hurt one of his friends, or worse, a member of his congregation, there wasn't enough dirt on the planet to bury yourself in.

"Can I help you?" the man said as Bart approached him.

"Show me," Bart demanded, thrusting the Bible he held into the man's face, missing his narrow and bespectacled nose by mere centimeters.

"Show you what?" he asked.

"Where in this book you find the spirit of homosexuality. I want to
191

know where you came up with such a cockamamie idea, because it sure isn't in here anywhere."

"Sir, you have me at a distinct disadvantage. Perhaps if we introduced one another like civilized human beings, we could resolve this matter more quickly. My name is Philip K. Sax. And you are?" he asked, putting out his hand for Bart to shake.

"Mad as heck that you would tell a child that he has the spirit of homosexuality after only speaking with him for a couple of minutes. What kind of arrogant, pompous jerk would do such a cruel thing?" Philip looked over at the sedan, where Oliver still sat in the back seat as he was told to. Jake and Cassandra had joined Bart, both for back up and because Jake wanted to be close enough to pull Bart off if it became necessary.

"You're speaking of the Cratch child?" Philip asked, although it was more of a statement than a question.

"His name is Oliver," Bart corrected. "And he's not homosexual, and furthermore there is no spirit of homosexuality. Now I want you to either show me where in the world you find such a fanciful notion or you can go over and apologize to Oliver for your reckless stupidity."

"Are those my only choices?" Philip asked disdainfully. Jake wasn't surprised to see Bart's hands ball up into tight fists that had his knuckles turning white and the veins running along his forearms bulging like swelled water hoses. He wished he had brought a stun gun with him. He was thinking that he might need it in a minute. He was even surer of it when Bart stepped forward, placing himself nose to narrow nose with Philip Sax.

"Your only other option is for me to beat some sense into that arrogant head of yours."

"What? With the sheriff standing not two feet from us? I hardly think he would be willing to stand by while you manhandle me." Philip smiled, thinking he had the upper hand over an ignorant opponent, an unarmed man in a battle of wits. To him, Bart Rancher was not much more than a common Neanderthal

"I'll let you in on a little secret," Bart said, leaning forward to whisper in Philip's ear. "I'm not afraid of going to jail, and I can knee you in the groin and stomp that pompous nose so deep into the ground that you can smell people's feet in China before Jake can pull me off you. So are you going to cooperate, or what?"

"God save us from ignorant peasants," Philip said.

"Don't forget that it was ignorant peasants that wrote a good portion of the New Testament," Bart corrected.

"Very well, I'll be glad to share my knowledge with you. I assume you understand Aramaic and Hebrew. Otherwise, you'll never be able to discern the hidden insinuations placed between the lines of the original writings."

"I do read both those languages. And I also read Greek, which is what most of the New Testament was written in. Want to try again, Sparky? Because I'm running out of patience." Bart sized up his opponent. He was about four inches shy of six foot, with spindly arms and legs that didn't look like they had done an honest days labor at any point in their lives. He had the narrow face and beady eyes of a rodent, not quite a rat, but something close; a ferret maybe. Yeah, that was it, he was definitely a ferret. Either that or he was a lawyer. In each case, he was a member of the rodent family.

"Most scholars would agree with you," the ferret squeaked, "but after exhaustive research on my own, I have determined that much of the New Testament was actually written in either Aramaic or actual Hebrew. And it's in those languages that one finds the spirit I was speaking of." Bart was disgusted. He had seen this kind of religious research zealot before, many times in fact. There were always people who claimed to find more in the Bible than was there, when they wouldn't even accept what was written right in front of their noses. The plain language and forthright message of love and peace with God eluded them while they sought hidden messages written between the lines or encoded with a code that they had naturally cracked while the rest of the world remained blissfully ignorant. Because of his own inclination toward seeing codes where no one else did, he had gotten caught up in the whole count every other vowel or skip two consonants, then read the

194

third one hysteria. It was actually much more complicated than that, but it boiled down to an elitist group of men being able to read the code while the masses had to have the Bible interpreted for them. It wasn't what God had intended. It had happened for thousands of years because of the illiteracy of the masses and the lack of printable type, but once those problems were rectified, everyone could read for themselves what God had to say to them.

"All I know is that there is a confused young man sitting in that car who trusted you for sound advice based on the plain language of this book and you gave him some nonsense that only you can see. So from now on, if you run across a member of my church that needs help you send him or her to me or another trusted pastor. But don't you dare answer them yourself or you'll have to answer to me." Bart backed up a step to give Philip an inch or two of breathing room, but he was still close enough to make his threat of kicking him up an octave a viable possibility.

"And just how am I supposed to distinguish between your flock and the rest of humanity?" Philip asked with an air of superiority.

"Good point," Bart conceded. "I guess you just need to keep your opinions to yourself."

"Well, I never," Philip sniffed haughtily.

"Is there a problem here?" a man wearing bib overalls and a flannel shirt with its sleeves cut off asked. He was a big man, built like the trunk of an old oak tree, with powerful limbs that knew the value of hard labor extending out from its base. He had a shock of unkempt strawberry blond hair protruding out from a baseball cap that was advertising one of the new power drinks. He removed the cap to wipe the sweat from his forehead with a red handkerchief he pulled from one of the many pockets on his overalls. He removed the cap to dab the top of his forehead, revealing the fact that the hair extending beyond the borders of his cap was about the only hair he had, other than, of course, the thick mass of hair that popped out from his shirt at various places.

"No problem," Philip answered. "Just a minor disagreement about counseling techniques. I'd like to introduce you to Pastor Bart Rancher." Philip offered Bart over as if the two of them were old classmates who had just run into each other on the street one day.

"Pleased to meet you," the big man said, stepping forward to shake Bart's hands. "And it's nice to have our good sheriff stop by and see our work here. It's not big city fancy or nothing, but we do get results."

"It's nice to meet you, Shane," Bart lied. He knew the man on sight, even though the two had never been formally introduced. Bart had avoided him since that initial contact, mainly because of the emanation of evil that surrounded him like a swarm of gnats. It was still there, just as Bart expected it would be. He might be a little off balanced, maybe even slightly crazy, but he wasn't insane and he knew what he saw the first time and that it wasn't his imagination and that it was likely a permanent mark of Shane's character.

"I'd also like for you to meet," Jake began, but then cut himself off as he realized that sometime during Bart's confrontation with Philip, Cassandra had disappeared. He regained his composure and motioned for Oliver to join them. Oliver didn't have any inclination to see Philip again, but he was glad to get out of that stuffy sedan. The fall air was beginning to cool some, especially in the evenings, but they had parked in the full sun and even with the windows down he was beginning to sweat.

"This is why we're here," Bart stated. "I wanted to clarify some counseling Philip gave Oliver here."

"Sometimes Philip does overextend himself," Shane agreed, much to Philip's chagrin. A knowing glance let him know that they would take care of this later after the visitors had left and that the rebuke was only temporary. "Why don't the three of you feel free to look around the camp? Philip will be glad to give you the guided tour."

"I'd rather look around on our own," Bart said, "if that's okay with you." Bart could tell that it wasn't okay with Shane, but that he didn't dare say otherwise.

"Of course," Shane agreed reluctantly. Without another word, the trio turned and began their investigation of the camp, knowing that while they were looking at different aspects of the camp, they themselves were under the scrutiny of mounted cameras and posted guards.

"I wonder what's inside those warehouses," Bart asked Jake, who was already walking towards the nearest one looking for a box or something else to step onto so he could see in one of the high windows. He finally found something, only to find that the windows had been painted over so that no one could see in. The doors, of course, were locked. They found other curious items as well, including an area that was fenced off from the rest of the encampment, but nothing that would cause an immediate alarm and certainly nothing Jake could take to a judge to ask for a search warrant. That was especially true since most of the judges in this area gave of their time and talents to the camp.

They were about to give up and go back to town when Bart heard a noise coming from the bushes to their right. He told Jake and Oliver to go on ahead so he could investigate. His suspicions proved to be true. Darryl and Leonard were scuffling around in the bushes trying to get his attention.

"What are you guys doing here?" he demanded.

"Sorry," Darryl explained, "but you were gone so long and well we just kind of got lonely sitting around the house. Besides, we were both spooked out by that woman you were talking about."

"You saw her too?" Bart asked.

"No," Leonard answered, "but we weren't sure if she might show up again and she might be like a serial killer or something. You never know about people like that."

"You mean like imaginary people that pop in and out of people's lives at inopportune times and won't leave."

"Yeah," Leonard replied. "Hey, wait a minute. I see where you're going with this."

"We've been looking around," Darryl said, changing the subject. "And we think you should go play some volleyball."

"I've been by the court," Bart countered. "Nothing but a bunch of sand."

"Arrrr, matey," Leonard said, doing his best pirate imitation, "but what treasure there may be buried in that sand." Bart didn't feel like going back in a direction he had already come, and he was getting worried about Cassandra. He knew she was a reporter and that she was probably just off snooping in a way that only reporters can snoop, but that didn't stop him from worrying. In fact, the knowledge that she was probably off snooping and might very well get herself caught made him worry even more. The other thing he was dreading was trying to convince Jake that they needed to check out the volleyball pit which they had only recently left based on the word of two imaginary people. Still, Jake knew that they served as his extra set of eyes, spotting things he seemed to have missed. It was a weird, almost symbiotic type of relationship. They certainly wouldn't be around without him, or at least he didn't think they would be. He sometimes wasn't sure. He knew that God didn't waste anything, so it was possible that if he weren't around, they would be someone else's imaginary friends. That was a hard concept to deal with at the moment, but he made a mental note to talk to God about it later in prayer. That thought made him wonder if Darryl and Leonard prayed, perhaps voicing concerns that Bart didn't in the same way they paid attention to things that he would have let go by unnoticed.

"Are you coming?" Jake asked.

"No," Bart replied. "I think we need to go back and check something out. Are you willing to trust me?"

"You or them?" Jake wondered. Oliver didn't know what he meant and thought it was a rather odd question.

"Does it matter?" Bart replied. "Me and them are one and the same, so to speak."

"Not in my book," Jake countered. "But I'll go with you anyway. I don't care if it is instinct or voodoo, it works. So lead on, McDuff. By the way, though, where are you leading us to?"

"The volleyball pit," Bart answered. "I guess I saw something there that didn't register at first. I'm not sure what it was, but there was something out of place that needs to be investigated."

"Well then," Jake answered, "let's go play some volleyball. I'd like to spike one down Philip's long nose."

"Personally, I'd like to drive one down Shane's throat, but I don't see that happening."

"I don't want to hear you preaching on loving your neighbor for awhile," Oliver said.

"I love my neighbor," Bart said. "I'd just love him a little more with a volleyball down his throat." They walked back to the pit, where a game was already in progress, but they were willing to put a couple more on the court. Bart took the side Darryl pointed to. While they were discussing whose serve it was, Darryl pointed to a dark stain on the sand.

"It looks like blood to me," he told Bart, who was moving around in rotation at the direction of his teammates. That drew him away from the spot he wanted to be in and he had to wait 15 minutes and several serves before he got back into position to do what he wanted to do, which was get a large enough sample of the sand to take back with them to have it analyzed. It wasn't kosher in the eyes of the law, and it certainly wouldn't pass a chain of evidence muster, but at least it would give Jake a direction for his investigation to follow. He waited for the right ball to come towards him, and then made a flying leap for it as it went by his head. It looked spectacular, even though it served no purpose other than getting him on the sand so he could gather the sample he dove for in a Ziploc bag he had brought along for just such an emergency. It wouldn't hold up in a court of law, but it might serve to draw enough attention to get them a search warrant, especially if he had it tested himself rather than give it to Jake. He could use some of his contacts from his former life to have the sample analyzed, and then accidentally leak it to the local paper. On the other hand, it might be better to leak it to one of the larger statewide papers. The camp had some kind of positive story in the local paper at least once a week for the last couple of years. Between the money the camp brought in and the wealth of Angus' church, Bart wouldn't be surprised if the paper wasn't an extracurricular ministry of the church by now.

When he got up, he feigned an injury to his shoulder, withdrawing himself from the game. By that time, Jake was into the action and didn't want to leave, the competitor in him having been drawn out. Reluctantly, he withdrew and joined Bart and Oliver by the bleachers. They headed back to the car, hopeful of finding Cassandra there, when Jake began the questioning.

"So what did you find?" he asked.

"Nothing you need to know about," Bart replied. He didn't want Jake's fingerprints to be on the evidence at all. If he didn't know what Bart was having analyzed, then he could have plausible deniability. As far as the courts were concerned, Jake was just a friend giving another friend a ride while his car was broken down. If they found anything, then Jake could step in

and head up an official investigation, but that wouldn't be until much later.

"I'll buy that for now," Jake replied. Then, changing the subject,

added, "Where do you think Cassandra has been all this time?"

"You probably don't want to know that either," Bart said.

"She's probably been sneaking into those warehouses or using her

feminine wiles to seduce answers from some of the guards," Oliver added.

Jake and Bart both looked at him oddly, dumbfounded by his probably keen

observations.

"Where did you come up with feminine wiles?" Bart wondered. "I

don't remember teaching that in Sunday school."

"Sorry, pastor," Oliver answered sheepishly. "I guess I watch too

many late night movies." That confession started the trio down a path of

conversation that included all the genres of the late night movie set. Jake

loved the spy movies, especially of the sixties and early seventies. Bart liked

them too, except the concept of the spy having to sleep with practically every

woman he met.

"Not every woman," Jake countered. "They usually have at least one

that wants him, but he says no."

"That's because he's too busy saying yes to everything else with two

legs and panty hose," Bart replied. "It's not realistic to think that one man could have that much attraction for all those different ladies."

"Hello," Jake answered sarcastically, "it's not realistic for him to escape the bad guys or for the bad guys to put him in some kind of ingenious trap instead of just putting a bullet in his head. That's one reason I like them, because they're not realistic."

"Touché," Bart conceded. "What about you, Oliver. What kind of movies do you watch?"

"Everything really," Oliver answered. "I'm like Jake, I guess. I just want the escape from reality that comes with watching a movie. Sometimes I pretend I'm one of the characters in the movie as I'm watching it. It doesn't even have to be the main guy, just as long as I'm in the movie and not at home. It's kind of dumb, huh?" Neither Jake nor Bart thought it was dumb at all. Part of the draw of a good movie was to take you to places you might not ever see on your own, and to put you in circumstances that weren't your own. They didn't have to be better circumstances, just as long as they were different from your own, and as long as someone else was scripting the response to them. Part of the struggle of life was writing your own script, which was especially difficult when you didn't know the dialogue of the other characters in your life and how they would respond to you. Life was a constant ad-lib.

"I like the old horror movies," Bart offered. "The black and white movies were the best, before they discovered how to make blood look real. I liked it when the bad guy would hide behind the door, or in a dark basement, and then when the unsuspecting victim passed by, they would cut to another scene. You knew what happened, but it was left to your imagination to fill in the blanks. It was actually scarier than those slasher films they put out now."

"Yeah," Jake agreed. "The same goes for the old love scenes in romantic movies. You knew what happened when the two went towards the bedroom, but you didn't have to watch. I always feel like a peeping tom when we watch romantic movies, even if they're rated PG or PG-13." By that time, they reached the car, where they found Cassandra waiting in the front seat, using the rear view mirror to check her hair for strays and makeup for smudges. As far as Bart could tell, there were neither. She was perfect just the way she was. He didn't know for sure, and wouldn't until or if they were married, but he thought she probably looked that good coming out of bed in the morning. That thought triggered a memory of another woman in another time. Her name was Anna, and she was every bit as beautiful physically as Cassandra, but here beauty was only skin deep. The ugliness in her ran straight to the core of who she was. The only reason Bart thought of her now was that she could come up out of the pool after a spectacular dive in which she looked like a swan in flight, shake her head slightly to and fro, and have every hair fall perfectly into place. He heard later that she had married a man who emotionally abused her, causing her to develop either bulimia or anorexia, he wasn't sure which. Either way she had almost died before getting

help and later becoming a minister of sorts. She spoke to women's groups

about the trappings of beauty.

"Didn't you lock the car," Oliver asked Jake.

"I thought so," Jake replied as he opened the door, which was indeed

unlocked.

"What took you guys so long?" Cassandra asked innocently, diverting

attention from her self in the process.

"Well, it might help if you let us know you're leaving us so we don't

waste valuable time searching for you," Jake replied with more than a hint of

irritation in his voice. "I brought you out here, which makes me responsible

for your actions and well being."

"Aww," Cassandra cooed. "You care about little ole me. How sweet of

you." She leaned over and gave him a wet, audible kiss on the cheek. Jake

blushed and forgot any thoughts of irritation or questioning her about her

whereabouts for the last couple of hours.

"Feminine wiles in action," Oliver whispered to Bart. The drive home

was uneventful, mostly filled with conversations about old movies and which

stars were better looking, the ones from back then or now. The men naturally

chose men from the past, although they all felt a little weird talking about

guys being good looking or attractive.

"You'd never hear Bogie talking about which guy he found more attractive, Cagney or Tracy," Jake observed. "There's just something fundamentally wrong with men talking about whether other men are attractive or not."

"Oh, come on," Cassandra scolded, slapping his shoulder, "it's not like anyone is wanting you to date them or anything. It's just a matter of an opinion or two."

"Fine," Jake conceded, "but I still haven't heard you talk about which women you find more appealing, old school or new. So let's hear it. Which group is better looking?"

"Depends really," she observed. "The ladies from now look better longer, with a few exceptions. Most of that might be plastic and botox, but it still looks good on the screen. I'm not sure I'd like to see any of them really close up. It might ruin the image I have of them. The imagination is always better than reality. Don't you agree, Bart?"

"Huh? Sorry, I was kind of drifting when you were talking about the women looking better longer. I was just sort of wondering what Marilyn Monroe would look like now. I gotta tell you, there ain't been a woman yet come from Hollywood that can hold a candle to her."

"You got that right," Jake agreed readily. "I'd step on the faces of today's stars just to stand next to her."

"Isn't she the one that sang 'Happy Birthday' to President Kennedy?" Oliver asked.

"She sure was," Jake answered. "How did you know about that? Wasn't it a little before your time?"

"Before yours too, Jake," Bart countered. "It was just about before mine, but we all know about it."

"Oh you men and your testosterone," Cassandra complained. "A girl shows up with blonde from a bottle hair, some curves, and Vaseline lips and you all go gaga. Even Oliver is practically panting and he doesn't even know her."

"Sounds like someone's a little jealous," Bart observed. "It didn't bother us when you talked about Cruise and Gibson."

"You said something about both of them," she replied.

"Well, you got to admit that one of them is a few bananas short of a bunch," Jake answered back. "In fact, I'm not sure his tree goes all the way to the top."

"Maybe not," Cassandra replied, "but I wouldn't mind climbing up just to see."

"And I wouldn't mind Marilyn singing 'Happy Birthday' to me," Bart countered, "but I don't see it happening any time too soon."

"At least I can still have hope since my choice is alive. All you've got is some black and white memories of a woman that would be old enough to be your grandma if she lived."

"Eww," Oliver said, "it sounds disgusting when you put it that way."

"It does sound kind of sick when you think about it," Jake agreed.

"You sure know how to destroy a fantasy," Bart observed dryly.

"Well," Cassandra said, "why should you worry about a ruined fantasy when you have reality sitting in the seat in front of you?"

"Are you going to sing to me?" Bart asked coyly. She didn't answer, but a knowing glance between the two of them let him know that in the right time and place she would sing to him if that's what made him happy. At the moment, he was happy just to be in her presence. She made him feel like no other woman had, at least not in a very long time. The initial burning desires he felt for her were still there, but he had managed to draw them down to a slow simmer, ready to be turned back up if the situation became right, meaning they were married. As he forced the flames of desire to cool, other feelings came in that fed the fires of emotions burning within him. He found a greater attraction to her mind and heart, and found himself wanting to know more about whom she was and what made her tick. He wanted to know all about her background and her family, even if he wasn't ready to meet them yet. He also wasn't ready to talk about his past, but knew that it wasn't fair to ask about hers unless he was willing to talk about his own. Whether or not the stars of yesterday could compete on looks with the stars of today, one thing

remained unchanged in Hollywood, situations were always easier to handle

when you had a good scriptwriter and a director telling you what, how, and

when to do what you had to do. He knew God was the ultimate director and

scriptwriter, but he still felt like he was going through life in a virtual state of

constant improvisation. Just once he would like to see an angel with a cue

card telling him what to do or say next. Since that wasn't likely to happen, he

just shut-up and enjoyed the ride.

CHAPTER EIGHT

Bart woke the next morning feeling fuzzy and confused, which was how he ordinarily felt the first thing in the morning so he assumed everything was still right in the world. His heart was torn between the reality he enjoyed with Cassandra and what might be a fantasy with Shalina. On the one hand, Cassandra was a wonderful, vibrant, beautiful woman who seemed to not only accept him with all of his faults and idiosyncrasies, but actually seemed to enjoy him all the more because of them. On the other hand, if Shalina were real, then he couldn't pass up the opportunity to at the very least get to know her and find out what she was truly like. He enjoyed her company, too, and she was pretty as well, if in a different way. It was kind of like comparing Ginger and Mary-Ann on Gilligan's Island. Each of them was a beautiful young woman, and each brought a different kind of beauty to the small screen. It was an apple to oranges comparison that wasn't fair to either woman. He decided against deciding on anything at the moment. The matter, though pressing, wasn't urgent. It not only could wait, but it would have to wait while he continued, along with Jake and Cassandra, the investigation of Megiddo camp.

Bart looked in on Darryl and Leonard, who were both still asleep in the den. Darryl was on the love seat and Leonard was sprawled out on his usual spot on the pool table, with a trail of drool spilling down on the green

211

canvas below his face. He decided against waking them for the moment. He hoped this would be one of those rare days when they slept practically all day. He didn't understand why imaginary people needed to catch up on their sleep from time to time, but both of them needed to recharge their batteries every now and then with a full day of non-stop, snore like rolling thunder, drool a river sleep. Whatever the reason behind it, he was going to take full advantage of the situation.

After assuring himself that his compatriots were probably out for the duration, he decided to make the best of an already good situation. The first order of business was getting to the Post Office to make an overnight delivery to a friend in the state crime lab of the sample he had collected the previous day. He doubted that any real evidence would be produced. The sample was too small, had been out too long and had a high rate of contamination, not only from the sand, but from the drops of sweat and possibly even other people's blood as well. Still, it was worth a try. Maybe if they couldn't get a full DNA analysis, they could attempt to get some mitochondrial samples. It wouldn't be as good, but it should provide the evidence they needed to get a judge to issue them a search warrant. Most judges in this area had pretty much sold their soul to Megiddo in one fashion or another, either by making public appearances with and for the camp, which connected them to the camp in the eyes of the voting public during November, or by making and receiving contributions to the camp. One thing Cassandra found out about while she was making like the proverbial wandering minstrel was that many of the political candidates in the region had a revolving door type of account when it came to financially backing them. The strange thing about it was that the money returning to them was always twice of what they gave or more, and not all of it went into their campaign chest. Most of it, in fact, went to the politico's personal hope chest. Basically it meant they hoped they didn't get caught taking underhanded bribes from less than scrupulous preachers.

Some people referred to preachers as men of the cloth. Bart would say that far too many of them were men of the green. One of the things he saw hurting the church, more so with those outside the walls of the church than those who were within and had gotten used to such shenanigans, was the amount of salary being pulled in by those in the larger churches. In some ways he felt split about the subject. He knew the Bible called for those in the ministry to receive the double honor, but he didn't think that included receiving salaries comparable to high priced CEO's and living in homes that could shelter several large families, with some that compared to Presidential mansions of third world countries. And they received all of those things while many members of their congregation had to make the hard choice between food and medicine. In the end, whether you held political office or a church office, it came down to personal scruples and character.

213

After making his deposit at the local Post Office, Bart headed to the mini-mart for some coffee and breakfast. Besides serving the best biscuits and gravy in the area, along with gas, oil, and various sundries, the mini-mart served some of the best wisdom of the ages. The White House conference room had never gathered the amount of wisdom which came almost daily from the forum held at the breakfast tables there. Retirees, along with those who had never seemed to hold steady work, yet still managed to get by, gathered around coffee and each other to share the gossip of the day, news they had seen that morning on television, and solutions to the problems of the world, which usually began with us getting out of the United Nations and kicking their backsides so hard that they skipped across the Atlantic until they landed back in Europe where they belonged. Bart didn't totally agree with that entire notion, but he couldn't deny the temptation.

He decided to leave the VW in the Post Office parking lot and walk the few blocks to his destination. It was a beautiful sunny day, with temperatures nearing seventy, and he was sure that the bite of a fall chill couldn't be very many days away, so he needed to enjoy it while he could. Besides, there were other people making their way up and down the sidewalk and it gave him an opportunity to interact with them without the dynamic duo of Darryl and Leonard interfering. He hoped they would spend the rest of the day snoozing, but he couldn't count on it. It was kind of like the chill of fall he was anticipating; it was coming, he just wasn't sure exactly when or where it would be.

He was passing by one of the myriads of cell phone distributors that had popped up in the last couple of years, most of them closing within weeks of their grand opening, when something caught his eye. He hated the fact that he was forced by the circumstances of timing to carry a cell phone. People expected it of him because they all had one. They could be reached at a moment's notice, whether they were in conference with an associate or just sitting down to dinner with the family, and they expected the same from their pastor. But the object he saw the store owner setting up a new display of may just be the answer to prayer. It was a separate earpiece that connected wirelessly to his cell phone. With that tucked behind his ear, he could talk to either Darryl or Leonard and those around him would only think he was talking to someone on the phone. Why didn't God think of this before? It was brilliant.

"Hello, Bob," Bart called out as he entered the store. Bob Seavers, a likable man in his fifties who still looked, and sometimes acted, like he was in his twenties, looked up from the window display he was setting up.

"Hey, there, Bart," he called back. "What can I do you for?"

"I was looking at that new toy you got," Bart answered. "How much does it sell for?"

"Well, the going price to the general public is fifty dollars, but I've got a special pastor's discount that brings the price to an even hundred, taxes included." It was the usual banter between the two of them. Bob always pretended to give a discount, and then quote an unreasonable higher price. Bart had done quite a bit of business with Bob over the years, mostly buying special order surveillance equipment from him. He only asked why once, and Bart told him it was to spy on members of his congregation he suspected of having affairs. Bob chuckled nervously, but Bart had such a deadpan expression that he wasn't sure if he was kidding or not. The only other time he hinted at wanting to know why, Bart told him there were a couple of members of his congregation that had decent bodies and he wanted to see them up close and personal. Once again, his poker face didn't reveal whether or not he was kidding or not.

"I'll take it without the discount, if you don't mind," Bart replied. Bob showed him how to work the ear bud, as he called it, and sold him a few necessary accessories, like a car charger, then showed him how to work it. Bart thanked him, hung it over his ear to get used to the feel of it and then proceeded down to the mini-mart. He had barely made it out of the door and onto the sidewalk when he heard a hauntingly familiar voice speak to him over his newly acquired ear piece.

"Hiya, handsome. Longtime no see," Shalina said playfully. Bart was shocked and just a little perplexed because he hadn't heard his phone ring.

Maybe he had it on vibrate and just hadn't felt it, or maybe it was a feature of

the new ear piece. If that was the case, he wasn't sure he liked it. He wanted to

be able to screen his calls a little. There wasn't anyone in particular that he

didn't want to talk to, but there were some members of his congregation that

he didn't want to talk to all the time. He felt terrible that he felt that way about

people that he was supposed to be shepherding, but he also knew that people

could be, if you let them, a terrible and avoidable distraction. He thought of a

line from A Christmas Carol.

"People are our business," the ghost of Marley stated. Now he couldn't

remember Marley's first name. Bob kept popping into his mind, but he didn't

think Scrooge had a Rastafarian business partner. But, then again, stranger

things had happened.

"Are you going to talk to me or what?" an annoyed Shalina asked.

"Sorry, mon, I was spacing a little or something like that," he

answered.

"Huh?" Bart realized he had adopted a reggae accent, cleared his

throat and tried again.

"Sorry, I was just a little preoccupied in my thoughts. To what do I

owe this pleasure?"

"No charge," she replied. "For now anyway, but you owe me. I was just wondering when your birthday was."

"Are you planning on buying me something?" he asked. He liked this new toy. He could imagine himself talking to any of his imaginary playmates, or even several of them at a time and no one being the wiser for it. He was also thinking of ways to incorporate it into his sermons. Every once in awhile he would borrow a routine from Bob Newhart and pretend to be talking on the phone with someone, sometimes Gabriel or another angel, and sometimes just another person. Leonard and Darryl helped him during those routines by playing the other role. He had done it a few times without them, but it was really better when he could play off of one or both of them.

"I might, if you play your cards right. But I had something else in mind. So are you going to tell me or not?"

"I'd love to, but to be honest, I'm not too sure."

"Not sure of when your birthday is? Weren't you there?"

"Kind of, but I was awfully young then and didn't have much of a concept of time. Besides, I couldn't read the days on the calendar until I was several months old and by then I was worried about premature graying more than I was about silly things like birthdays. I do remember that it was sometime in the fall," he confessed.

"Are you telling me that you don't celebrate birthdays?"

"Sure I do. I celebrate birthdays all the time. I just don't celebrate my own." Bart stopped at one of the benches the city had placed in a grassy area off of the sidewalk and sat down. Now that he was engaged in conversation with Shalina, he wasn't in a hurry to get to the mini-mart. Besides, there were parts of this conversation that were not meant for public consumption. They weren't talking dirty or anything like that. They weren't even sharing private little secrets. But he didn't want just anyone to know that he didn't know when his birthday was. That would lead to questions about why, which would lead to more questions about his childhood that he didn't want to answer. As a pastor, his current life was pretty much under a microscope all of the time, but his past was meant to stay back there in his past if he could help it. If not, then some well meaning, but definitely misguided, church member or fellow pastor would try an intervention, find the woman who gave him birth, and try to get them together for reconciliation. He forgave her, but that didn't mean he wanted her to be a part of his life.

"Since you remember your birthday is in the fall, and its fall now, today could be your birthday, right?"

"I suppose," Bart conceded, unsure of what to expect next.

"Are you alone?" she asked coyly. He looked around and answered that he was. People were driving up and down the road, but only eccentrics like him actually walked any farther than from the parking space to the store.

"Happy birthday to you," she began singing in a husky voice

219

reminiscent of Marilyn Monroe singing to President Kennedy. Bart sat back to relax and enjoy the show, but soon found out that was an impossibility. He had never really thought of the affect of having a beautiful woman sing in your ear could have. It was almost as if she were standing right there beside him, her breath coming in heated gasps as she reached each note of the innocent song, one that lost it's innocence somewhere along the way. His hair stood on end and his skin began beading in little droplets of sweat, despite the cool breeze now blowing. His heart was racing faster and faster with each soft exhale of breath tickling his ear. Despite his best efforts, he found himself moving almost uncontrollably, sometimes stretching out like a rubber band on the verge of popping, then tightening up into a hard rubber ball. He was like an old hound dog whose belly was being rubbed enthusiastically. He was glad the streets were deserted. There wasn't even very much vehicle traffic. He was really glad Shalina was on the phone and not here in person. She could hear his soft groans that escaped his lips despite his trying to keep them imprisoned, but at least she couldn't see him gyrating around like an epileptic cat. Then the siren's song was over, ending much too quickly, but mercifully so for Bart's sake.

"Hello," he called tentatively, afraid that the call might have gotten dropped.

"Hello," Shalina said, but not in his ear piece. She was standing right behind him. Bart stood up suddenly, nearly stumbling off of the sidewalk and

into the path of a furniture delivery truck. He caught hold of a lamp post just

before falling backwards.

"Where did you come from?" he said, having gathered his wits again,

both from the near collision and from the very real collision of Shalina's

husky voice crooning to him.

"I was standing back there in the alley the whole time," she confessed.

"I guess from your reaction you like my song." Bart shuffled his feet and

blushed almost violently. He felt like the blood vessels running along his skin

on his cheek bones were about to burst. He broke out into a cold sweat and

was shivering like a wet dog.

"I guess you could say that," he admitted. If he were to tell the truth,

he loved and hated it at the same time. He knew exactly how Jason and the

Argonauts felt as they listened to the maddening tune of the siren's song.

There was something about the emotional pull of a song, even one sung in a

nearly erotic fashion that connected to the heart of a man the way that nothing

else did. The old saying that the way to a man's heart was through his stomach

was a bunch of unadulterated hogwash. A man could get a decent meal at any

diner or restaurant in town, but to have a woman sing to a man was a once in a

blue moon activity. Bart remembered the first time he heard a girl sing a love

song. It was at a high school talent show and the girl sang <u>Wind Beneath My</u>

<u>Wings,</u> and Bart knew that as he sat on the front row center that she was singing only to him. The only problem was that there were around forty other guys in the audience, including the principal, who knew she was singing to them. As it turned out, she was singing to her Algebra instructor, who was subsequently fired shortly after that for fraternizing with female students.

"Yeah," she said, "I guess I could say that, especially since you still haven't stopped shaking."

"Well, I was nearly run over by a truck a few minutes ago, as you recall. That might have a little to do with me shaking." It was a lame excuse at best, but it was the best he could do on a moment's notice. The palpitations and shaking could rightly be blamed on nearly becoming a hood ornament, but the blushing and convulsions could only rightly be attributed to near fatal release of male hormones swimming through his body like a school of devouring piranha.

"Uh-huh," she said impishly. "And I don't suppose it had anything to do with little old me, hmm?" She cocked her head slightly to one side with an impish grin. Her soft brown hair flowed like sand in an hour glass, softly landing on her bare shoulders. The baby blue sweater she wore had an enlarged neck, allowing one shoulder or another to escape from its woven confinement. Bart noticed and appreciated her self conscious act of tugging first this way and then that as the sweater would dip down over one shoulder or another. Then she would pull at the front, in case something else might be accidentally revealed. He purposefully focused on her eyes, both to show her the respect she deserved as a fellow human being and to stop himself from being tempted in case she did have a wardrobe malfunction.

"I suppose I might as well fess up," he agreed. "Especially since my reaction is so obvious. But how did you know about the birthday thing? Jake and I were only talking about it yesterday, and I don't recall you being anywhere around."

"Oh, come on," she said, "Monroe is a universal language to men. If I was wearing a white dress instead of these blue jeans, I could really blow your mind by finding a way for it to blow up." She was referring, of course, to the famous scene of Marilyn walking over the steam grate. She was right; certain things in life spoke a universal language, even when they didn't say anything at all. The two of them settled in on the park bench to talk about universal languages and anything else that might cross the paths of their minds.

From their vantage point, they could see several local shops, including a donut shop, a small café that they decided to visit in just a little bit, a pawn shop, and several other assorted small stores. They watched people come and go for close to an hour, observing the strange habits of the animals called human beings. It was funny to see people duck in to get donuts like men secretly ducking into an adult book store. They saw several people going into the pawn shop with some sort of merchandise, only to return moments later with a small amount of cash and a scowl on their faces. Bart couldn't read lips from this distance, and he was glad because he was sure from the expressions he saw that he didn't want to know the words that were being said. They watched cars circle the block several times like vultures hovering in the hot desert air waiting for a poor animal to breathe its last breath. And when a car pulled away from the curb, the vulture swooped in to claim its rightful prey. The sad part was that other parking spaces were available only a few hundred feet away, but they weren't willing to walk that far.

"Sad, isn't it?" Shelly commented. "I've seen people do the same thing in mall and department store parking lots. They waste a gallon of gasoline to find a parking place up front, then go in and by a treadmill, which they have an assistant from the store load for them."

"Silly girl," Bart commented. "They aren't buying a treadmill. They've run out of closet space and need somewhere to hang their jackets and throw their dirty clothes. I know, because I've got one setting in my den at this moment collecting clothes and dust."

"Well, maybe so," she said, "but you are also out in the fresh air walking about for your business instead of driving everywhere you need to go. I don't blame you for letting that treadmill collect dust. After all, who wants to walk about in life and not get anywhere?" It made perfect sense to Bart, even though the treadmill was actually an apt illustration of most people he knew. They did walk about their lives, conducting business like busy little ants and at the end of their busy little lives they had made very little progress. Most of the time the problem was that very few people had a specific destination in mind. They wandered from place to place, thinking that each one they went to would bring them the happiness they knew they deserved. Children strived for the destination known as adulthood, women marched towards marriage, and men climbed the hills of success. And when they finally got to where they thought they wanted to be, happiness had moved on to another time and another place farther away.

"Well, I'd like to get someplace," Bart stated, standing up. "A place of complete satisfaction where the conversation is good and my belly gets full. I already have the good conversation, and if you'd let me buy you lunch at the café, I'd have my wish of a full stomach."

"How could a girl resist such a charming invitation?" she replied. "Besides, I didn't want to say anything, but my belly button is gnawing at my backbone."

"Really?" Bart asked. "I wanna see." He reached over to tug at her sweater, but she batted his hands away.

"That's private property, mister, for me and my hubby only."

"I didn't think you were married," Bart commented.

225

"Not yet," she answered, "but who knows, maybe after lunch we could find a willing preacher."

"Whoa, girl. I think I'd like to get to know my future wife a little better before we settle down to a house and white picket fence."

"First of all," she corrected, "I want a farm and barb wired fence somewhere so far out that we know folks who come by the house are either lost or coming to see us. And second, you know my name and that you care for me, what else do you need to know?" The question, as strange as it was, took Bart off guard. In the old days, when marriages were arranged as a matter of conveniences for the sake of the families involved, men and women chose to love one another over any other feelings they might have. And those marriages lasted for decades. In modern, so called civilized times, people dated for years, sometimes even moving in with one another before marrying, and those marriages lasted months. Maybe she was on to something. It sounded preposterous, but so did a schizophrenic preacher with a slight tilt to anti-social tendencies like ducking out of services before shaking hands and avoiding parties that were designed to introduce him to some of the more eligible single women within a three county range. He wasn't sure, but he suspected they even brought in some ringers from out of state at one point. Sometime on the walk over to the café, which was less than three blocks away, he found his hand being held by hers. Or was he holding her hand?

Who had grabbed hands first? And did it really matter since they were obviously together now and he liked the feeling it brought him? It wasn't much really. They were just friends holding each other's hands. People did it every day. It reminded him of something though, something just beyond the horizon of his memory. Then it came to him. There was an older couple that lived just up the street from him. The man had some heart problems and the doctor had prescribed a regimen of walking every day to strengthen his cardiovascular system. Bart watched them almost every day, walking hand in hand.

"I would like to know a little more about you before we get hitched," he told her as he held open the door for her to enter.

"I'm an open book for anyone willing to take the time to read," she replied. "Ask a question and I'll either tell you the answer or tell you it's none of your business. Of course, since we'll be man and wife soon, I guess there won't be much that's none of your business. Still, there might be a few things that I'd like to keep secret, just so there's an air of mystery about me."

"Is that important?" Bart asked. He was enthralled with her soliloquy and wasn't sure he would be allowed a word in edgewise and wasn't quite sure whether he cared or not. He liked the sound of her voice. It was harmonious, like the whisper of the wind carried through the woods on a late summer night.

"Important? How in the world can you preach about marriage and relationships when it's painfully obvious that you don't know the first thing about women?"

"I have a hard time balancing my checkbook, but I still preach on tithing and managing your money."

"That's different," she stated and let the matter drop as if the simple fact that she said it was different made it so. Bart couldn't argue with logic like that, and he wasn't inclined to try. If she said it was different, then that's all he needed to know. Before he could pursue the matter any farther, she told him she needed to powder something or other and that he should go ahead and order for the both of them because he should know by now what she would like. He ordered two cheeseburgers with matching orders of fries and large drinks. The order came while she was still in the restroom, but he waited for her to return before starting so they could ask a blessing on the food.

"How thoughtful of you," she commented. "And the order is absolutely perfect. I just knew I could trust you to order for me."

"So," he started between bites, wiping away a bit of stray mayonnaise before continuing, "why don't you start by telling me about your childhood. You could start with where you were born, what your parents were like, did you have siblings or were you an only child? I want all of the intimate details."

"Those will have to come later," she said. "For now, I'll just tell you about my childhood. Actually, now that I think about it, there's not many intimate details to tell. I've kissed a few boys, even made out some in high school, but I'm still a virgin and proud to say it to whoever wants to know. As for my childhood, I have a twin sister, both my parents are dead, but not until after I grew up, and that's about the story of my life. Now where can we find a preacher around here? You're one, but I think it would somehow be illegal or immoral or maybe both for you to perform the ceremony, so we'll have to find someone else."

"Don't you want to know something about me?" he asked.

"I suppose, but there will plenty of time for that after we're hitched." She took another bite of cheeseburger, sipped some cola through her straw and smiled at him like she was waiting for him to ask her to the prom or to be his steady girl. At first he thought she was kidding, just playing some kind of silly game and he was happy to play along with her, but now he wasn't too sure that if he backed out she wouldn't get a lawyer and sue him for breach of contract or something silly along those lines.

"Why don't we finish lunch before going to find a preacher?" he asked, hoping he hadn't somehow teased himself into breaking a young woman's heart. He liked Shalina. He was totally comfortable around her and he wanted to know her better, and might consider marrying her someday in

229

the future, but he also liked Cassandra, who was another marital option. He

wasn't as comfortable around Cassandra as he was his present company, but

most of the discomfort came from a rising passion boiling up inside of him

like a long dormant volcano becoming active once again. The problem with

volcanoes, however, was that they tended to cause destruction and mayhem in

their wake. With Shalina he felt some passion as well, but it was subdued,

easily controlled, or it was until she started singing in his ear. But even then, it

was fairly easy for him to put the genie back in the bottle and put the cork

back on without too much of a fight. He wished that somehow he could take

the ease and comfort he felt with Shalina and morph that into the passion and

fire he felt with Cassandra to have one woman. As it was, someone was going

to be hurt and he felt certain that no matter how it turned out he was going to

be feeling that pain as acutely as anyone.

"Fine," she managed between healthy bites of burger. "But I suppose

that if we're going to wait that long, we might as well postpone the whole

thing for now."

"Oh," Bart said over his straw as he sipped the last of his soda, causing

a slurping sound that seemed to echo through the whole dining area.

"Yeah," she answered. "I've got an appointment with a lawyer this

afternoon and I need to do some research at the library. So we'll get married

another day."

"That wasn't a divorce lawyer, was it?"

"Don't be silly, I won't need one of those if we get married. I'll just kill you." Her delivery was so nonchalant, so deadpan that Bart wasn't sure when she was just kidding and when she was absolutely serious. He had been almost sure that she was serious about the marriage until a few minutes ago, and now he was almost as sure that there wouldn't be any alimony or child support involved if they ever separated, which might explain why she wanted a place far out in the country far away from prying eyes and ears.

"I'll remember that. But an appointment with a lawyer might have put a little crimp in our honeymoon, don't you think?"

"I would have rescheduled that, silly. But you could have helped with the research I'll be doing at the library. We could make such a good team, like Batman and Robin. Do you look good in tights?" Once again the question was asked in such a carefree manner that Bart was caught off guard and wasn't sure if he was supposed to honestly answer or avoid the subject altogether. Considering that he was in the throes of middle age and the corresponding spread that goes with it, he opted to change the subject.

"I could still help you with the research. What are we looking for?" He wanted to help her, if he could. For one thing, it would help him to learn more about her and spend more time with her. For another, it would just be one friend helping another with something as mundane and common as library work, which would help him explain to Cassandra, if necessary, why he was spending so much time with another woman. That, of course, brought a whole new train of thought with it. Was she another woman? Could she be another woman unless Cassandra was the first woman? Bart wasn't sure about anything at the moment, and to make matters worse, all he could think about was an old joke about a man taking a driver's exam. He was told that there was a train heading west at thirty miles an hour and another one on the same track heading east at fifty miles an hour. They would meet within minutes and the instructor wanted to know what he would do. The man answered he would call his brother because he hadn't ever seen a wreck like the one that was about to happen. He guessed Jake could be the man taking the exam because he was about to see Bart crash like no one else had before.

"Do you really want to help or are you just looking for an excuse to spend time with me?" she asked.

"Does it matter?"

"I suppose not," she replied. "I'm looking through the family histories here. I told you that I had a twin sister, which is true. What I didn't tell you is that we were separated at birth. Our birth mother couldn't take care of us so we were adopted out. She went to live with some of our birth mother's family, but they couldn't afford both of us, or didn't want both of us, I'm not sure which. I was sent to an orphanage, but I was adopted out pretty quick. That brings us to present day and me looking for my sister."

"So Lucy is your sister? Sister Agnes says she hasn't seen her for years. The only niece she sees regularly is Bonnie, and I don't think she sees her very often. I've been here for quite awhile and I've only seen her a couple of times. Of course I don't see Sister Agnes as often as I should."

"I think Lucy is the woman I'm looking for, although I can't be sure because like I said, we've been separated basically since birth. I've been looking for clues, but the records have either been sealed, destroyed, or missing. It's been pretty frustrating trying to find out anything."

"Did your adoptive parent's tell you anything? Maybe they kept in touch or tried to find out more about your family."

"I doubt it. What started out as a good thing ended up going south pretty quick. My dad was an intern who couldn't handle the long hours and ended up hooked on speed. Mom coped by taking her own version of mother's little helpers. After that, I was just a kid in their way that cost money they would have rather spent on drugs. Dad became abusive, mostly because he was angry all the time. The anger was mostly at himself, but since you can only beat yourself up so much, he had to have another target. Mom started having affairs while he was out on binges, and I was sometimes forced to watch. She invited me to participate, but never forced me to." It was no wonder that Bart felt a kindred spirit with the woman standing before him.

She was recounting the details of a painful and sordid life as if she was reading someone else's biography, but the pain was all hers.

"Where are the tears?" he asked, pulling her into his chest. She heaved somewhat against him, but no tears or sobs followed. A couple of heavy sighs came and then she pulled away again.

"I cried a lot when I was younger; maybe I've cried myself dry. I really don't know. Besides, if it weren't for all of that happening, I might not have found God the way I did. I needed a father figure, and God showed me he was available. Since then, I only looked back long enough to forgive my parents for being human. They were pretty screwed up, but any of us can be." That made Bart think about the woman who had given him birth. Had he ever really forgiven her? He said he had. He went through the motions of doing so, but was that enough? He still wasn't ready to have her back in his life, but he didn't want her to pay for what she had done anymore either. There was a slim line between forgiveness and reconciliation, and he was walking that line, but wasn't about to cross it just yet. Maybe someday soon he would welcome her back into his life, not as a mom, but just another woman who needed a friend. For now he had to concentrate on the task of helping Shalina find out what he could from the library's genealogical resources. Fortunately for them, after the big shake your family tree and see what falls out craze of the late seventies and early eighties, the library teamed up with the local body of the Latter Day

Saints. Bart couldn't even come close to agreeing with their interpretation of

the Bible, but he couldn't fault them for their genealogical record keeping, or

their focus on family values.

Shalina walked out ahead while Bart picked up the tab for lunch.

Together, once again hand in hand, they walked over to the library, which was

over a mile away, but neither of them seemed to mind the use of time or the

exertion. It was a good way to rid themselves of the excess calories offered by

lunch.

CHAPTER NINE

After a couple of hours of searching through dusty books and flipping through newspaper articles archived on microfiche files, Bart was ready for a break. Unfortunately for him, though, Shalina had found her zone. She was flipping from article to article, back to the original, and then on to a book or other manuscript in wild eyed fashion. Bart said goodbye, and even gave her a light kiss on the forehead, but he didn't think she had even noticed when he left. He was glad that she was so consumed with finding a sister that she had never met, but also felt a sense of unease and apprehension at what she might find when she finally reached her destination. He knew that the destination people reached often failed to live up to the thrill of the journey. He hoped it would be different for her. Maybe she would be the one in a million that found a pot of gold at the end of her biological rainbow.

Sometime during his self imposed imprisonment within the confines of the county library, dark clouds had crept in, bringing with them an impression of an early sunset. What had been a pleasant and warm afternoon had morphed into a drab, dreary, and altogether uninviting evening without stars or other natural lights. The first emissaries of the fall chill were in town for an early visit before inviting in the rest of the winter entourage. It wasn't cold by any means, but Bart had dressed for what felt like a warm spring day and he was now facing the prospect of walking at least the next fifteen minutes in chill night air and would count himself lucky if he could end the walk before getting wet. The western horizon flashed an ominous portent of things to come that lit that half of the sky for several seconds before fading again to black. He ducked back into the library and warned Shalina that she might want to cut her studies short and come back with him, but she wouldn't hear of it. He offered to come back after her in a couple of hours when the library closed, but she declined, telling him that she would just call a cab when the time came. She told him that she was trying to persuade the librarian to let her stay late and continue her research, but Bart didn't see any chance of that happening. Ms. Flount was a stickler for the rules that made Captain Bligh seem like a rebel in comparison. Still, Shalina held to an unimpeachable hope. Bart could do little to dissuade her or otherwise talk reason to her, so he left her alone in the back corner of the library, looking absolutely radiant in the glow of the microfiche.

He walked down the street alone in his thoughts of the previous days events. Sometimes in times when he had a few moments alone, which was a rare thing between his imaginary and real friends, he would glance skyward and begin talking with God. This was one of those times. They talked from the library to the convenience store parking lot where Bart had left his car parked, with Bart doing more listening than talking. He didn't hear God's voice audibly, which considering his peculiar set of circumstance seemed rather odd to him. He thought that since he could talk to Darryl and Leonard, along with a various assortment of other people that popped in and out of his life like movie stars doing cameos in "B" movies, he should be able to hear the voice of God, even if it was his own imagination. There were times when he even tried to force the issue and pretend that he was hearing the voice of his Creator, but it would never come. Instead, the message that came through to him was like a series of impressions that left him with a feeling of knowing what he should do next. In this case, the message was almost one of God telling him that he had made the bed; it was time for him to lie in it. Bart was pretty sure that he had formed the wrong impression of what God had truly said, but he couldn't quite make out what he should do next. He didn't want to hurt either woman, and he also didn't want to make a wrong decision and be stuck with a woman who either didn't want him, wasn't right for him, or even worse, turned out to be a figment of his own somewhat distorted view of reality. He could, he supposed, perform a wedding ceremony between him and an imaginary fiancée, with Darryl as best man, and Leonard as the usher who would seat all of his imaginary guests. It would cut down on the cost of the wedding, especially the expense of food served at the reception. For a honeymoon, he could just imagine them in Hawaii or some other tropical paradise. But he wasn't ready for a relationship that wasn't founded squarely upon the foundation of reality. Maybe someday he could resign himself to that fate, but not today. If Shalina weren't real, and at this point he wasn't sure whether or not she was, then he would have to somehow find the courage within himself to rid his life of her forever. He had seen her eat, watched her pick up books and work the contraption that read the old newspaper articles, but he had seen Leonard and Darryl do almost the same thing over and over. He felt them as if they were a physical presence within the room, even knowing they were only manifestations of his own design. He tried to think if the waitress at the café had interacted with her during lunch or whether the librarian had made any gestures that would have suggested to him that he wasn't alone in the knowledge of her existence. She was in the restroom when he ordered, and had walked outside while he paid for lunch. In the library, she sent him to the front to ask for assistance when it was necessary. Of course that was the gentlemanly thing to do, so he didn't protest when it happened, but it now gave him cause for hesitation in moving forward with her in any meaningful manner. Maybe he needed to concentrate on Cassandra, who drove him absolutely insane physically and was meeting him on an emotional plane as well. Shalina, on the other hand, enmeshed him in an emotional net that drove him to almost the same degree of distraction that he felt with Cassandra physically, and was beginning to meet him physically as well, especially with her imitation of Marilyn.

"Wait up," he heard someone call. It was Shalina, who looked like she had run the last ten blocks. "Are all preachers deaf, or are you a problem child? I've been hollering at you for the last five or ten minutes. Are you that deep in thought?"

"I guess I was. I was about as deep in thought as you were in your research. What happened to your idea of camping out under one of the tables until the librarian left so you could continue your research by flashlight?"

"Was I really that bad? Sometimes I get a little intense when I focus on one thing. It's kind of a fixation thing I've been trying to work on."

"I don't blame you. Actually, it's kind of nice to see someone care about someone else enough that they're willing to put out that kind of effort. Kind of rare in this gilded age of me first mentality."

"Who says I'm not putting me first?" she responded. "After all, I may have ulterior motives of which you are unaware. And even if I don't, the thought of finding my sister may have more to do with satisfying a thirst within my own soul than with connecting with another person, especially a stranger that just happens to share my DNA."

"Ouch, talk about bursting my emotional bubble. I had you up on a pretty good pedestal, and I'll be doggone if you don't go and kick it out from beneath your own feet. What's that about?"

"I don't belong on a pedestal," Shalina stated flatly. "I'm just a woman who happens to be looking for someone I can share a piece of myself with, and hopefully someone who can share a piece of what someone else has to offer. I'd like to do that with Lisa if I ever find her, and I'd like to do that with you, if you're willing to think about it." Bart was willing to think about it. In fact, the thought of him being together with either Cassandra or Shalina had occupied the greatest majority of his time. The only other thought that competed with it was the mystery surrounding the young girl's death and its connection to Megiddo camp for drug rehabilitation.

"I've let it run through my head a couple of times," he confessed. "I really like you and all, but," he said, letting his thoughts trail away like vapor caught in a sudden gust of wind.

"But there's another woman who has your attention as well," she finished for him.

"It's that obvious, huh?"

"I was born at night, but it wasn't last night," she replied. "I've seen the far away looks you get at times, especially when I bring up any notion of commitment. I know we've only just met and that I don't have the right to claim you for my own just yet. All I'm asking is that you don't count me out without giving me a fighting chance. Can you do that much for me?" Bart couldn't believe what he was hearing. She wasn't making herself a door mat for him, but she was giving him the freedom to explore both doors before deciding which one to step through, if either was right for him. He didn't deserve a woman this good, and he wasn't sure that Cassandra would be

willing to be as compatible. He saw her more as the type of woman that would

tackle Shalina, claw her eyes out, and then raise her bloodied fist in triumph

before claiming Bart as her prize. His thoughts were so focused on that

imaginary scene that he didn't notice that the two of them had picked up a

couple of rather large shadows. He continued to ignore their presence until he

bumped into a third presence that had just stepped out from the shadows of a

dimly lit alley way that separated one of the oldest theaters in the state and a

storefront non-denominational church. It was the ferret man from the camp

who had spoken with Oliver about his problems.

"Good to see you, Pastor," the ferret hissed. Bart wasn't sure how it

was that a ferret could hiss, since they were supposed to be a snake predator,

but he was sure of what he heard. It came out as a weird combination of

whistle and whine that met at the ear with the definite impression of a snake

hiss. Either that, or Bart just thought of the man as a snake. Either was likely

to be equally true.

"Wish I could say the same about you," Bart replied. "But to be honest

I wouldn't care much if I never saw you again. Hope that doesn't hurt your

feelings too much."

"Not at all, but it may hurt my colleagues feelings. They're a lot more

sensitive about these things than I am." It wasn't until then that Bart realized that the shadow that had fallen over them was not from some passing clouds, but from a couple of goons that had fallen in behind them and looked big enough to require their own zip codes.

"Let me guess," Bart said, "graduates of the rehab program that just want to show their gratitude for your good work?"

"Very astute of you," the snake hissed. "They're also grateful for the good sum of money we pay them, but that makes it sound dirty somehow, doesn't it? It's much nicer to think of them as grateful people." Bart had directed Shalina to his left so that he could put her against a building, leaving her exposed only on one side, and he stood there, ready to fight and die for her if necessary. He hoped it wouldn't come to that, of course, but he was ready for whatever might be coming his way. He continued to walk forward, pressing his unwanted company backwards a few steps. It wasn't much, but it did allow for him to slip Shalina into an open shop door. He thought it was a shoe and leather goods shop, but it didn't really matter. All that mattered is that she was out of the way and could possibly get help. She obviously didn't want to go, but he gripped her arm and gave her a look that said there really wasn't much of a choice. She gave back a look that seemed to say something about not forgiving him if he did something stupid like get himself killed. He had no intention of doing anything that stupid, but the road was paved with people who had good intentions.

"It's just you and me now," Bart stated.

"Let's not forget my friends," Philip corrected. "Remember, they're the sensitive type who hurt easily. You really wouldn't want to hurt their feelings, would you? Because there's no telling how they might react if you did. Now, why don't you join me in this alley so we can have a little chat in private, hmm?"

"I suppose it would hurt their feelings if I declined," Bart offered.

"I'm afraid I couldn't say," Philip said. "But I wouldn't risk it if I were you. Besides, what possible harm could there be in having a little conversation about doctrinal issues with a fellow brother?"

"I ain't your brother. Like Jesus told the Pharisees, you're of your father the Devil, and the works of your father is what you'll do." That comment earned him a swift punch to his left kidney. While he was recovering from that attack, he found his right arm trying to reach a place between his shoulder blades that would be impossible for anyone but a contortionist to reach. He tried to put it back in its normal place at his side, but it refused to move. He assumed the vise like grip he was feeling on his wrist might have something to do with his arm's inability to correct itself, but he didn't have time to contemplate that theory for long before being elevated upward and shoved forward into the alley. Once there, things only got worse, much worse.

"We don't think you should return to the camp anytime soon," Philip stated, with an exclamation point provided by a hard kick into Bart's stomach. Sometime in the last few minutes he had been slapped, punched, kicked, and maybe bitten. That last part he might have done himself, thinking he had the other man's arm instead of his own. He remembered thinking that there must be more to this visit than just to deter him from coming back to the camp. Someone must have seen him get that blood sample. There couldn't be another explanation for this kind of brutality. There was one, but he didn't think Philip had that kind of pull. If Philip were the egocentric maniac that he appeared to be, then he might be working on his own, and this little show of force was for naught, except to stroke one man's overactive ego. Looking at the sneer on Philip's face, Bart thought that there might be more to that theory than he had originally considered. Of course, either way, his ribs were still broken and he was pretty sure someone else would have to fill in for him that coming Sunday, which was a shame since he had been practicing a sermon based on Humpty Dumpty, which was someone he could entirely relate to at the given moment. In his tirade, Philip hadn't mentioned anything about the blood sample, or any other evidence gathered against the camp, so Bart wasn't about to bring it up. Besides, he was too busy bringing up blood samples of his own at the moment to be too concerned about those he had sent to the crime lab. That meant that the only alternative was that the snake man was working on his own, something Bart would remember and use to his

advantage later. If there was enough anarchy in the ranks for someone to act

on his own just over a bruised ego, then there might be room for someone to

plant and foment the seeds of rebellion. And judging from the man's rage,

Bart was sure the snake could fertilize anything that was planted.

They left him in a heap next to a dumpster, alongside an empty

whiskey bottle and what appeared to be the recycled remains of someone's

pastrami on rye, although it was actually hard to tell. It looked more like

spaghetti and meatballs, with lots of sauce and not much meat. Bart felt like

adding to the collection, but the boot that had stomped his chest felt like it was

still there and he wasn't sure he could force any regurgitation past it. Instead,

he thought he might just pass out. On second thought, he considered dying.

After all, he was in pain here, with a dilemma of being caught between two

wonderful women, neither of which he wanted to hurt. Jake could manage

without him. His congregation could find another pastor. They weren't a dime

a dozen, but they weren't much more expensive than that. He started to laugh

at his own little joke, but the vibration on his diaphragm reminded him of why

he was thinking about dying. He wondered if he would get an angelic escort,

or maybe Jesus himself would come to take him. He wasn't being egotistical.

It was a theological thought that since Jesus said he would come and receive

those who were his unto himself that meant He would literally come for his own when they passed from this life into Heaven. Bart wondered if that was true or not, and he wondered if within the next few minutes he would find out for himself. He had decided to at least pass out when he heard the unmistakable sound of a woman screaming.

At first he thought whoever it was might be screaming at the sight of him. He knew that if he came across someone as bloody and beaten as he currently was that he would probably scream like a little girl. But then he realized that the scream was coming from somewhere farther away, outside of the alley. He wasn't sure how far away, the blood trickling in his ear gave everything he heard a sort of muffled sound, but it didn't sound very far from the edge of the alley. It took him a few minutes for the impact of the scream to connect with the events prior to his beating. He was trying to remember what had happened just before he had bumped into snake man and before snake man's two henchmen had repeatedly and violently bumped into him. The second scream brought everything back into perspective. It was Cassandra! No wait, that was wrong. It was Shalina. They had shared lunch together and then went to the library for research on her family. She had just caught up to him when he was attacked. He had sent her away to get help, but she must have returned just as Philip and crew were leaving the alley. He had to get up. He had to help her somehow. If nothing else, he could stain Philip's nice clean suit with a gallon of blood. He didn't think he lost that much. He wasn't sure

247

how much he lost and how much was still inside of him, but in the wrong

place. It was squishing around just beneath his skin and sloshing around his

lungs instead of running laps through his circulatory system like it was

supposed to be. But none of that mattered at the moment. All that really

mattered was getting to the end of the alleyway and helping Shalina. He

forced himself to move. The best he could do at the moment was a slow,

slithering crawl. He thought he was doing a wonderful imitation of a crippled

slug, running in slow motion. He needed to move faster, but he knew this was

his best gear for now. The only other alternatives were park and reverse, and

he wasn't too sure about reverse. He could see the end of the alley through

blood filled eyes. There was someone standing there, but he couldn't make out

whom.

It might have been Shalina, but then again it might have been The

Queen of Sheba or Jimmy the Greek for that matter. Whoever it was, they had

their hand over their mouth like they were about to puke. He couldn't blame

whoever it was if he ended up with a bellyful of bile on top of his back. He

knew he felt like puking, so how could he blame someone else for doing it at

the sight of him? He was close enough now to see that it wasn't one person,

but a couple. He had his arms tight around her, but not in a threatening

manner. He was holding her, comforting her, trying to hold her steady and

upright. She wasn't Shalina, though, but some other young woman, probably in her early twenties. From the way he was holding her and the look of

concern on his face, the man was no doubt her husband or boyfriend. Even in

his beaten stupor, Bart couldn't help but be envious and maybe even a little

jealous of what these two were sharing in this freeze frame of time. She clung

to him like a piece of ivy climbing a college fence and he stood there, firm

and as unmovable as a rock. He held her in the steely clench of comfort that

told her he would be her prince, her knight, her hero. Even through his matted

and swollen eyes, Bart could see how beautiful the picture before him was,

and he could see how strongly the yearning was inside of him to be that hero

for someone, he just didn't know who would be standing at his side when this

day was done. He decided to instead be the western hero and take this time to

ride off into the sunset. Actually, he didn't decide, his body decided for him.

His elbows gave way and his chin hit the harsh pavement with a resounding

thud. That was the last thing he remembered until waking up in the saloon

with the bewitching Miss Sally, the redheaded barkeep and owner of the

Flaming Star.

As it turned out, Miss Sally neither owned a saloon, nor had she ever

had the pleasure of serving as barkeep at the Flaming Star. As strange as it

sounded, Miss Sally wasn't even named Miss Sally at all. Instead, her name

was Beatrice and she was the charge nurse on the sixth floor of Mercy General

Hospital, which generally was not known for dispensing mercy and was not even known at times for the proper or timely dispensation of medicine.

"Howdy pardner," he heard Wyatt Earp call out from the swinging doors of the saloon. No doubt he was there to wet his whistle and maybe dance with Miss Sally on his way to the OK Corral. Then again, it might be Sheriff Jake stopping by to see how his best friend was doing after receiving a beating that nearly cost him his life. Bart liked the idea of the saloon scene so much that he was having a hard time shaking the illusion. He looked over and forced himself to focus on the piano player with the toothpick stuck in the corner of his mouth like a perpetual growth. He gradually became Darryl sitting on the piece of sadistic furniture that the hospital passed off as a chair. The drunken cowboy crying in his beer and singing some old trail song was none other than Leonard, who actually was singing an old trail song. It figures. Melissa, Jake's wife, was there as well. She was one of the saloon girls dancing on stage. In fact, she was the only girl on stage, but it sure was one heck of a costume. Bart felt bad about how he had checked her out earlier and hoped that anything he might have done or said earlier was all in his mind. He didn't need Jake being mad at him for wolf whistling at his wife.

Something was wrong, though. There should have been at least one more dancing girl on stage, maybe two. He sat up suddenly, remembering Shalina and her screams for help. He couldn't remember reaching the end of the alley. The last clear, coherent thought he had was of her screaming for help.

"Where is she?" he cried out, causing his nearly collapsed lungs to choke and cough in protest. Unashamedly, he leaned over the bed and coughed up what was no doubt a large piece of lung that had fragmented from the main piece. Regaining his composure and setting himself upright again, he asked the question one more time, calmly as he could manage.

"She's been taken," Jake replied. "We're not sure where or when, but no one has heard from her since that day we visited the camp. She hasn't been seen around town and I checked out her room at the hotel. The maid says she hasn't slept in the bed since that day."

"Who are you talking about?" Bart asked, confused about what he was hearing. As far as he knew, Jake didn't even believe Shalina existed, and he wouldn't know what room she was staying at in the hotel. Something strange was going on, something far stranger than being beaten, left for dead, being semi-rescued by a panicked young couple, and imagining yourself in an old west bar. Jake was talking about the abduction of a woman he didn't believe existed and using terminology that not only denied that belief, but suggested that he knew she was real all along. Bart had to gather his wits about him quickly if he was going to be any help.

"I'm talking about Cassandra, of course," Jake answered. "What other woman do you know of that I might know of?" He paused for a minute, and then continued after having a thought dawn upon him, "You're talking about Shalina, aren't you? Did something happen to her as well?"

"What do you care?" Bart said with a little more anger than he meant to have in his voice. "You don't even believe she's real."

"I may have my doubts about her existence," Jake admitted, "but until proven otherwise, I'm going to treat her and her abduction or disappearance or whatever like she was just as real as you and me."

"Thanks," Bart said. "You don't know how much that means to me."

"Alright then, tell me everything you can about what happened to you and about Shalina. It may be that she was taken as a hostage to keep you from testifying about whoever did this to you. By the way, you did see who did this didn't you?"

Bart spent the next half hour recounting his afternoon with Shalina while Jake answered questions about the disappearance of Cassandra. By the end of the afternoon, the two men had worked out a plan of action which included Bart spending the night in the hospital with one of Jake's deputies standing guard.

"We can't just lay around and do nothing," Bart protested feebly.

"We won't be," Jake promised firmly. "And you won't be just doing nothing. You'll be here recuperating and thinking about where the girls are, how we'll find them, and what we'll do when we find them. In the meantime,

I'm going to pay another visit to our friends at the camp and demand some answers from Phil the Ferret."

"I doubt you'll find him there," Bart warned. "But thanks for trying. I guess you're right about getting some rest. I can feel the drugs taking over now."

"And I don't guess you're in the mood for sharing, huh?" Bart smiled and let his head fall back on the pillow with a soft thump. Melissa shooed Jake out the door and looked towards where Leonard and Darryl had been sitting when Bart spoke to them as he came out of his sleep earlier.

"I don't know if you two are still here or not, but you better behave yourselves and leave Bart alone or you'll have to answer to me. I don't care if you are just figments of his imagination, there'll be a high price to pay if you bug him. Is that clear enough for the two of you?"

"Yes, mam" each replied in turn, although Leonard did so with his fingers crossed behind his back. Even so, he had no intention of bothering Bart, but he wanted an out for any mischievous behavior he might consider later that night when he got bored. Darryl was already planning on watching the Twilight Zone marathon that was coming on later that night, so he would be too wrapped up in Rod Serling to bother anyone.

Jake and Melissa walked down the hall to the elevator, with Jake stopping by to speak with the doctor before beginning the slow descent to the

253

first floor. He also paused to leave instructions with Deputy Charles Lamb, a heavy set man who had seen enough death and carnage in Vietnam to last several lifetimes. He didn't talk much, but Jake knew he was solid as a rock and that he was leaving Bart in good hands for the night.

"Do you think he'll be alright?" Melissa asked as she pushed the button for the first floor.

"No, but he'll recover from the beating," Jake responded honestly. He was concerned that his friend was slipping slowly but surely into an abyss of dark imagination from which there would be no escape. All he could do at this point was support him the best he knew how and hope beyond hope that he was wrong.

Bar T. Rancher

CHAPTER TEN

Reverend Angus McFarland, as he liked to be called, sat at his expansive wooden desk and slowly sipped a brandy. He looked down at the dark wood and wondered again what kind of wood it was. Not that he really cared. All he knew is that it was what he liked and it cost more than most of the people in town made in a year. Who cared? His church could afford it and as the pastor of the largest and fastest growing church in town he deserved to have the very best. Those in the congregation would just have to dig a little deeper and sacrifice a little more. How could they expect him to speak for God if he had to hunch over a small, secondhand, metal desk the way he had to do when he first began preaching. He remembered those days with a shudder.

Those were hard times for him. He would spend days, sometimes the better part of a week pouring over the Bible, commentaries, and other material. He would sift and sift through concordances, flip through references, study the masters, all in an effort to preach to a congregation that was already thinking about lunch while he was trying to disseminate a weeks worth of study into the space of two short hours, and most of those interrupted with singing, bathroom breaks, and note passing between people in the pews. He didn't mind the teenagers passing notes, that much was to be expected. It was when he caught the adults doing the same thing that bothered him. It was

256

when he found his sermon interrupted by a flock of turkeys that his deacons were pointing at that the camel had one more piece of straw than it could handle. He quit that church and vowed never to set foot in another one again. People didn't want to hear about God and be taught his word. They wanted to be coddled and entertained. He walked away from church, walked away from God, and walked away from everything that had ever meant anything to him. Everything, that is, except his brother. In his running away from God, he ran right back into the hands of his no-account brother. At about the same time that Angus had found release from the prison of pastoring, Shane was being released from one county lock-up and was no doubt headed to another.

Shane convinced his brother that he had a gift that shouldn't be ignored. All it needed to reach its full potential was a little training and practice and Shane knew the people who could provide that training, for a small price of course. Angus worked his first con on a small church in rural Alabama. He came in as a traveling missionary on his way to work the fertile fields of Mexico. The people there took him in and treated him as one of their own. It took several months, numerous pie auctions, bake sales, fish frys, and other minor fund raisers, but John Trotter, as he was known at the time, left with over ten thousand dollars, and was last seen traveling north. Although he did most of the work, his take on the first haul was less than a thousand. He could have been bitter, but he considered the cost of six months a small investment on what would turn quickly into a large source of revenue. Shane, his brother, became a permanent part of his ministry team. They didn't think that most rural people of the south, who were by far the easiest marks for them to hit, would readily accept an ex-con preacher, or at least one claiming to be a pastor. But they would gladly embrace an ex-con who allowed God to turn his life around and was now trying to spread the good news to others who were trying to make it on the outside. Later, after having taken several classes on drug rehabilitation, they shifted from being just ex-con to recovering addict, even though the hardest thing he had ever ingested was liquor. He didn't even drink heavily. The stuff made him violently ill, but that didn't stop them from letting everyone believe he was a recovering addict who wanted to help others get free the way he had done. It worked and it made money hand over fist, which all the brothers McFarland cared about.

Those days were a million miles and a thousand lifetimes ago. The brothers were working their final scam, one that would pay off well enough for each of them to retire, if they chose to. But Angus, for one, had no desire to play shuffleboard, bingo, or any other old man's game. He was on top of the world and intended to stay there for as long as he could ride the wave. If he crashed on the beach or went under at least he had enjoyed the ride. One thing, though, was sure in his mind. No one, not his brother, not any of the lowlifes they were forced to deal with, nor any government official of any capacity was going to knock him off of his board before he was ready to relinquish the wave. He would ride it straight into the gates of hell and let the flames devour the water in a frenzy of steam, but he would not be taken down prematurely. And he certainly wouldn't be taken down by a nosy woman with ink flowing through her veins and a laptop for a heart. He looked at her over his massive desk, sitting before him like a mouse before a cat. No, it was more than that. He was no mere house pet or alley stray, he was a lion among the tame, de-clawed, purring pussycats who called themselves men. Few of them could look at a woman such as the one before him and think about anything else other than how to please her, have her and make her all one's own. But Angus didn't think about how he could please her. She was there to please him. She was there to become his toy, his plaything. In short, she was there for him, not him for her.

"Welcome, Miss Green. I assume it is Miss Green, since you've been seen cavorting with one of our fine city's most eligible bachelors."

"It's miss," Cassandra informed him. "But I don't think welcome is the right word to us for a kidnapping victim."

"Oh, come, come, Miss Green. Kidnapping is such a harsh word. Next thing you know you'll be speaking of yourself as a prisoner."

"So I'm not a prisoner?"

"Let's just use the phrase involuntary guest."

259

"Oh, you're good. I suppose you're not really evil, just morally challenged?" Angus laughed, causing Cassandra to shudder slightly. There was something more than sinister in his laugh. She thought of people who dealt drugs or robbed banks as being evil, and possibly even sinister, but there was a higher category, or maybe to be more correct, lower, category of wickedness that went beyond those kinds of people. There were malevolent men and women who made the normal, run of the mill, crook look like choir boys and saints in comparison. Hitler, Stalin, and Nero were among those who held a place in history's hall of shame. Somewhere among those men a place would have to be made for the name of Angus McFarland.

"I might think of myself that way, my dear woman, if I thought of myself as being held to those bonds that chain other men. I removed those chains long ago and haven't looked back a day since."

"I don't understand," Cassandra said. "I thought you were supposed to be a preacher, a man of God."

"David was a man of God, and he committed adultery and plotted the murder of a man. His son, Solomon, had a harem of wives and concubines that would take more than three years for a man to satisfy. That is if he were capable of performing well each night for more than three years." Angus chuckled, obviously pleased with his own estimation of Solomon's prowess with women. Either that or he inwardly placed himself in that category of men that would be capable of such feats of wonder and stamina. Judging from the smug look on his face, there was no doubt in Cassandra's mind that he placed himself not only in that category of men, but with the Titans of old. Names like Samson, Hercules, and Troy would find themselves paling in comparison in the estimation of a man like Angus. Cassandra didn't think that she would get anywhere in a head to head confrontation with a man of his ego. She knew that she also needed to be careful if she decided to play coy with him. She knew he didn't get to this point in life by being stupid. She decided the best course of action to follow was to be almost totally honest, which brought her into territory that she was almost unfamiliar with. There were few people, and not many of them men, with whom she had even been close to being honest with. She vowed to add Bart Rancher to that list if she survived her current crisis.

"What is it you want from me?" she asked with perhaps just a bit more defiance in her voice than she intended. He was a big man, and although they were alone in this room, she wasn't fool enough to believe there weren't guards nearby. Again, a man of his status didn't get to where he was without making enemies, and without being able to handle those enemies when they opposed his plans.

"Want?" he asked, feigning innocence. "Why my dear Miss Green, it should be obvious what I want. You are by all standards of comparison a beautiful woman, and although I may be slightly older than you, I am still a

virile, capable man, with attributes of my own that are not undesirable." She

had to admit that despite her circumstances and her own personal repugnance

caused by his character, she found him to be an attractive specimen of

manhood. He stood over six feet tall, with a body that looked as solid and

thick as any she had seen, and she had seen plenty in her younger days. His

hair was a vibrant, but not shocking, shade of red, with a neatly trimmed

matching mustache. A scar that ran along his left cheek should have detracted

from his good looks, but it only served to give him an appearance of

ruggedness. She felt like a rodent finding itself trapped within the confining

stare of a cobra. But she was determined that the snake in front of her would

at least feel her bite before he consumed her.

"Mr. McFarland, are you trying to seduce me?" she asked coyly,

hoping to appeal to something in him that might be a weakness.

"Two corrections, Miss Green, first, I prefer the title, Reverend. I

know it's a bit presumptuous of me, but after all I've done and all the sermons

I've preached, I feel like I deserve it. Secondly, I have no intention of

seducing you. I'm going to rape you. I'm going to do it slowly, with great

relish and delight on my part and with great pain and agony on your part.

Sorry to break the bad news to you, dear, but that's simply the way it is. Oh,

by the way, this is the part where you say I'll never get away with it."

"Why would I say something so stupid? If you're planning on it with me then no doubt you've already done it with others. I suppose that after I've finally met all of your sick, twisted, demented desires that you'll kill me and dispose of my body with the other women who've been trapped in your web." She was scared, but she was determined not to show it. There weren't many things in life that frightened a woman like the prospect of being violated by a sexual predator. In fact, she couldn't think of any. The very thought of his hands, much less anything else, being on her made her want to vomit. But she also knew that rape wasn't about sex at all. It was about power and domination. He would break her down, force her to scream, yell and cry. He would bring her to a point when the only thought that brought her any comfort at all would be the single thought of death, but he would have to work for it. She wasn't going to make it easy for him. She forced her mind to go to another place, far from the dirt and filth it was forced to wallow in at the moment.

"Once again you use words that force a sense of normality on me. I can't be sick, twisted, nor demented if those terms have no meaning for me, and they can have no meaning for me if I am not constrained by the values of other, lesser men. I set the standard for my behavior. I determine the validity of my actions. I alone am the master of my destiny." She couldn't believe what she was hearing. He had set himself up as his own god. She knew that most people held a spark of rebellion, with some of them allowing that spark to fan itself into a flame, but Angus went a thousand steps further. He added fuel to the spark, brought in the gasoline of self determination and fanned the flames until they consumed any vestige of humanity that might have once resided within the shell of his body. Cassandra hadn't been a religious person, and she still wasn't sure if she bought into the whole concept of a benevolent god and a malevolent devil, but as she compared the goodness she found with Bart to the evil she saw with the man setting at his desk before her, she hoped with all of her heart that there was a god and that he would hear the prayer she was already sending his way.

"So what are you going to do, spread eagle me on the floor. That ought to leave some stains on the carpeting that might be hard to explain to your congregation." She didn't want to unnecessarily upset him, but she also didn't want to be the compliant schoolgirl in front of the principal, which is what he was trying to make her feel like. She found herself wondering how many other women, and how many girls had sat in this same chair, and how many of them were now a semi-permanent fixture within the earth's outer crust. How was he getting away with it? He would have to be using women outside of the pool of local talent. Even prostitutes, especially in a small town, were missed by people around them. She couldn't imagine a small southern town harboring a red light district for the entertainment of its men, but she wasn't naïve enough to think that there weren't women in the town who made their living in a horizontal position. Her thoughts about the night life in a small town were interrupted by a soft caress from Angus on the back of her neck. She had been so caught up in her musings that he had somehow managed to move his massive frame from behind the desk to behind her chair without her noticing. His touch was smooth, practiced. He knew exactly where to touch a woman to stir feelings within her. She was almost moaning, in spite of the circumstances she was in. There was something unearthly, almost supernatural within his fingertips. There was something else as well; something she couldn't quite put her fingers on. It was so.....evil! She sat up abruptly, pulling herself away from the trap of the spider's web.

He pulled her back by the hair of her head and grabbed her arms, pinning them behind her with such force that she thought both of her shoulders would be dislocated. She wanted desperately to pass out from the pain. She wanted this to be a horrible nightmare, but she couldn't force herself to either pass out or wake up.

"I almost had you, didn't I? Don't lie; I've been down this road far too many times to get lost. You found yourself yielding to me despite what your heart or your mind said. Your body wanted to give in to the temptation. And why didn't you? I'll tell you. It's because you've been indoctrinated into an archaic moral code that you truly don't believe in. If you did, then you wouldn't have broken its laws so many times. Those men you've slept with, the alcohol you consumed in college and high school, the abortion you had in your twenties." Her body stiffened against his grasp, causing her further pain. But she didn't care about the physical pain. He had touched an emotional nerve that she had to keep covered constantly in salve just to get through life, and he had ripped away that salve and the scab that was keeping it covered.

"How?" she asked through gritted teeth, not wanting to give in to the tears that were pushing against the dam of her eyes.

"How did I know? I didn't actually, but it's one of those things that so many professional women have gone through that I took an educated guess and it paid off. I hit a nerve, didn't I? And again, I ask you, why do you care about a mass of tissue that you never even held? Could it be that you formed some sort of instinctual maternal bond with this little parasite that was going to feed off of you directly for nine months and then continue to feed off of you for the rest of your life? I hardly think so. It's more likely that you feel something because you have been told to feel something. No more, and no less than that."

"You're a monster. You're nothing but a sick, twisted, sociopath with delusions of your own worth. In the great scheme of things, you are no more than a pimple on the nose of the world, and one day soon you'll find people squeezing you out of existence." She knew better than to banter with such a man as him, but she couldn't help herself. He had hit a nerve, and it was sore and painful. She had hid that pain for years. She had calmed it, soothed it, even tried to drown it at one point in a bottle of rum, but nothing held it in check for long. So when he opened himself to be exposed to that pain, she was determined to give him everything he was asking for. She had already determined that she wouldn't be leaving alive, so she might as well make the best of a horrible situation.

"A monster? I don't think so, Miss Green. I'm simply a man who has allowed himself the luxury of doing what other men have dreamed of doing, but have been too stifled and too emasculated by an overly feminine society that they lack the courage to grab life as it comes to them and take what it is that they want. Look in the Bible, Miss Green, and you'll find men who were willing to do as I have done."

"Cain comes to mind," she quipped.

"Yes, yes, of course, as does Nimrod, Nebuchadnezzar, and other kings who were maligned by the writers of the scriptures because they dared reach for more than other men. But I'd like to remind you that among those who sought for more and found it was Solomon, the son of David and in the lineage of Christ. He did everything his heart desired."

"And if I recall the Vacation Bible School lessons correctly, he found out that having everything left him with nothing. Or do I remember that wrong." He had relaxed his grip on her and moved back to his desk, resting his backside on the edge for support as he seemed to ponder her last statement. Maybe he was finding life was just as empty of meaning as Solomon had discovered. Or maybe he was just toying with his newest quarry, the way a cat toys with a mouse before finally killing and devouring it. He was as hard to read as a runic stone.

"Solomon was a fool who was given the gift of ultimate moral latitude and chose instead to be defined by a set of rules meant for lesser men. I won't make that mistake." He went to the bookshelf and seemed to be perusing the massive collection for a particular book. Maybe he wanted a book of poetry to read to his prey before devouring her. He might be looking for a book of prayers. Exactly what was the proper blessing to ask before raping and maiming a woman before dismembering her and beating her to the point of being unrecognizable? More than likely he was looking for a book of spells to find an incantation for non-virginal sacrifice. She wasn't sure if spoiled meat offered to the gods of lust and desire would gain their favor or displeasure, but she wasn't really in the mood to find out either.

"You asked where you and I would find privacy for our rendezvous."

"I did?" He chuckled, allowing a broad smile to sweep across his face. It was gone almost as quickly as it came and Cassandra was unnerved by its brief presence. There was something within that smile that was more sinister than anything else she had previously encountered. It was almost as if the grin

wasn't his at all, but belonged to another being, devil, demon, or spirit, that

was controlling him. She wasn't much on the spirit world. She had always

thought of those who believed in such things as either harmless eccentrics,

dangerous zealots, or one of the mindless masses that needed someone or

something to lead them about because they had no real thoughts of their own.

But since encountering Bart, she had begun to change her mind about the

reality of something beyond the realm of sight. He had something within him

that was real, and as tangible as the wing back chair that supported her weight.

She was rapidly coming to the point where it wasn't seeing is believing, but

believing becomes seeing.

"I believe you said something about me having you spread eagle on

the carpet. How crude. Besides, one of the members of my congregation

might come in for counseling and interrupt us. Wouldn't that be awkward?"

He chuckled at the thought as he continued to walk the perimeter of the room,

pausing at times to skim the contents of a book or wipe the dust from one of

the many artifacts that dotted the literary landscape.

"I wouldn't want that for us. So let me fill you in on a little history of

our town. At one point it was the home of one William Jennings Bryson.

Heard of him?" She shook her head no.

"I wouldn't think that you would have. He's not really known at all outside of the county lines. Regardless, he was a political mover and shaker in these parts. He could have used his money and influence to gain his own political office, but he preferred to remain shrouded in the curtains rather than take center stage. His one drawback was a bit of paranoia. He was sure that the communists were coming for him, mostly because he backed McCarthy and others like him. So he built a large underground bunker beneath his home. It was the ultimate safe room, complete with stocked pantry, kitchen, living quarters and enough space for several guests. Would you care to guess where he built that deluxe bomb shelter?" Again she shook her head no. She wasn't in any mood for guessing games. She wanted to be either saved miraculously or dead. The space in between those two was a wide gap and it was torture to live there.

"Well, I'll tell you anyway. He built it right under his home, which used to set where the church currently resides. I discovered it quite by accident during the excavation process for the foundation. I had it restored, restocked, and ready for my use. Those who were a part of that particular construction project either retired to a home overseas or they retired permanently. Either way, there are only a handful of people who know of its existence. My brother is one, and soon you'll be another. Of course, your knowledge will be short lived since it will die with you." He paused in front o a bust of someone that she assumed was famous, although he was too far away for her to be sure and even at that she might not recognize him. For all

she knew it could be a caricature of the original owner of the property,

William Jennings Bryson. Angus turned it first one way, and then the other. It

was almost as if he were a schoolboy fiddling with the combination tumblers

of his locker. After an interminable amount of time, the shelf in front of him

slid backwards and then to her left. She felt like Nancy Drew, only she didn't

think that the erstwhile teen detective ever came into a situation quite like this.

She wasn't a big fan of Carolyn Keen, but she was fairly sure that the teen

sleuth never faced rape and torture at the hands of a maniacal preacher with a

bent toward the macabre.

He grabbed her, jerked her to her feet and tied her wrists with a large

plastic cable tie, all in one swift move, and then shoved her toward the small

room that had been revealed by the sliding book shelf. It wasn't much larger

than a closet, and was completely bare of any type of decoration, other than

the wooden quarter panels on the bottom half of the three walls. The top half

was polished stainless steel, as was the ceiling. She guessed he got his kicks

looking in the mirror as he tortured and maimed his hapless victims. It was

funny, but she was somehow slightly disappointed. She hadn't known exactly

what to expect. After all, torture chambers hardly ever made the covers of

Good Housekeeping or Redbook. She thought that Cosmopolitan might be

tempted to put a how to section within its pages, but she couldn't recall ever seeing that instruction manual, although she had seen quite a bit in that magazine that might have led her to similar circumstances. That was hardly fair. She had been given to more encounters than she should have had, but she couldn't blame a magazine or its editors for her lack of discretion. She hoped that if she somehow managed to survive this encounter that Bart could lead her to a closer relationship with the God he knew and loved.

"This is the big secret?" she asked, her tone showing the disdain for both the man and the room.

"Hardly," he answered and inserted a key card into a slot that she hadn't noticed before. The bookshelf slid back into place and another door slid in place behind it from the other direction. Her legs nearly buckled as the room began a slow descent into the abyss, a place she felt herself going as well, although she didn't think her descent was nearly as slow or as controlled. She was sure of it when the doors opened again at the bottom. If she had been slightly disappointed with her surroundings in what she now understood to be the elevator, it was apparent that what greeted her upon her arrival more than made up for it. There were torture devices beyond the realm of a normal human mind's comprehension. Some of them she could only assume were used for that purpose since she couldn't think of any other piece of furniture that needed so many leather straps and pointed metallic studs attached to the backs, legs, and arms of chairs and tables. Along the shelves were various artifacts that were far different from the ones found on the shelves of his private study. Above them were books, various statues, knick-knacks and trophies. Down here were trophies as well, but they weren't engraved by any of the local merchants. There were shoes of assorted styles and sizes, along with articles of clothing, gloves and pictures. One jar caught her eye. It was the kind she remembered from junior high biology class. She wandered towards it, hypnotized by the glare of light reflecting off the glass jar. Angus made no attempt to halt her progress. There was no need. He had all the power he needed to overpower her, especially since her hands were still strapped behind her back. And she had no where to run or anyone to hear her scream, but she did scream as she realized what the jar held within its glass walls. A baby, or to be more politically correct, a fetus stared back at her. Thoughts of her own baby burst forth on her mind's eye, unlocking the floodgates of her tears. Before she could recover, she felt a pinprick in her left arm. She cried out in surprise and alarm.

"Sorry, my dear, but although you've been fairly compliant up to this point, I can't continue to count upon your generosity."

"What is it?" she asked dreamily.

"A mild sedative, one that will insure that you are awake for the next several hours, but will keep you groggy enough so that you're easy manipulated for my viewing pleasure," he informed her.

"No," she protested, but not at the use of the sedative. She had actually expected something like that from him and was surprised it had taken him this long to use it. Her cry came at the thought of someone other than a medical laboratory keeping a baby on display like a prized deer head hung upon the wall.

"Oh," he said, realizing she was still staring at the glass jar. "That is my nephew, or niece. I'm not sure because we've never really looked close. It came out of some woman my brother impregnated. He wanted a legacy, a name to carry on for him when he leaves this life. I don't care anything about that. This life is all I need. After that, there'll be hell to pay I suppose. But I digress. Shane wanted a child and seduced a young woman so that she'd have his child. But she found out what he was really like and was about to leave with the baby. She was welcome to go, but Shane wanted his baby."

"Even if it means keeping it in a jar?" she asked groggily. Her words were slurred and she was having a problem staying on her feet, which didn't go unnoticed by Angus.

"Let me help you," he offered, as if she were a guest in his home instead of a prisoner in his torture chamber. He led her to a bed. It looked like the kind of bed used in hospital delivery rooms, complete with stirrups for her legs, which Angus directed into place. In hospitals they were used to keep the expectant mother's legs apart for the purpose of facilitating delivery.

Somehow, even as Angus strapped her legs to the fixtures, she suspected that

they had a far more sinister purpose here. She wanted to scream, to yell, to

call out until her throat bled in protest, but no sound would come forth from

her lungs.

"You're a monster," she finally managed.

"So you've said," he commented as he pulled over a cart that looked

like it came from a Josef Mengele yard sale. There were syringes, needles,

medical instruments and other instruments of torture on the cart. Some of

them Cassandra could only guess the use of. She was about to die and all she

could think about was her own baby, the one she had paid another monster to

take the life of. Even now, as she watched Angus pick up first one toy and

then another, her attention was held not by his gleeful musings of torture, but

by the little glass jar on the shelf. She wasn't sure if it was the drugs talking to

her or her own conscience speaking, but she would swear that the child was

looking down at her with an expression that said he forgave her. She needed

that. She needed to know that she was forgiven for all of her past mistakes.

No, she corrected herself. A mistake is when you forget to carry the one and

end up with a wrong answer on a math test. She had deliberately taken the life

of another for her own convenience. She had slept with several men, searching

for the one that would give her love, happiness and acceptance. She wasn't

sure if he would listen to her or not, but she had to try.

"Jesus, forgive me," she pled.

"Even he can't hear you down here," Angus told her as he approached her with his first instrument. He was about to descend upon her when he heard the elevator doors open.

"Who dares to approach the dragon's lair when he's about to devour a maiden?" he yelled. In spite of the circumstances, or maybe because of them, Cassandra laughed at his melodramatic response.

"It's me," a timid voice replied. An older man approached. He was bent and permanently hunched. Cassandra found herself wanting to laugh again. In black and white he would look like Igor to Angus' Dr Frankenstein. That made her, of course, The Bride of Frankenstein.

"What is it?" Angus demanded.

"It's Philip," Igor answered. "He and some of the men went to town and beat Bart Rancher to a bloody pulp in an alleyway."

"Did they observe the usual precautions?" Angus asked, irritated that Philip would dare to do such a thing without prior authorization, but still pleased that Bart was dead and out of the way. He had been a thorn in his side for too long. The church he pastored was one of only a handful that failed to support their cause. With him out of the way, they could install one of their own in the pulpit. And the other pastors might receive the message so they would quit impeding the progress.

"Yes, they did. But there's a problem." Igor responded.

"What is it?"

"He survived. He's at the hospital now with a guard and he's already identified Philip as the attacker. I'm afraid Philip is on his way to being arrested."

"Why isn't he at the camp?" Angus roared.

"He was, but he left in a hurry without telling anyone where he was going."

Angus paced the floor, still holding the torture instrument in his hand, like a cigarette in the hand of a nervous smoker. This unfortunate incident could cost him everything he had planned for. There was little time to act.

"Find Philip and kill him. Do the same to the preacher in the hospital. Never mind about Philip, I'll take care of that myself. You just get someone to the hospital." They left without another word, leaving Cassandra drugged and strapped to a hospital bed with the ghost of her aborted child staring at her from a glass jar. She wished for sleep, but the drug or her own thoughts kept it from her. Besides, even when she closed her eyes, the eyes behind the glass stared back at her. Then something wonderful happened. As she thought about Jesus and the forgiveness he offered, she felt him take her hand and lead her to a place of peace. There, she met with her child and the three of them shared a picnic and played games in the warm afternoon sun. It was her last memory

Bar T. Rancher
for some time as she did gradually give way to a peaceful slumber.

CHAPTER ELEVEN

Even as Cassandra was beginning her evening with Angus, Sheriff Jake Plunkett was dealing with problems that although paled in comparison to hers, nevertheless included her as a problem. He left the hospital wanting to go in several directions at the same time. He trusted the deputy he left with Bart for protection, but felt as his best friend that he should be there with him while he recovered. At the same time, however, his best friend needed him to look for two missing girlfriends, one of which may only be a figment of Bart's imagination. It wasn't as if he needed complications in his life, and it wasn't as if he looked for them in his spare time. Complications were like balls of lint in your belly button. You didn't search for them. You didn't manufacture them. They just appeared out of nowhere when you needed them the least. Another complication in his life was the arrest of Philip for the beating of Bart. Jake knew how he would like for that to go down, but he couldn't allow the temptation to beat a sniveling rat to further complicate his life and cost him the job he loved. By the time he had made the descent down the final flight of steps and stepped out onto the first floor of the hospital he had set in his mind his priorities for the next couple of hours.

His first priority was to arrest Philip. He had been present at the time of Shalina's kidnapping and may have information on the abduction of Cassandra as well. Like it or not, he was the key that might unlock the mystery of what had transpired in the previous evening. The problem, though, was how to get to him. There was no doubt that he was safely snuggled away at the camp. Jake knew there was no way for him to go in to that place with guns a blazing like some kind of western hero, snatch the villain and ride off to save the women folk before riding off into the proverbial sunset. The only sunset he would be riding off into would be his final one. The thought of obtaining a search warrant for the camp to search for the missing females crossed his mind as well. He let that thought cross and keep on going. No judge in this area would be willing to give him a warrant based on his suspicions. He wasn't sure a judge anyplace would be willing to go there, but he was sure none around here, most of whom had their pictures in the paper at one time or another with either Angus or Shane, would put his political future at stake for the whims of the local sheriff, who might very well be voted out of office come the next election.

He needed a way to bring Philip out of the camp. He needed to bring the rat to the cheese instead of trying to get the cheese to the rat. The problem was how. How could he get a man to risk several years in jail, not to mention the wrath of Shane McFarland? What would be powerful enough, offer enough temptation to make him do that?

He shoved the keys into the ignition and slammed his fist against the padded dash of his car in total frustration. He had a million things to accomplish and no tools to accomplish any of them. He knew what needed to be done, but no idea how to do it. He was like a one legged duck, constantly swimming in circles, hoping the crumbs of bread would come to him since he couldn't make it to them. He missed his friend. He knew that was part of the reason he felt the helplessness and despair wash over him. He was a small town sheriff dealing with big city problems, but that wasn't unusual. He had done so before. But before he had always had help. Batman was in need of Robin. But, to be honest, that wasn't the problem either. Batman dealt with the Joker and Penguin for years before Robin came swinging into his life. It wasn't that Robin wasn't here, it was that the reason he wasn't here was that he was lying in a hospital bed and Batman was totally helpless to do anything for him. He was in the hands of the doctors now and Jake didn't like that at all. He wanted to be up there ordering medicines, checking charts and observing the patient's vital signs. He wanted to be with his best friend. He told himself to concentrate on the problems he could solve and ignore those he couldn't touch at the moment. It was the kind of advice that Bart would give, so he decided to follow it. He started the ignition and headed out of the parking lot at a breakneck turtle speed. No matter how hard he wanted to press toward justice, the anchor of wanting to be with a friend he might not ever see again held him to the pavement of the parking lot. It wasn't until he had made the left turn onto the highway that he gained any speed. Once there, his mind clicked along with the spinning of the wheels. As his mind sped towards a solution to the many problems at hand, he found himself having to hit the brakes. It wouldn't do for the sheriff to have to write himself a ticket for doing ninety in a fifty-five mile an hour zone.

He kept thinking of Philip as game. Not as a game, like Monopoly or Chess, but as game, like deer or squirrel. He thought of him as an animal that needed to be baited to draw it out into the open where a clear shot could be made. But what kind of bait would it take to draw a man like that into the open? What could he do to bring Philip to him? It would have to be something enticing, alluring, something that would make his mouth water in anticipation. Jake thought about his first and only encounter with the rat faced little man. He thought of what brought the two of them together. They had nothing in common and might not have ever met if it hadn't been for Bart. Philip could have lived his entire life in this county and the two of them would have remained perfect strangers, which would have suited Jake just fine. He wasn't exactly the kind of person that Jake could see hanging out with the guys, maybe kicking back watching the big game or sitting around smoking a cigar and playing Texas Hold'em. He was more the kind to watch a cooking show or one of those how to shows about decorating. It hit Jake between the eyes like a shot of mace. It wasn't Bart that brought Philip to his attention. It was Oliver. He was supposed to meet with Philip alone to discuss his spirit of homosexuality or whatever it was that Philip called it. They were supposed to

meet alone, at the camp on the predator's home turf. Jake had his bait. That is,

of course, if his bait was willing to cooperate. Oliver wasn't a worm to be

dangled on the end of a hook without choice in the matter. He was a human

being. And he was only a young boy. Jake would have to risk his career, and

worse, the life of this young boy if he was going to bring a shark to the shore

and maybe, just maybe, save the life of at least one young woman that his

friend cared for. He slammed on the brakes and spun the squad car around,

heading back to town and straight to Oliver's house.

"Mrs. Cratch?" Jake asked through the barely open door.

"Yes. Who is it?" she replied.

"It's Sheriff Jake Plunkett, mam. I need to speak with Oliver if I could,

please?" He had to be careful not to spook this woman. He was fairly sure that

Oliver would cooperate, especially since his friend and pastor would be

depending on him, but he wasn't at all sure that Mrs. Cratch would be as

likely to participate if she knew all of the rules of the game they were about to

play. He didn't like leaving her out of the loop, and wouldn't have if these

were ordinary circumstances, but lately in his little town, there was little that

could be called ordinary.

"What do you need with Oliver?" she asked through the cracked door.

"Is he in some kind of trouble or something? I knew that boy would end up in the pen some day. He doesn't act like other boys do, if you know what I mean." Jake knew exactly what she meant, and he knew why. Other boys didn't have a shrewish mother circling around them like a hawk looking for prey every hour of every day.

"No, mam, he's not in trouble." He had to think quickly. He figured he was about one minute from the door being shut in his face. "There's a job coming open soon at the jail. It doesn't pay much, but Bart told me that Oliver was a good worker and needed something that might keep him out of trouble, so I came here to interview him."

"At this time of night?"

"My schedule is a little crazy at this time, mam. I'll have him back before too late."

"He has to come with you? It's a school night, you know?"

"Yes, mam, I realize that, but I'll have to show him the job for him to be able to tell me whether or not he'd be interested and whether he'll be able to do it." He was skating on thin ice and the weather was warming with every minute, but he kept circling around the rink.

"I'll get him for you." Oliver appeared a few minutes later, obviously fussed over by a mom who wanted him to make a good impression for a job interview. She wanted him to look strong and mature, which he usually did. Her fussing only served to make him look primped on. When he opened the car door, Sheriff Jake was on the phone, giving directions to someone named Charlie. Oliver didn't know who Charlie was or what the phone call was about. He pretended to not be listening, but it was kind of hard to ignore when you're in the same car as one of the people on the phone. Finally, after an uncomfortable and awkward moment, Jake said he'd call Charlie later and turned his attention to Oliver.

"I need your help, Oliver, but it's kind of dangerous and I won't blame you if you just want to get out of the car and head back home to the safety of your house and bedroom," Jake stated.

"What is it?" Oliver asked, his curiosity aroused. Tell any teenage boy that you have a dangerous mission and he's pretty much hooked on whatever it is you want him to do. That wasn't Jake's intent, it just happened to work out that way.

"Bart's in the hospital. He's been beaten pretty severely and will probably be there at least a few days. We know who did it, but he's at the camp and if I go in there to arrest him they'll just hide him from me. We need some bait to draw him out into the open."

"And you want me to be that bait?" Oliver asked.

"Yeah, that's the idea. Philip is the one behind this and I think he's gay and I think the reason he wanted you at the camp alone was so he could start to seduce you."

"Gross! I'm not that way," Oliver protested his hand on the door handle, ready to run back to his bedroom.

"I know you're not," Jake assured him. "But Philip doesn't. When you stop to think about it, it's the only thing that makes sense. He's mad at Bart because Bart cost him something that he wanted. That something is you." Oliver squirmed around in his seat like he had an old man with flaming hemorrhoids.

"What does that have to do with me helping you?" Oliver asked, not at all sure he wanted to hear the answer. He had already formed in his mind the reason that Jake called on him to help instead of a deputy or some other adult.

"I want you to go with me to the library and e-mail or even better instant message Philip. Did he give you a card of some kind?" Oliver reached around his right rear pocket where he kept his wallet. There were only four things in there. One was his student ID, another was his lunch ticket, the third was his learner's permit, and the fourth was the business card Philip handed him when he wanted to arrange a counseling appointment. Written on the back of it were two e-mail addresses, with one highlighted. The first one was a link to the official website of the camp. The other one, the highlighted one, was a hotmail address that could be used for instant messaging. Oliver wasn't at all comfortable with the idea of even pretending to be gay, but if it would help bring Bart's attackers to justice, he was more than willing to do whatever it took and told Jake that.

"Great," Jake said, reaching for the ignition key. "But we'll have to hurry. From what Bart said, Philip acted on his own. That means those in charge at the camp might not know about the incident just yet. Once they do, they'll clamp the leg irons on Philip to protect him and themselves. I hope you're ready for some good acting." They drove away from the safety and security of Oliver's home into a night that was dark on every level. Oliver wasn't one given over to too much in the realm of the supernatural. He believed in angels, and so he had to believe in demons as well, but it was more of a philosophical type of belief. He realized that the Bible spoke of them, and he believed the Bible to be true, but sometimes he wondered about parts of it, like angels and demons, being relevant to modern times. But now, as he headed towards the library and possibly a date with a man who wanted to seduce him and turn him over to a homosexual lifestyle, he couldn't help but feel they were being accompanied by a multitude of angelic forces as well as a myriad host of dark, demonic forces. He could almost feel their fetid breath hiss its way into the car through the vents. Jake broke through his morose thoughts.

"When you talk to him, I need you to have him meet you at a secluded cabin I'll give you directions to. The seclusion will make him feel safe."

"What about me?" Oliver asked. "When do I get to feel safe?" Jake laughed.

"You can back out at anytime. Remember this is strictly voluntary. If you don't do this, then I'll find another way to get to that weasel."

"But this was your first and best choice, huh?" Oliver asked. Jake wanted to tell him that he had a thousand other plans, all of them equally good, but he couldn't lie like that. If he was going to use that boy as bait, then he needed to know the whole truth, not just part of it.

"Actually," Jake admitted. "It's my only choice at the moment. I've racked my brain trying to think of a different path to take, but every other way I tried to walk down ended up in a dead end. And I might be totally wrong about Philip's intentions. I've been known to be wrong before. Just ask Melissa, she's got a whole list of times I've been wrong written down on a calendar and filed away in her head for future reference."

The laughter they shared over that comment was short lived as they approached the gothic castle that held the county library. The structure was imposing during the daylight hours when it was a bustle of activity with children's reading times and various literary outreach programs, not to mention the county officials who spent breaks and lunch times perusing the magazines or doing research for government projects, but at night, when darkness permeated throughout the building like the air they breathed, it was absolutely terrifying to behold.

"How will we get in?" Oliver asked, hoping they wouldn't have a key and would be forced to turn around and find another computer to use.

"I am the sheriff, don't forget," Jake reminded him. "One of the perks is that I get a key to almost anyplace in town. That includes the library. Now come on. We don't have much time to lose." They entered through the front doors and made their way to the computer stations located at the back of the library. Jake didn't want to draw attention to them, so he opted to use his flashlight instead of turning on the overhead lights, much to the dismay of Oliver, who would have rather had every light in the building turned on and floodlights brought in to brighten any and all shadows that might have remained. The warm glow of the computer screen flickering on brought him some comfort.

"Sign in to your normal e-mail account and send Philip a message that you're online," Jake instructed.

"It'll be better if I instant message him," Oliver corrected. "I can go to my message service and invite him to join me for a conversation. I think it'll be quicker that way."

"Whatever you say," Jake agreed. "I'm just along for the ride. If he seems interested, tell him about the cabin and that you can meet him there in about an hour." Oliver went to work, signing in to his account and sending out an invite for Philip. Several of his friends were online, but he ignored them as they chatted about the latest movie or that day's pop quiz. It was hard to resist talking to some of them, especially a couple of girls that had started showing an interest in him, but he was there for one reason and one reason only. He was afraid that reason wasn't going to respond when he heard a familiar ding that indicated his invitation had been accepted.

"Hello," the screen said.

"Hi," Oliver typed back.

"Didn't expect to hear from you," Philip said through the glow of the screen. Oliver asked Jake how he should proceed. They wanted Philip to incriminate himself on the message board and ask Oliver to meet him for something more than casual conversation. It made Oliver uncomfortable and Jake wanted to make sure they didn't go so far that a judge would throw out any charges because it might be considered entrapment. They really needed a couple of weeks, or maybe even months, to set up the kind of sting they were considering, but they didn't have that kind of time. If either Shane or Angus got wind of Bart's beating and Philip's hand in it, they would clamp him in leg irons for their own protection. Jake couldn't risk that happening. He had a chance to bring in one of the inner sanctum and possibly turn him against the others. It might also be the break he needed in the murder case. Bart was sure that whoever committed the murder, those who worked at and for the camp were helping to cover it up. Jake didn't know if it was just one of the clients and they didn't want or need the bad publicity or one of the staff was responsible. It might even be Shane himself. Later questioning of some of the neighbors indicated a man fitting Shane's description was seen at the house quite a bit. It was possible that he and the young woman had been having an affair. Maybe he wanted to break it off and she played the trump of pregnancy too soon and he responded by slamming her hand with a murder. Or maybe it was him that wanted to end the affair and she planned to go public with the pregnancy. Either way, she ended up dead and Jake was going to see to it that whoever was responsible would pay.

"Do you mind?" Oliver typed.

"Not at all. I was kind of hoping you might get in touch."

"Why?"

"You're a special boy. Even your pastor should see that."

"He does, I think. What do you mean special?" Oliver thought he was going to be ill. He was pretty sure what Philip meant by special. He meant that somehow or another Philip was turned on by him. Oliver couldn't understand that in the least. There wasn't a single girl in the whole school that thought he was even cute in a weird, almost geeky kind of way, but this freak had the hots for him. The thought that if Pastor Bart hadn't intervened he might have ended up in this guys manipulative clutches occurred to him, and made him even more grossed out. He was glad that Jake was here now. Even through the anonymity of the internet, this guy had a hypnotic aura about him that made up seem like down and left look right.

"You look thirsty," Jake said. "There's a soda machine downstairs at the foot of the stairs. Why don't you get us both a cold one?" He handed Oliver a handful of change, much more than would be necessary for two colas. Oliver had the distinct impression that Jake was trying to get rid of him for awhile, and he was absolutely right, of course.

"How special am I?" Jake typed as Oliver after the boy had left the room. He had waited until he saw the beam of the flashlight bob on down the stair case at the far end of the library. He hated sending the boy out into the darkness for no more than just a cold drink, but he couldn't let him go any further with this conversation. It was okay for Oliver to cast out, but it was up to Jake to hook the slimy fish onto the line.

"I think you're very special. I'd like to get to know you better."

"What do you mean by know me? I'm very shy."

"I can help you with that. I'll take good care of you."

"I think you were right."

"About?"

"You said I had a spirit. Are you saying you have it too?"

"Yes, and I want you and I to explore that together. Are you willing?"

"I guess, but where can we get together?"

"Not here. How about a hotel?

"My parents would find out. My uncle has a cabin for hunting. It's not being used right now. I can give you directions."

"Is it secluded?"

"Yeah, we'd be alone. Would you like that?" It was Jake's turn to be ill. The only problem was that he was too angry to be sick. He had been in law enforcement for too long not to know that there were people like this in the world and he had been forced to deal with them from time to time, but this was the first one that had come close to someone he cared about. He had actually only known Oliver for a short time, but he was a good kid and deserved a break from the hardships of life. He already had a hard enough home life to deal with. An overbearing mother and a wimpy father could drive any kid into the arms of a predator like Philip. Jake was just glad that Oliver had someone like Bart in his life. That thought only served to spur his anger a little higher. Bart, who had overcome his own adversities to help others, was lying helpless in a hospital room because this jerk was stopped from getting his jollies seducing a naïve young man.

"Maybe. What did you have in mind?" He didn't want to appear too eager, but he wanted Philip to condemn himself on something that couldn't be refuted. Normal conversations could be refuted. If Philip claimed he didn't say something, then it would be the word of a teenage boy against a respected counselor, but e-mail conversations, even instant messaging was recorded by the server and could be pulled up with little effort. Just in case, he was filing it away on the computer he was using.

"You're the adult, why don't you lead?"

"Alright, I'll bring some wine. Do you drink?"

"I could start."

"Good boy. I'll bring the wine, you bring your body, and we'll get the two of them together. How does that sound?" Jake thought it sounded like Philip needed a bullet between his eyes, but that wasn't an option at the moment. Of course, later, if Philip decided to make an escape attempt it might become more of a possibility. His first priority, though, was to get Philip convicted of both Bart's assault and the sexual advances on Oliver. He was sure that once he had him charged with that, others would come forward who had also been victimized by Philip's predatory nature. He was much too smooth, too natural, for this to be his first time. His other priority was to get Philip behind bars so he might provide information about Cassandra's whereabouts.

"I'm e-mailing you the directions. See ya soon." Jake sent an e-mail directing Philip to the quiet, secluded cabin that hopefully would just be a temporary stop on his way to more permanent quarters in the state prison. He hollered at Oliver, who was just coming up the stairs, doing some hollering of his own. His hands were full of not one, but several sodas.

"Stupid machine!" he exclaimed.

"What's the problem?" Jake asked.

"No matter which button I pressed, it kept giving me diet sodas."

"So you kept pressing anyway?" Jake inquired.

"Well, yeah," Oliver answered sheepishly.

"Bart says the real definition of insanity is to keep doing the same thing and expecting different results. I guess since you pressed different buttons, it doesn't really apply to you."

"Maybe it does," Oliver admitted. "I pressed one button five times before moving to another." They set the extra sodas on the counter for the librarian and took one each to the car for themselves. They each took a drink before getting in the car and decided to toss the cans into one of the garbage cans the city had provided along the sidewalk for just such emergencies.

"Gross," Oliver exclaimed, spitting the excess from his mouth like he had been siphoning gasoline and accidentally sucked a little too hard. "That's about the nastiest stuff I've ever put in my mouth."

"About?" Jake asked, opening the door to his squad car and sliding in.

"Uh-huh," Oliver answered as he buckled his seat belt. "Once, in third grade, someone dared me to eat a bug. I think that might have been worse, but I can't really remember." The two of them spent the journey to the cabin talking about things people had dared them to do and sharing exploits of

school adventures. Oliver was glad to find that Jake hadn't always been a

straight and narrow person, and Jake was glad to have the distraction as they

drove out of the city and down a long country road that seemed to last well

into eternity. After making the final turn down a road that looked like it hadn't

been in use since the time of the cattle drives, Jake paused long enough to

grab some tools out of the trunk and pull down a sign that was posted

alongside the road.

"Need some help?" Oliver asked through the window he had lowered.

"Nope," Jake answered. "You stay in the car, or you'll be an

accessory."

"Whatcha doing?" Oliver wondered.

"Just getting you a souvenir for your trouble," Jake answered as he

tossed the tools and the sign back into the trunk. They drove the next few

minutes in silence, with Oliver being curious about Jake's actions, but also

being too afraid to ask.

The cabin was built out of cedar logs, giving it the appearance,

especially in the dark, of being a part of the woods. It was recessed in an

enclave of towering pines that swayed back and forth in the October breezes

like a group of gypsy dancers. The pines bowed down over the short

driveway, giving it an appearance of a deep tunnel. Oliver half expected a beautiful woman to be living there with seven short miners. He started

humming heigh-ho, heigh-ho to himself as Jake pulled the car around to the

far side of the cabin and down an old logging trail where it couldn't be readily

seen from the cabin. Oliver wasn't sure, but he thought he saw the lights of

their car reflect off of another pair of headlights further down the trail. He

figured there was probably another cabin further down in the woods. The

place was probably covered with hunting cabins, like ticks on the back of an

old hound. Either way, Jake didn't seem too upset by it, so he wasn't going to

be.

"Make your self at home," Jake told him as they entered.

"I'd be glad to, if I could see what home looked like," Oliver said,

standing still in the open doorway until some light was brought into the

situation. Cabins like that made comfortable temporary dwellings for critters

like possums, snakes, and spiders. Until Oliver could be fairly sure that he

wouldn't be interrupting their sleep, he wasn't moving any further. Jake

accommodated him with a pair of oil lanterns that lit up the room pretty well.

Jake chose to use the oil lamps instead of turning on the lights because they

wanted to keep the atmosphere dim so Jake could easily hide in the shadows

of the loft bedroom. There wasn't much to the cabin. The bottom floor

consisted of a fireplace with an assortment of couches and chairs gathered

around it in a semi-circle. Behind the furniture was another room that served

297

as kitchen and dining room. Tucked in one corner was a small bathroom, complete with working toilet and shower. Oliver was impressed with that. Above the kitchen area was a loft bedroom, with a steep set of stairs leading up to it.

"That's where I'll be," Jake assured him. "You won't be alone even for a minute."

"I'm glad to hear that," Oliver said. He was about to say something else when they saw headlights coming down the tunnel drive. Jake headed up the stairs and hid in the darkness, pulling his gun out as he went. He didn't want to take any chances of this developing into a hostage situation. His career was on the line, that much was for sure, but that wasn't what concerned him. Oliver, and his safety, was his main concern. If anything happened to him, Jake would never be able to forgive himself for placing a good and innocent kid into the hands of a madman like Phil the Ferret.

"Knock knock," the ferret called, opening the door before anyone had a chance to invite him in. He walked into the room as if he owned the place. It reminded Jake of an old Carly Simon tune, something about being so vain. In this case, he was walking into a rustic cabin instead of walking onto a yacht, but the effect was there all the same.

"Come in," Oliver, his voice breaking from the flutter of butterflies in his stomach. For Brother Bart's sake, he was determined to go through with the plan, but his brain was having a hard time convincing his feet not to run.

To keep them from bolting out of the still open door and dragging the rest of

his body behind them, he plopped down hard on the nearest piece of furniture.

Unfortunately, it turned out to be the love seat, with just enough room for two

people and Philip was already heading over there. Oliver looked up at the loft

to make sure that Jake was in place and able to get a good shot off if he

needed to. He realized just in time that he needed to move closer to the

fireplace to make sure it was Philip that stayed in the line of fire and not him.

He scooted over and let Philip make himself cozy in the seat beside him. He

felt like a mongoose inviting a cobra over for dinner.

"Quaint," Philip commented about his surroundings as he poured each

of them a glass of wine. He had brought the wine and the glasses in a picnic

basket. From Oliver's vantage point he could see that the basket also

contained some cheese, crackers, fruit, and several objects that he couldn't

identify and wasn't sure that he ever wanted to. One thing he did identify was

a pair of handcuffs. Oliver would be glad when he saw another pair of those

wrapped around Philip's wrists.

"It's not much," Oliver explained, "but it gives us some privacy, and

isn't that what you wanted?"

"Exactly," Philip said as he maneuvered his arm around Oliver's back

and gave a friendly squeeze on the young boy's shoulder. "I wanted the privacy so we could have the chance to know each other better; so we could

explore each other without interruption from bothersome parents and pastors.'"

"Is that the real reason you wanted me to come to the camp?" Oliver

asked, snuggling up into Philip's embrace. He felt like he was about to lose

any food left in his stomach, so he grabbed the glass of wine to swallow it

back down with. Jake started to protest, but he held himself back. They still

didn't really have enough evidence to convict the creep, and he wanted to

make sure that the ferret was kept in a cage for a long, long time.

"Yes, it is. I have a private suite at the camp that we could have used.

It has a Jacuzzi and a very large, soft feather bed. We would have been much

more comfortable there, but I'm sure the bedroom here will be adequate

enough for the two of us. You can think of this as our honeymoon."

"And who am I supposed to be, the bride or the groom?" Oliver asked,

barely able to disguise he total disgust and revulsion.

"Doesn't matter," Philip answered nonchalantly. "We can start out

with you as the groom, if that will make you feel better. And I'll be the bad

bride that needs punished." He pulled out the handcuffs and started to put

them on himself.

"These will fit better," Jake called as he started down the stairs, his

gun already drawn and pointed at Philip's chest. Oliver had quickly moved

over to a point past the fireplace, putting as much distance between the mongoose and snake as he could in the small cabin.

"So that's it," Philip said, seemingly unconcerned about the sudden change in circumstances.

"Yes, that's it," Jake stated flatly. "Philip, you are under arrest. You have the right to remain silent."

"Oh, please," Philip interrupted. "Let's dispense with all of the melodrama. I know my rights."

"So you're waiving the reading of your rights?" Jake asked.

"Yes, yes. I'm waiving the reading of my rights. It won't matter since I won't be in jail long enough for any of them to be abused anyway. I'll be out of jail and you'll be out of a job in the same day. Angus and Shane will see to that."

"And how are they supposed to do that?" Jake asked as he spun Philip around and patted him down, still keeping his weapon trained on the predator.

"They own Stony Ridge. They probably own the county by now and are well on their way to owning the state. They've bought enough judges and politicians to start their own state if they didn't like this one so much."

"There are bound to be some who couldn't be bought," Jake protested. "I'll be able to find one who doesn't have a price tag stuck to his collar."

"Oh, there were plenty of those. Some couldn't be bought for love or money. But people are people and most people have vices that can be

301

exploited."

"Really? Enlighten me."

"For one, there are plenty of people who share my interest in the welfare of young boys like Oliver." He looked over at the young man and winked. Jake had to step between the two to stop Oliver from smashing Philip's nose into a bloody pulp. He did hesitate long enough for Oliver to get one good shot at Philip's jaw.

"Must be getting old," he apologized. "My reflexes aren't what they used to be."

"I'm sure your reflexes are as good as they've ever been," Philip stated, wanting desperately to rub his soon to be swollen jaw. Oliver was back in the corner between the fireplace and the front door, rubbing his fists. They hardly ever showed in the movies how much it hurt for the person throwing the punch. He wasn't entirely sure that he hadn't busted a couple of knuckles. He was pretty sure at least one was in a place that it didn't belong and he tugged on it in an effort to get it to pop back into place.

"Go to the kitchen and see if there's some ice in the freezer," Jake instructed him. Oliver trotted over to the kitchen to do as Jake told him. The cold of the ice stabbed through him at first, but it eased the pain and seemed to take down the swelling.

"I could use some of that," Philip said, rubbing his chin on his shoulder.

"Cry me a river," Oliver shot back.

"So Angus and Shane are blackmailing the politicians they couldn't buy? Is that it?" Jake asked.

"For a small town sheriff, you catch on quick," Philip responded. "There are honest ones, of course, but not enough to matter at this point. So you might as well take these handcuffs off. I'll never stand trial, not at Stony Ridge anyway."

"Well then," Jake said thoughtfully, taking time to stroke his chin in a manner reminiscent of the great philosophers, "I suppose the thing to do then is take you somewhere else. You know what would be great? It would be great if we could get you on federal charges, like crossing state lines for sex with a minor."

"I suppose that would work out better for you," Philip said uncomfortably. He was painfully aware that Jake knew something that he didn't.

"It would be great if somewhere along that dirt road you crossed the state line unawares. It doesn't matter, of course, in the eyes of the law. After all, ignorance is no excuse. But then we'd need a federal agent here to arrest you." As if on cue, someone knocked at the door.

"Who could that be?" Oliver wondered aloud from the kitchen.

"I don't know," Jake answered innocently. "Let's see." He left Philip standing at the edge of the fireplace and went to open the door. A man in a dark suit stood there, smiling.

"I'm FBI Agent O'Neill. And I assume you are going to be my guest for the next several years," he said, looking directly at Philip, who had sagged hard against the wall in defeat.

Bar T. Rancher

CHAPTER TWELVE

"Bart, Bart," Leonard called out, shaking Bart by the shoulders as he tried to rest peacefully and finish the dream he was having about him, Shalina, and Cassandra living happily ever after as man, wife and wife. He wasn't sure, because there isn't much in dreams that are sure, but he was thinking that in his dream he was Solomon, Shalina was the Queen of Sheba, and Cassandra was a queen as well, but she wasn't the Queen of Sheba, which made absolute sense since Shalina was already fulfilling that role. On the other hand, it didn't make any sense at all since in dreams there aren't many things that make sense. He decided to lay back, smile, and enjoy the ride while it lasted, which, as it turned out, wasn't nearly long enough. No matter how hard he tried to ignore it, Leonard's voice kept calling out to him. The rooster that sat outside his window called out his name in Leonard's voice instead of crowing at the rising sun, which was blue and looked amazingly like Oprah Winfrey. His loyal basset hound, who usually howled at anything that came within inches of his nose, making him a royal nuisance and an absolutely useless watchdog, was speaking with Leonard's voice as well. The last straw was when each of the women came to him and whispered to him in his ears using the voice of Leonard. He decided that the only way to get rid of that voice was to wake up, sit up, and slap the source.

"Hey!" Leonard shouted, rubbing his stinging left cheek. "I'm just trying to help."

"Help me what?" Bart asked. "Help me to wake up and join a world of pain and suffering when I could be cavorting with the two women I love the most?"

"First of all," Leonard corrected, "you shouldn't be cavorting at all, even in your dreams, with women you hardly know. And you sure shouldn't be cavorting with two women at the same time."

"I know," Bart admitted. "But it hurts too much to be out here, physically and emotionally. It hurts to think that I don't know where either of them are right now and that I can't do a thing to find them."

"That's just it," Leonard said. "I think we can do something, but you have to get out of this hospital."

"What makes you think we can do anything?" Darryl demanded. "Bart is injured and needs to rest. He doesn't need to be out there doing the sheriff's job. Jake is doing the best he can to find the girls."

"No," Leonard protested. "He's doing everything he can to find Cassandra. He's not looking for Shalina because he's not even sure she exists." It was hard for Bart to admit, but Leonard was right. Jake was a good man and he was good at his job, which included at this moment looking for Cassandra and Shalina, but he would focus on Cassandra first, and then look for Shalina if he had time. If someone was going to do something for her, it

307

would have to be up to him and the boys. He began to flex his muscles
around, starting with his legs and working his way upwards. Each movement
brought a new onslaught of pain, but it was bearable and it meant that he was
able to move, which was an improvement over when they brought him in.
With concentration he was able to make the move from reclining to sitting.
After a few deep breaths and some even deeper concentration he was able to
stand and make his way slowly to the door, which was being guarded by
Deputy Lamb. That was a tough break for Bart. He knew Deputy Lamb and
knew that there was no way around him and his no nonsense approach to law
and order. He was strictly by the book and would follow whatever orders Jake
had given to him, which more than likely included keeping Bart in the room
as well as keeping others out. They would need a plan.

"If," Darryl offered, "Leonard could distract him long enough, I could
tackle him from behind." Bart had a hard time not giving into the laughter that
wanted to bust out of him in a thousand different directions.

"That would never work," Leonard said.

"And why not, if I may be so bold as to ask?" Darryl countered. Bart
was proud of Leonard for recognizing that the plan wouldn't work because he
and Darryl were only imaginary characters.

"Because, silly, that guy's twice your size. You'd never be able to take
him, even if I distracted him with a Fourth of July's worth of fireworks and

half the showgirls from a Vegas chorus line."

"Ha! That shows what you know. I'll have you know I can turn my body into a living weapon." He did some karate chops at a shadowy opponent in front of him. Bart decided he had been too quick in his assumption of Leonard's intelligence. He would have to devise a plan of his own, one that didn't include one of his imaginary friends doing a Barney Fife imitation. They were right about one thing. He would need a distraction to divert Deputy Lamb's attention while he snuck out of his room, past the nurse's station, down the elevator, and out of the front door. And he had to manage to do all of that while being shackled to an IV tower and trying to pull the flaps of his gown together so he wouldn't moon everyone as he passed by. It should be easy as pie if he just put his mind to it.

Why did pie click in his mind so much? There had to be a reason, but his mind was refusing to work despite his most stubborn insistence. He supposed that it was normal for people who had been beaten silly to suffer at least a temporary form of brain damage, but it sure was coming at an inconvenient time. Of course, he couldn't think of a convenient time to have your head used as a soccer ball and your body as a tackling dummy. The funny thing was that he felt like a dummy. There was no good reason to go down that alley with Philip the Ferret and his gorilla buddies. He should have stayed out on the street. No doubt they would have grabbed him and Shalina

309

and forced them to go, but they were on a public street and might have been able to attract some attention before the goons grabbed them. There was no point in chastising himself over lost moments. It was a lesson he had learned the hard way with the agency. They believed in the saying the Marines were fond of using from time to time, which said that any movement or decision was better than none because at least then you were making forward momentum. Right now Bart wasn't too sure about how much forward momentum he had made, but he also believed in another saying, one that had much better backing than even the U.S.M.C. He believed the Bible when it told him that all things work together for good. He couldn't say it was good, and he wasn't sure how God would work it out, but he still trusted that he would. He tried to stay focused on the task at hand. He needed someone from the outside to aid and abet in his escape. But who could he call? Then the pie hit him in the face.

"Hello, Marc," Bart said into the telephone after dialing the number he had found in the phone book.

"Hey, my man, how's it going?" the big man responded cheerfully. It was obvious from his response that he hadn't heard about Bart's predicament, so Bart spent the next ten minutes explaining where he was and how he got there. Then he spent the next twenty minutes trying to calm the big man down so he wouldn't rip the ferret's head off.

"Jake's got that under control," he assured Marc. "Besides, we need him to bring down the others in the organization."

"You make it sound like some kind of Holy Ghost mafia," Marc chuckled.

"Yeah," Bart agreed, "but there's nothing holy about these people. I think they're responsible for at least two murders."

"Two?"

"A young woman was found in the ruins, or at least what was left of her. I think she was pregnant at the time."

"That's worse than disgusting. What are we going to do about it?"

"Right now what I need is to get out of this hospital, but Jake put a guard on the door."

"To keep folks out or to keep you in?" Marc wondered.

"I'm guessing both," Bart replied. "He knew I wouldn't be content to sit on my hands while he does all the work. That's where you come in. I was hoping you could help me get out of here." They spent the next several minutes formulating a plan of escape, complete with pecan pie, young men on roller blades, a getaway car, and some clothes for the half naked preacher.

It seemed like days, but it was only about a half hour later when Bart heard the big, booming voice of Marc. He was offering Deputy Lamb a piece of Georgia's homemade pecan pie. Bart took that opportunity to pull out his

IV tube and pull off any tape or monitors still connected. He didn't think any of them would set off alarms at the nurse's station, but he held his breath with every tug. After what seemed like a long Christmas night of waiting for Santa Claus, he breathed a deep sigh of relief. He listened at the door to see if their plan was working.

"You know what would be good with this?" he heard Marc ask Deputy Lamb, who was too busy shoveling in another bite of pie to give a coherent answer.

"Hmm-hmm," he managed to mutter.

"A good cup of hot, black coffee," Marc answered himself. "That would make this perfect, or at least as perfect as anything can get this side of heaven."

"There's some hot black liquid at the nurse's station down the hall, but I don't think I'd go so far as to call it coffee." Deputy Lamb laughed at his culinary critique.

"Well then," Marc asked, "where can we get a cup of the good stuff?"

"The doctor's lounge on the fourth floor has about the best coffee this side of Starbucks, but you won't be able to get in there. Too bad."

"Can you?" Marc asked.

"Sure, but I've got to guard this door. Jake will have my head if anything happens to Brother Bart."

"I see," the big man sympathized. "But I'll watch the door. Ain't no one gonna get past this preacher. Not without me pounding a sermon into their heads first, anyways." Deputy Lamb looked at the mountain sized preacher and decided he was right. Besides, it would be a terrible shame to try to wash down such delicious pie with less than adequate coffee. He made sure Marc intended to stay and trotted off to the elevator around the corner to head up to the fourth floor. Marc made sure he heard the ding of the elevator before stepping into Bart's room unannounced. He handed Bart his clothes and gave his new old friend a gentle bear hug.

"Good to see you, too," Bart said after catching his breath.

"Hope I didn't hurt you none. I'm just so doggoned glad to see you. I wasn't sure what I was gonna find when I got here. Are you sure you're up to leaving this place? I mean, you ain't gonna do that lady no good if you run your car off into a ditch or something stupid like that."

"I'll be alright," Bart assured him. "I'm starting to catch my second wind, believe it or not."

"I ain't so sure I do believe it," Marc countered since Bart had to balance himself on the bed to regain control of his legs while trying to put his pants on.

"Just a little shaky, that's all," Bart said, trying hard to persuade Marc that he was okay. He also had to convince himself, which was no easy task

313

since it was his brain sensing the pain, along with the agony of defeat and every other body part. He was sure that at some point in his life he had been in worse situations, but he was hard pressed to remember any of them at the moment. With Marc's help, he managed to finish getting dressed and within five minutes he almost looked like he might be presentable enough for the rest of humanity. Marc stepped out just as Deputy Lamb was stepping out of the elevator with two freshly steaming cups of coffee. He didn't want to, but there was no choice but to put phase two of the plan into effect. Before Lamb got there, Marc ducked his head back into the room to tell Bart to have him signal the others. Bart flashed the lights off and on twice, then waited for the fireworks to begin.

Just as the elevator doors opened, the parking lot became a flurry of activity. Car horns honked, stereos blared and tires squealed across the black pavement.

"What the heck?" Deputy Lamb cried out, looking through the window at the end of the hall. He started calling out questions into his handheld radio, but didn't get the answers he was looking for. Most of the deputies were busy on the other side of the county and the sheriff couldn't be found anywhere since going on radio silence earlier.

"Go on," Marc urged. "I'll take care of our man here."

"I can't do that," Lamb protested. "Jake will have my head if something happens to him." He felt torn between the chaos occurring in the parking lot and keeping order with Bart. He started to turn toward the elevator, but felt pulled back to the post he was supposed to be keeping. Bart was beginning to think he would never leave. He hated getting the kids involved in something illegal, even if it was just some joy riding and doing donuts in the hospital parking lot.

"Go," Marc urged again. That command, along with the sound of more squalling tires in the parking lot, was all Lamb needed to make his decision. He ran for the stairs, descending them two or three at a time. Despite his large frame and age, he moved quickly down the stairs and was out of the front door in mere minutes, barely giving Bart enough time to call Mikey and the other kids to warn them to get out of the parking lot before Deputy Lamb was able to see them and get their license numbers. By the time the good deputy was back at the elevator pressing the button to go back upstairs, Bart and Marc were at the emergency room entrance where Marc had his car parked for their great escape. It wasn't a complicated plan, but it worked and that's all that counted in the minds of the two preachers who were waiting at the last stop light going out of town by the time Deputy Lamb was cursing himself for being so gullible and wondering if that security job his brother-in-law offered was still available.

"Where are the kids supposed to meet us at?" Bart asked Marc as they headed towards the camp.

"They're supposed to be at the Glacier Creek Bridge, about a mile from here. It's where we do a lot of our baptizing in the summer time. Wouldn't want to use it any other time, though. It's cold enough then, but it's downright unbearable any other time."

"It's spring fed, isn't it?" Bart asked.

"Yep, and colder than blue blazes. Used to be the only way to dunk folks back in the day. Some of the die hard folks still want it the old-fashioned way, but I draw the line at having to break the ice." Bart couldn't imagine people actually wanting to dive into frigid water just to have a deeper religious experience, but each person had their own quirks and turns that made them who they were. That included those who not only wanted to be baptized as one of God's flock but as a member of the polar bear club as well.

The boys were already there, waiting in their cars parked under the bridge. One of them had started a fire in one of the homemade barbeque pits that were spotted along the narrow strip of sand that passed for a beach. Other creek side beaches in the area were spotted with broken glass, along with beer cans and other sundry pieces of trash, but this one was almost considered sacred, even by those who didn't hold much of anything sacred. They were busy munching chips and going on at each other about what a blast they had at the hospital.

"Can you believe we got clean away?" Mikey was asking one of his friends.

"What I can't believe is that Pastor Marc wanted us to get away with it. What's up with that anyway?"

"We'll find out now," Mikey responded. "Here they come now." Bart and Marc were approaching.

"How's it going, Mikey?" Marc asked.

"It's hanging, preacher man," Mikey replied. "Now how about you and this pale preacher tell a brother what's going down. We done brought the stuff you asked for. So what gives with y'all anyways?"

"I'd like to tell you, Mikey," Bart answered, "but then I'd have to kill you."

"Oh, no. I know he didn't just try to score on me. That ain't happenin' preacher man." Mikey's friends laughed as the embarrassed Mikey tried to think of a quick come back. He was usually on his feet quicker, but Bart's deadpan humor and his off the wall answer caught him totally by surprise.

"One up for the preacher man," one of his friends said as they drew an imaginary one on a scoreboard in the sky.

"I see how it is," Mikey stated. "Preacher man gets one up and y'all go dissin' on me. Y'all ain't even playing by the rules."

"Ain't no rules in these woods," Marc corrected. "You know that much."

"Yeah, I know," Mikey agreed sullenly, "but that just means old preacher man best watch his back."

"Oh, I'll be watching it all right," Bart said. "But right now I'd like to see yours helping haul that stuff to the creek, if you don't mind."

"I got you," Mikey said, with just a gleam of mischievousness in his eyes that told Bart he really should be watching his back for the next several days at least. His off the cuff remark, which should have been totally ignored, had cut across the bow of Mikey's manhood. It wasn't what average, tie-wearing, have your kids in bed by ten Christians would call good clean fun, but it was for the most part harmless. It would probably end with a "momma" joke from Mikey, which would be pretty much useless since there wasn't anyone on earth who thought less of the woman who gave him birth. Either that or he'd spend a Saturday afternoon cleaning toilet paper from his yard. But that was okay with Bart because he had access to a garage full of campaign signs from the previous mayor's race. The incumbent, who lost in a landslide, contributed them to the church, thinking they could be repainted and recycled for a more sacred purpose.

"Seriously," Bart said, "thanks for all your help. We couldn't have done any of this without you."

"Y'all just remember that the next time your church has pizza and movie night."

"You know you're always welcome for our special nights," Bart said, hurt that someone might not feel welcomed at his church.

"Yeah, but next time I want to pick out the movie." Bart looked over at Marc, who gave him an approving wink.

"You got it," Bart agreed.

"One more thing," Mikey added.

"What's that?" Bart wondered.

"Where'd you get all this stuff? We're talking about some serious hardware. Night vision. High powered rifles and scopes. Y'all ain't going deer hunting."

"Let's just say I used to have friends in low places. Now I got friends in high places," he said, looking up to the sky. "And I've got friends in between, too. Friends like you and Marc. And I've got a lady friend that might be held prisoner at Megiddo, so me and Marc are heading down there to see if we can find her. Are you sure this creek will lead us inside the camp?"

"My daddy and granddaddy hunted down this creek for years before them guys built that camp. That creek goes right under the southern fence. With them wire cutters, you shouldn't have any problem getting in there."

"Just like getting into Babylon," Marc said. Bart let that last thought flow the waters of his mind as they floated down the chilly waters of Glacier

319

Creek. Babylon fell at the judgment of God; perhaps Megiddo could do the same. He was sure, although he couldn't tell anyone how he knew, least of all himself, but he knew that Angus McFarland and his brother Shane were as dirty as the ancient kings. He was also sure that when, not if, they found Shalina, she would be at the camp as prisoner of one of those two evil men.

The float trip was quiet. The lack of summer rain had depleted the creek's resources to the point that at times they almost had to get out and drag the two man rubber raft. They didn't mind though. Even though every molecule of Bart's body screamed to hurry, they knew their only hope of getting into camp without being noticed was to wait until after nightfall, which wouldn't come for a couple of more hours.

Bart spent the time letting his mind drift back to another float trip, one he took with his friend, Sheriff Jake. He wasn't really sure though that it could be called a float trip. The dry wash they walked down only had waters in them a couple of times during the year, during the monsoonal rains that swept through Arizona each year as a reminder of what God had done during the days of Noah. If he could bring flooding to that barren landscape in mere minutes, it shouldn't come as any stretch of the imagination to believe he could flood an entire world in forty days and nights. During their travels, however, Bart and Jake could only find themselves wishing for a four minute shower. Instead, they found an unrelenting sun beating down on them day after day and cold nights that threatened them with hypothermia because of the thirty to forty degree temperature difference that came with the setting of the desert sun.

"Remind me again of how we ended up here?" Jake said to Bart as they trudged along in the soft sand of the dry wash. It was like walking on a beach that went on forever with no water in sight.

"What you want to hear," Bart replied as he ploddingly picked up one foot to set it in front of the other, "is how this is all my fault because I don't listen to the advice of well seasoned professional law enforcement officers."

"No," Jake corrected. "I don't care if you don't listen to other officers of the law. But you ought to listen to your best friend when he says he hears someone coming up behind us."

"How was I supposed to know they had another team out there? I had accounted for everyone from our intel."

"Well," Jake stated the obvious, "it doesn't look like your intel is too intelligent. Who gave it to you anyways, Darryl and Leonard?"

"No, I gave them some time off. They're back at the motel sipping tea and soaking up the sun at the pool. It's a good thing for them too, because Darryl burns easily." Jake wished he had been given the day off as well. Instead he was trudging along in hot sand with a semi-sane preacher, no water, and no idea of where they were or where they were going.

"Why are we going this way?" Jake asked after what seemed like hours of marching along.

"Because this will lead us back to their headquarters where we were ambushed," Bart replied in a matter of fact manner.

"Excuse me, but I remember being knocked out before I was blindfolded and thrown into the back of a panel van. Did you get shotgun after I lost consciousness because as I remember it you woke up next to me?"

"It's a gift I have," Bart explained. "Even when I'm asleep, my body records it's movements. I haven't been lost since I discovered the gift when I was about twelve. And I've looked at all the maps of this area, including topographical and geological. We're somewhere between the Santa Cruz and Gila rivers, only a little over five miles from the headquarters where they ambushed us."

"Why didn't they take us farther?" Jake wondered. "It doesn't make sense to leave someone within walking distance of your base of operations." He stopped to drain the sand out of his shoes, a ritual he had become way too familiar with over the course of the last several hours, and one he didn't want to repeat once they were back home. He sat in the soft sand for a minute, the sides of the wash providing shade from the blistering sun so that the sand was almost cool to the touch. He leaned back against the short canyon walls, painfully aware that they were probably home to any number of desert denizens, including spiders and scorpions, two of his least favorite animal visitors. His least favorite, though, was the rattlesnake. As far as he was concerned, anything that slithered on the ground and had leathery skin was poisonous and deserving of a swift but very painful death.

"There was no need to take us any farther in their minds," Bart answered. "They expected the desert to finish us and when it did, they could say we were just a couple of stupid gringos who should have stayed in the woods back home."

"I'm not so sure they weren't right," Jake replied. "How much longer?"

"We should be there within an hour," Bart answered. "So why don't we fix up some shelter here and try to get some sleep before going after them?"

"About that," Jake wondered, "just how are we going to go after them when neither one of us have any weapons and they're armed to the teeth?" He was really starting to have misgivings about the whole mission. If it hadn't been for the look of emptiness he had seen in the little Hispanic girl's eyes he probably wouldn't have even considered coming with Bart across Texas and into Arizona just to catch a group of people called coyotes that transported large groups of illegals across the border into the United States. That was the job of the INS or border security. It wasn't the job of a simple county sheriff from the Ozarks of Arkansas. Who was he kidding? Nothing had been simple about his life since he met Bart Rancher. He had a way of transplanting the abnormal into the everyday and making it seem perfectly normal.

"Most of them should be gone into town. And besides, we'll have the element of surprise on our side."

"Yeah," Jake agreed. "Most people don't expect to be attacked by two dead white guys."

"Exactly," Bart agreed. "So let's get some sleep for a couple of hours." They found a piece of old tin the desert had claimed for its own years earlier and stretched it across the gap of the wash to provide them some shade. It wasn't much, but after Bart put a thin layer of sand across the top, it dropped the temperature underneath by an appreciable amount. When they awoke almost three hours later, both of them were shivering from the cold.

"What's the deal?" Jake complained. "Bake us during the day and then put us in the freezer at night like a couple of leftover meat loafs? I really don't get this place."

"It'll be worth it in the end if we can help some of those girls escape the prison they've been in." They continued their desert trek, each step they took illuminated by a high desert moon. In the cool of the evening, the trip that would have seemed like it took an eternity during the day passed relatively quickly.

"What now?" Jake asked, leaning his hard, lean frame against a chain link fence. There was only one building inside the compound, an unassuming white stucco ranch style house that could have blended into any suburban desert development without too much notice. The guards on top, along with the top end cars that filled the drive might have caused some nosy neighbors a cause for questions, but as long as they took out their trash and didn't have barking dogs, they probably would have been welcomed and asked to join the neighborhood watch committee.

"The wash runs through the middle of the compound," Bart replied. "It should come out close enough to the Corvette over there that I should be able to use it to cause a distraction while you sneak into the main house."

"And then?"

"Do I have to think of everything?" Bart asked. Jake thought it would have been nice for him to think of little details, like weapons, back up, and escape routes, but didn't have any illusions about those things magically appearing out of thin air. They crawled along on their bellies until they reached the designated car, which happened to be the Corvette that was parked close enough to offer them cover after their release from the wash. Bart crawled up to the back and used a wire he pulled from one of his shoes to pop the trunk. Inside he found more than he could have hoped for. Along with a nine millimeter, there was a roadside emergency kit that included the flare he was hoping for. He gave Jake time to crawl as close as he could to the house, using the cover of the parked automobiles, before popping the flare and shoving it down the gasoline filler tube. He barely had time to throw himself back into the shelter of the wash before an explosion shook the compound and everyone in it. During the ensuing chaos, Jake was able to sneak inside while everyone else was running out to see what had happened. Bart, in the meantime, managed to snag one of the guards who carelessly stepped a little too close to the ditch where he had been hiding. Now that he was armed with the guard's weapon and uniform, he made his way to the house to help Jake.

Jake quickly made his way to the rooftop access and called up to the guards.

"What's going on?" he demanded with such force that they didn't think to question who he was or what authority he possessed that allowed him to question them.

"Not sure," the first one answered.

"Well get down here and help with the search," he demanded and then slid back into the shadows. When they were both down the ladder, he popped both of them with the back of the nine mil, collapsing their bulky frames to the floor. He struggled to get them back into the obscurity of the shadows before going back into the building to search for more guards. Bart was already there and had found a phone to call for back up. He thought about calling the local police, but decided instead to call 911 and report the fire. That way he knew they would send police, fire and ambulance. The latter would be needed for the young girls who filled the brothel and unfortunately filled the fantasies of the high priced clientele.

"I think we have them on the run," Bart told Jake when they caught up to each other.

"Let's hope so, pal," Jake replied. They did have the guards going in several different directions. The original exploding car set off a nearby Cadillac belonging to a state senator and threatened to set off a chain of events that would have destroyed the compound. By the time the police arrived, there were enough local officials to host a city council meeting running around in their underwear wondering who had set off WWIII while they were trying to get their kicks with underage girls smuggled across the border. Jake and Bart caught a ride back with an ambulance driver, preferring not to stick around for the aftermath.

"You ready?" Marc asked him, bringing him back to the reality of the mission ahead of them. This time, however, they would need more than a wire and an exploding Corvette.

Bar T. Rancher

CHAPTER THIRTEEN

Shalina ducked into the shoe store, ashamed by her actions, but unsure of what else she could do. Immediately after entering the small shop that smelled of leather and machinery oil, she grabbed the cell phone out of her purse. She almost cursed when she couldn't get a signal. She didn't know if it was the steel and block structure of the old building or just where she happened to be in town, but it didn't matter to Bart. She wasn't able to help him when he needed her most. Her next move was to try to find the shop owner. Since she didn't see him at the front, she ran to the back, calling for help.

The front of the store was almost bare, there was only a small countertop that held a display of hand tools and an old fashioned cash register. Her shoes echoed loudly on the hardwood floors as she ran around looking for the proprietor to gain his help. Unfortunately all she found was a couple of industrial strength sewing machines for piecing together leather, some machines she couldn't identify and a plethora of leather goods, including shoes, purses, and wallets. But there wasn't anything she could use to help Bart. She thought about grabbing a can of something to spray into one of the goons eyes, but she was sure that would be a one shot deal and there were two men to deal with. Besides, all she found was a can of spray lubricant, which might irritate his eyes a little, but probably wouldn't do anything more than that. At the very back, down a narrow hall, she found a restroom and a metal spiral staircase. She took it, but it only led to a small landing with a locked door. It spoke of most of her life in that one moment, which consisted of a long climb going in circles with a locked door at the end of it. She was beginning to panic and wasn't thinking straight. Her only friend in town was probably getting the beating of his life less than a hundred yards away and she was totally helpless. She wasn't even capable of getting help. She was about to succumb to the desperation of the situation and just lay in a crumpled heap on the landing in a puddle of tears when she felt a renewed strength flowing into her from somewhere. Taking the stairs two at a time, despite the narrow steps and circular pattern, she determined to at least find a phone she could call from to get help.

In her earlier panicked state, she had spotted a phone line running along the white concrete wall at the back, but hadn't really thought about the possibility of calling from a land line. Like everyone else in the world she had grown accustomed to having the world at her fingertips and the idea of using a wired phone simply hadn't occurred to her. Now she followed the painted brittle cable first one way to the junction box where it was hooked to the outside world, then back the other direction until she came to a mobile base with the wireless receiver missing. She almost laughed at the absurdity of it all. People bought exercise equipment from the home shopping network that would be used as an expensive coat rack when all they really needed to do was throw the remote in the trash so they would have to get off the couch to change channels. She finds a telephone base, but can't find the receiver because the stupid owner of the shop, who can't be bothered running his business even during business hours, has carried it to Timbuktu or some other remote corner of the galaxy and she can't even buzz it using the base's button because it's been off the base too long and doesn't have enough charge to respond. Life wasn't fair.

Who was she to complain? She wasn't being kicked in the groin or having her head used for a punching bag. Her complaint was that the technology that was supposed to make life easier for everyone was making her life impossible at the moment, but that was a temporary setback. It was a grain of sand being crushed through the great cogs on the gears of the universe. Then again, as far as speed bumps along the highway of the universe went, she wasn't much more than a pebble on an eight lane highway herself.

"Enough self-pity," she told herself. "Bart needs my help and I guess I'll just have to handle things myself." She went back outside and raced down the alley to where she assumed he had been taken, but by the time she had searched for a phone and an invisible or non-existent shop proprietor, the young couple had arrived and called for an ambulance. The EMT's were loading him into the back even as she approached. She thought about asking if she could go with them, but that would mean questions and she wasn't sure

she was ready to give any answers at the moment so she decided to take care

of some other things and go to the hospital after he was seen to and settled in.

She hated not being there for him when he needed her the most, but it

wouldn't matter in the long run if she were at the police station instead of the

hospital with Bart.

Her first order of business was to see what she could find out about

Shane McFarland and his camp for wayward boys. They were tied in with

her…; her what? She wondered what she should call him. He wasn't a

boyfriend, at least not yet, although she could easily see him filling that role.

He was kind, compassionate, funny and good looking, which was always a

plus. She didn't have to have movie star good looks, but it didn't hurt if he

was easy on the eyes and Bart certainly was all of that. What he wasn't,

however, and what she wanted him to be more than almost anything was a

steady boyfriend. She wasn't ready for the two point five kids, dog, and white

picket fence, or she didn't think she was anyway. She was ready, though, for

someone she could talk with, someone to have dinner with more than

occasionally and more than anything someone to share her heart with.

Instead of focusing on what she didn't have or might want, she

decided to focus on going to the camp and seeing what she could find out

about what really went on at the camp. From her talks with Bart, and her recent encounter with some of the so called graduates from the camp, she

suspected that they had a greater interest in helping themselves to something

than in helping their students from breaking free from something. Her

direction was clear; the only choice ahead of her was how to proceed. She

could try sneaking in the back door, but she suspected their security would be

a little tighter than she could fit into. She was about to crumple into an

indecisive ball when the bells from Riverview Church interrupted her lack of

thought. The peals of the bells inspired a plan within the folds of her mind.

Instead of making a frontal assault on the camp itself, she would sneak

in the extreme back door of the church. She needed information and she knew

that there was a symbiotic relationship between the church and the camp;

neither of them would have existed, or at least thrived, without the other one.

In her mind, they were like two ticks sharing a straw while sucking the blood

out of the dog, represented in this case by the town and surrounding area.

They would, no doubt, end up sucking the very life out everyone and

everything they could before they ended up turning the straw on each other.

As she considered the prospect of what the future might hold, she didn't like

the possibility of what the final outcome might be. There were two headstrong

and highly egotistical people trying to share the reins of a single buggy. That

kind of dualistic hierarchy couldn't last. In an alpha male society, there had to

be a top dog to lead the pack. Even the Bible recognized that truth when Jesus said that no man could serve two masters, he would serve one and end up hating the other. Jesus, of course, meant that people couldn't serve God and money at the same time, but the principle held true under any circumstance. Shalina thought she might even be able to turn that principle to her advantage if she needed to.

With a steady clip to her gait, she walked back to the library where her car was parked. She double checked the back seat before entering the car. It was a habit she picked up after seeing a television program about a woman being raped by a man who hid in the back of her van. It was an unlikely possibility, but one she couldn't ignore, especially after her and Bart's encounter with the goons from the camp. After assuring herself that the backseat was free of boogiemen or other malcontents, she entered the vehicle and headed for Riverview, not at sure that she would find the church as free of boogiemen.

It was a short drive from the library to the church, but time seemed to warp around her. Somehow, in a way that was beyond her comprehension, the drive took forever and yet was over so quickly that it was as if she didn't even put the car into gear. There were two cars in the parking lot, besides the huge fleet of buses and vans in the fenced area to the west of the church. She couldn't believe her eyes. The church had its own maintenance garage for servicing the multitude of vehicles owned by the church, including the

Mercedes parked in the pastor's spot near the front by the doors. There was no cute sign about coveting the pastor's parking space, but she was fairly sure no one attempted such an affront. That would be an act of blasphemy worthy of stoning the offender. In either case she thought her best option would be to park out of sight behind the bus garage. Fortunately for her the gate was closed but not locked. She was able to park her car in the fenced area without anyone noticing. It was just in time, too, because as she was killing the engine when she saw Quasimodo coming out of the front door of the church. She hoped that meant only one other person was in the church, which might allow her the opportunity to sneak in and look around without being noticed. Of course, that other person happened to be Angus McFarland, the pastor of the church, so there would be several places that would be off limits to her. But she hoped to get in there and possibly wait him out. She could hide in the ladies room if necessary until he left, which she hoped would be soon.

As soon as the hunchback clambered into the bell tower of his Volkswagen Bug and headed off to find Esmeralda, Shalina made her move for the front door. It occurred to her that he might have locked the door behind him, but she thought that since Angus was still inside, the door would still be open. Fortunately for her he left the door not only open, but slightly ajar, as if he were expecting someone to follow closely on his heels. She was glad to oblige him, although she was following his footsteps in reverse.

She was stunned by the opulence exhibited by the members of Riverview Church. She wasn't expecting to find the usual vaulted ceiling with faux beams and indirect fluorescent lighting, but she wasn't expecting the entrance to St Paul's Basilica either. The foyer was larger than many of the smaller churches in the area and contained furniture that would rival most of the fancier homes in town. Somehow all of the money that surrounded her in the form of gold inlays and marbled statues made her heart hurt for those in town that might have benefited from a week's worth of groceries or having an electric bill paid that would have made the difference between having lights or going hungry in the dark. With winter only a few short months away, she was sure there were plenty of people in the ruins and other areas of town that could benefit greatly from having their propane tank filled before the first chill of the season. She knew they would defend their spending by saying something along the lines of it takes money to make money. They would also pull out their budget and show the vast number of social and missionary programs they supported. She understood that for most churches, especially with the new trend toward ever larger mega churches, the balance between the display of wealth and the distribution of aid to the poor was delicate at best and totally out of hand, as it appeared to be with Riverview, at the worst. But she couldn't let the philosophical debate going on her head distract her from her task at hand. She pushed open the double swinging doors leading into the sanctuary and peaked inside.

"So far, so good," she whispered to herself, which turned out to be a huge mistake. The large empty room proved to be a huge echo chamber that would have rivaled the biggest canyon for the ability to send a person's voice back to its source. She paused, waiting to see if the voice was heard by any ears other than her own. Again, it was so far, so good, but this time she declined to say it aloud. Instead, she ventured farther into the sanctuary, following along the path between the outer wall and the plush padded pews. There were doors near the front that she hoped led to either the church clerk's or treasurer's office. Either one might contain information about the financial ties between the camp and the church. It was common knowledge that the church supported the camp. What she hoped to find was how much the community was supporting both and if the money was being spent properly.

She was reaching for the door labeled, "Timothy R. Douglass, Church Treasurer", when she heard the doorknob on the next door begin to twist. It figured, since she didn't trust people with double first names. The connection between the opening door and a person with two first names was illogical, but since she was alone in the room, there was no one to argue the counterpoint. Instead of doing so herself, she dove underneath a pew, embracing the thick carpeting like it was a long lost cousin at a family reunion. Her two fears now were being spotted by Angus and finding someone's bubble gum with her hair. Fortunately, neither one happened.

Angus sped out of the room like a cat with kerosene on its tail. He was moving so fast that he didn't take the luxury of looking back even for a moment, which allowed Shalina the break she had desperately hoped for. She crawled as quickly as she could along the wall toward the door, which was closing all too quickly in front of her. Its shutting would shut out any prospect she might have for finding any real evidence of impropriety going on. God must have been smiling on her that day, because the door was being held open by the automatic cylinder that had gotten stuck just before the latch found its home in the door jamb. With just a little prying, she was able to swing the door back open and enter into the inner sanctum of Angus McFarland, hypocrite extraordinaire.

She had heard stories of other preachers who begged for money in the name of God from poor parishioners while living in the lap of luxury, but she couldn't believe that whatever they had could rival the spectacle of extravagance before her. Some widows in the church gave their mites so he could savor brandy and eat caviar from silver trays while they drank tepid tap water and ate potted meat, if they could afford that much. And all the while, they hung on every word he spoke from the pulpit, whether it came to them live or through one the multimedia formats the church put out on a weekly basis. Some of the gracious grannies probably scraped together pennies and nickels so they could afford to send in their monthly contribution, thus guaranteeing them a constant stream of sermons from the good man of God. She almost puked at the very thought.

She redirected her thoughts to what she had come here for, trying to think of where a man like Angus McFarland would hide his secrets from the rest of the world, including most of the people in his own flock. Riverview was a prime example of a flock being shepherded by not just a wolf, but one of the biggest and baddest wolves of all time. He misled almost everyone he came into contact with, making him one of the most dangerous animals, a man born to be both a pathological and sociopathic liar, which was a very dangerous combination. He not only felt the compulsion to lie, but then didn't feel any remorse for doing so. And there was no doubt in her mind that such a man as Bart had described to her was not only a liar, but much worse. She had more than her fair share of contact with such men as she thought him to be and found that people like that began their careers as liars because they had something to lie about. The practice of constant lying wasn't the disease, just one of the many symptoms of a disease of their psyche that was buried under layer after layer of cover up upon excuse until they no longer thought of themselves as being the sick ones. In such minds as his, the normal people around him were the sick ones, while his mind had found the freedom it so richly deserved.

The question then was, "Where do sick, twisted individuals with psychotic thoughts and paranoid tendencies hide their deepest and darkest secrets?" That was some question. The only problem was that she didn't have a clue. It was hard enough to think like an evil person since she wasn't one, but it was near impossible to channel the thoughts of someone as hateful and twisted as Angus. But she had to try, so she looked around the room, hoping for a visual clue that might lead her to where the "X" might mark the spot. It seemed to her that Ms. Drew always had a map or a treasure trove of clues to sift through by the time she had gotten this far in the mystery. All she had was an empty office, little in the way of time, and a blank, deer in the headlight look on her face. It was hopeless.

"No," she said aloud, unafraid at this point that someone might hear her. She had closed the office door behind her and as far as she could tell she was alone in the vast expanse of Riverview Church. She probably could have sung an aria from The Barber of Seville without it being noticed.

A man such as that probably wouldn't hide anything in obvious areas like his desk. Even the common places that are seen on mystery movies like taped under the drawers or safes hidden behind copies of masterpieces would be past his ego. There was no way he could be considered to be like the rest of common society. She poked around the room, hoping beyond hope that God would send her a sign telling her where to work. She didn't need a flashing neon sign, but it would not bother her too awful much if God decided to work

that way just this once.

Even though she didn't expect to find anything there, she had to start

someplace, so she poked around the desk. Not surprisingly, it was locked.

That didn't stop her from looking, though. She took a letter opener from the

desk caddy and used it to pry the lock open. A quick glance through the files

she found her first assumption proved true. There was nothing there that

would indicate any sort of wrong doing on his part. Most of it had to do with

mundane church business, including sermon outlines and files on members.

There was nothing there that would help Bart.

She looked around the rest of the room. There were several

bookshelves, containing everything from sermon outline books to

commentaries to classics by great preachers of yesteryear. There were also a

number of books that you wouldn't expect to find in a pastor's library. She

studied that section particularly hard, thinking that possibly the pastor was a

little more common than he cared to admit. It would figure that a compilation

of books that stood out from the ordinary would be the place to hide valuable

materials from prying eyes.

She was headed over there when she tripped over her untied shoelace

and stumbled into another bookcase that contained classic literary

masterpieces. Catching herself on the edge of the shelf, her fingers wrapped around the wood, allowing her to regain her balance. But something seemed wrong about the whole thing. It took her a moment to realize that the shelves were supposed to be a singular unit, going from wall to wall. There was a gap in this particular shelf that shouldn't have been there. She tried prying on it to open the gap wider, but although it creaked and groaned some, it didn't give any. She ran back out into the sanctuary and out to the foyer, where she remembered seeing a broom closet. Grabbing the stoutest looking mop handle she could find, she rushed back to the pastor's study.

Her heart was racing with excitement. She wasn't sure what she might find behind the shelf. It would probably be a locked safe, which wouldn't help her in the slightest, but she couldn't think negatively right now. Something had held open the shelf so she could spot the gap and possibly find the evidence she was looking for to incriminate Angus in whatever dirty deed he was up to. Peeking down into the gap, she saw a piece of trash there, possibly a bottle cap that was stopping the shelf from coming together the way it was designed to. Other people might say it was a bottle cap that allowed her to see the opening, but she knew it was the finger of God that was the real reason for her hopeful success.

Using the mop handle as a pry, she tugged and tugged at the shelf, finally feeling it move slightly just as she was at the point of exhaustion. Buoyed by her inch of momentum, she gave a gargantuan pull on the handle.

With her knuckles white from exertion and a torrent of sweat pouring from her brow, she felt the shelf move back into the recess of the wall, revealing a small room inside.

Her elation, however, was short lived when she realized that the room was devoid of anything. It was completely empty. There wasn't even a picture on the wall or anything else for him to hide things behind. She decided to inspect the room more closely anyway. There had to be a reason to hide the room with such an elaborate masquerade. No one in his right mind, even a diabolical mind, would spend that kind of money and time to hide an empty room.

The only thing she found to give any indication that something was amiss in the room was a small slot that looked like it might take an ATM or credit card. Maybe the good shepherd was concealing an ATM machine used for money laundering. Or maybe it was some kind of booth to use for phone sex and the slot was for a credit card. Those were stupid ideas, of course, but as silly as those ideas were, she couldn't think of anything else that was any more feasible. Just on a whim, she took her debit card and slid it into the slot to see what might happen. She half expected the slot to eat her card and return it to her in pieces, but instead it returned it to her. She almost squealed in delight. The idea was far fetched, but it had almost worked, and more importantly, it told her that the slot was a working mechanism of some kind. It wasn't just an empty hole leading to nothingness.

With that thought in mind, she returned to the desk for another search. It was possible that Angus, in his haste to leave, had been careless enough to leave the card that activated whatever it was that needed activation behind. It wasn't likely, but then again, it wasn't likely for her to trip over her own laces and just happen to catch her fingers on an opening of about an inch in width. She prayed quickly even as she scanned the top of the desk.

She couldn't believe her eyes. There, right on the corner of the desk was what looked like a hotel key card. She had almost knocked it to the floor while she was rifling through the desk moments before. With baited anticipation, she grabbed the card and carefully slid it into the slot.

Her knees buckled beneath her as the room began its descent. Of all the reactions she might have anticipated, the room sinking into the ground beneath her feet was the farthest from her mind. It was an elevator of all things! She had no idea where the ride would take her, so she steeled her mind for almost anything.

The sight that greeted her as the elevator finished the descent was far greater than what she had prepared herself for. Row upon row of women's clothing, mixed with body parts in specimen jars, together with pictures and other memorabilia were on shelves. It was like a macabre, twisted version of a junior high biology laboratory. Instead of frogs and snakes in formaldehyde, however, there were ears, fingers and toes, and what looked like a baby in a jar. She was so taken with the whole scene that she failed to notice at first the woman laying on the table in the middle of the room. It wasn't until she moaned in pain that Shalina took notice of her.

She was on the type of table used in hospital delivery rooms, situated in there as if she were ready to give birth at any moment. There was only one problem with the scene. She didn't appear to be the slightest bit pregnant. She was groggy, almost asleep. Shalina ran to her to see if she could help. She felt like an actress in a bad B-movie. She hoped that if this were a horror movie that she was the lead role instead of one of the supporting characters who gets killed just before doing something heroic. So far the plot line indicated she was more of the leading role type. She hoped that would continue to hold true as her shoes clicked along the concrete floors.

"Are you all right?" she asked the woman on the table. She got a muffled groan in response. She always felt so stupid asking a question like that. A woman is laying on a table with her legs up in stirrups, obviously in a drugged stupor, and all she could do was ask if she was alright.

"Uh-huh," came the drugged response. "Are you the angel I've been praying for?"

"If that's who I need to be," Shalina responded. "Do you think you can walk if I take the straps off?" Cassandra answered with a slow but definite nod of yes. She didn't want to be on that table any longer. It was a horrible reminder of what almost was. If that man hadn't come when he did, she was sure to have become another trophy on the wall of shame that Angus kept. She wasn't sure if the woman helping her was really an angel. All that mattered was that she was a messenger of God sent to save her in a desperate moment. It was her first moment as a new Christian, and it was destined to be a memorable one. She tried to concentrate on the woman's features so she could memorize her face but the drugs refused to allow her eyes to work at full capacity. No matter how hard she tried, she couldn't see much more than a head of sandy blonde hair. If someone were to ask her later what the person looked like who helped her, she wouldn't be able to tell them much more than a blonde haired woman. For all she knew, it might actually be a man with a really high pitched voice. None of that mattered though in the heat of the moment. What did matter is that within minutes she would be free again.

"Come on," Shalina urged. "I'll help hold you up." With a little struggle and a great deal of pain, Cassandra managed to get to her feet and was walking to the waiting elevator. Together the two women made it to the door leading outside without incident. Shalina leaned her charge against one of the marbled pillars on the porch while she retrieved the car. She hated leaving the young lady alone, but neither one thought she could make it the distance from the church to the car.

After loading her into the passenger seat, where she promptly passed back out, Shalina drove her to the hospital she had seen earlier. It was a short drive from the church to the hospital and Shalina spent it trying to figure out who this woman was. She didn't find a purse or any other personal effects around the area she found her in. She didn't spend a whole lot of time looking, of course, but in the quick scan she made there was nothing to be found. That made sense. After all, an abduction victim hardly has the chance to gather her belongings before being kidnapped.

When they arrived at the hospital, Shalina pulled up to the emergency room entrance, aided a half asleep Cassandra into a wheelchair, honked the horn several times and then pulled away, looking into the rearview mirror to make sure someone was coming out to help her. She hated not staying around to explain and possibly help more, but there wasn't much more she could do to help. She didn't know for sure if the woman was drugged or just drunk. She didn't know who the woman was or why she was being held prisoner in an underground bunker beneath the church. There were several questions she couldn't answer about the woman and several more she didn't want to answer about herself. Still, her conscience was bothering her and she was about to turn around when she heard a terrible commotion coming from the other side of the hospital. Horns were honking wildly, tires were squalling, and stereos blaring as loud as any rock concert she heard. With all of the turmoil in the

Bar T. Rancher

area, she was sure there were bound to be police in the area quickly. That

made her decision easy. With all of the tires burning rubber on the other side

of the hospital, no one noticed as she left her own set of marks on the parking

lot as she left.

CHAPTER FOURTEEN

Sheriff Jake was as nervous as the proverbial long tailed cat. He was also being pulled into several different directions at the same time. Bart had recently been teaching during their home Bible study about the evils of allowing cloning for the purpose of harvesting parts or stem cells from embryos. Jake didn't understand the science behind what Bart was talking about and he trusted his pastor and friend with his life, but right now he would gladly allow himself to be cloned so he could go in three different directions, including staying where he was.

He was hearing over his radio the disruption that was going on at the hospital. Even though he desperately wanted to check out what was going on there, he knew that he was too far away to be of any use if there was a problem. By the time he would have arrived, the action would have been over if there were any action to begin with. Judging from the report he was getting from Deputy Lamb, it sounded like a bunch of kids who just happened to pick a bad night to act like a bunch of idiots. Hopefully Lamb got some license plates and they could trace down the culprits later.

He also wanted to be looking for the wraith known as Shalina. So far as he could tell, Bart was the only one in town who had seen her. Although out of the ordinary, it wasn't totally out of the question. People bumped into more strangers than they realized every day of their lives and never

349

remembered seeing any of them. It was one reason, he suspected, that people had a hard time finding the things they looked for even though they had just seen it the day before. Because they weren't focused on the object when they saw it, they didn't catalog the surroundings they saw it in. So when they began looking for it, they couldn't remember where they had seen it. It was the same with people. People saw people every day, but because they aren't important in their lives, they don't imprint on the registry of the mind. Bart said she was real, and that was good enough for him. Besides, even if she were a fantasy, Bart's friendship meant that he deserved the benefit of the doubt.

Then there was Cassandra. There was absolutely no doubt that she was real and there was no doubt that she was in danger. Jake wanted to go to the camp, raze it like Sherman over Georgia and sift through the debris until he came across Cassandra's living and breathing body. The problem was that if he did try a raid on the camp, neither her nor he would be likely to come out alive. If there were no connection between Megiddo and the disappearance of Cassandra, then it would only be his career that was killed. On the other hand, if there was a connection, which seemed more likely at this point, they would have him outgunned and definitely outmanned. He knew from their previous visit to the camp that it would take a Ranger unit to infiltrate that area without raising the alarms.

His only real option was to stay where he was and take care of the moment at hand. As hard as that was for him to accept, he knew he didn't really have a choice. Phil the ferret was taking center stage on karaoke night and everyone loved the tune he was singing. Once he realized that he was up on federal charges and out of the reach of either Angus' or Shane's sphere of influence, he began throwing information faster than they could catch. He was spilling the beans on several prominent officials, from local county judges to people connected in the governor's office and all points in between. Some of those exposed reminded Jake of one other destination he wanted to go to. He had some house cleaning of his own to take care of. There were two of his deputies named in Philip's indictment of government corruption. He wanted them taken down as quickly as possible. Agent O'Neill had a theory about that subject.

"If you were Angus, how would you react when you found out Philip had Bart assaulted?" the federal agent asked.

"I don't know," Jake answered. "I suppose it would depend on whether I ordered the hit or not."

"Let's assume you didn't. After all, is it in your interest to disrupt whatever you're doing by beating up on a local pastor? I mean, to have him killed might be a possibility if you think he's getting too close, but to have him just abused is personal, not professional."

"So you think Philip acted on his own, using Shane's guys as his own personal resource?"

"That's my professional opinion," observed the elder agent. He was in his fifties, a no nonsense baby boomer who had seen his generation drug, drink, and degenerate themselves into the annals of history as one of the most decadent group of individuals since the time of Nero and Rome. He wore a plain brown suit with a matching tie and a white, neatly pressed, highly starched shirt. Jake assumed, and rightly so, that he had several other outfits in his closet to match. He wasn't in this business to win friends or influence people. His objective was to remove scum like Philip from the sole of America's foot and he would do whatever he could to make sure it happened. Jake knew he chose to serve in Vietnam even though he had a chance at a college scholarship. When he returned from the conflict overseas, he had to face it all over again when he finally had the chance to return to campus. Even while working to pay for his education, he managed to shove a four year degree into three and went to work immediately with the Bureau, where he remained for the last thirty years. He was already eligible for retirement and the easy life on a beach in Florida, but he felt like he still had something to give.

"If I were Shane or Angus for that matter, I'd order a hit on Philip," Jake commented. "He's nothing but a liability now."

"That's what I thought. I also thought that if you're game, we'd give your two deputies the chance to make themselves a bonus from the McFarland

brothers by making the hit."

"What are you talking about?" Jake wondered. "I don't like Philip and

there's nothing more I'd like than to attend his memorial, but I can't use him

as live bait when he's going to be the star witness for the prosecution." Jake

looked in at Philip, who was sitting at a makeshift desk writing down details

of the McFarland brother's operations in full detail. Oliver had gone upstairs

to the loft bedroom to see if he could get some sleep. Jake heard him

occasionally roll over in the bed, obviously getting troubled sleep, if any. He

had really come through for himself and for Jake, as well as for Bart. It was

too bad Philip didn't know anything about Cassandra's abduction, other than

the fact that she hadn't been brought to the camp. The way he was spilling his

guts about the financial and criminal activities of the two brothers, Jake had

no doubt that he wouldn't hold back anything about Cassandra if he knew it.

Still, there were some questions they might have failed to ask.

"Is this the first time they've taken a woman hostage?" he asked the

ferret, interrupting his writing.

"If she's been taken by them," Philip said, "it's not as a hostage, at

least not in the normal sense of the word. I've heard about the boy's insatiable

desires, especially Angus. I've heard stories about him that would make me

seem normal, even desirable, in comparison to him, if you know what I

353

mean."

"No," O'Neill said dryly, "we don't know what you mean. Why don't you enlighten us?"

"I wanted to have sex with Oliver, okay? I've already confessed to that and to several other counts that you wouldn't have known about. But I just wanted the companionship of a young boy for awhile. When I was finished with him, he could go back to his normal life, relatively unharmed."

"I don't want to know your relatives if that's how they define unharmed," Jake commented. "But what do you mean by that? Does Angus kill his victims? And if so, how has he been getting away with it?"

"Let's just say that he usually is more selective in his companionship. Usually he picks those who no one will miss. He picks through the rubble of society until he finds one without those who'll ask questions later."

"What about the bodies?" O'Neill wanted to know. "He has to be able to dispose of the bodies."

"That's where his boys in blue come in," Philip answered.

"How so?" Jake asked.

"Let's just say they know where to pick up the trash," Philip responded.

Jake and O'Neill went back to the kitchen for more coffee, leaving Philip to finish his writing. Both of them hated having a dirty cop on the force and Jake was kicking himself for not seeing it earlier. He had seen them disappear at times they couldn't, or wouldn't, account for later. One of them had recently bought a new speed boat, which should have given him a clue, but he just put it off to his wife working and having good credit.

"I should have seen it," he spoke to his coffee.

"You were too close to the forest to see the trees," O'Neill commented. "It happens."

"I wasn't too close to the forest. I live in that forest everyday. I have lunch with those trees. I've been to their kid's recitals and kindergarten graduations. I was even the one that introduced one of those cedars to his wife."

"Cedars? Why do you call them cedars?"

"Cause I hate cedars. Ever since me and Melissa have started clearing our farm property we've run into nothing but scrubby, nasty, itchy, stinky old cedars. I swear for everyone I cut down, two more grow up in its place."

"Well," O'Neill stated, "when we cut these down, we can use them as kindling for starting a forest fire. Now, how about our plan?" Jake left Philip in O'Neill's capable hands while he went and talked to Oliver.

"Hey, sleeping beauty," he said, nudging the sleeping boys shoulders. "I need to ask you something."

"Uh-huh," Oliver said, rubbing the sleep from his eyes. Jake was amazed at how quickly the young man had been able to put the events of the previous few hours out of his mind so he could sleep. Or maybe it was the other way around. Maybe the events wouldn't leave him alone so sleep was his only refuge.

"Agent O'Neill and I have to leave for a little while. Would you be okay here on your own?"

"All night?" Oliver wondered.

"Yeah, but O'Neill is calling a relative of his who lives nearby. He'll be here about fifteen minutes from now. Could you handle that?" Oliver assured Jake he could. He didn't feel good about spending the night in a cabin that could have been used as a backdrop for any number of horror movies, but with another federal agent in the house, one who hopefully carried some heavy fire power, he figured things would be all right. Besides, one more night here meant one less night at home. He had the days numbered until graduation and college. He loved his mom and dad; he just couldn't stand to be around either of them. They needed some serious help, and so would he if he had to live there much longer.

"We'll drop Philip off along our way to the safe house," O'Neill instructed Jake. "Then we'll call your guys and have them meet us there."

"Will that give us enough time?" Jake wondered. "It's a long ride back to town on these dirt roads."

"Don't worry. I've got my guys already in place if we don't get there in time. They know what to do. I know you want to be there for the collar, but we need to think more about getting the job done instead of who's doing it."

"I know," Jake admitted. "I just don't want to see anyone get stupid and get killed. I know those guys and if anything goes wrong, I think I'd be able to talk them out of doing anything."

"Correction," O'Neill stated. "You don't know those guys. The men you know are honest, hard working cops who pay their bills, love their families, and do the job they've been paid to do. These guys aren't any of those things."

"You saying they don't love their families?" Jake asked.

"Would they shame them this way if they did?" O'Neill replied. It was hard for Jake to admit, but he knew O'Neill was right. A person that was willing to cheat, even if his excuse was his family, would probably be willing to cheat on his family. There had to be honor in a man's soul for him to truly care about those he loved. That didn't mean that everyone had to be a paragon of virtue or that everyone who ever violated the law was a despot of evil, but it did mean that there needed to be at least a part of that person's make up that could tell wrong from right and was willing to decide on the side of right when the chips were down. He knew that careers in law enforcement tended to attract a certain kind of individual. It was usually those who saw the world in terms of black and white, without shades of grey. Maybe that's why he and

Bart were able to get along so well with each other; they knew that the world,

despite what the majority of people in their respective careers said, didn't

operate in a strict black and white fashion. There had to be shades of grey for

true freedom to exist.

"I've contacted Johnson and Allen. They're supposed to meet us at the

safe house like you wanted. I told them not to go in, just stand watch at the

door."

"Good," O'Neill complimented. "If they're clean, they'll do as they're

told and stay outside. If not, my men know how to disarm without killing

them. We don't want them dead any more than you do. That would only serve

to make them martyrs and you the fall guy for a police corruption scandal. If

we can contain this with those two, we might avert a public relations fiasco."

"I'm more concerned about them being able to tell us where Cassandra

might be," Jake corrected.

"Me too," O'Neill agreed. "But if we can keep a lid on this as well,

then so much the better."

"I doubt the lid will stay on for very long once his testimony begins,"

Jake said, pointing to Philip, whom had just been handed over to another

agent. O'Neill was about to comment on that possibility and that as long as

the lid stayed on long enough to get a grand jury convened it was fine with him, when the crackle of the radio interrupted his thoughts.

"This is Agent Bruner," the radio said.

"Go ahead, Bruner," O'Neill replied.

"We've got visitors, both in plain clothes, and both of them carrying. They're like mice heading for the cheese," he stated. Jake wasn't surprised, but he was disappointed. He had hoped that Philip had been wrong about his two men. There were times when he had disagreements with Allen, but he always thought he was a professional. In fact, most of their disagreements had been about Jake's lack of protocol in running the office in a more professional manner. Allen especially hated the times when Jake called Bart in to help with an investigation. To Allen, it was conduct close to mutiny or treason for the Sheriff to bring in an amateur to a crime scene or investigation. Jake remembered the last time they had words. It was at the Swenson girl's murder. As Jake thought about that scene, he remembered having to scold the other man for denigrating a crime scene. Maybe as he looked at it, it wasn't as much of an accident as he had originally thought.

Johnson came as a real surprise. There were more times than he could remember that Johnson had been his only back up. It was that way with the Holden's. Johnson was on the scene then, ready to respond in a flash to a radio call from his Sheriff and friend.

Friend? Could he really use that word about a man who had betrayed him and everything that both of them had supposedly stood for during all of

the time they had known each other. He didn't think he ever had associated

that word with Allen. He was a colleague, an acquaintance, but not a friend.

And as it turned out, neither was Johnson.

"Where are they now?" O'Neill demanded.

"Heading down the hall for the back room where our prisoner is

asleep," Bruner replied. "They've opened the door and are aiming their

pistols."

"Hold fire until they've shot," O'Neill instructed. He knew he didn't

have to tell them how to do their jobs. They were all experienced officers who

had been highly trained to do the job they were doing. But he wanted to be in

charge in case anything went wrong. That way, he could take the blame for

any fallout that might occur. They heard two shots come through the radio.

Jake was even more disappointed. He figured his men would know enough to

use a silencer when they were in town so they wouldn't attract attention to

themselves. He didn't want his guys to be crooked, but he especially didn't

want them to be crooked and stupid. There was yelling coming over the air,

and then silence.

Jake and O'Neill could both imagine in their mind's eye what the

scene must look like. Johnson and Allen were just inside the room with their

nine millimeters drawn. Two shots echo through the room as each of them put a blazing hot projectile into the dummy that's "sleeping" on the bed with its back toward them. They move forward slightly, lowering their weapons, but not holstering them. One of them, probably Allen, reaches forward to make sure that they've gotten by with a clean kill. That's when, in that unguarded moment where each of them is slightly relaxed, they'll hear the voice behind them ordering them to drop their weapons and lay flat on the floor. They're smart. They know that even though they only hear one voice, there are at least six different guns on them. They don't want to go to prison, but that's still to be decided. It's a possibility. It's a good possibility, because they know they've been caught with their hand in the cookie jar of corruption, but the only other possibility is a firefight with six men they can't see. That outcome is decided before they have a chance to react. They might be good enough to get one, possibly wing another, but then they'll be dead. Even if they're not dead, the list of charges would include killing a cop, which means the death penalty is on the table. Neither man wants that, so they drop their weapons on the bed next to the dummy they've just killed and lay quietly on the floor so federal agents can come over and put handcuffs on them while their rights are read to them. It's a familiar scene to each man, but in other times, at other places, it was them reading the rights and putting on the handcuffs.

"We have the suspects in custody," Bruner reported with a tinge of regret in his voice. Normally when a collar was made, everyone was elated.

361

That was, of course, until judges and defense attorneys became involved it should be a simple matter of catch bad guy, put bad guy in jail, don't let bad guy out for long, long time. This time, however, it was one of their own that was going down for the count. That stained the reputation of each of them, and it hurt each one of them to the core to find out they were right.

"Keep them there until we arrive," O'Neill instructed. "We're around five minutes out. Don't talk to either and don't let either one talk to each other until we arrive."

"Got it," Bruner responded. "Any further instructions?" He knew that normally O'Neill wouldn't have been micromanaging each detail as he had been this operation. It was a good thing for the Sheriff that the agency had been using this place as a safe place for some time. That meant that an operation that should have taken a week of preparation was able to be implemented within an hour. It was highly unusual, which meant that O'Neill wasn't trying to grab glory, but take blame if necessary.

"Yeah," O'Neill said. "Let our boys in blue know they're getting a visit from their boss sometime tonight. It might put them in a more talkative mood if they know he's coming."

When they arrived at the safe house, Jake was taken aback just a little by its location. It was the farm house he and Melissa had been looking at earlier that summer. It adjoined the farm property they had been clearing and planned to build on soon. They had hoped to buy the farm house and its one and a half acres so they would be able to move out to the farm while they worked on their new home. Melissa had even wanted to stay in the old place and fix it up rather than build a new place. She said it had character. O'Neill agreed.

"It's a great place," he assured the young Sheriff. "New plumbing was installed last year, and all of the downstairs floors were redone recently. It'll be coming on the market soon, if you're still interested."

"I don't know if Melissa will still want it knowing someone was almost killed in it," Jake said.

"Just a dummy," O'Neill corrected. "There hasn't been a drop of blood shed in any room of this house except the kitchen. And that's just cause Bruner is a klutz with a knife."

"Boy, a guy tries to put a little extra meat in with the chili and you guys won't let him ever forget it." Bruner stood in the open doorway. He was everything in a federal agent that O'Neill wasn't. He looked more like an extra on <u>Miami Vice</u> than a bona fide federal agent. He had on a white shirt with huge billowy sleeves, tight jeans that looked like they were grown on his body, and a big dangling earring hanging from his left ear.

"One of these days I'm gonna grab that thing and use it as bait," O'Neill told his partner.

"You ain't getting it out of my ear," Bruner told him.

"I wasn't planning on it. I like deep sea fishing for barracuda and shark. Now, where's our guys?" Bruner led them to the same back room where Roscoe, the dummy, had been shot only moments earlier.

"He takes a lot of abuse," Bruner informed Jake. Some other time, Jake would have found that funny, but at the moment he didn't think the Stooges could make him laugh.

"Where is she?" he asked Allen, who was the one left in the room. Johnson was taken to a room upstairs.

"Who?" Allen shot back. Jake had to resist the urge to smack his former deputy. He didn't want anything like a civil right's infraction to jeopardize the case they had against the two.

"Cassandra Green," Jake replied. "We know Angus snatched her earlier. What we don't know is where he'll hold her, at the camp or somewhere else."

"And you expect me to be able to help?" Allen snapped.

"I expect you to help yourself, but I'm not waiting forever. I gave you first shot cause you were down here and I didn't want to climb steps. But that's fine. I could always use the exercise." He turned and left the room without further comment, with Allen calling his name behind him. Jake figured if Johnson wouldn't talk, Allen would. It didn't matter to him who ended up with the deal as long as he got the information he wanted.

"Guess I stepped in it this time," Johnson said, refusing to raise his head for eye contact.

"You're covered in it from head to toe," Jake agreed. "You're only hope of not drowning in it is to tell us where Angus is holding Cassandra Green."

"I don't know the name," Johnson said, still staring at the patterns in the old linoleum, "but if he has her, she's at the church."

"He'd defile the church that way?" Jake asked in disgust.

"He'd defile Heaven given half the chance," Johnson answered. "The only thing Angus McFarland cares about is Angus McFarland, and God help anyone who gets in his way."

"Then you better start praying for me," Jake responded. "Because I'm getting in his way and I ain't moving until he goes down."

"You haven't got a prayer, Jake," Johnson said sadly. "He knows people. He buys and sells people like some guys buy and sell cars. He bought my soul and I didn't even know it."

"He's got no right to you or your soul," Jake said in defiance. "Whatever you gave him you can take back, because it still belongs to you. Now tell me the best way in to the church without being seen."

"How long has the girl been missing?" Johnson asked.

"Several hours. Why?" Jake said in response.

"Because you're probably going there to collect a body." Before Jake could respond, a knock came at the door.

"Just a minute," he ordered. He wanted a chance to ask Johnson what he meant by them just collecting a body, but the knock was persistent.

"What is it?" he almost yelled at Deputy Lamb, who should have been at the hospital.

"Sorry, Sheriff," the older man said with almost a tear in his throat. "I failed you."

"Has something happened to Bart?" Jake barked.

"Not yet, sir. He and that black preacher from across town engineered an escape. We think they're looking for Miss Green."

"Or Shalina," Jake said.

"Who?" Deputy Lamb asked.

"Never mind," Jake replied. "It doesn't matter now. What does matter is how long it will take you to get the rest of the guys together so we can go rescue that idiot pal of mine before he does something stupid like getting himself killed."

"There's something else you should know," Lamb said, shuffling his feet back and forth like a schoolboy waiting in the principal's office for his spanking.

"What is it, Lamb?" Jake asked with a little more irritation in his voice than he intended. It had been a long day, his best friend should be laying in a hospital room but was too busy playing Rambo, he was looking for one girl who he had recently been told was probably dead, and needed to be looking for another girl who probably didn't even exist. On top of all that, he had learned earlier that most of his state was a spider web of corruption and that two of his fellow officers were a part of that tangled web. So he felt a little more than justified in being irritated.

"It's Miss Green, sir. She's at the hospital, but I don't know how long she's going to stay there."

"She's all right?" Jake asked, elated at the news that one of his worries was off the list, for the moment anyway.

"She was drugged, but she's recovering quickly," Lamb reported. "But if you want to talk to her, you better get over there fast. She was talking about going to the camp, kicking butt and taking names."

"Is that all she said?" Jake wondered.

"She said something about nuking them all and letting God sort them out," Lamb answered. "I didn't know what else to do, so I called dispatch and they told me where you'd be. What's up with Johnson and Allen? I seen Allen downstairs and he don't look so good."

"I'll explain later," Jake assured him. "Right now, I need to find Agent

367

O'Neill and have him take me to the hospital before Mrs. Rambo joins her husband."

"Huh?"

"Like I said, never mind. Just get back to headquarters and wait there for word from me. Call in every deputy and reserve we have. It looks like it could be a long night."

"It already has been, sir, and it's just now eight o'clock." Jake found O'Neill and Bruner. He explained the situation as best as he could and asked them to give him a ride to the hospital. If there was going to be as much trouble in his town as it looked like, he was going to need all the help he could get. Unlike other policemen, he didn't have a problem letting the feds take over where they could.

CHAPTER FIFTEEN

Oliver went down to the kitchen to get a soda or something. He wasn't really all that thirsty, but he was bored and tired of tossing back and forth like a ping pong ball in a league tournament. He wished he had asked Sheriff Jake to take him back to town, even if it meant sitting in the station by himself. There was no sense moaning about it at this point. Soon an agent would be coming to keep him company and then maybe he'd be able to go back to sleep. It was impossible to slumber when the room you're in is closing in on you while you snore. Besides, he heard noises out here that he never heard in the city. His mind told him those noises were just blowing breezes, bugs and beasties that make their home in the wild. That was the problem. He wasn't a beastie and the closest he had been to the wild was a walk his church sponsored at the park. He didn't even go to church camp, which was through no fault of his own. His mother preferred him to be close enough to hear her yelling, which meant he couldn't leave the county.

Someone knocked at the door, causing him to jump and nearly spill his soda all over the front of his shirt. Regaining his composure, he went to the front door and opened it. He closed it almost as quickly.

"Hello," a female voice called out. "My Uncle Tipper sent me here. My name is Jackie. Didn't he tell you I was coming?"

"Sorry," Oliver apologized after reopening the door. "I wasn't expecting someone like you."

"What should I look like," she wondered as she pushed back the screen door and welcomed herself into the cabin. She sat on the fireplace and poked at the fire. Oliver thought she was probably the prettiest girl he had ever seen.

"You should be old and ugly," Oliver spat out clumsily. "I mean, well, I just wasn't expecting someone as young and pretty as you." She smiled shyly. Oliver couldn't believe she didn't know how absolutely gorgeous she was. She had short blond hair that hung in little ringlets over her ears and down the nape of her neck, stopping just short of covering her collar. Her skin was tan, but not with the unearthly glow that most of the popular girls at school had. This looked more like a natural tan, one that came from time spent in the sun doing things like hiking or swimming. As her collar slipped down, Oliver noticed that she did have tan lines, something the girls at school wouldn't tolerate.

"Well," she said, "sorry to disappoint you. Maybe I should just leave."

"No," Oliver shouted. "I mean, no, please don't leave. It's been so boring here, and I can't sleep." He felt like such an idiot. Most guys his age would have killed to be in the situation he was in and all he could think about was how long the day had been and how he wouldn't be able to sleep now that Uncle Tipper sent his bodacious niece over to baby sit him. He must look like the world's largest nerd to her. Why shouldn't he look like a nerd? He was one after all. Even his pastor thought he lacked some of the necessary social skills needed to function in society. The problem wasn't as simple as all that, however. He had the skills needed to survive, and possibly even thrive in an ordinary setting. He could cope with light conversation and small talk. He didn't even have a problem with social events like dances and sports. He was fairly good at some sports. He wasn't first string, but he wasn't the last one picked at recess either. In high society, he might actually stand a chance someday, if that chance ever came his way. In high school society, however, he was on the lower order of the evolutionary ladder. So the attention of someone like Jackie made him feel awkward and less than adequate to say the least.

"Would you like me to tuck you in?" she asked teasingly. His mind screamed yes. In fact, it screamed yes a thousand different times in over thirty four languages. Just the thought of him being in a bedroom with a beautiful girl was enough to send chills down his spine. He wasn't really contemplating going to bed with her, not in a sexual way anyhow. He had determined early in life that he was going to be a virgin when he married, something else that ended up as a black mark in the social register of high school. Still, the thought of her setting on the edge of the bed as he drifted off to slumber land gave him a warm fuzzy feeling all over his body.

"How about watching some TV instead," Oliver suggested. He didn't see a television in the room, and hadn't noticed one upstairs, although he might have missed it.

"There's not one here, silly," she stated. Bingo!

"Oh, well then how about we walk to your place. I'll come back over by myself when it's time for bed. Does that sound like a deal?"

"You're smarter than you look," she told him, but agreed to the deal. The idea of staying in a cabin with no television, computer, or any other electronic means of entertainment didn't exactly appeal to her either. The night was still young and she didn't want to spend it playing cards, if they even had those in the cabin. She was sure they must have someplace, but she preferred Oliver's idea over hide and seek with a deck of cards. Her house was just about a mile away, so she walked to the cabin, and she wasn't relishing the idea of such a quick turn around. Still, she thought she would rather take another mile hike rather than sit around and twiddle their thumbs together.

"I'm game if you are," Oliver offered.

"So what are we waiting for?" she said. Oliver grabbed his hat and headed for the front door, where he was grabbed by Jackie.

"What's that about?" he quizzed her.

"It'll be quicker through the woods," she explained.

372

"But its dark now," Oliver protested. "We won't be able to see our way through there."

"Don't be such a worry wart. I know these woods like the back of my hand. I could walk through them blindfolded."

"Fine for you," Oliver said. "But I'm all out of blindfolds."

"Just hold my hand and you'll be fine," she told him. They slipped out the back door and began their trek towards Jackie's house. With no light, they tumbled over some firewood that was stacked by the back porch, but after brushing themselves off and assuring each other that they were alright, they headed off into the woods without further incident.

CHAPTER SIXTEEN

Bart and Marc were set up next to the fence. The angle of the small valley that guided the creek kept the cameras from focusing on this area, giving them the cover they needed to plan their next step. Despite Marc's greater size and his obvious ability with weaponry, made evident from his handling of both the handgun and rifle that Bart had brought for the bigger man, Bart still wished he had been able to bring Jake along for the ride. Unfortunately, though, Jake was still a man of the law above everything else and was held by that code. Bart respected that and that respect meant that he couldn't allow Jake to compromise himself on a mission that although totally necessary, was mostly illegal.

"It's straight up eight," Marc told Bart, glancing at his indiglo watch. "What time did you want to move on this place?"

"I'd love to go in now," Bart said. "But when I was here the other day, I noticed the new guards were coming on at two. Hopefully, they work a straight eight hour shift, which means they'll be changing shifts at ten. We'll wait for the shift change when the new guards are going over paperwork and the old guards are in the showers."

"I hope the day guards will be in bed, too," Marc added. "Maybe we'll be lucky and they're the kind of folks that go to bed with the chickens."

"Yeah, but you and I don't believe in luck, do we?" Bart added.

"We're the kind of folks that believe God answers prayers. So why don't we use our time doing something useful." Marc wholeheartedly agreed so the two of them spent the next couple of hours praying, sometimes silently, at other times vocalizing their prayers. Marc tended to be more emotionally responsive than Bart and there were times when Bart would have to calm his friend down so they wouldn't end up being caught during their revival time.

While the preachers were spending their time in prayer, the good sheriff was spending his trying to talk sense into one Cassandra Green.

"We can't bust in there like storm troopers, Cassandra, no matter how angry you are," Jake told her. She was defiant, however, and refused to be dissuaded, no matter what logic or argument was presented to her.

"I can have a team ready within the hour," she proclaimed. "I've been working undercover with the ATF for a year now trying to get into that camp and now that Angus McFarland has been stupid enough to give me just cause, I'm not going to let a little thing like my emotions get in the way."

"Boy," Agent O'Neill interjected, "I'm sure glad we don't have a young woman in charge of our nuclear warheads."

"How's that?" Cassandra demanded.

"I was just thinking that we'd all be in trouble if Russia or someone else started playing games at the wrong time of the month, if you know what I mean."

"No," Cassandra said sharply, narrowing her eyes on the elder agent, "I don't know what you mean. Why don't you try explaining that totally sexist remark so I can get it right when I report it to the EEO?"

"Hold on," Jake interrupted "We're all a little edgy tonight."

"Really," Cassandra stated. "And how many other people here were nearly raped and dismembered by a madman, hmm?"

"You know what I mean. I just think that if we're going to go into a camp that we suspect is filled with armed men carrying high powered rifles, we ought to go in with a plan rather than going in with our guns a 'blazing like Wyatt Earp and Doc Holliday." Although she would have preferred going in with the idea of shooting anything that moved and explaining to her superiors and the EPA why there wasn't a single animal alive within a mile radius of the camp, she knew Jake was right. Maybe, in his own Neanderthal way, Agent O'Neill was right as well. Women tended to allow emotion to carry them too far at times, while some men she knew didn't allow their emotions to carry them far enough. Where was Bart at? Why hadn't he even come to check on her or call the hospital to find out if she was alright? Jake said he was out trying in his own way to facilitate her rescue, but for all she knew that was a case of one friend covering for another, which wouldn't be unusual. Normally, their stories weren't as creative as Jake's, but she knew Bart wasn't a normal, usual kind of person so it made sense that Jake wouldn't make up normal, usual kind of excuses to cover for him.

"The first thing we need to do is gather the evidence from the church," Cassandra offered.

"Already on that," Agent O'Neill said, "I've got men and women all over that place. Sorry, but I have a hard time calling it a church now that I know what went on there right under the noses of the congregation."

"From what I understand," Cassandra said, "it wasn't just under the noses of some of them, but with their permission and help. I don't know how good people can get so twisted by one man so easily." It was a hard question to answer, but it had happened time and time again. There were monuments of mankind's misguided attempts to manipulate their fellow men throughout time and the known world. Places like Guyana conjured images of death and destruction because one man twisted the emotions and wills of other men until the line that distinguished good from evil became lost in a maze of smoke and mirrors. After the dust settled, it was hard to tell where the will of the masses left off and the will of one man took over.

"Then the camp is our next move," Jake stated, "but we still don't need to go in there like gangbusters. Anyone got an idea on how we can get in without being party crashers?"

"How many people saw you come in the hospital?" Agent O'Neill asked Cassandra.

"Don't know for sure," she said. "I was pretty out of it how I got here. In fact, I'm not even sure how I did get here. I remember something about an angel coming for me, but I don't know for sure if she was real or if somehow I managed to get myself out of there. People here tell me I just kind of showed up during the ruckus in the front parking lot. For all I know one of those guys saved me and then used that distraction to get away without being noticed."

"Someone engineered a mob scene just so they could remain anonymous about rescuing you?" Agent O'Neill asked.

"I know," Cassandra admitted, "it doesn't really make sense to me either. But I don't know how else to explain it other than maybe it was really an angel that rescued me. That couldn't be, could it?"

"We'll leave that for Bart to answer," Jake responded. "For now we still need a plan to get into the camp."

"I was coming to that if we could focus for a little bit," O'Neill said. "As far as we know Angus doesn't know about her escape and he still thinks Philip was killed by your crooked cops" The words stung Jake. He couldn't bear the thought of two of his key officers being on the payroll of the McFarland brothers. On top of that, he had no idea where Bart was or what he was doing at the moment. His best friend was hurting and should still be lying in a hospital bed instead of...doing what whatever it was he was doing.

"Your point?" Jake asked.

378

"My point is that we could use the dirty cops to get into the camp. One of them, whichever one you trust the most, can drive right into the camp to report on Philip's untimely demise. I'll be in the trunk, Miss America here can squat down in the back seat, and I think with you in uniform, you can ride shotgun."

"And once we get there, then what?" Cassandra asked.

"Then your team and mine can come in behind us and clean up the mess."

"Sounds like a plan to me," Jake said, "or at least the start of one. We can make up the rest as we go along. I'll begin by talking to Johnson. I think Allen would be more of a hindrance than a help. Allen's been a little jealous and very bitter since I've been elected Sheriff. I should have seen this coming, but I've always been one of those to see the best in people and I guess I wanted to see the best in him too, even if it wasn't there to see."

It was a long trip to the camp, made all the longer by the tension in the car that increased exponentially with each mile marker that clicked by. O'Neill was on the radio, organizing a strike force to be on standby just outside the fence. Cassandra was speaking to her people as well, informing them that they would be coordinating their efforts with the FBI, which went over like steak at a conference of vegetarians. Still, they would do what they were told, whether they liked it or not. Jake kept on radio silence. As far as he knew, Johnson and Allen were the only dirty deputies on his force, but there were a lot of incidental people that he wouldn't trust until he had a chance to check them out. There were dispatchers, lawyers, court reporters and others that hung around the station and could call the camp to warn them. Besides, half the people in the county entertained themselves by listening to their scanners and talking about what they heard about the next day over the fence or over coffee at the café the next morning. Either way, they didn't need that kind of news going out over the original information super highway.

They arrived at the camp just after ten, but decided to wait another fifteen or twenty minutes before approaching the gate, using those precious moments of peace to finalize plans and prepare mentally for the challenge ahead of them. Johnson tried to use that time to apologize to Jake for all of the wrong he had done, but he made the mistake of trying to excuse his behavior by telling them about money problems he and his family were facing.

"You've got to be kidding me," Jake exclaimed. "I've been skiing behind that boat of yours. I've been to your house that I couldn't afford on my salary. I've eaten steak at your house when Melissa and I were scraping by on hamburger. Don't give me that noise about not being able to make ends meet. Your problem is that you haven't even begun to try to introduce your ends to one another. Instead, you've kept both of them burning for so long you don't know which end is up." Johnson hung his head over the steering wheel, nearly honking the horn with his forehead, ashamed at both his past actions and at the lies he was telling Jake as well as himself.

They entered the gate at a quarter after ten, with the team in place as they had planned. With Jake hunched down in the passenger seat, the guard at the gate assumed that Allen had fallen asleep on the way out. It wouldn't have been the first time the old timer allowed Johnson to drive out there basically on his own. The guard commented on that fact to Johnson.

"Asleep again," he asked, shining the flashlight across the interior of the car over to where Jake was slumped against the door with his, or rather Allen's nametag reflecting back the beam of the guard's inquisition.

"You know it," Johnson responded. "Like usual, he stuffed himself with Irish stew and then headed for sandman land." Johnson liked the man he was talking to. He was a former SEAL who had fallen on hard times after his time in 'Nam and ended up using his training to rob convenience and liquor stores to pay for his drug habit. During years of armed robbery, even when the demons were driving him like a team of stallions, he never harmed a single person. It wasn't much of an accomplishment, but considering the stories other men in the camp told of years and years of constant violence and mayhem.

"I thought you cops all ate donuts and coffee."

"That's after the ride home," Johnson answered with a chuckle. Before the guard could keep the conversation going with another response, Johnson

took off, accidentally kicking up a spray of gravel with his nervousness.

"Careful," Jake muttered. "We don't need to raise anyone's suspicion,

especially a gate guard who's fresh on duty."

"Sorry," Johnson said. "Guess I'm just a little edgy about the

possibility of being shot down in a hail of bullets."

"You make it sound so dramatic," Cassandra said from her position in

the floorboard of the backseat. "You've got your vest and a team each from

the FBI and the ATF standing by outside for our signal. What more could you

ask for?"

"To be at home with my wife and kids," Johnson answered honestly.

"You should have thought of that before you started taking dirty

money," Jake stated. Johnson couldn't argue with that kind of logic.

The team of FBI, ATF, and local law enforcement had Johnson pull

the car over to a locked shed he informed them was used for storing

explosives and munitions. Fortunately, those in charge were a tad bit

overconfident in their outer defenses and hadn't considered that someone

would be able to breach them. The only thing between them and enough

firepower to feed an army of Rambo's was a small lock that was easily

thwarted with a pair of bolt cutters. It was also in a secluded area that was

dimly lit, the greater portion of lighting being allotted to the living areas of the camp. With a quick squeeze on the handles, Jake was in a gun lover's candy store.

"Good thing your trunk has that emergency handle in case anyone gets locked in," Agent O'Neill stated. "I would have still been in there if it hadn't been for that."

"Sorry," Jake said. "I guess I got a little lost in here."

"I don't blame you," O'Neill said with an appreciative whistle. "There's enough powder in here to start your own war."

"That's the idea," Johnson said. "Their ultimate goal was to take over the state and have it secede from the union."

"You can't be serious," Cassandra said. "What makes them think they can get away with that?"

"Several generations of graduates from the camp, for one thing," Johnson replied. "They've been quietly taking over some of the smaller towns across the state. That, coupled with government officials who either owe their souls to the brothers, or even worse, those who actually believe in that nightmare."

"And what about you?" Jake asked.

"It's like you figured," Johnson finally answered honestly, "I got greedy and couldn't see past the dollar signs. I rationalized at first, but the honest truth is that I liked the money and I liked the things it could buy. That's all there is to it." Finally Jake heard the words he wanted to hear. It was still hard for him to swallow that not one, but two of his own, were dirty, but what Johnson had just admitted to helped wash down his bitter little pill.

They tied Johnson to a support pole even though he swore he wouldn't go do anything to hinder their efforts. As far as O'Neill and Cassandra were concerned, he should have been tied, gagged, and stuffed back into the trunk of the car, but Jake didn't think they needed to go that far. After tying him up, Jake and his fellow officers went through the munitions like a bunch of drunks going through a wet bar. Stuff went flying off the shelves quicker than merchandise went through the check out at Wal-Mart's day after Thanksgiving sale. They all agreed that it was so much better than the handguns issued by their respective departments.

While they were stocking up, Bart and Marc were coming in behind them, still making their way down the shallow creek. As they floated by the storehouse, Darryl called out to them.

"Hey, over here," he shouted.

"Shh! Do you want everyone to hear you?" Bart warned.

"Hear me what?" Marc asked. "I didn't say anything."

"Sorry, Marc, it's not you." Then to Darryl, he asked, "What's so important, anyway?"

"There's an inlet over here where you can hide the raft. There's enough cat tails around here to keep it hidden while you guys get in place."

Darryl was right. He and Marc pulled their tiny home away from home into the inlet and began to mount up equipment, including night vision goggles, two way radio headsets, and enough C-4 to blast a hole to China if they needed to. Bart took most of that, along with the primers and timers he would need to set the charges. He wasn't a man prone to physical violence, if it could be avoided, but he had lived long enough in the world and seen enough of its gory underbelly that he knew there were times when the only way to answer violence was with violence. It wasn't something he did on a personal level. He lived up to the principal of turning the other cheek as much as he possibly could, but that's when it was his life and limb on the line, not the life of someone he cared deeply for, and possibly even loved.

Once they were in place, with the charges set, Bart and Marc met back at the rendezvous point to await the distraction they had called for. Minutes later, they had what they were looking for. Marc's boys, as Bart had come to call them, started shooting fireworks from the nearby hillside into the camp. They were firing from so many different directions at the same time that it was hard for anyone to get a fix on their location. Squads of would be soldiers poured out of barracks, where they had been sitting sipping coffee and watching the news while waiting for Letterman or Leno to come on. It was as Marc suspected, it had been so long since the camp had dealt with an incident that the guards had gotten soft and careless. They ran around like a bunch of headless chickens, going to and fro in the darkness hoping they'd bump into something that would explain the chaos exploding around them.

Fortunately, none of them came close to the munitions storehouse where Jake and crew were just exiting their cover in order to perpetrate their assault on the camp.

"What the…" Jake asked. "Is this some of y'all's doings?" O'Neill and Cassandra both shook their heads no. The blank expression on their faces, as well as the negative response they gave to his question told him they were just as much in the dark as he was. Both agents were on their handheld radios, trying to ascertain who was responsible for the light show in the sky. One of the ATF agents reported seeing some teenagers in the area that might be responsible. So far, though, no one had been able to catch up to any of them to see for sure. It was obvious that the teens knew the area around the camp better than the agents and were able to blend in their surroundings with little to no effort.

"What do we do?" one of Cassandra's team asked over the radio. This was unprecedented in her short career with the ATF so she looked over to Agent O'Neill for his advice. This was one time when she would gladly pass the reins of control over to someone with more experience.

"Round 'em up and move 'em out," came O'Neill's reply. He called in all of the agents, who began to quickly round up and corral the guards, most

of whom weren't even carrying weapons at the time of their capture. Some of

them were still in shorts, others had only towels wrapped around themselves

since they hit the ground running straight out of the showers. Some were still

in bed, wearing headphones and totally oblivious to the cacophony of sights

and sounds that had gathered about them.

While the two agencies cleaned up the mess outside, Bart and Marc

stormed the mansion that was Shane's residence. Bart, although a bit

confused, was glad to see that uniformed men and women were rounding up

people from all over the camp and escorting them to staging areas for

processing. Because of the combined efforts of both teams, along with the

surprise intervention of teenage assistance, the sweep went remarkably well.

Bart suspected that his part in the melee wasn't going to be as easy. The

guards who patrolled the outer perimeter of the mansion were still on duty,

keeping to their assigned posts regardless of what was going on around them.

It was like the old football mantra of protecting the quarterback and Shane

McFarland was the team's number one man. He was to be protected at all

costs and that meant the most experienced and reliable men were kept with

him.

Marc was in place on top of one of the now empty barracks that was

closest to Shane's home. He signaled Bart, who was watching him through the night vision goggles, and then took two quick shots, eliminating the gate

guards with tranquilizer darts. Bart approached the gate stealthily, and then

took out the two door guards in similar fashion with his air powered

tranquilizer gun. He didn't want to kill anyone if he could help it. Marc was

clambering down the side of the building when he heard the voice behind him.

"Hold it, big man," the voice demanded. "What were you doing up

there?"

Marc turned around slowly, wanting to face his adversary rather than

getting shot in the back. When he did, the two of them immediately

recognized each other as Marc Johnson looked down into the face of Sheriff

Jake Plunkett.

"You son of a gun," Jake shouted. "How did that renegade preacher

rope you into something like this?"

"He asked," Marc replied. "That's all friends have to do. Besides, I get

tired of sitting on the sidelines. It feels good to be back in the action."

"When were you in the action, as you say?" Jake wondered.

"Alright, so I haven't done anything more violent than paintball. But it

does feel good to help Bart do something. That boy is some kind of weird, but

he's all heart."

"Yeah, weird with heart, that's my man Bart," Jake agreed. "Do you

know where he is now?" Jake was worried about his weird, full of heart friend. He was acting impulsively, and he was still hurting from the beating he took earlier that day. He was probably running on mostly adrenaline, and even that would run out eventually. When it did, Bart would crash and burn like a kamikaze pilot. He had to be sure he was there when it happened so he could pick up the pieces.

"He's headed for the mansion," Marc answered, pointing to the lavish house encircled by the chain link fencing. "The outside guards are already out. I got the two at the gate; Bart got the ones by the door."

"You didn't kill them, did you?" Jake asked, somewhat shocked at how easily a preacher was bragging about taking out two guards. Even if they were the bad guys, he shouldn't be gloating about taking two people's lives.

"Nah, Bart hooked me up with a tranquilizer gun. All those days practicing at the county fair finally paid off." Marc chuckled about his marksmanship. He was really feeling good about being part of something that was bigger than his everyday life. Most people lived their lives in the mundane existence of everyday. They rarely took the opportunities that passed by them on an almost constant basis to grab hold of something bigger than themselves. Most people lived as if this life was all they had and so they were never willing to let go of the little they thought they had in order to take hold of something that was grander and greater than anything they could imagine, and once they had it they could never lose it.

"Okay, watch my back here so I can go in and get Bart's back. Can you handle that?"

"I'm on it like white on rice," Marc assured the sheriff. Jake, feeling secure in his back up, trotted up to the gate. Luckily, Bart had already cut the chain, making his entrance even easier. Of course, the guards lying on the ground dreaming of better days also made for a straight forward entrance. He ran from there to the front door, not bothering to knock as he went in without a second thought about what danger might lay beyond.

Despite the danger of the situation, Jake couldn't help but be impressed by the vast amount of wealth he had just walked into. He couldn't be sure in this light, but he thought the hardwood floors his boots were tapping against were either mahogany or some South American exotic. The chandelier hanging from the raised ceiling had enough crystal in it to make a thousand different prisms for a thousand different elementary schools. He had to force himself to focus on the job of searching for Bart instead of getting caught up in looking at décor that looked like something out of the Smithsonian.

"Looking for this," Shane shouted from across the room. He had stepped out of the shadows and might have been able to shoot Jake if it hadn't been for the fact that he had his hands full of a squirming, writhing preacher.

"It's gonna be alright," Jake said, unsure of whether he was trying to assure Bart or himself.

"Sorry, Jake, got stupid and got careless," Bart said.

"Shut up," Shane shouted and beat the butt of his gun against the side of Bart's head. It was hard enough to cause a great deal of pain, but not hard enough to knock him out. It was hard enough for Jake to pull up his sidearm and take a bead between the eyes of Shane McFarland. He hesitated just a moment, giving his opponent just enough time to get a better hold on Bart, who had slumped low enough to give Jake the window he needed to get his shot.

"Take the shot, Jake. I trust your aim. Besides, he won't shoot. He's a coward. A sorry, low down, cowardly scum of a man who doesn't deserve to live."

"Shut up, you," Shane shouted. "I will shoot."

"And then what," Jake asked. "There are hundreds of FBI and ATF agents swarming all over your precious camp like bees on honey. You won't get out of this room alive. Are you ready to die?"

"I am," Bart answered. "Shoot the scum. He killed Holly. He deserves to die. A life for a life, that's what the Bible says." He was purposefully goading Shane, trying to keep him off balance, hoping he'd make a mistake, maybe relax his grip just enough for him to slip away. He was also hoping Shane would get rattled enough to make a confession of his guilt in the murder of the young Swedish girl. He had already confessed to Bart, but there was no way that was going to hold up in court. It was hearsay at best. It might not do any good for him to confess to Jake under these circumstances either, but at the worst it would give them probable cause for search warrants to get the evidence they would need to get a conviction.

"Shut up, I said," Shane shouted, raising his gun for another blow against the preacher's head, but opted against it. He didn't want to knock him out and have to carry a dead weight hostage. He wasn't sure how he was going to get out of there, but he was determined that he would and that it would be in one piece, not in a body bag. Sure he had killed that little tramp. She deserved it. Besides, why should they worry so much about the one he had killed when his brother had killed dozens, maybe hundreds. He wasn't sure how many prostitutes had walked through the doors of the church only to end up being carried out after Angus had used them as his personal voodoo dolls. In comparison, his killing of one girl wasn't nearly as bad as brother's cold blooded murder of hundreds. Yes, he was sure it had to be in the hundreds by now; there might even be a thousand by now. After all, he had been at it for close to a decade. Surely there were thousands of women's souls screaming in agony over the misery.

"You won't kill me," Bart taunted. "You didn't even have the guts to kill Holly by yourself. Your brother had to clean up the mess when you got that poor woman pregnant. What was it, Shane? Did she want money? Was she going to expose you and your perversions?"

"Angus didn't have a thing to do with it. I killed her. I did it all by myself. All Angus did is help me cover it up." Jake couldn't believe it. Shane had not only confessed to his part in the murder, but had implicated his brother as well.

"Why rip her apart?" Bart asked. "There was no need to do that?"

"It was Angus' idea. He wanted the baby for some sick twisted reason only he knows about. I think he still has it somewhere." He started sobbing slightly. Bart could feel the shudders of emotion pass over him.

"You loved her, didn't you?" he asked.

"What do you know about love?" Shane yelled, stiffening at the thought.

"I know about love, and I know what it's like to have that love taken away from you," Bart said. It was hard carrying on a conversation when the person you're talking to has his forearm around your neck, but it wasn't impossible. He had to keep it up, keep the pressure on Shane as long as he could.

"She was taken from me," Shane agreed. His arm relaxed. The grip on Bart's neck wasn't nearly as tight as it needed to be for the bigger man to maintain his control. With a sudden drop, Bart fell to the floor before Shane could even begin to react. He started to raise his pistol to threaten Jake, then pointed it back at Bart and then fell just as suddenly as Bart had, crumpling to the floor in a sobbing heap. Bart grabbed the gun from his hand before he could react and within minutes Jake had him back on his feet with the cuffs on him. All in all, it was a good night for almost everyone.

"Has anyone heard from Angus?" Bart asked as he settled his very sore carcass back into the hospital bed where he belonged.

"Disappeared without a trace," Jake answered. He started to say something else, but then stopped just short of the words exiting his mouth.

"What is it, friend?" Bart asked.

"I hate when you call me that, in that way," Jake responded.

"So tell me what's on your mind," Bart told him. Jake hesitated again, shuffling his feet back and forth, looking for the right words to say. He loved his friend as much as he had ever loved any other man in his life, and he hated to see him hurt, but he knew the best thing for him was the truth. It wouldn't be pleasant, but it needed to be out in the open for everyone to see and examine.

"It's Shalina. We've searched the town for her. I've had every deputy combing every nook and cranny of the town, the church, and the camp. There isn't a sign of her anywhere. It's as if…" He let the words trail away to nothingness.

"As if she never even existed," Bart finished the sentence. "Like she was a figment of my imagination."

"Maybe," Jake replied. "And maybe she just doesn't want to be found. I'm thinking that Cassandra's angel might be Shalina."

"You're not serious."

"I am, and Cassandra agrees. She thinks Shalina is for real." Bart wasn't sure what to think anymore. He had come to a place within himself that accepted the fact that Shalina might not be real. Now even those who had doubts from the beginning were trying to convince him that maybe she was real, but for some reason known only to her, didn't want to be found.

"Don't mess with a man on morphine," Bart warned half heartedly.

"He's not messing with you, Bart," Cassandra said from the door.

"Et tu, Brutus," he said through a drugged slur.

"Me, too. Bart, I want the two of us to work. I want us to build a relationship together, if that's possible. But I know that's not going to happen if there's a third person coming between us. I want you to do all you can do to find her. Once she's out of your system one way or another, I'll be waiting for you. Not forever, but I will give you the time you need." Bart drifted off into a morphine mist, wondering how he had ever won God's favor so much that he had not only one, but two women who cared for him, even if one was more suspect than substance.

Bar T. Rancher

CHAPTER SEVENTEEN

The days when the train turned its wheels through the town like a terrible tyrannosaurus were over. Bart heard that expression over and over as he wandered the depot turned train museum. It was true. There were still trains coming and going through town, but they were the exception rather than the norm they used to be. Stony Ridge used to boast of one of the highest used passenger services throughout the mid-south, but that was before the regional airport was built just south of town. That, coupled with the cheap gas prices of the sixties, led to the decline and eventual demise of the passenger rail. Bart left the museum, depressed by the death of an era, and went to the combination bus station and restaurant across the road.

He sat down at a booth and ordered a cup of coffee along with a piece of cherry cobbler. It wasn't that it was the best thing on the menu, but rather the only thing that was actually edible. The only reason the small café stayed in business at all were the bus passengers who had traveled hundreds of miles without a drop to drink or a morsel of food. Those who traveled the route frequently, such as salesman, knew enough to carry a cooler with sodas and sandwich fixings when they came through town. Some of them even made a little extra money by selling to those unfortunate ones who were unprepared for the journey.

His mind and legs were restless, so he deserted his dessert to walk about viewing the overpriced merchandise in the gift shop. He was amazed

how many people bought trivialities simply because they were emblazoned

with the state motto or had the name of the town imprinted on it someplace.

The only thing that was worse in Bart's opinion was those pieces of plastic or

wooden trinkets that were supposed to be made by southern craftsman. The

only way they could be considered to be made in the south is if they were

made in southern China or southern Korea. It really shouldn't concern him

that nomads from far away and distant lands paid much more than they should

have for junk that might not ever make it back home without breaking, but for

some reason he couldn't quite fathom, the whole thing stuck in his throat like

a jagged little pill. Maybe it was the stupidity of the buyers, or perhaps it was

the greed of the merchandisers. Either way, he hated the whole concept.

Economic reform, however, was not his mission of the day. He was

there to ensure himself that he wasn't crazy. Or that he wasn't as crazy as

everyone seemed to think he was. Shalina had told him that she would be

leaving today, and for some reason he was under the impression she would be

taking the bus. He knew she walked everywhere while she was in town, so he

assumed she hadn't rented a car. Since the airport was more than your average

walking distance from town, he deduced she didn't fly in to town. The only

other way in was by bus, so here he waited, nibbling at the cherry cobbler

while trying to wash it down with tepid coffee. It wasn't a pretty existence,

398

but it was all he had at the moment.

"The schedule shows the bus doesn't come in for another half hour," Darryl said, looking at the board showing all the departures and arrivals. Unlike busy airports with their electronic displays, this board had been only recently upgraded from a chalkboard to one using dry erase markers.

"I know," admitted Bart. "I just couldn't handle hanging around the house and I didn't really want to see anyone else right now."

"I know just how you feel," Leonard said, clucking his tongue.

"How's that?" Bart wondered.

"Probably cause I'm part of you," Leonard said. "Either that or I'm just saying something to make you feel better or I couldn't think of anything else to say. You know, now that I think about, I'm just saying that because I can't think of anything else to say and I didn't want to be left out of the conversation."

"You're a big help," Bart commented sarcastically.

"What else are imaginary friends for?"

"We need to do more than offer lame advice," Darryl chided his counterpart. "He needs real advice, not just platitudes with attitudes." Leonard knew his partner was right, but the problem was that he didn't have anything else to offer. When it came to solid, sound advice or even decent morale boosting he came up totally empty. He wanted to give more. He really did. After all, Bart gave him a voice, a chance to do things, a life. He was given a smart mouth at times, a decent sense of humor, even if it was slightly off color at times and needed to be held in check every now and then, and a proclivity for trouble. But somewhere along the way he didn't pick up the necessary wisdom for occasions such as these.

"I know," Leonard told the others, his head hanging low in shame. "I just don't know what to say sometimes, but I still feel like I should say something, so something stupid comes out of my mouth before my brain can stop it." Bart looked at his friends with a renewed appreciation. He was aware that having imaginary friends after the age of five or six was definitely a social stigma, but there were times when he felt like everyone should have one or two special friends to call their very own. Perhaps if people had other people to talk to that they knew wouldn't or more precisely, couldn't, talk to anyone else about what they shared, everyone would bare their souls more. And, as everyone knows, confession is good for the soul. The problem is that although confession may be good for the soul, it's terrible on friendships and marriages at times.

"I understand," Bart told his friend. "There are times when I need to counsel with people who are going through a situation that goes beyond anything I can comprehend. How can I explain or even comfort someone going through something that horrendous when I don't understand it myself?"

He wandered again from the gift shop to the café, took another bite of his now totally cold cobbler, held the coffee cup to his lips, but drew it back when he felt the chill of the liquid as it neared his mouth. He thought about ordering more, but his stomach was already tying itself into several kinds of knots. He ate the last of the cobbler, forcing it down his throat with the table water. Afterwards, he went outside to pace around there for a while, his nervous energy feeling confined by the four walls and crowded aisles.

Where was she? If she was going to take the bus, shouldn't she be here by now? He desperately wanted to see her; he wanted to know for sure she was real. That wasn't strong enough. He had to know if she were real or just another character in the drama playing across the theatre of his mind. Sure, he loved Darryl and Leonard. And even though there were times he would gladly trade them for nothing more than a stick of gum and a decent cup of coffee, in all actuality he wouldn't trade the world for either of them. At the same time, though, he wouldn't give a plug nickel for another one like either of them.

Of course, he might be totally off base on every assumption he had made. Maybe she left the night before, while he was still in the hospital recuperating. He just didn't think she could do that to him, though. On the other hand, he had half expected a visit from her sometime during the time he had been there, even if it was sometime in the wee hours of the morning when no one else was there. Well, that wasn't exactly true. Jake, Melissa, or

Cassandra had been there around the clock, including the wee hours of the morning. Maybe she had come sometime during his stay, seen the visitors, and opted to remain anonymously discreet. He knew from his earlier encounters with her and her famous disappearing tricks that she wanted, for reasons known only to her, to remain in the background, a nameless face in the crowd.

There was really no way of knowing without proving or disproving her existence and the only way to do that for sure was to find her. His only hope to do that, whether he liked it or not, was to wait around and hoped beyond hope that she showed up to get on the bus for home.

"Could you use some company?" someone asked him from behind. The voice belonged to Sheriff Jake Plunkett.

"Yeah," Bart answered. "Darryl and Leonard were keeping me company, but I forgot the earpiece for my cell phone, so people were starting to give me a strange look."

"What people?" Jake wondered.

"Okay, it was just the guy from the café, but he was definitely looking at me strangely."

"Bart, that guy is a couple of bananas short of a bunch. He looks at everyone strangely because he's strange."

"Just the same," Bart said, "I didn't think it would be a good idea to continue talking to them when it looked like I was just talking to myself."

"You got me there, pal. I know what goes on between you and those two and it still freaks me out sometimes. But, hey, I'm sure there are things I do that probably freak you out, too. It's part of the price of being human I guess." Jake reached over and gave his partner a friendly hug over the shoulder. It might not have been a manly thing to do, but it was the right thing to do, just like being here to reaffirm his friend's sanity was the right thing to do. As far as he was concerned, the jury was still out on whether or not Miss Shalina was a real person or not, and as long as the jury was out, he would stand by his friend until the very end. In fact, even if she were nothing more than a wisp of smoke in the fog of Bart's mind, he would still stand beside his friend. Heck, he would serve as best man at their wedding if it made him happy.

"There's the bus," Jake stated. It came rolling down Main Street like a lumbering elephant. Bart and Jake waited for her to come to a stop and disembark her passengers before boarding to make sure that Shalina hadn't boarded at some point before. It was a long shot, they knew, but they couldn't allow any mistakes if they were going to be sure. Afterwards, Jake did a search of the station, including the women's restroom after asking another woman there to make sure the room was empty. He wasn't about to take any chances on her hiding in a stall or anywhere else. He went through the small building with a fine toothcomb, not wanting to miss any opportunity to find the missing woman. He was going to do his very best to help his friend find the answers he was so desperately looking for.

"She's not here, is she?" Bart asked his friend.

"No, I'm afraid not," Jake answered. "I really wish that she was, or that she was somewhere, anywhere. It's the not knowing that's driving me crazy."

"Oh, no," Bart said. "This town can handle only one crazy person at a time. And I'm the token candidate for the mental institute."

"Sorry, but the fact is you don't have a commodity on mental imbalance. You just happen to be the one I know the best." They both laughed and then decided to head back to Jake's place for some lunch. Jake wanted to stop by the office to see if anything had come in from the feelers he put out to some of the larger offices in the state along with a few out of state that were close by, but Bart put the kibosh on that. He told Jake it was time to drop it. There came a time when things, and people, had to be let go so that others could be taken hold of. Bart knew that Cassandra was real. She could be touched, felt, and seen by him and everyone else. He had done everything in his power to find Shalina and prove her existence, but the time had come, to paraphrase the walrus, to talk of other things.

Bart took one, final look back at the bus as Jake pulled back onto Main

Street. He was about to turn back around when something caught his eye. It was movement in the back glass. He couldn't be sure, but it looked like someone was waving. He craned his neck, nearly turning around in the seat to get a better look.

"What's up?" Jake asked. Bart didn't answer at first because he couldn't believe his eyes. He didn't want to believe his eyes, and he didn't dare share what he was seeing with Jake. He was seeing Shalina wave goodbye.

www.ingramcontent.com/pod-product-compliance
Lightning Source LLC
Chambersburg PA
CBHW020253030726
47499CB00001B/184